GO**O**SE
HUNT

GOOSE HUNT

DENNIS OGDEN

For Paris, Kathy and Jiri

There is no snow; it's the frozen dew that rimes the trees above the hovering cloud of vapour exhaled by the huddled mass ruthlessly herded beside the rail tracks. Tired, confused and fear-drenched eyes stare ahead into the mist as they pass the mortuary built into the rampart where so many friends and family lay. Those leading crack the icy ground that quickly turns to mud under hundreds of leaking, worn-out shoes that follow. Families clutching small bundles struggle to stay together, infants are carried, older children hold onto coat tails and the old and frail are propped up even if vapour barely rises from their trembling lips, for if the rumours are true that they're to be sent to their death, they should die together.

But one prisoner, Ignaz Kravitz, has other ideas.

Over the nine months since he and his family were interned at Theresienstadt Ghetto, there was no longer belief in the Nazi deception of a comfortable existence in the purported paradise spa town once called Terezín. His memory of an elegant life as a fine gentlemen's outfitter in Prague, and his pride in serving his country with distinction in the Great War, are all he has left to remind him of the humanity he cherished and fought for. Now, weakened by hunger and lingering war injuries, he has become useless as a worker for the Nazi war industry and he, his wife Zdenka and their nine-year-old son Evzen have been selected for transportation to an unknown, yet suspected destination.

With his son huddled close to one side and his wife on the other, Ignaz is determined that Evzen will not die a child and has concocted a plan. The boy is big for his age; tall and quite solid thanks to the little extra food his father had given him from his own pitiful rations. This made the young Evzen appear older and still capable of hard labour. It was the role of the camp police—the Kapos—to get as much work as

1

possible out of the Theresienstadt inmates or share the same fate as those who could no longer pull their weight. And Ignaz knows just the right Kapo to approach. Like all Kapos, he too is a prisoner and, like most of his kind, a criminal. But this Kapo was far more corrupt and desperate to prove his newfound allegiance to the Nazi regime, so, as heart-wrenching as it is, Ignaz hopes to persuade him to keep a healthy young worker in the camp.

As the two thousand men, women and children are roughly jostled along to await their transportation, Ignaz becomes frantic in his search for this particular Kapo. It's dangerous for him to even look around as the guards could take it as an act of aggression and bring him under control with a rifle butt to the head. But continue to search he must, for in the distance, the train whistle is heard. Suddenly pushed from behind, he turns slightly. An old man falls to the ground and is repeatedly kicked in the head until his skull cracks with a stomach-turning crunch. Risking the same fate, Ignaz looks up at the perpetrator as he delivers a final stomp onto the dead man's collapsed face. He has found his Kapo, but, seeing the fierce thrill of the kill in his dark eyes, Ignaz wonders if his plan to save his son may be worse than their ultimate destination. But his determination to extend young Evzen's life is stronger and he turns to face the Kapo placing his son between them.

Ignaz was not only a superb tailor, but also a skilled salesman. As the train approaches, its whistle louder and louder, his pitch for the life of his son becomes frantic in the fast-dwindling minutes. The Kapo knows only one thing, his own survival, and a young worker could go a long way to secure this. With a firm grip on the boy's shoulder, the Kapo pulls him to his side. Unaware of Ignaz's scheme, Zdenka lunges for her child but is elbowed in the face and topples back into her husband's arms. Panic begins to spread through the crowd as the train emerges through the mist. In a last attempt to bid farewell to his hysterical son, Ignaz reaches out to give him a final caress, but the Kapo notices him placing something into the boy's hand. He wrenches the boy away and forces his hand open. Ignaz can only watch as the platinum and gold ring, his last, carefully hidden asset of valuable disappears into the Kapo's pocket. All his plans are unravelling. With his last reserve of strength Ignaz lunges at the Kapo. Zdenka joins in the fray, setting off more panic and confusion among those close by. As the four figures struggle closer and closer to the tracks, the dark, menacing bulk of the steam engine passes with a shrill whistle and an engulfing hiss of steam. When the steam clears, Ignaz and Zdenka are gone, dragged and tumbling under the steel wheels and iron undercarriage as the engine slows. Evzen makes a frantic lunge towards the grinding wheels, desperate to join his parents in their final moment, for he too believed they should all die together. But the train has come to a stop and all he can do is crawl under the carriages in the desperate hope of finding his parents alive.

Attracted by the commotion, the camp commandant, flanked by two guards, approaches the Kapo as he drags the struggling, hysterical child from under the wheezing, motionless train. Assessing the situation, the commandant is impressed by the strength shown by the now orphaned Evzen. With a frivolous wave of his hand, he orders the Kapo to find someone to care for the boy.

Josef Veselý and his wife are hiding their two young daughters' faces from the horrific sight. The Kapo had tried, unsuccessfully, to take their names off the transportation list as Josef, having been a resident of Terezín before it became the Ghetto, was of some use to him —one of the many resources he was able to discover and keep secret for his own purpose. With the commandant gone, here was an opportunity to preserve his source of local knowledge. He pushes the traumatised boy at his new family and sends them back to their barracks as the solid doors of the freight cars are unlatched and opened.

CHAPTER 1
Melbourne, Australia, April 2008

I like this time of the morning. I'm not much into crowds and noise and this time of the year's the best. Yesterday's late summer heat is now a gentle warm breeze and when I close my eyes the softest of sounds become, like, so intense at three a.m., I reckon I hear birds talking in their sleep. I love birds. Not *Lovebirds*, they're too, you know, like Hollywood poodles, not real. I like blackbirds and magpies and those crazy honeyeaters that fly around like they're in a computer game, love'em. I wonder what kind I'm hearing up in this tree?

'Shit! Come on Bri. What the fuck ya doin'?'

The birds go silent. Bloody Zac's spoilt the moment. I really don't know why I'm with him, but then I don't know why he's with me either. I think on the street, ya just sorta, like, link up for company or something. Never really thought too much about the why, it just happens. Anyway, I feel a bit safer with someone around at this time of the morning, not that Zac would be much help if anybody threatened, he's so skinny. Or maybe he's one of those, what is it, wiry types who don't look strong but are. He's always bragging about how good he is in a fight, but then he's so full of bullshit I don't know what to believe.

The embankment down to the train tracks is steep and I slide down holding down the flap of the old canvas bag to stop any spray cans falling out.

'Not too far', I call out, but not too loud. 'Lose the light from the street.'

I smile to myself as I look up at the embankment just before it hits the tunnel. Whoever decided to cover the side with concrete to stop rocks and stuff falling onto the tracks has left a great surface to paint.

'Here, this'll do.'

'There's no space.'

I look over the wide stretch of concrete now covered in all sorts of good, bad and indifferent graffiti then point to a piece a few metres from the tunnel entrance. 'There, that one's had its day…time for it to go.'

I used to, you know, sorta feel strange painting over someone else's piece. But that's the way it is. I paint over someone's piece and someone paints over mine. Mine ain't meant to last anyway. If they don't serve their purpose over a couple of days, they deserve to be painted over.

'Just leave that one. I like it' I say, pointing to a tag next to the condemned piece. It's got a bit more originality to it than most graffs that are just copies of whatever style's in or are just plain depressing, ya know, jagged edges and Jagger-type mouth vomiting everywhere, or blood and guts and decapitated bodies, why's that? Like, I'm not a prude or anything and I paint my fair share of heavy shit, but I kinda think if ya gunna paint something people will see, you might as well give them something to make them think or like rather than make them sick, know what I mean?

Zac ties a disgusting rag over his mouth, picks up a can and starts spraying a white cover over the outdated piece. It only takes a minute. Everything only takes a minute in this game. In and out quick before you get caught. With a clean space to work on, he steps back onto the train tracks and with his finger pointing and waving about, he maps out the invisible word for an idea of size and proportion. Once he's satisfied he's straight into outlining the word. He's not much good at anything else but I like his style for letters and that's why I let him do the outline. Even though it's always the same, by the time I'm finished it'll look totally different…and that's the point…the same word but filled with different detail has become, sorta, recognisable over the last year or so. I mean it's not really a real word, more like three words in one actually, but SECRETSINCITY has a musical ring to it, like synchronicity, and that's where I got the idea. I'm not, like, you know, literary or anything, it's just that I was tossing around ideas and came up with a short list of words, three of which were 'secrets', 'sin' and 'city', you know, the three little words that I reckon describes the urban race. I wrote them down in that order and they just seem to jump out as one, so I Googled it and up came *do you mean synchronicity?* Couldn't get my head around the meaning until I saw a reference to *Through the Looking-Glass* by Lewis Carroll. You know, *Alice in Wonderland*. Well, that's one of the few books I've read, and probably the only one I've read more than once. Loved it. So when I saw this mentioned, my ears pricked and I read more. Seems this guy Jung came up with the word and his favourite line from the book is when the White Queen is talking to Alice and says, '*It's a poor sort of memory that only works backwards*'. I'm still not sure what synchronicity means, but that quote planted itself inside my tiny brain and wouldn't bloody well go away. So I tossed it around and decided on my own meaning that if I came up with something that suggests secrets in the city, anyone looking for hidden clues would start digging into their own secrets. Like the White Queen said, *going backwards into their own dark, guilty past*. And because everyone sees graffiti as bad, so must be the message and thinking the worst is the only way my audience can unravel what I'm teasing them with. And now, a year later, I'm like so stoked at the response but bloody stunned at some of the reactions I get. Jeez, we're a fucking sick race.

Just then, a car crosses the road bridging the tunnel.

'Drop, Zac' I call out, crouching low as the headlights flicker through the wrought-iron fence sending light patterns across the decorated embankment.

'Wha?' he says before shaking his head and turning back to finish his work. Don't know why I bother.

I put on my grotty mask, and, as I always do, say to myself I need a new one, but then I forget about it. Can't be an age thingy yet, can it? Not at the tender age of twenty-four!

'That'll do, Zac.' I'm eager to get started and if I don't stop him, he'll keep going with all sorts of fancy shit that I'm gunna cover anyway.

'Yeah, just gotta…' he replies.

I can see he's getting into his own little creative world. 'Now!' I snap. It always works.

'Whatcha gunna do?' he says, stepping back so I can take over the canvas. He always asks but I never tell him. Most times, I don't even know myself until I start. It just sorta flows once I have a can in each hand and start spraying. I reckon it must be the same as any other artist painting on canvas or stuff. Yeah, I know, Graffiti's not seen as art, but I disagree cuz I've been drawing and stuff ever since I was little and if what I do makes people think, then I reckon I'm an artist, so there!

Anyway, here goes.

————

In a paint-splattered, frayed and sweat-stained grey singlet bearing the word STREETSCAPE with a hand-written (ES) inserted between STREET and SCAPE, shorts cut down to the barest minimum from worn-out jeans and a pair of seriously scuffed Blundstone boots that seem far too big and heavy for her long, slight legs to lift, let alone walk in, Briney Ruza paints with ease, speed and confidence. On her left arm, just below the shoulder, is a small tattoo of a red rose with a twisted barbed wire stem piercing a heart. Her lean, athletic figure darts from one side of her chosen space to the other, pausing only to brush some of her mousy-coloured, crudely cut shoulder-length hair from her eyes and pick up another can from the palette of colours arranged in order on the ground. It's as if all the elements have been carefully planned to link up at the conclusion of the painting. But nothing is planned, it just happens, and over the past year, her work has been seen by hundreds of train commuters on their way to work. Her interwoven detail that fills in the word SECRETSINCITY is the talk amongst the city's office workers. What *is* the latest hidden secret?

A growing number dedicated to the challenge scan the broad stretches of trackside graffiti searching for *The Word*. If nothing else, it helps pass the time for these 'poor creatures of habit as they attempt to lighten their tedious task of getting to their tedious task', as Briney describes them. Over morning coffee or between displaced, windswept groups of smokers huddling in the street, the discussion is of the morning's observation.

After each session, Briney and Zac will return to their hovel, the only remaining barely liveable dingy bed-sit in a failed factory conversion at the end of a service laneway in the oldest part of Prahran. Once a liquorice factory where the raw, pungent black ooze that was used to flavour chewing tobacco before being sweetened for candy continues to exude its trademark bouquet from floor and walls. At around nine o'clock, Briney will upload a photo of her latest graff to her MySpace page for those who did not see it and those wanting another look. Her experienced followers understand the rules of the game. The answer to the hidden secret will never be revealed. There will be no clues and no conclusion just a process of elimination. The following day, a list of what the answer is *not* will be released. A list of words, phrases and sometimes actual gossip randomly selected by Briney from discarded magazines, newspapers and an old dog-eared pocket dictionary scavenged from wheelie-bins left out for collection.

For some strange reason the list satisfies most participants in this fantasy. They're more interested in what is *not* the answer than in having their day ruined by a finality that leaves nothing to occupy their minds but their work. The hidden message, if indeed there is one at all, may be guessed correctly but never acknowledged—a challenge without a conclusion. For many, Briney's game is the catalyst to revisit their past, some come through with a sort of cleansing of spirit, a release of inner demons. Some do not. To some, the process adds further poison to what is eating away deep inside them. The pain endured is the pain they believe they deserve with relief coming from their self-chastisement.

But Briney Ruza, the creator of this inner-exposing fantasy, is by no means immune to the perils of her own game.

———

I must be finished cuz I can smell the paint. Strange, but like, when I paint my sense of smell and hearing shut down and I'm only left with sight and feel. Yeah…feel! I love using my fingers like a kid with finger-paint. Get in a mess like a kid too. It's like a fluid connection with the wall that touches me back. Crazy I know, but I kinda feel that the wall's trying to talk to me.

I reckon these fumes are getting to me. Just gotta add my tag, not too big, just enough to be seen from a moving train—*MySpace/MyRuza.com*—there. Used to be just MyRuza until I got my page up.

'What do you think, Zac?'

I never get an answer straight away from him. When I start painting, he sorta goes wandering then comes back, sits down and switches off until I'm finished.

'Zac!' I don't want to call out too loud.

'Huh?'

'What do you think?' I repeat taking a couple of shots with my little digital camera.

'Yeah, cool. Can we go now?' he says, after giving the piece a quick once over.

No bloody appreciation. All he wants to do is get back to the pad, go to bed, do the grope thing in the hope I'll let him. Haven't made up my mind about that yet. See how I feel later.

'Wait!'

'What?' I ask, sensing some urgency as he looks down at the train track he's standing on.

'I feel something coming.'

I put one foot on a track and feel it too.

'Gotta be freight this time of the morning.'

The tingle rising up from the iron rail, its shiny surface catching a hint of the distant streetlight is getting stronger. We look at each other.

'Cool,' he says under his breath. 'Wanna?'

I give a silent nod and start stuffing cans back into the bag but one slips outta my paint-covered hand.

'Leave it, quick it's nearly here' he calls, seeing me fumbling in the semi darkness.

I manage to grab it, stuff it into the bag with the others and rush to his side with our backs pressed against the outside of the tunnel entrance. We wait. I can hear his heart beating and wonder if he can hear mine? It's not as if this is the first time we've done it, but it still gets the blood pumping.

Hearing a distant rumble and the sound of the wheels chatting over

9

the track joints we look into the tunnel and see a faint light hitting the bend in the wall.

'It'll be goin' slow cuz of the bend in the tunnel' says Zac.

As the sound of the diesel engine increases, its wheels begin to squeal taking the bend and its headlight creeps along the wall. I see the cracks and cables and a rat or two scampering away. Then in a flash, the engine's single light is facing us. We straighten up out of view of the driver and wait for the train to exit.

'Third one' Zac suggests.

'Yeah' I agree, hooking the bag's shoulder strap over my head so it's across my chest.

Then, with a rush of air and a roar that shatters the stillness of the early morning, the huge bulk of the diesel engine passes us at a slow steady speed allowing the many cars in tow to navigate the bend.

We count, one, two…

'Now!' Zac calls out as he pushes himself off the wall, and after a few strides, grasps the steel frame of the ladder attached to the back of the third car and heaves himself up and onto the coupling.

I'm right behind him and swing up and into the space between the two cars just as the diesel picks up speed. With both hands covered in wet paint I lose my grip and slam into the back of the car. Something digs into my side. It hurts. I try to grab hold of something else but in the semi-darkness and with the train increasing speed it's difficult and I lose my footing on the greasy coupling. Zac grabs me by the arm, but I'm slipping down. I can see the blurred ballast rushing below as I desperately search for something to stand on. I look back up to Zac as his hand slides along my paint-smeared, sweaty arm.

'Hold on, Bri.' He's panicking…it's him I want holding onto me.

'Zac!' is all I can get out before I drop.

I don't think I was knocked out, just stunned when I slammed face down onto the hard ballast. I must have tumbled over somehow cuz I'm now on my stomach facing back towards the tunnel as the train rushes overhead. The clackety-clack of the steel wheels running over the track joints each side of me keeps time with the constant rumble of the massive bulk an arms length above. I want to close my eyes and wait for the monster to pass, but I can't. I'm not allowed.

Between each car I get a flash of light from the street above. Another flash of light and another. How many cars are there? Then the noise dulls but the cars keep passing overhead. Everything becomes blurred. Am I passing out? I feel different. I feel cold. I feel company.

Images appear, images of a different time, a different place, in a different life. I sense pain and suffering. Rat-tat, rat-tat go the wheels, softer and not the clackety-clack as before. I try but can't close my eyes as the images become clearer. I see arms and legs flayed and dislocated at unnatural angles as a head is cracked open, spilling its contents onto the rocky ballast. Then I see another figure, crushed and separated into sickening pieces. I'm paralysed with fear, forced to witness this horror as rivers of blood trail towards me. Screams rebound around me, yelling, shouting, orders, orders, more orders until finally I'm allowed to close my eyes.

The train's no longer running over me, its sound fading into the distance. I look around expecting to see blood and bits of body everywhere, but even in the dim light from the street above, there's none. But I know it's there all around me and I desperately need to get away from the creeping gore.

I can hear the brittle tinkle of stones settling under someone's weight as they kneel over me. I see a halo of light outlining long, straggly hair. It's familiar. It's Zac.

'Hey man, you okay?'

I'm wet…blood…I'm covered in blood.

'The blood! Stop the blood!' I hear myself screaming. 'Get me away from it, quick!'

'Don't move' he's telling me while he pokes and prods. 'Can't see any blood and I don't think anything's broken.'

Bullshit! I saw so much and can still feel it.

'Can ya move ya legs?'

Shit, if I could move my fucking legs I'd get away from the blood. But they are moving. I don't understand.

'Ya fingers?'

I stick one index finger up.

'Fuck you too. Ya head, move it slowly'

It hurts, but I can turn it gently from side to side.

'There's a cut on ya head and some scratches and bruises, that's all I can see. Let's get ya off the tracks.'

I manage to stand on shaky legs and look down and around. There's no blood to be seen on the ground. The wetness I feel is yellow paint from a can in my bag that must have flipped its lid and sprayed me.

All's still and quiet again.

I look into Zac's face. 'It was horrible.'

'You bet. Shit, I really thought you were a goner for a moment.'

'No, it was horrible. What I saw and heard was horrible.'

'No shit! But it was a fuckin' buzz though, hey?'

'No, Zac! I saw other things, awful things, like I was seeing something from the past.'

'Like duh, ya just got run over by the longest fucking train I've seen. Shit, that'd send anyone's brain into orbit. Like, they say when you face death your life passes before ya.'

I push away from him with an icy glare. 'It wasn't my life I saw.'

'Yeah, right, let's go. I reckon ya need to rest after that little trip.'

He has no idea what I'm talking about. How could he? I mean, now, thinking back, I'm not bloody sure of what I saw either.

We head back to where we came down from the street and as I pass my graff, I feel something weird…like it's calling me. Nah, I must be in shock or something. I shake my head but it's still there. Then, as if guided by some other force, I reach out and press the palm of one hand into the still-wet paint. The jolt of energy sends me into a cold, heart-thumping sweat. What have I discovered?

'You okay?' asks Zac, noticing my frozen pose. 'Looks like you've seen a ghost?'

'Yeah,' I reply, knowing he has no idea how true those words could possibly be.

I feel my hand relax and I take it away from the wall.

'I'm just gunna take some more shots,' I say, staring at the handprint I've now added. Shit, I hope the camera didn't break!

CHAPTER 2

Zac's snoring, my head hurts and after pulling off the bit of shit paper I stuck on the cut last night, it's bleeding again. I check it out in the cracked mirror above the sink. Probably needs a stitch or two but I'm not that fussed about retaining my good looks, and anyway, the odd scar's sexy I reckon. But the sight of blood brings back the horror under the train and a shiver goes through me. But nothing's clear anymore. All I remember is coming back here and washing all this yellow paint off me, and then I must have collapsed.

My singlet's dry enough to put back on and it looks sorta cool with the squirt of yellow. I find my knickers on the floor next to my old travel clock. Can't remember taking them off or if we did anything, oh well, whatever. But it's time I uploaded the latest graff.

Funny, after doing SECRETSINCITY for a couple of months, I didn't worry about all the people who missed seeing my piece until I saw this article in the paper that's free at train stations. I often spend a day travelling around on trains to see what others are doing on walls and shit. Anyway, one day I pick up this crumpled copy of *mX* that was left on a seat, and in amongst all this celebrity shit I spot a small article about graffiti. Well, you know, your eyes tend to grab onto anything you're into. But, fuck me if this piece isn't about me—well my graffs that is. Shit, I'm a celeb in my own lifetime, I thought. Like, I've had some things about my work in street mags and grunge stuff, but not in any major paper for the whole world to see. Well, at least the transit world anyway and that's the target audience, right?

Anyway, because I only paint beside two lines near where I hang out, this article said something about limited exposure. So I got to thinking and set up a MySpace page to upload a photo each time I did a piece. That's when the game really got started. Instead of revealing a hidden secret, I'd put up a list of what it's *not* the next day. Great, I thought, but, duh, I had to get the MySpace address out there, so I found the paper's website and got in touch with the reporter and filled him in on the details without revealing who I was or anything. I didn't see the reply in *mX*, but heard about it. Then I started getting all these comments back and, well now, I have a growing band of dedicated subscribers.

I boot-up the laptop. Yeah, I know it sounds strange, a street kid like me having a pad, a laptop and a camera, but they were given to me. Not from social welfare, fuck no, but from the government in a sorta roundabout way. This guy was a government bureaucrat or something who spent five minutes with us on the street for a photo op to show he cared about the homeless. Well, after the shots were taken, bugger me if he doesn't chat me up. Made it look like he was interested in *our* welfare but all he was interested in was *his*. So what the hell, if a bureaucrat wants to cheat on his wife he's up for paying something, right? And he still does. Not much, mind you, and I've never asked for anything and I'll never tell anyone. I think his conscience got to him. But we did have some fun. He was about fifty something and wasn't all that good looking, but he was clean and that's something I wasn't used to. It's sorta like a backpacker roughing it through all those poor countries and one night in a clean, fancy hotel is, like, heaven. Well, that's how I felt, anyway. He had money and he liked to spend it on me and that's something else I never had, so I thought why not take advantage. It was a short fling thing, but he did take me overseas once to some fucking conference thingy in Asia. I had to stay invisible, mind you, so he gave me money to keep busy during the day. I'd just walk around the streets looking for local street art and stuff and hardly spend anything, but that's all gone now. And this place, well he got it for me so he could sneak around sometimes for a fuck. He wasn't all that comfortable here. Not his normal up-market style but it was all he could afford without the cost showing up somewhere. That is until his wife got wind of something and he suddenly split. Anyway, with his conscience money, the bit of welfare I manage to squeeze out of the government and whatever Zac comes up with since he moved in a few months ago, I can just hang onto this place.

14

Anyway, the photos are uploaded and I click on the first thumbnail to see it full screen. It was taken before we jumped the train. So was the second. Either is good enough to upload. Then I bring up the third and fourth shot taken after the train thing and I'm jolted back by a flash of blood and gore. Confused, I hit the back arrow to see the first two photos. Nothing! Nothing but the graff as it should be, no blood, nothing. I feel my gut tighten as I go back to a thumbnail view of all four images together. Except for the last two showing where I put my hand, they all now look the same. It's my mind. I'm going fucking crazy. I enlarge the second and third photo so they fill the screen side-by-side. Both shots look the same apart from the handprint. Or are they? I feel there's something else different. I look from one to the other, back and forth, back and forth. What is it? What can I see? It's the handprint! It seems to have changed the overall image like the last piece in a jigsaw puzzle revealing the full picture. I look up close then lean back in the chair for a distant view. I even squint. There's something hidden in the painting that's trying to show itself to me but I can't make it out.

There's a loud snort from the bed, then a sniff. Good, he's waking. I wonder if he can see anything?

'Zac, can you look at this?'

It takes a moment for him to register before coming over.

'What?'

'Can you see any difference in these two?'

He stares at the screen for only a fleeting moment. 'Na!'

'Look again, closer.'

He leans forward. His breathe stinks because of bad teeth.

'What am I supposed to see?'

'Can you see the one with the handprint?'

He rests his head on my shoulder to get a closer look. I wish he wouldn't do that. Now I've got his dandruff over me.

'Oh, Yeah, there.' He points. 'Hardly see it though.'

'That all you see?'

'Why, ya done something, like add a secret for a change?'

'Never mind. Just go and have a bloody wash will you?'

'Yeah, well, I need a piss anyway,' he mumbles heading to the bathroom.

The bang on the head must be playing tricks so I decide to upload the one with the handprint to MySpace. Maybe someone out there will see what I almost saw.

CHAPTER 3

Plenty of suggestions have come in about yesterday's hidden secret. I usually look over them before uploading the NO LIST so I can cancel out all the guesses. Naughty I know, but hey, it's a game, right? But this time I can't. Not that I don't want to or anything, shit, quite the opposite, I'm so fucking hanging out to see if anyone saw something that'll trigger off what I may have seen.

Zac's just come back. I bet he's been out telling his dickhead mates all about me falling under the fucking train. Why is it all his stories are about me? Maybe it's a bloke thing or something, or it's just that he never has anything interesting to say about himself. Yeah, that's probably it. I know all the guys on the street think he's a wanker and a fucking loser, but I also know that he's got a connection they rely on for their score. Yeah, he deals in dope. Not real heavy stuff. I wouldn't have him around me if he did. Just grass and hash. Old hat shit these days, but anyway it's something that keeps him in with the mob he knocks around with. I reckon he sorta knows he's out of place on the street and needs to brag, boast and blackmail himself in. There's something about Zac that says *this is where I want to be*, not like me with no bloody choice.

'So, what sorta crap's come in, Bri?' he says leaning over my shoulder.

I get up to make a coffee. 'Dunno.'

'What, ya haven't checked them out? What about ya list, loaded that yet?'

'Not yet.' I really don't feel like talking about it. 'Want a coffee?'

With my back to him, I can hear him pull the chair up to the computer and there's a pause before he answers. 'Na.' He's reading. 'Fuck! Doesn't anyone have anything creative to say? It's just the same fucking shit as always. Sex shit…political shit…end of the world shit…religious shit…more religious shit. Jeez, ya attracting some real weirdos lately.'

I pour hot water into the chipped mug with some cheap instant coffee and a couple of tubes of sugar I knock off from the tables outside cafés, then turn to face him with my back against the sink while I stir.

'Yeah, usual deep and meaningless crap.' He pauses. 'But ya list's growing. What is it…um…up to three hundred and thirty-four.'

I put the spoon in the sink and take a sip of coffee while trying to remember what it was last time, but I can't, my minds on other things.

'Whoa! That's refreshing?'

I watch him lean closer to the screen and for some reason a chill ripples down my spine and I feel goose bumps popping out, even with hot coffee inside me.

'What?' I ask both hands wrapped tightly around the hot mug to calm the chill.

'That's new. Fuckin' weird, but different at least.'

'What?' I ask again, tensing up and slopping coffee over the side of the mug.

'Just says, *what you know of Goose?*'

I watch the coffee mug fall to the floor as if in slow motion. My hands still wrapped around the space it fell from.

'Fuck!' Zac yells. I didn't hear the mug break but he must have. 'Shit, Bri, ya scared shit outta me! Whatcha do that for? Now we just got one mug left.'

'Say it again,' I can hear the words in my head but I'm not sure if they came out right.

'What?'

'Say it again,' I repeat louder.

'What? That we've only got one fuckin' mug left?'

'No! No! The words, the comment, what was it?'

He turns back to the computer.

'*What you know of Goose?* That one?'

That's it! That's what I saw. Don't know exactly what a Goose looks like, I would have said a Duck or something, but I'm sure that's what I got a flash of before it went away. I mean a Duck! Shit, no wonder I couldn't figure it out, that'd be the last thing I'd bloody paint.

'Ya gunna, mop up the mess?'

'What?' I can hear his voice but my mind's far away.

'Ya gunna just stand in coffee and broken mug?'

I step over the broken pieces and puddle of coffee. 'Get outta the way Zac,' I say almost pushing him off the chair. 'I wanna look at my graff again.'

'What about the fuckin' mess?'

Why's he only now worried about a bloody mess? I ignore him and sit down and scroll back to the photo. First I study it up close, then lean back, then up close again and squint.

'Can you see anything?' I ask before he goes.

'What? ya mean a Goose?' There's a pause. 'What the fuck do they look like?'

'Like a Duck...I think.'

His head's now beside mine and we both stare into the screen.

'Nah, just ya usual shit of roses and stuff.'

What does he mean, usual shit?

'Look closer.'

'I told ya, don't see any fucking Duck, Goose, whatever. Anyway I thought a Goose was sticking ya finger up someone's bum.'

I ignore that.

'Ya not gunna take any notice of that, are ya? I mean, shit, ya get lots of fuckin' crazy comments.'

'No, this is different. This is telling me I've added something that's a secret even to me.' I pause. Do I tell him? Gotta. 'Zac, Something happened after the train and when I put my hand back on the wall. I like, felt something strange then, and I feel something really strange about it now. Did anyone else mention a Goose, a Duck or anything like a bird?

'Com'n Bri, ya only get one fuckin' duck crazy weirdo who thinks like that.'

I take that as a no, but I don't think this is from some weirdo. I just sense it.

'Anyway, do we have Goose here in Oz?'

'Geese,' I correct him.

'What?'

'Geese. One Goose, two Geese.' Funny how while thinking of one thing your mind's got a broader range.

I look at the sender's username. *R. Veselý*. Don't mean nothing, but they never do.

'Do we?'

'What?'

'Do we have *GEESE* in Australia?' He always gets pissed off at being corrected.

'Yeah, Yeah, I'm sure we do,' I impatiently snap back, unable to take my eyes away from the name. *R. Veselý*. Looks foreign. Why am I starting to sweat? What's with this *R. Veselý*? I never worry about checking who sends in comments, but for some reason this name is starting to have a familiar ring to it.

'Zac, can I tell if this, um, *R. Veselý* has sent in any other comments?'

He was heading to the bed. He huffs, 'Fuck, what now?'

'I want to know if this *R. Veselý* has sent in comments before.'

'Only by going through all the past entries, I think.'

'Fuck! You mean over the last year?'

'Well, since they became a subscriber.'

I feel a bit stupid at not knowing much about this, never did worry about getting into the nitty-gritty of how these programs work. Not my gig. Give me a wall and a can of spray paint any day.

Before I know it he's reached over and clicked on the page's control button. 'There…My Readers.' He clicks again. I want to stop him. This is too fast. I need to think. A list of subscribers appear, some with photos, some without, but most with obscure graphics that, if I was interested, would tell a lot about their mentality.

'There,' he says, scrolling down to *R. Veselý*. Under a blank image are the words, *Subscribed 16 Nov 2007*.

'Ya only got about four or five months to look back.'

'Zac, would you do it?' I ask, leaning back and away from the screen.

'Fuck, Bri, what's wrong with ya, crippled or something?'

'Just fucking do it for me will you?' I snap, probably a bit unfair I figure.

'Well, let me sit down then.'

I get off the chair and step back, arms crossed and a hand to my mouth feeling sweat on my top lip. This is so weird and probably all for nothing. What's he doing? Why's he taking so long?

'Zac?'

'Yeah, hang on will ya?'

Why is the name sounding more familiar? Is it the mention of a Goose? Nah, that doesn't make sense.

'Zac?'

'Fuckin' wait will ya, jeez!'

What's a Goose got to do with anything? Yeah, he's probably right, just another weirdo. But that flash of an image could've been a Goose. Maybe it's one of those psycho things when two completely detached minds see the same thing for no other reason than it's what they see. I mean, like those inkblot tests they give people and how they see images that no one else does. Well, I'm sure there must be at least one other who'll see the same thing. Shit, I wonder how the shrinks interpret what people see in those inkblot tests? They gotta be just as nutty, I guess.

'Just the one.'

'What?'

'They've made just this one comment about the Duck thing.'

I think for a moment. 'So they've been looking at my graffs since November and never made a comment before.'

'That's what I just fuckin' said, right!'

He's so bloody testy.

'Boring fuckin' page though.'

'What?' Shit, no, he hasn't has he?

'Their page ain't got nothing on it except the name and where they're from.'

'Fuck Zac! Will they know you've checked out their page?'

'Nah. Don't think so.'

'You…you don't think so? You're not sure?'

'Yeah, well, pretty sure…I think?'

Oh, fuck what if he's wrong and they've seen I've checked them out.

'Hey, why the panic? Shit who cares if ya check out someone who's, you know, a subscriber.'

'Where?'

'What?'

'Where're they from?' I'm holding my breathe with a hand across my mouth in anticipation.

'Um, Prague, Czech Republic. Where the fuck's that?'

I almost trip as I spin around and grab the old travel clock lying on the floor by the bed. It's so long since I've taken the clock out of the fold-up case, and shaking hands aren't helping. There, got it. I hesitate before turning it over. Will I be disappointed, relieved or shocked? Shit, here goes. Fuck, there it is. Fuck, it really is!

'Bri? I said, where's this place?'

Keeping my eyes glued to the clock, I answer, 'It's where my old lady came from…Zac…Veselý used to be her last name!'

'Get a grip, Bri. Shit, mothers don't go on MySpace!' He looks up at me. I'm sure I've gone white as a ghost. 'Listen, you sure ya shouldn't go see a fuckin' doctor or something. I reckon that knock to ya head's gotta be worse than it looks.'

'Look at this,' I say, offering him the clock.

'Yeah, it's ya fuckin' clock. I've seen it before, so what?'

'Just look at it will you!'

'Who cares what the fuckin' time is. Anyway I can see it on the computer.'

'Would you fucking look at this!' I yell. 'The name, *Veselý*, it's engraved on the back. This was my grandfather's clock…see, *Josef Veselý*.'

That got his interest and he takes it for a closer look.

'But whoever sent in the comment is *R.Veselý* not *J.Veselý*.'

'No, it's gotta be her.'

'Could be just a fuckin' coincidence, Bri.' He pauses…his mind ticking over. 'So, what…you're saying ya Czech or something?'

I have to think before answering. 'No, born here.'

'So, how did ya get this then?'

'From…it's a long story.'

He hands the clock back.

'Well, there's an easy way to find out if it's her, just ask.'

I can't! No, the words didn't come out. 'I can't!'

'Why not? Just reply to the comment and ask, simple.'

Maybe for you shithead, you don't know.

'Look, I'll do it for ya.'

Fuck! He's turned back to the computer.

'You do it Zac and I'll cut ya fucking balls off!'

That worked.

'Well, what ya gunna do then? Just accept it's ya old lady without actually finding out?'

He's not supposed to say sensible things. Shit!

Before I can stop him, he's clicked on the word 'reply'. A blank box appears with the little text insertion mark blinking for attention. He gets off the chair for me to sit. I remain standing, holding the clock close to my chest while staring at the blinking mark synched to the seconds as they tick over. It would be easy to just shut down the computer. But all I can do is stand and stare. I can hear Zac behind me starting to pick up the pieces of broken mug. His silence is deafening. Fuck you Zac. Why did you have to do that? Deep down I knew why. Deep down I also know what I have to do. Deep down my stomach is aching. I pull out the chair and sit. Zac stops gathering up the broken pieces. He's won.

My hands are hovering over the keyboard but I've no idea what to say. Sure, I could simply ask if this is my long lost mother. No way, it's just not that bloody simple.

I can feel his eyes burning into my back. Yeah, Yeah, I'll do it, just let me do it in my own time, hey!

I don't know why, and I've never done it before, but for some reason I place the palms of my hands onto the screen. Instantly I feel some magnetic pull. Is it electricity or something? Maybe, but whatever it is, my hands drop to the keys and before I know it I've typed in, *Who are you?* then hit the send button. Shit! 'Shit!' I repeat out loud. 'I've done it.'

CHAPTER 4
Terezín, Czech Republic, April 2008

Evzen Kravitz is a patient man. Not by nature—far from it—but from many decades of despair, repression and struggle. All his life he has learnt to wait. All his life he has constantly asked…wait for what?

But today, with a winter chill in the air even though it's into the second month of spring, his patience has deserted him. He's learnt to endure his painful bone-grinding hip and arthritis in the knees, but this morning his slowness is annoying him. The broad empty streets of the bleak fortress town of Terezín, north of Prague, are silent at this early hour. An old couple pass and bid him a good morning. With a quick nod he hobbles on for fear he'll miss the 8.05 bus to Litoměřice.

Arriving without a moment to spare he breathlessly hoists himself up the two steps into the bus, wincing from the pain he pays his eight crowns to the driver then slumps breathlessly into the nearest seat.

Ten minutes later the bus pulls into its terminal beside the Litoměřice railway station. For the past week this has been a daily routine for Evzen, except today he's caught an earlier bus. Normally he'd change to a local bus that would stop at the hospital, but this morning he's not going directly there and he looks grimly towards the challenging hill that leads to the town centre.

After stopping several times to rest and ease the pain in his joints, Evzen finally arrives at the Tourist Information Office under the arches on the west side of the vast central square. As he expected, the Office will not open till nine-o'clock. With almost half-an-hour to rest and regain his energy, he flops into a chair at a cafe table on the south corner facing the Office. Much to the annoyance of the waitress, Evzen dismisses her offer to take his order while concentrating on the Office door and the clock set into the Gothic church tower opposite.

At five to nine, four young tourists arrive at the Information Office, try the locked door then peer through the window. Evzen is on his feet instantly and hobbles hurriedly across the corner of the square to take up first position at the door, ignoring the foreign comments. The thought of waiting for this mob to be served first is intolerable at such an urgent time.

Evzen shuffles and taps his fingers on the door while watching the young man inside preparing to open. Finally the door is unlatched.

'Computer!' Evzen snaps in his native Czech. 'You help me, yes!'

The young man, not in the mood for such rudeness this early, holds up his hand while backing away, allowing the four tourists to enter. They pass him with a satisfying nod and go directly to the map and brochure display by the counter. Having no time for today's youth, Evzen is insistent.

'Computer! You help me before. You help again, yes?'

Seeing his other customers are happily browsing through the display, he gives the old man a nod, well remembering the last visit.

'I need to boot-up the computer first,' he says, going to one of the two free public computers and tapping the power button. The screen turns blue and he keys in a password.

"It will take a moment, sir. I'll attend to the others and come back,' says the young man noticing two of the tourists have made their selection and are waiting at the counter.

Evzen watches the young man walk away, annoyed at his lack of understanding of the urgency, then turns back to see the blue screen transform in a photo of the town square with a row of icons on one side. Seeing the real Square just out the window, Evzen is fascinated and reaches out to touch the screen. Suddenly there's a loud *BING* and a small window appears in the centre of the screen. Alarmed, thinking he may have done something wrong, he glances back to the young man serving his customers and showing no concern at the sound. This new technology terrifies Evzen and he steps back from the computer and watches with a mix of fear and wonder for the next surprise.

Having finished serving the others, the young man returns to the computer and readies his fingers over the keyboard.

'Okay, what do you want today?'

'Same,' Evzen replies, peering nervously around the young man's back.

'Umm, that was MySpace, right?' he asks with a questioning glance at Evzen who nods, still confused.

The MySpace home page opens.

'And your name is…?'

'My…my name? Why you want my name?' stutters Evzen.

'To open your page, sir, I need your username and password.'

'Oh, yes, ah?' says the flustered Evzen as he remembers and pats the pockets of his old, weathered coat. 'Yes,' he says, pulling out a crumpled piece of paper and hands it over. The username and password is keyed in and the paper handed back.

The page opens and there's another *bing*.

'It seems you have a message, sir. Do you want me to open it?'

'Message?' mumbles the old man nervously. Even though it was what he was hoping for, the speed is bewildering

'You want me to open your message?' repeats the young man.

'Yes, yes, you open, thank you.'

The young man smiles at finally getting some civility.

'It's in English and says, '*Who are you?*''

Evzen is confused. This is not what he expected.

'Do you want to reply?'

But there's no response. The young man turns to see Evzen shaking his head, his lips trembling.

'Sir, are you all right?'

'I, I no understand,' Evzen says in a quavering voice. 'I…I don't understand all this…this…' He waves a crooked finger towards the computer screen.

The young man shows some compassion. 'Sir, yesterday when you come in I helped you as you had not used a computer before. Just tell me what you want me to do.'

'Your name?' asks Evzen.

'My name? My name is Jiri, sir.'

'Thank you, Jiri…I…I need to explain.'

'Please sit,' says Jiri, pulling out a stool from under the computer bench.

'Thank you,' Evzen says accepting the offer. 'My name is Evzen… Evzen Kravitz. I am here as instructed by a friend who…who is unwell and unable to get here. This, this…'

'MySpace page,' assists Jiri.

'Yes, that…that is hers. Yesterday you help me find it.'

'Yes, and I remember opening up another page and you became very upset at what you saw.'

Evzen clears his throat, the image still vivid in his mind.

'You said something about a Goose.'

'Yes, Goose,' says Evzen, his voice becoming raspy. 'I saw the Goose.'

'You then asked me to add a comment about that image, saying, um, let me see…' He brings up the comment. 'You asked *what you know of Goose?* He turns to the old man. 'Sir, I hope you take no offence at me saying this, but I looked at that image and could see no Goose.'

Evzen is silent in thought for a moment before mumbling aloud to himself, 'I not see that Goose for sixty-four years until…until that painting.'

Jiri is beginning to suspect this poor old man is showing signs of dementia. Not wanting to upset or confuse him any more than he already is, he decides against further discussing the invisible Goose. 'Do you wish to reply to this message, sir?'

Evzen looks blankly at Jiri as his mind has slips into the dark past.

'Sir,' he says a little louder. 'The message, you want to tell who you are?'

Evzen snaps back to the present. 'No!' he replies with an urgent shake of the head. 'No, no I'm just messenger. It not me they need know. He pauses for a moment, a trembling hand stroking the white, prickly stubble on his weathered chin. 'Say…say…*I am your mother.*'

CHAPTER 5

The sun's just up and it's bloody hot already. The old grey blanket's been kicked down to the end of the bed and Zac's blissfully snoring away. I've been listening to him all night cuz I haven't slept thinking about yesterday's message from Prague. If I'm right about this Veselý being my old lady, I've tossed and turned wondering if it'll actually change anything? I could've got up any time to check if I've got a reply, but I don't know, it's like I want it to be her, but then at the same time I don't. No point putting it off any longer, so I roll outta bed and boot up the laptop. Shit I'm nervous. I mean, who wouldn't be nervous at finding their old lady after sixteen or seventeen years. What if I frightened whoever off with the straight out *'who are you?'* Anyway, thirteen comments have come in, that's gotta be a bad omen. Shit, here goes. Let's see, the first one, no not that, nope, not the next, or that, or that. Shit, there it is, *R. Veselý*. Oh, fuck!

There's a small dead-end laneway down the Windsor end of Chapel Street where I come to sit and think. It's only used for deliveries and by now, ten-thirty, they've all been made so it's nice and quiet. Except for a couple of small doorways down a bit, the walls each side are solid old bluestone. There's a few tattered posters stuck on but only near the corner cuz no one would see them otherwise. There's the odd crappy graff, mostly small tags and stuff, nothing creative or anything. So the old bluestone is pretty much bare and, I don't know, there's something hand-made and personal about old bluestone walls. It's as if the walls have sucked in something from all those who cut the stones and built it. Sometimes I reckon I can see faces in the texture of the stones. Yeah, crazy, I know, but I have a special feeling for this place. Until recently there was this old homeless guy who camped here sometimes—I only knew him as 'Sarge'. Sometimes we'd talk and sometimes we'd just sit on the ground and stare at the wall. He was a Yank who came back after the War looking for the Aussie chick he promised to marry when he was posted here. But seems she couldn't wait, and I think because he was sorta screwed up by a war injury, he never got over it. Anyway, we got on all right. I have a feeling I reminded him of her. Then one day I came here to sit with him and all I found was a pile of his belongings and a note saying, 'FOR BRINEY'. I didn't know what to think, though I had a pretty good idea. I've never seen or heard anything about him since. So now I always wear his old Blundstone boots and use his old army bag he called a 'musette' to carry my paints and stuff around in. When it's cold, I wrap myself in his old battered and faded greenish fleecy lined nylon jacket I call my Yank Top. Yeah, I miss the poor old bugger, and right now I could do with him around to talk to.

I'm sitting only a few metres down from the Chapel Street entrance. While I like the solitude here, I need to feel and hear the real world, and the traffic and constant parade of those with a better life walking past the laneway helps me put things in perspective. It's like the small entrance frames portraits of everyday life for an instant, and while I'm only a couple of metres away, it's the distance of a lifetime.

'Thought I'd find ya here,' says Zac sitting down beside me. 'Thought I'd bring a friend along to keep us company.' He hands me a bottle of cheap Georgi Vodka.

Zac doesn't have the same feelings about sitting here like I do. He just watches everyone walking past the laneway and makes stupid rude comments.

'Fuck, did ya see that? Don't know about you, but Goth guys are real fuckin' weird.'

'Zac! I gotta tell you something.'

'Yeah, what?'

He wasn't really listening, just watching the passing parade.

'You know we don't talk about our past, right?'

That seemed to grab his attention and he looks at me real strange as if I'm about to break the golden rule, and I probably am. Sensing I'm about to open up to something, he takes out his tobacco to roll a cigarette. I watch and wait till he's finished rolling, licks the end, puts it between his lips then pats his pockets for a light. He never has one. I wait, knowing what's gunna happen. He's up, goes to the corner and stops everyone who passes until finally someone helps him out with a light. I wait. He's back sitting down beside me, takes a long drag and blows out a stream of smoke that catches the breeze directly into my face.

'Yeah?' he says, finally ready to listen.

We're sitting on the cobblestones with our backs to the wall that's warmed by the sun and the bottle of Vodka is between my legs. I'm looking down at it, fingering it as if it's all ears and won't talk back.

'What I'm gunna to tell you, Zac, I don't want you blabbing to anyone else, right!'

I can feel him looking at me, sensing I'm serious.

'Yeah, sure.'

That doesn't sound convincing. A tram passes in the main street channelling a rush of wind down the laneway. I get another face-full of smoke.

'I want you to promise, Zac. Do you know what a promise is?'

'Yeah, of course I know what a fuckin' promise is! Whatcha think I'm stu…' He stops short of finishing the sentence. He knows deep down what others think of him. I can sense his mood change and he's retreating into his protective shell. It's sorta one of those crazy things that's, you know, like a bond between us.

'I know you never asked, and, like, it's not the done thing, but right now I need to tell someone about my past.'

He looks away and stares down at the cobblestones while flicking ash from his cigarette. I take a quick glance at him, sensing his unease.

'Zac?' I question his mood.

He remains silently flicking his cigarette.

'Zac?' I repeat.

With his head slumped low, he finally speaks. 'If I tell you about my past, then, like, you'll have that over me to stop me telling anyone about yours. Right?'

I never expected him to come out with that, but the way he said it, I reckon he honestly wants someone to hear *his* story.

I take a long swig of Vodka then tap him on the shoulder with the bottle. He looks at the bottle, then me, and accepts it.

I try and break the ice and lighten the mood. 'We're both here in this shit-hole not because we want to be, right?'

He doesn't nod but gives a hunch of the shoulders and takes a drink from the bottle, wiping away a dribble running down his chin.

'And we'd get out if we could, right?' I add.

He lowers the bottle just as a trio of giggling late-teen girls pass the laneway in their bling outfits, totally absorbed in their own identities and loudly wanting the world to know.

'It's not that bad,' he confesses, looking at the girls.

I say nothing.

I'm nudged with the bottle, take it and down another mouthful.

'Do ya want me to go first?'

'No,' I snap in reply. I don't want his story to interfere in what I need to get out. 'No, I want to go first.'

He turns his attention to a piece of paper floating down with the breeze. Good, I don't want him to look at me.

I take a deep breath and hold it in for a moment to help me relax. Strangely I'm conscious of the wall at my back sucking all the tension out of me.

'Well,' I cough to clear my throat. 'Well, as I said, Prague is part of my past.' I take a glance at him. He's still looking at the piece of paper that's now trapped under his dirty, worn sneaker, but I know his listening. 'Not that I know much about Prague, like. I mean I've never been there. As I told ya, I was born here in Melbourne somewhere. But because my mu…my old lady's Czech, I sometimes Google or go to the library and read up about the place.'

The sun is now high, hot and soothing. The warmth from the bluestone is spreading through me like I'd imagine those hot rocks at a health spa would be like.

'She never married, so I don't know who my old man is. Doubt if she ever knew herself.'

Why have I stopped? Fuck! I don't want to cry. I clear my throat to continue.

'All I remember was that there was always men around, you know, like, different men. I'd be in the same room, mainly cuz there was only one, and there was this curtain drawn to stop me seeing who she was with. But I could hear everything, and I mean everything, the swearing, the grunting, the groaning, the arguments, the slapping, everything...'

Fuck, I can't hold back the tears any longer and feel them roll down a cheek. I sniff and give out a cover-up little cough. Shit, this is too much of a girly thing but I can't stop now.

'Anyway, that didn't last long though, cuz I was taken away from her when I was about seven or eight, I can't remember exactly, and I've never seen her since.'

I can't help it but I gotta wipe away the tears.

'Well, that old clock of mine, that's the only thing I have to remind me of her. She once told me it was the only thing she had to remind her of her parents and where she'd come from and...'

Just then, this guy, a real wanker mate of Zac's, spots us and comes down the laneway.

'Hey, dude,' he calls out. 'Just the one I gotta see.' He's obviously desperate for a hit and always looks sick, you know, like he's got Aids or something. Probably has. Fuck, now that's stuffed things up.

'Fuck off, Twig!' snaps Zac. 'Not now!'

His abruptness is a surprise to both of us.

'Hey man, like it's a fuckin' need, right?' He's always angry and his anger scares me. He can turn real violent with so much as a look in the wrong direction.

'I said fuck off, Twig, ya interrupting, got it?'

Whoa, I've never seen Zac so macho before. He's still sitting but the look he's giving Twig makes him six feet tall.

'A second, man, just a fuckin' second,' says Twig, confused at Zac's response. I'm sure he's never been told to fuck off by Zac before. Not Zac, he's so desperate to keep in with that mob.

'Look, I said fuck off Twig or you can forget me for ya supply forever. I'll catch up with ya later, right?'

Twig gives me a filthy look as if I'm to blame, and I probably am. I can see the rage building in his bleary eyes. He's about to erupt.

There's a movement as Zac drags his right leg back, ready to give him leverage up.

The breeze feels cooler or is it the standoff between the two. Twig's bent, lean body is quivering with rage and withdrawal, a very dangerous combination. But then, to my total surprise he sees his position, his supplier is calling the shots.

'Later, right?' he questions, anger still in his voice.

Zac only nods once and then twitches his head towards Chapel Street, indicating where he should piss off to. Twig gives me one more seething glare. I respond blankly. Never liked him and never will and I wish Zac wouldn't mix with him or his mates.

Finally, with head bowed, hands stuffed in empty pockets, Twig drags himself out of the laneway into Chapel Street, probably to take his anger out on some poor innocent bugger minding his own business.

We wait a few minutes to make sure he doesn't come back and to get our minds back to where we were.

'Fucking shit! Sorry Bri, go on,' says Zac, placing a hand on my knee. He turns his attention back to the paper still trapped under his sneaker and slides his foot back to a more relaxed position. 'You were telling me about ya clock.'

He *was* listening.

I try to remember where I left off. The tears have dried and I grab the bottle to add to the reassuring warmth I'm still feeling from the wall.

'Yeah, umm, well when I was being taken away from my old lady, rescued from her is how they put it, I grabbed the clock, you know, like, just out of impulse, cuz for some reason, even at that age, I knew I'd probably never see her again. And I never have. In fact I hardy remember what she looked like. You know, I was always told to stay behind the curtain even when she wasn't with anyone. I sorta felt like that curtain was not just to hide me from her…you know…activities, but also from her sad, secret world.' I can feel a lump growing again in my throat. Zac's hand is still on my knee and I feel a slight tightening of his touch.

32

'But worst was to come cuz I was put into fucking foster homes left, right and centre.' I need another drink. 'I never stayed in the same place more than six months. If I wasn't moved, I'd have run away anyway, and that went on until I sorta found my place on the street.'

I can feel his hand tighten more on my knee.

'What age?' he asks, lifting his foot to allow the paper to escape on the breeze.

'Sixteen,' I answer, sniffing back a tear. 'Thought about it years before and tried but the law was against me until I turned sixteen. Though the fucking law never was there for me anyway. It never protected me from those fucking so-called foster fathers. They would leer at me and touch me and presume that just because my old lady was supposed to be a whore meant I was born to be one as well. Well, what they didn't know was that I'd heard all their fucking bullshit before, from behind the curtain when guys with the same fucking mentality would beat up my old lady till she was blue and bleeding. At least she never laid a hand on me.'

'Did she ever try to see you, do ya know?'

'Don't know. She may have, but no one said anything to me.'

He sniffs and wipes his nose with the back of his hand. I dare not look to see if he's shed a tear cuz I feel I may have hit on something similar in his past.

'Did *you* try and find *her*?'

I wait for the sound of another tram to pass.

'Yeah, but without any luck cuz she never went by her real name, ya see.' I take another swig of the bottle and hand it to him. He releases his hand from my knee to take the bottle. Shit, why'd I do that? His hand felt kinda supportive there.

'But ya knew her last name from the clock, right?' He hands me back the bottle. I take it and place it down between my legs again and wait for him to put his hand back on my knee, instead he starts to roll another smoke.

'Yeah, well, didn't know about the name on the clock then. All I knew was she called herself Mimi Rose and was from Prague.' I pause to see if he laughs. He doesn't. 'Anyway, I adopted the name Ruza cuz

I reckoned it's Czech for Rose, and from then on I've used MyRuza on all my graffs. Sorta in the hope she might see one of my jobs one day. Bloody ridiculous I know, I mean, why would she be looking for me through fucking graffiti, right?'

'Right,' he agrees. 'So, ya wanted her to find you, or was it you wanting to find her?'

I look at him. What a question? I mean, sure I wanted to find her. I couldn't believe she just dropped me and forgot me...I just couldn't.

'Both, I suppose,' I finally answer.

He's silently staring down at the cobblestones playing with the unlit cigarette in his hands.

'I mean, haven't you ever wanted to know what your family are doing?' I didn't mean to ask him that. Not yet. He doesn't answer anyway, or maybe no answer is the answer.

'Zac!' It's now time to tell him. 'I got a reply this morning.' I wait for a response, but he's just staring down at the cigarette rolling between his fingers. 'It's her.'

'So what, ya just gunna believe it, are ya?' he says after a stretch of silence.

'Fuck Zac, everything fits, don't you see? I mean, like, the name, coming from Prague, and...' I try to think of other reasons.

'And what about all this fucking shit about a duck?'

'What?'

'The duck or goose, or whatever. What's that got to do with ya old lady?'

Shit, he's got me. I've no answer to that.

He returns from hustling another light from someone in the street and flops back down beside me. I get another face-full of smoke. He's not saying anything. I think he realises he's got me stumped by the Goose. But there's more I need to tell him, but shit, where do I start?

'Zac, I like, saw things the other morning. Ya know, while I was under the train. Things that totally freaked me out.' I need to gulp in some air. 'I saw two bodies under that train being ripped apart. Blood...so much blood...and...bits of bodies being flung all around me. But...but...they were bodies from another time and place.' I shiver as the awful images reappear. 'I know you're gunna say it's because I hit my head and you could be right, but Zac, with all this weird stuff since…I think something's happened to me.'

I wait for some response but all I get is another face-full of smoke and a cough while he stares down at his feet while flicking ash. What's he thinking? I bet how fucking off the planet I am, that's what.

'Look, I know you think I'm crazy and all, but…' I can feel the wall at my back urging me on. 'Zac…when I put my hand on the wall after the train thing…' I pause. 'It…it…sorta talked to me!' There, it's out!

The reaction from Zac is what I expected. He's stopped flicking ash and looks up at me with a snort of a laugh.

'Fuck Bri, ya pissed. Like, I can sorta understand seeing ya life passing before ya under the train, but fucking walls speaking to ya, shit come on?' He takes a draw of smoke. 'I know ya used to say that what ya paint is what ya feel from the wall, but I thought that was just creative shit.'

I'm not angry at his doubting. Shit, I'd do the same if things were reversed. 'Yeah, I am getting pissed. And yeah, if I did see parts of my life before me under that train, well…those bodies have some connection.' He's shaking his head at me. But the wall at my back won't let me stop. 'Look, what I felt when I touched that wall I can't explain. All I can say is that I can't ignore it. I know it sounds fucking crazy, but I really can't ignore it cuz it…' Shit, will I say it? 'It's…it's to do with death!'

This sounds crazy even to me, but the words just came out.

'Whatcha mean death? Whose?' He looks down to the bottle between my legs, grabs it and puts it between his. I reckon he thinks I've had enough.

'Don't know!' I say with a shake of the head and a shrug of the shoulders. 'All I know is that it's got something to do with me and… well…my old lady.'

He gives out another disbelieving snort. He's back looking down at his feet again. 'That's fuckin' crazy, Bri. Geez, someone ya don't know from shit mentions a fuckin' duck…'

'Goose!'

'Yeah, whatever, goose, duck, shit it could be a fuckin' elephant for all I care, and they come out with '*I'm ya mum*' crap! And then just like that, you believe em. Jeez, that knock to the head should've been checked out.'

Why am I so calm? Why is it the more Zac thinks I've gone crazy, the more I believe in what I'm feeling? And why does this hard bluestone wall feel so soft and reassuring?

'Zac, you're wrong!' I blurt out, jumping up and step over to the shady side of the lane. I reach out and rest both hands on the cold stone, unlike the opposite sun-warmed wall. I can still feel the force and the sense of voices. I know it sounds weird, but that's all I can make out, not words, or anything like that, but I can sense the wall is trying to tell me something and is relieved to have finally found someone it can release its secrets to. My hands recoil from the wall at the sudden realisation. All my graffiti, my little tricks on people, are all about hidden secrets. It was something that caught on and gave people a reason to think about their own secrets. It was all a joke. But…was it? Do I really have some sort of insight? That wall was trying to communicate with me— taking me into its confidence. I'm not crazy. I'm not that pissed. I'm not imagining this. I'm in just as much shock as anyone would be. I want to reach out and touch the wall again but I hesitate. Am I scared at what I've discovered? And anyway, what *have* I discovered?

'Bri!' Zac breaks into my cloud of self-interrogation. 'What the fuck ya doing?'

I take a long pause to look at the wall. All of a sudden my head clears of all this confusion. A sense of total control and certainty washes over me. I turn to him.

'I need to do something Zac.'

He's just sitting there looking at me, his hands still holding the bottle between his legs, his cigarette, barely alight, hanging limply between his fingers.

'I gotta go to Prague.'

Silence. Not even a passing tram or passing shoppers in Chapel Street.

'What?' he finally gets out.

'I gotta go to Prague, Zac.'

'Wha…why?'

How do I tell him? What do I say without sounding like I'm a total nut case?

'Just gotta, that's all.' Shit, what a chicken.

A smirk appears on his face. 'Yeah, right.' He's getting up. 'I'm hungry, let's get a pizza.'

CHAPTER 6

How can anyone like pineapple on a pizza? At least we got a dual one with my favourite Margherita on one half and his awful insult to pizza, a bloody Hawaiian on the other. Shit I hate it when bits of his fucking pineapple invade my half. I heard that the Margherita was created for Queen Margherita cuz it's sorta the colours of the Italian flag. I'm sure she would've spat chips if they'd put pineapple on it.

Since getting the pizza and returning to the laneway, there's been no mention of me going to Prague. I reckon Zac thinks the knock to my head is making me talk a lot of shit and I don't blame him. But I don't think I am and I'm determined to follow my instincts. I've always had this thing about trusting yourself. That gut feeling that only pops up when important decisions need to be made…and it's telling me to go.

'Zac, we had a deal, right? I don't want you telling anyone about what I've told you, right!'

'Jeez, Bri, they'd think I was fuckin' making it up. No way I'm gunna tell anyone all that bullshit.' He pauses as he realises what he's said. 'Yeah, well, not about ya old lady, I mean about the wall, the goose and going to Prague crap.'

I accept his sorta apology, but he's just lost out in getting the last bit of my Margherita. Not only that, but I'm having growing doubts about him keeping his loud mouth shut.

'So, like, what's your story then?' Thinking I might get something over him that'll shut him up.

He wipes the remains of his pizza from around his mouth with the back of his hand and leans back against the wall with a cold distant look in his eyes. I study him for a moment and see pain and anger flush over his face. Shit, maybe I'm being unfair. I mean, like, it was my decision to tell him my story and I guess I shouldn't force him to tell his, and going by the look on his face, it could be worse than mine.

'Look…um…like if it's bad you don't have…'

'Yeah, I want to,' he snaps back before I can finish. The tone of his voice has a ring of maturity I've never heard before.

Like I needed a hit of Vodka before opening up, Zac prefers to get his courage from a joint he takes from his shirt pocket. He always has a ready for emergencies, and I guess now's the time. A quick visit to the street for a light and he's back taking a long, slow inhale and holding it in until he needs some more air. After another long draw, he hands it to me. I accept to keep him company on the journey ahead.

'Not sure where to start,' he says, while holding in his breath for as long as he can. 'I mean, there's no real starting point like you. Cuz, ya see, I didn't have the same problem.' He reaches over to take the joint back for another drag. 'I had all the trimmings, ya see. Anything I wanted, I got. We were the perfect example of the pseudo-rich with a fuckin' big house in Doncaster and boat and holiday house in Portsea —everything to be better than the Joneses—as they say.' He's into it now and hands the joint back. 'My old man's a fuckin' property developer… cheated on everyone, couldn't give a shit about the environment, cut costs with cheap work and cheap materials just to get a quick build and sale and move on.' He wipes his nose with the back of his hand. Is that a sign of emotion? 'Anyway, Yeah, I had every fuckin' thing that was in fashion and all just to show everyone we was rich.' He sniffs and wipes his nose again. Is that the dope doing that or is he starting to choke? 'The fuckin' thing was, even though I had everything…I didn't have what I really wanted!'

I can sense anger coming into his voice. 'What was that?'

He gives a little laugh 'Freedom!' I wait for more. 'All I wanted was freedom to express myself. Ya know, like, live my own life without all that fuckin' pretentious bullshit.'

'So, what did you do?'

'What did I do? Fuck, what do ya reckon? I started to rebel. Hated school and all the fuckin' rich kids, so I reckon that's when things started to go fuckin' haywire.' He looks at the stub of the joint I've passed to him and delicately holds it between the tips of his fingers, takes short puffs to stop his lips from burning then stubs it out against the bluestone wall.

'So I used to stay away from school, ya know, hang out at the shopping centre and all that stuff. And that's where I noticed other kids hangin' out, nothing to do, just hangin' out. It was then I realised that I wasn't gunna play the game everyone wanted me to play and become some fuckin' rich successful creep like my old man or turn out just like my fuckin' shit of an older brother did. I wanted to find my own way in my own time and fuck society.' He coughs back a growing lump in his throat, his eyes becoming watery.

I reckon he needs a bit of support. 'Yeah, I can understand that.'

'Yeah, well, I knew I didn't have the fuckin' brains to get where I was expected to go. Like, the more spent on ya education the more ya expected to perform. It's the fuckin' expectation from everybody and nobody gives a shit about whether you want it or not.'

'Yeah, no one gave a shit about me either. All the fucking authorities kept saying to me was that everything was for my own good. How the fuck do they know? Like you, no one fucking asked me what I wanted.'

I reckon he feels we understand each other and a sorta excitement creeps into his voice. 'Yeah, no fuckin' way did anyone ask me what I wanted, I was programmed from day one by my shit of an old man.'

I see an opportunity and take it. 'And what *do* you want, Zac?'

He looks at me, his expression changes from anger to confusion.

'I mean, you gotta have some aim no matter what.'

He has to think for a moment and looks down at his sneakers. 'Fucked if I know, and fucked if I care. My old man kicked me out. He was a real prick. He had to have total control over everything and everyone. I think he got it from *his* old man. Now there was a real hard bastard. Had more clips over the ears from him than anyone. He had this, I don't know, ruthless European attitude. Kraut, I think he was.' I wince at the word—never liked it. 'And if I didn't do what he or my old man said I got a beating from both of them…and my mum. She was just as bad. A real social climber she was. Had none of those graces and shit the real social crowd put on.' He pauses to sniff and wipe his nose on the back of his hand. 'So I was disowned by my whole fuckin' family, thrown out with nothing and told never to come back until I…what'd he say, '*accept my responsibility*', Yeah, that's what he said, accept my fuckin' responsibility. So I fuckin' hit him with something hard that was nearby, and left. Didn't kill him or anything, not that I cared if I had. Anyway, zip, nothing, not a fuckin' thing. I walked out with nothing and no fuckin' where to go.'

'When was this?'

'When?' He thinks. 'Umm, I don't know, a couple of years ago, I guess.'

This convinces me of what I've always felt deep down, that we really don't have anything in common. I mean, I had no choice and always had a strong want to better myself, you know, starting from the lowest of bases, limited options and no family at all and a strong need to get out of this sordid existence. While Zac had everything and choices, despite what his family was like, and chose to opt for a lazy life. Now I understand why others on the street are wary of him and his persistent, over-energetic and annoying attempts at being accepted. I find I've become disinterested in his story.

'I'm going to Prague, Zac, so you better start thinking about what you're gunna do and where you're gunna go.' I'm surprised at how cold I said that.

He gives out one of his snotty laughs. 'Yeah, well where ya gunna get the money?'

'I'll sort it out somehow.' That's so unconvincing and he knows it.

'Anyway,' he says grabbing up my last piece of Margherita. 'I still reckon ya fuckin' crazy to get up and go based on two unproven messages.'

That's got me angry. Not him taking my last bit of pizza, but maybe he's right. Anyway, whatever, I'm not gunna let him talk me out of it. At least I have something to aim for even if it all turns out to be bullshit. I just want to get out of the rut I'm buried in. And you never know, just maybe, I will find her.

'I can get the money.'

He said that in a bloody smug way and with his mouth full of my pizza. What's he on about?

'I'll manage.' I snap back.

'What, it'd take probably a couple of grand to get there, so where ya gunna get that sort of money without being stopped at the airport by the fuckin' cops, hey?' His voice has gone up an octave and he's like a bloody predator circling his prey.

He's right, but I don't want to hear it. 'I'll think of something,' I say under my breath.

'And even if ya do get a job, it's gunna take forever to save that much. Ya won't be seeing Prague for more than a year.'

I feel he's ready to strike. He's lying back smugly stuffing the last bit of pizza into his mouth just waiting for me to accept what he's said is true.

'I can get the money and we can be in Prague in a couple of weeks.'

My head's spinning trying to think of something. Being arrested for stealing will never get me to Prague, and with a charge forever hanging over me I probably won't be allowed into any country in the future, so it's a risk I don't want to take.

Then it hits me. '*We!* What do ya mean, *we*? Oh no, thanks for the offer, Zac, but if I'm going to Prague, I'm fucking going alone, so thanks but no thanks, hey!'

I can see a glint in his eyes. Fuck, whatever he thinks about his old man, he certainly taught him that money is the answer to everything and he knows he's got me fucking cornered. Shit, shit, shit, what'll I do?

'I need to go for a walk and think.'

He's just sitting there looking down at his fucking feet knowing he's got me. He's certainly inherited his father's conniving.

I stand and start to walk away. He says nothing to stop me…that's unsettling. Then I do something fucking stupid. I turn back to him, instantly falling into his trap.

'So how would you get the money without stealing it yourself, anyway?'

I can see the smirk on his face even if he's still looking down at his feet. 'Can't tell ya that, but I won't be stealing it.'

This gives me a chance to hit back at him. 'So then, why haven't you used this money for yourself before if it's so fucking easy?'

He wasn't expecting this question but is quick to answer. 'I didn't say it was easy. And anyway, I didn't need it until now.'

I'm stumped for a smart reply.

'Yeah, well, I'm going for a walk.'

I like to walk around the older parts of Prahran. The laneways are narrow and the old houses, apart from their simple charm, have managed to keep some of their original gardens and trees. But I'm not thinking about gardens and trees. Bloody Zac's got me by the short and curlies and he knows it. Shit there's no way I'm even gunna get enough money to go to bloody Hobart, let alone Prague on the other side of the world. But the bastard's managed to raise some doubts in my mind. Why was the first message just about a Goose? I mean, if my old lady was really looking for me, and she must be to notice a graffiti blog at her age, why not start off by asking if I was her kid or something, not about a Goose, it just doesn't add up. So what, am I accepting all this to be true just because it's something I've always hoped for? Maybe.

Suddenly a little kid on a three-wheeler bike flies around a corner, swerves to avoid slamming into me and grazes a wall with the handlebars. He continues on as if nothing's happened, his little legs peddling like crazy to get as far and as fast away from me as he can. I watch him turn into a house and out of sight then look back to the wall and the streak of yellow plastic he's left behind. I place my hand on the fresh scar. It takes some concentrating, but I reckon I can feel it. I shake my head to clear it of any wishful thinking, but the feeling's still there. The wall felt that brush with the bike. It's faint, but I can sense it. That minor collision is now part of the wall's history, its little secret that will last a lot longer than the yellow streak that'll disappear over time. Yeah, I can feel it and I turn and head back to the pad.

Zac's not here, probably fixing up that prick Twig. Good, cuz I didn't want him around while I send off a reply.

With the computer on, I've read both messages from Prague over and over and I'm starting to feel something isn't right. I'm getting a sense these words are not from a woman, and that's made me reconsider the reply I'd worked out on my walk. Now, with the little text thingy flashing and waiting for me to type something, I'm stumped. Damn it, just be blunt, and my fingers start hitting the keys, then the send button and I quickly shut down the computer.

CHAPTER 7

An influx of tourist to the royal town of Litoměřice are making the most of the clear blue sky and midday sun to lounge in the variety of cafes facing the central square, Mírové náměstí. Still rugged up against the chill air, they linger over their coffees taking in the eighteenth-century baroque architecture. Others are underground in the web of cellar bars and restaurants that can descend down three levels. Whether underground or above, Litoměřice is full of life—a far cry from it's nearest neighbour, the darkly depressing Terezín.

But crowds are not to Evzen Kravitz's liking, especially when entering the busy Tourist Information Centre with a number of Germans in the mix. The urge to turn and walk out is strong, but his urgent mission is stronger and he must overcome his ingrained emotions and wait to be served. Ever since his childhood, waiting in line constantly stirs up painful memories of queuing for food, for a job, for medical treatment or, worst of all, transport to the unknown.

It takes an agonising seventeen minutes of anxious shuffling forward as the crowd thins to finally front the counter.

'Good afternoon Mr Kravitz,' says Jiri, much to Evzen's surprise that he's remembered. 'Is it the Internet again today?'

Evzen nods a rationed once; enough for acknowledging the greeting and for the reason he's here. Jiri walks around the counter with the slightest smirk towards the two computers situated beside the entrance to the Centre. One computer is being used by a young girl loudly chewing gum while reading through her list of emails and quivering to noise coming from her plugged ears. Evzen is unsettled by someone other than Jiri being able to see what he's about to do, but there seems no choice in this world of sloven youth, technology and now urgency as more people enter the Centre.

'Same MySpace page?' Jiri asks, catching the sharp nod from Evzen. Eager to quickly serve the old man and get back to the counter, Jiri flicks through the process until the page opens, and without asking, enters the username and password. He remembers everything about this strange man and his strange ways and his strange messages.

'You have another message. Do you want me to translate again?'

Evzen glances at the young girl next to him and believing no one could possibly hear anything above the racket surrounding her head, looks back to Jiri with a nod.

'Says…' Jiri pauses as he tries to make some sense of it. 'It says, *I need more proof you are my mother.*' He looks back at Evzen with a quizzical frown, as does the young girl who stops chewing for an instant to give Evzen a once over with her suspicious eyes.

This modern world of the computers, the Internet, MySpace pages, words and images that appear out of nowhere demanding instant action and the lack of privacy gets the better of the stressed Evzen, for now he has another message that requires yet another answer.

'I…I return,' is all he can say with a shaking head and hurriedly hobbles out the door.

Jiri is busy sorting and restocking the display of postcards before closing when the front door opens. He had given up on Evzen returning, but on closing time it annoys him to see the old man enter

44

with a look of desperation and weariness added to his usual sour demeanour.

'I have answer,' says Evzen, heading directly to the computer with a crocked finger waving at the keyboard. Jiri gives the wall clock a quick glance before joining the old man at the computer. It doesn't take long for the MySpace page to appear.

'Yes,' asks Jiri, his fingers paused over the keyboard.

Evzen unfolds a piece of paper in his trembling hands.

'You say, *do you still have grandfather's clock.*'

The words are keyed in.

'Is that all?' asks Jiri, hoping it is.

'Yes,' replies Evzen stuffing the note back into his coat pocket.

Relieved that he can now lock up and go home, Jiri is about to hit the send button.

'No!' Evzen says suddenly. 'Goose!' he adds, his quavering voice almost breaking up. 'What you know? Why Goose?'

Jiri is confused. 'Sir, you want me to add *what you know of Goose*?'

'Yes, why Goose? You say why Goose too!'

Jiri shrugs his shoulders, unconcerned if the old man sees his bewilderment.

'Is that all?'

There's no answer, just the usual unfriendly nod from the old man in his haste to leave.

Outside, Evzen rests against a colonnade arch dabbing sweat from his brow with an old, frayed and stained handkerchief. The effort of the day has taken its toll on his patience and his weary body, for two visits to the hospital in one day and two nerve-racking confrontations with the Internet was never anticipated.

When Evzen woke this morning in the simple two-bedroom apartment in a quiet back street situated at the south-west corner of Terezín that many year ago housed a butcher shop, he sensed the day would not be without surprises and his daily visit to the Litoměřice Hospital would again be an unhappy one.

Ever since Ruza Veselý returned to Prague, almost two months ago and thirty-nine years after her self-exile to Australia, he has cherished every minute of having her back. But it wasn't long before her debilitating illness required her to visit the hospital on a regular basis. Initially, she rejected Evzen's offer to accompany her to the nearest hospital at Litoměřice, but as her illness weakened, not only her body, but her resolve, she accepted his support. This is when Evzen became aware that while Ruza was in Litoměřice she not only visited the hospital, but also the Litoměřice Tourist Information Centre.

Evzen was always instructed to stay outside while she entered to *do some business*, she would say. That business, he later discovered with much anger and disappointment, was to view the website of someone called *MyRuza*.

But now, confined to hospital and her condition possibly terminal, this *business* she carried out could no longer be kept a secret from him. She had no choice but to ask him to continue her online observation of her daughter, a request that was instantly rejected by Evzen without any explanation. His refusal had devastating consequences as Ruza's health declined rapidly forcing Evzen to back down and agree. This resulted in reversing Ruza's decline and Evzen promising to never again refuse her requests.

The first day he nervously carried out his promise was the day he found he had much more than Ruza's interest at heart. That was the day his sight was blinded by hatred and loathing, the day that revived his promise of reprisal, the day he saw the Goose.

He could not tell Ruza what he had seen, and he did not tell her he had sent a message asking what this person, this girl, this supposed daughter of his long, absent love, knew of the Goose she had painted.

The next day came the reply asking who *he* was. Who *he* was! No, no he must not reveal himself, but he had now opened communication that was not meant to happen. He had allowed his emotion to interfere with Ruza's secret observance and now must confess he'd made contact for he needed to ask her what to say in reply. Without telling her the Goose was the reason for his rash action, Ruza readily forgave him, much to his surprise and relief. In fact there was an easing of the deep emotional pain in her eyes, for she had secretly hoped that someday a connection would be made.

'Tell her…' She pauses to consider her choice of words. 'Tell her… I'm your mother.'

Now, mopping his brow, his breathing laboured after the stress and exhaustion of the early morning visit to the hospital, then to the Tourist Information Centre, back to the hospital and back once again to the Centre, Evzen wipes the dribble from his nose, pushes himself away from the arch and hobbles off to his lonely room, aware that this can only be the start of more unforeseeable surprises to come.

———————

CHAPTER 8

It's typical of Melbourne weather, bloody hot sun yesterday and now I'm woken by the sound of heavy rain on the window. It's stirred Zac too and he's flung an arm across my tits. I look at him. We're both naked cuz of the hot night and I get a tingle from his touch. Feels good. When was the last time we did anything? Did we do it after the last graff like we normally would? Shit, I don't remember. Things really have changed since then. The tingle starts heading south. The sound of rain, that's what it is, always gets me feeling horny. I turn slightly away from him and gently run a hand down between my legs twitching when I touch where the tingle has come to rest. Zac turns towards me and I feel his erection pressing into me. I reach behind to direct it to where it's most wanted.

Zac's lit a cigarette and we're both silently staring up at the ceiling catching our breath. I needed that.

'Zac,' I break the silence. 'I took your advice and sent off a message yesterday for more proof.'

Isn't it strange how after a fuck you sorta go all soppy and open up

47

and say things you weren't gunna say. I suppose sex is sorta trust and you ride on that wave for a little while after.

'And?' he says, waiting for more.

'Well, I ain't checked for any reply yet.'

He places a hand behind his head on the pillow. I glance over his stretched-out thin body, his cock resting, deflated to one side.

'Ya know, like, what I said yesterday about getting the money still goes.'

I don't answer in the hope I can work something out without him.

'I'm gunna check if I've got a reply.'

I have a pee and a bit of a wash while the laptop's coming alive then sit and feel the nerves return as I read over the nearly arrived comments.

My god, it's true!

'Zac!' He's dozed off. 'Zac!'

'Wha?' He stirs.

'It's true! It really is her.'

He grumbles, getting off the bed and comes to look over my shoulder.

'See, I mean, no one knows about that clock except her. Fuck, it's true!'

'Yeah, Yeah, okay. But what about this?' he says pointing at the message. 'Still on about the fuckin' Goose.'

Shit, you know, I never saw that. All I saw was mention of my grandfather's clock and that was enough to send me off. What's it say? *What you know? Why Goose?* Jeez, I dunno?

'What ya gunna say?'

'What?'

'The Goose, what ya gunna say about it?'

I'm stumped. Shit I wish this fucking Goose would go away. I mean, shit, I've got more important things to worry about, like, what am I gunna say to her after all these years. At least I can only text. Shit, there's no way known I could talk to her on the bloody phone, hell no.

'Well, whatcha gunna say?'

'Fuck Zac, don't push me...I dunno yet.'

48

'So, like, ya still wanna go over there then, hey?'

I can tell by his tone he's getting ready to pounce but I need time to think. Yeah, right, shit, that's all I've done since yesterday. But now he's annoying me.

'Zac, you stink. Go and have a wash.'

He hates it when I say that. But at least he takes the hint.

With him gone, I go to the bed and grab my clock, take it out of its leather case, turn it over and yeah, there it is, *Josef Veselý*. I go back to the computer and hold the clock up beside the message from *R. Veselý*. I look back at the clock…*Josef Veselý*…*R. Veselý*…*Josef Veselý*. I can't stop comparing the names. My name. I'm a *Veselý*! Never thought about it before. Fuck, I can't believe it…I have a family!

Zac comes back smelling a bit less. 'You replied yet?'

I'm sitting in silent thought with head bowed and leaning back so far in the chair it's almost toppling backwards.

'Fuck, Zac. What'll I say?'

'Just say, Hi Mum!' He laughs and yanks the chair back, frightening the shit outta me. He always does that when I'm sitting like this. I'll never learn.

I don't answer…but at least it's a suggestion. *Hi mum, how've you been these last seventeen or eighteen years? Whatcha been doing? I'm going great, thanks. Married with six kids and own a fucking enormous house in Toorak with servants and all that shit and worth a fucking fortune.* Yeah, right! More like, *hi mum, where the fuck you been for the last seventeen years and why the hell did you dump me…cuz I'm living in the gutter thanks to you.*

Shit, I thought I'd got that feeling outta me a long time ago. I wonder if I do go over there and meet her whether she'd tell me. Nah, don't think I could if I was her. Anyway, the fact is that she found me and made the first contact, so I suppose that's gotta go in her favour. Shit, what'll I say?

'So, what do ya reckon?' He gives the chair a shake.

'What?'

'Prague! Ya wanna go or not?'

I push the chair forward and out of his grasp.

'Look, Zac, I'm not saying yes or anything. I think we should talk about it more,'

'What's there to talk about?" He walks away to get dressed. "The only way ya gunna go is if I get the money, right? And if I get the money, I go. Simple. No discussion!'

I'm fiddling with the trackpad and watching the little arrowhead jerking wildly around the screen. 'Look Zac, I really don't see any future for us, you know, together, I mean.' I stop fiddling, waiting for his reaction. The little arrowhead pauses in anticipation.

'So, we're goin' then, right?'

How did he figure that out? And why no reaction to what I just told him?

'So, I suggest ya send a message to ya old lady telling her how excited you are at finding each other and that you're comin' over to see her asap, okay?'

I feel pressured. 'Look Zac, I'm not sure about this. I mean, like, I don't want to be in debt to you for the rest of my bloody life.'

There's a pause, he knows his got me, then says, 'I can get the money in less than four days, max. I've checked flights and we can be in Prague in a week.'

Shit, this really is starting to sound tempting. But, apart from the worry of going with him, something else is bothering me.

'Look, I need to know how you're getting this money, Zac. I mean, like, I don't want to be travelling with the cops after us.'

'Don't worry,' he says coming over and placing his hands on my shoulders. 'I won't be stealing it, trust me.'

Yeah, right! How can you trust anyone who says 'trust me'?

'Look, Bri, since we opened up about our past and stuff ya got me thinking, right, and like, I figure that I sorta need a change of scenery, so whatever ya decide I'm still gunna get the money and go somewhere. May not be Prague, but I'm going somewhere. So, I suppose what I'm saying is…take it or leave it.'

Shit! Is he serious? I think so.

I turn to him. 'Look, ya gotta promise me ya not stealing this money, right?'

'Cross my heart and hope to die I won't be stealing anything. There, satisfied?'

I watch his finger make a cross over his nipple ring and then look deep into his eyes. I normally can see through his bullshit but this time I feel he just might be telling the truth. I'm not absolutely happy with this but I'm not stupid either, and the reality is, the only way I'm gunna get to Prague is to accept his offer, shit!

'Look Zac, if I agree, I want you to understand that once we get to Prague you're on your own, okay? I mean I do what I want and when I want without the need to tell you, okay? I mean I'm there for a reason and I don't know what's gunna happen or where it's gunna take me.'

'Yeah, sure, that's cool,' he says raising both hands in surrender. 'But, hey, we can still have some fun though. I mean, you know, like, we can still be together, right?'

Fuck, he's got his way and any conditions I impose are of no immediate interest to him.

Suddenly he slaps his forehead. 'Fuck! I got one, but you need a passport. That's stuffed that then!'

'Got one,' I say, shaking my head. 'And, Yeah, I have been overseas once.' Should I go on further? No. 'Long story, Zac, but I've got one.'

We remain silent, just looking at each other. It's a done deal!

'So what do we do now?' I feel like my hands are tied and I'm uncomfortable that everything's up to him now.

He scratches his head, sniffs and wipes a hand under his nose. 'I gotta go out now.' He does up a couple of buttons of his shirt and grabs his scraggy beanie. 'I'll let you know when I come back.' He stops halfway out the door. 'Ya better tell ya old lady we're coming.'

The door closes behind him and I'm left to think about what I'm gunna say. Shit, this is gotta be the fucking hardest thing I've ever had to do. Like, I don't want to go into some great big spiel or anything, nah, something short and nothing gushy. I know, *still have Grandfather's clock and coming to Prague, will inform when.* Yeah, that'll do.

CHAPTER 9

Evzen steps from the bus and waits as it drives off. As if wiping one scene to the next, the passing blur of metal, windows and wheels suddenly reveals the Litoměřice Hospital. In front of the entrance, a bronze cast female torso is poised before a slab of white marble she appears to have been born from, while below, a pool of crystal clear water is tempting her. Evzen ponders how deep is the water he's got himself in to, how strong will the current of change be and what hidden snags will have him drowning in his own selfish vendetta and, above all, what impact this morning's message will have on the ailing Ruza. Will she take the news of her daughter's arrival as good or bad? Yes, she has finally located and made contact, but did she want it to go this far? He felt her intense lingering pain when she told him of abandoning her child and now with the likelihood of a face-to-face meeting, will she be made to explain her reasons why, or was she content to just know the girl is alive and well and leave it at that? And is *he* prepared? Torn between not wanting her around, a physical reminder of Ruza's past life without him, and the desperate need to talk to her, to question her, no, interrogate her and find out what she knows about the Goose. But where will this girl stay? The thought of being with her in the apartment terrifies him. She is of a generation that lacks values, respect and shows ignorance of life's cruellest moments. How will *he* cope?

Feeling the stress this is putting on his weakened heart, Evzen transfers his heart tablets from his shirt pocket to the side pocket of his jacket, gripping them tight as he takes the first nervous step toward the hospital entrance. Institutions, as he calls every building of authority no matter what their purpose, once entered will have a life-changing outcome, small or large, good or bad. And he nervously believes today will offer up the latter in both instances.

The long corridor is busy with patients and other visitors as he wobbles his way to Ruza's ward. A nurse who normally tends to Ruza is coming out of the ward and her usual warm, friendly smile dissolves as she approaches. A cold chill runs down Evzen's spine and he tightens the grip on his tablets.

'Ruza?' he says in response to her changed expression. 'What has happened?'

'Mr Kravitz,' says the nurse taking his arm and leading him to a nearby line of chairs against the corridor wall. 'Please sit,' she says easing him into a seat and feeling his rapid pulse through his frail arm. 'Mr Kravitz, are you all right? Maybe I should call a doctor?'

'No, no, Ruza! Something has happen, yes?' he says, tensing up and trying to brush her hand away.

The nurse doesn't want to add anger to his obvious stress. 'Mr Kravitz, Ruza Veselý has had a relapse and she has been taken to intensive care.'

The look that comes over Evzen's face is not of surprise or fear, but of panic. He shakes his head as all the questions and explanations he has pondered over become unravelled.

'But...but...she will recover, yes?' he stutters. 'I can see her, yes?'

'Mr Kravitz, she has been placed under heavy sedation to aid the treatment.'

'But I have important news she needs to hear...she...she must know what I have to tell her,' he pleads.

She pats his arm while her other hand is still feeling his pulse. 'I'll ask the doctors and see if you can visit her.'

Evzen covers her hand with his. 'She must know about her daughter before she...' He cannot say the word even though it is expected at any time, but not now, not before seeing her daughter after so many years.

The nurse is concerned about leaving this frail old man in his stressed condition, but doing nothing will only worsen the situation. She gives his arm a reassuring squeeze. 'I'll get the doctor to talk to you.'

Evzen watches the nurse walk away, turn into a reception area and out of sight. He looks back toward the ward Ruza should be resting in.

In both directions the corridor is suddenly empty and a wave of blame washes over him. The messages, the contact with her daughter after so many years, the emotional strain, all must have brought on this crisis. Finding her daughter could be the death of her and his resentment of this girl reaches a new high. Will she be the reason that after only such a brief reunion he will lose his Ruza once again…this time forever? This girl, this daughter of a stranger, this girl from another world has come between his life-long love and himself.

But scars from the past, no matter how long ago they were inflicted, can never be erased…and this girl also holds a secret. A secret he desperately needs to uncover.

'Mr Kravitz,' the nurse's voice breaks into his thoughts and looks up. 'I have talked to the doctor and he believes it is too early for you to visit. She is still very critical and it is best you go home and maybe tomorrow she will be in a better state for you to visit.'

Evzen can only stare at her, then with a shake of his head, whispers, 'No, she needs to know. I can't leave until then.'

The nurse is adamant. 'Maybe tomorrow…you come back tomorrow.'

'But…she may…' He looks pleadingly into her eyes.

'I'm sorry, Mr Kravitz, the doctors are doing all they can… tomorrow.'

How worse can this day get, accepting he has no choice. The nurse goes to help him up but he rejects her assistance. His love may be taken away from him, but he still has his independence. 'Tomorrow, Mr Kravitz,' she says as he slowly limps away, his head bowed in defeat.

Evzen is not a big drinker, unlike most Czech men, but he feels the need of a Pilsner to calm his nerves and drown his disappointment and the Hostinec na Vídraholci opposite the hospital beckons.

Sitting at a table in the shadows and away from any window overlooking the hospital, he withdraws the old handkerchief from his pocket and wipes his moist eyes and a drip from his nose.

His beer arrives and he takes a long, slow drink. Placing the mug on the table, he stares into the froth and puzzles over what to do now.

If Ruza were able, she'd tell him what to do. He would not like it, but at least it would not be for him to decide. But now it is. My dear Ruza, he calls out in the silent recesses of his heart, what should I do?

The beer is finished, unnoticed. 'Another,' he orders, for the isolation of the bar offers a degree of comfort from the confusion of the outside world.

CHAPTER 10

It's been three days since sending the message I was coming to Prague and still no reply. Have I frightened her off? She probably regrets she ever made contact with me. I mean, I've thought about it, you know, over there and all, and how I'd be and what I'd say to her. I could send another message, but all I'm getting back are short, cryptic replies and I still have this eerie feeling that I'm talking to someone else and not her.

Zac's gone out. I guess to get the money. He seemed a bit edgy when I asked him and he got a bit shitty and left without a word. I figured that if he gets himself into bloody trouble with the cops I'll just play the dumb girlfriend who knows bugger all.

Then, just as I'm contemplating being the dumb mousy blonde, the door flies open and Zac rushes in.

'Change of plans. We gotta get to Sydney tonight!' he says and starts scooping up his pile of clothes off the floor.

'What? Why? What the fuck have you done now?' comes my stunned reply.

'I got us on an earlier flight to Prague but it leaves from Sydney first thing in the morning, ya ready?'

I'm confused but obediently start gathering up all my clothes and stuff. 'So ya got the money?' A bloody obvious question I know, but I wanted to hear what he had to say and judge if there wasn't some other reason we're leaving so suddenly. Like, he did say once he got the money we'd be off, but I wasn't expecting it to be today.

'Shit man,' he answers in a surprisingly excited and cheerful tone. 'More than I hoped for, that's why I could get us on the next flight out, but hurry we've only got a couple of hours before our flight to Sydney. We can park at the airport there for the night.'

'Everything's, you know, okay, isn't it?' I can't hide my doubts.

'Shit, Bri, why all the fuckin' questions? We need to get to the airport pronto, that's all, now hurry.'

It doesn't take long to get our gear together cuz there ain't much. Zac shoves his stuff into an old school sports bag he had with him when he came here. He's leaving his really dirty stuff, which is most of it, cuz he reckons he'll buy stuff in Prague if he needs it. I manage to get most of mine into a Safeway's shopping bag and old Sarge's musette after I dumped the spray cans. Sorry to leave 'em, but I won't be allowed on the plane otherwise. Plus I need room in the bag for my laptop, which I check one last time if anything's come in from Prague, but nothing, shit!

I follow Zac to the door and pause for a last look around the crappy place. Well, when I say crappy, I mean less crappy than most other places I've shacked up in. Except for our clothes and stuff, everything else was here and the silly bugger who got me this place can sort things out with the landlord. I turn to close the door behind me and on another miserable chapter in my life. Then suddenly stop. 'Fuck, the clock!' It's still on the floor beside the bed under the kicked-off blanket. That would've been a total disaster, leaving behind what is now, more than ever, my absolute most valuable possession.

It was a bloody sleepless night in the Sydney terminal and the call's just come through to board our flight to Prague, well actually Bangkok first. I check one last time if any messages had come in and still nothing. But, as I'm about to leave the country I thought I'd better send a message. *I'm on my way and should be in Prague*...shit, what's the date? April 12, okay, I should be in Prague tomorrow sometime so that'll be...*April 13*. Then, after some thought, I add...*tell me where to go to meet*.

It was a nine-hour flight to Bangkok. We were so bloody tired we slept most of the way. On landing we had to rush to board the next flight to Budapest. Just made it so there was bugger all time to get on the computer and check for any messages.

The fifteen-hour flight to Budapest was a challenge to anyone's endurance. Cramped, down the back of the plane and Zac getting so pissed that I thought they were going to land somewhere and drop us off. He was flashing money around like crazy. Buying expensive drinks and duty-free stuff. I had to threaten him with crushed balls if he didn't stop drinking and behave himself. I knew accepting his offer was gunna be a problem.

So, after changing planes at Budapest and twenty-eight hours after leaving Sydney, exhausted, aching all over, totally pissed off with Zac and desperately in need of a bloody long hot shower and a good brush of the teeth, we finally arrive at Prague.

The slow progress through customs seemed to worry Zac and I had a sudden fear that he could be stupid enough to be carrying drugs. And, as it turned out, so did the customs officers who asked both of us to open our bags and lay everything out on this large table. Luckily, and I must admit rather surprisingly, he had the brains not to be carrying and they finally let us through. But even then I felt they weren't completely satisfied cuz I could feel their eyes following us until we disappeared into the arrival lounge.

With Zac off to change some money, I pause to look around and pinch myself that I'm actually here in Prague. The place looks, smells and sounds different, though airports can disguise the place you've arrived at cuz that's the way they are. But I'm getting a strange feeling that this is not altogether new to me and that I'm kinda returning home. Sounds bloody crazy I know, but I'm getting this weird sense coming from all directions.

I'm snapped out of my trance as Zac returns counting the money he's changed and I hope he'll hand me some, but he just stuffs it all into his pocket without a word and heads to the exit. I follow in a huff.

Someone back in Melbourne had told Zac of a backpacker's Hostel that's got graffiti all over it, so, of course, it was the obvious place for us to go, right? We manage to arrange a taxi to take us with the help of someone who spoke some English, then, once outside the terminal, we get our first taste of European weather. It's well after midnight and so fucking cold I expect to see snow. Inside the taxi isn't much better until the driver turns the heater on after seeing how much I was shivering.

We see very little as the taxi weaves its way into the city, across a river, past what looks like a lot of construction work until finally stopping. In the dim lights from the street made dimmer by a cold fog that gives the place a haunted feel, I can make out old buildings on the right side of the road and what could be shops a little further down. On the left, what looks like the blank back of a telephone booth blocks our view. There's no one around and even though it's built up, with no shop lights on it feels deserted and a bit scary.

'Tam, tam,' says the driver pointing towards the phone booth. What's he on about?

'Elf?' Zac questions the driver.

The driver nods and waves his finger more to the back of the cab. We turn our heads and almost obscured by the phone booth is an open gateway over which is an arched sign with the words HOSTEL barely visible in the mist and dim streetlights.

'Elf?' Zac questions the driver again.

'Ya, Elf,' he says, nodding.

Zac pays the driver and we watch him drive away leaving us alone in the deserted street. We step up to the gateway. Beyond is a dimly lit laneway leading to a flight of steps rising up a couple of levels to the back of the building. Zac leads the way and in the dull light I can just make out an endless display of graffiti covering the wall on our right. At the top of the steps we turn into what seems to be some sort of courtyard with light coming from a doorway and a widow where a small bearded Elf with a tall red hat is staring out and beckoning us to enter. We open the door and step into a small reception space and… oh yes…heat. It was like stepping out of an icebox and into a sauna. The ochre walls, lots of timber, books, posters and other homely bits and pieces add to the welcoming warmth. Behind a counter, a guy, not much older than Zac, sits relaxed and cosy in a t-shirt. He looks up from the magazine he's reading. 'Hi,' he says in a sorta broken English. 'Welcome to Prague, ya?'

CHAPTER 11

I haven't set my clock to Prague time yet, but I reckon it must be around mid afternoon so I've had a pretty good sleep, but Zac's still out to it. The only room available had two single beds. It suited me but Zac was pissed off until his head hit the pillow. I ease out of my bed, not wanting to wake him just yet, stretch and go to the window for my first look at Prague in daylight. There's a bit of a haze still lingering in the air, or is it pollution, never known how to tell the difference until you get out and smell it. We must be three or four floors up and in the street below there's a bit of traffic but not many people walking around. I guess the cold would be a bloody good reason for that.

So this is Prague? Not what I expected actually. I mean the buildings I'm seeing in front of me are probably older than anything in Melbourne, but they're not at all like the photos I saw when I Googled the place. Where's all the old shit, like the fairytale buildings and the cobblestones and the castles and stuff? But it *is* Prague, and again I feel there's something familiar about it. I part the curtains more and rest a hand against the window frame and the wall so I can lean forward to look further to the right. Immediately, I feel a tingling through the fingers that ripples right through me and I'm compelled to move and face the wall. With arms outstretched and fingers spread wide I shudder and close my eyes at the overwhelming sensation of giving in to the wall's force. I let out a deep sigh as I begin to slide along the cold, hard surface as if a magnet on the other side of the wall is manoeuvring me. The sensation of connection is overwhelming and I smile.

'What the fuck ya doin', Bri?' comes a voice from the other side of the room.

I'm instantly released from the magnetic attraction, and flushed with embarrassment, quickly push away from the wall. 'Nothing,' I answer casually. 'Just needed a stretch that's all.'

'Yeah, well it looked like you were having it off with the bloody wall.'

I'll ignore that.

The Elf Hostel seems a friendly place and popular with backpackers. It's near the Florenc Metro and the main bus terminal so it's easy to get to the Old Town centre or to other Czech towns or even out of the country. This information and more is cheerfully explained to me by a girl behind the reception desk wearing an Elf T-shirt and a broad smile. Even though her English is pretty good, her Czech accent gives it another dimension, clipped and precise, not the slow, lazy drawl I'm used to…quite sexy actually. I've come down to the front desk to find out if they've got WiFi or where the nearest Internet café is.

'Ya, free internet down stairs,' says the girl pointing to steps leading down to a lower level.

'Thanks,' and head in that direction.

I'm not uploading anything so I didn't bother bringing my laptop down. After grabbing the only free computer I login to MySpace. Quite a few messages have come in since leaving Australia but there's only one username I'm looking for, and there it is.

'*Midday tomorrow. Magdeburg Barracks. Terezín.*'

Shit, that's it? That's all? No look forward to seeing you or anything? And, tomorrow, shit, when was this sent? I forgot about time zones. Sent today, this morning…then it hits me. I'm now in instant contact. No more waiting a day for a reply. Tomorrow! Shit! Like that's *tomorrow*! 'Fuck!'

I didn't realise I'd said that out loud and sense all eyes have turned my way.

'Ba?' says the girl sitting next to me.

I look at her. What does *Ba* mean? I shrug my shoulders and smile at her and the others in the room. I get a quirky grin back from the girl beside me before she and the others turn their attention back to their screens. I do the same but can't help looking back. The girl with the quirky smile is dressed unlike the others in the room. They're all like me in tatty jeans, T-shirt and a sloppy jumper or jacket. But she's, I don't know, as quirky as her smile and giving off this vibe I can't explain. I can't stop checking her out with her short spiky white hair, pale face and dark red lipstick, until she tilts her head towards me. There's no eye contact, but she knew I was looking and I snap my attention back to the message. I need to write this address down and get the girl on the desk to tell me where it is and how to get there. I go to hunt for my notebook I always carry in my bag but realise I left the bag in the room. 'Fuck,' I say again.

'Promin?' says the girl beside me. Then rightfully assumes I'm not Czech. 'Sorry, excuse me. Is there a problem?'

I look at her, instantly struck by her amazing green eyes. I've never seen eyes of such intense colour before and it throws me. 'No! Umm, no, sorry, I…I came down without a pen and paper.'

'Here,' she says, tearing a page out of a small note pad she's taken from the pocket of her expensive-looking black leather jacket. I take the paper and the stub of a pencil she hands me and notice her fingers covered with an assortment of weird chunky rings and black painted nails.

'Thanks,' I say with a smile. 'You speak English?' Shit, what am I saying, of course she bloody does!

She politely ignores my dumb statement and gives me another quirky smile—this time showing perfect white teeth—and asks, 'Where are you from?'

'Um…Australia.' I can't unglue my eyes from hers.

'Oh, Australia. You're lucky to have sun all year. I'd love to be tan like you.'

I smile, not sure what to say next.

'You just arrived in Prague?'

'Yeah, we got here late last night,' Why am I feeling so bloody coy? 'Still a bit tired from the long flight.'

She smiles without saying anything straightaway, then, 'We? You travelling with your boyfriend or husband maybe?'

'Oh no, his not a boyfriend,' I hurriedly correct her. 'And definitely not a husband!'

There's a hint of a smile and I note an extra glint in those green eyes. She extends a manicured hand, 'My name is Zoja.'

We shake. 'Briney, hi, nice to meet you.'

I go to release my hand but her grip tightens ever so slightly and unexpected messages dart to interested parts of my body.

'Um, you Czech?' I ask, trying to stay reasonably composed.

'Yes, of course, pale skin, hey,' she replies sliding her hand away.

Pale skin's right, yet not sickly transparent like a vegan's, more like smooth, fine porcelain and I have to force myself to stop staring into those eyes.

'Um...Zoja, mind if I ask you something?'

'Of course not...ask me anything.' There's that quirky grin again.

I turn to the computer to write down the message then hand her back her pencil and the page from her notebook. 'Do you know where this is?'

She gives the note a quick glance, takes her pencil and turns to look out the window.

'Are you finished on the computer?'

'Um, Yeah, I guess so?' I look back to the screen and figure there's no reason why I need to reply to the message just yet, if at all.

'The sun's come out. Why don't we go outside to the beer garden? You drink beer don't you?'

'Of course, sounds like a great idea,' I agree, trying not to sound too eager to be around her a bit longer.

I didn't notice how bright the colours of the beer garden were when we arrived in the middle of the night. The outside wall's totally covered in crazy wild graffiti. The tables beside the wall and around the small paved courtyard are painted a bright warm yellow with some touches of red and green. A low fence of uneven planks separates the paved area from a raised garden dotted with interesting objects and sculpture pieces. Each plank of the fence has a hand-painted name of a city or a country, a statement left by visiting ambassadors, I guess.

I was so interested in looking around I didn't notice Zoja getting two bottles of beer.

'Here,' she says handing me a bottle. 'You can't be in Prague and not drink the best beer in the world.'

'Ta.'

'Just so you know, there's always cold beer in the refrigerator.' She tilts her head back toward the office where the elf in the window is on guard.

'You pick a table, ya.'

I opt for a table in the sunniest spot. There's a few others sitting around drinking beer and chatting, most likely about their worldly adventures. Zoja slides her bottle to mine and we clink them together.

'Na zdraví.'

I nod. 'Naz…um, naz drov…oh, fuck it, cheers,' I concede.

Those eyes smile back at me as we both down a large swig of beer. Unfortunately my swig was bigger than I expected and beer dribbles down my chin and onto my T-shirt. I give an embarrassed grunt and quickly wipe away the beer. She smiles at my clumsiness, but it's a different smile, more like a smile of interest. I take another more modest drink, allowing time to take in the effect that smile had on me. I feel relaxed. The most relaxed I've felt for a long time. The sun is out, the sky has a touch of blue and I've met someone who seems friendly… no fuck it…someone I'm attracted to.

'That note you showed me inside,' she says, interrupting my thoughts.

Shit, I've already forgotten about the address. I put the beer down and take out the piece of paper from my jeans pocket and hand it to her. 'Um, Yeah, can you tell me where this is?'

She gives the note a fleeting glance, again without taking it.

'Are you Jewish?' she asks, her expression slightly cooler, her eyes not as sparkling. Shit! What a bloody question?

'I'm sorry, none of my business, I should not ask.' She obviously saw the stunned, confused look on my face.

'Um, sorry, but I don't understand. Like, no, I'm not into any religion.'

'It's just that Terezín was a Jewish Ghetto under the Nazis during the war, and well, there is not much there to see but museums and depressing, deserted old buildings. I didn't think it is of interest unless you are Jewish. I'm obviously wrong and I apologise.'

'No, no, it's cool, no problem,' I reply. But what she said has rocked me. I mean, what's with this Jewish thing and this Ghetto, Nazis and deserted buildings? I had no idea what to expect, but shit, it sure wasn't this. Could I have written it down wrong?

'Look?' I say sliding the note back to her. 'You sure it's the place you think it is?'

This time she underlines the words with her black nailed index finger. 'Magdeburg Barracks, Terezín.' She looks back to me. 'It's one of two museums there. Why? What were you expecting?'

'I…I've no idea what I was expecting, but shit, nothing like this.'

We're both silent for a moment

'Have you been there?' I ask.

'Yes, but it's a regrettable part of our dark history.'

Regrettable dark history! Shit, something must be wrong here, but I'm sure I wrote it down right cuz the spelling was weird.

'There's a bus terminal not far from here where you get a bus to Terezín. I'm sure the girl at the desk here will have a timetable.'

I raise the bottle, hoping a drink will dull my confusion.

'You have someone there to meet?' she asks, having a drink herself.

I'm halfway through swallowing and cough at her question. 'No! Um, I mean.' I need to think. 'Maybe.'

'Is your travelling companion going with you tomorrow?' Is that a hint of cheekiness in her tone?

'No, no, he…'

'Fuck, there you are?' Zac's timing is perfect, but unwelcome. 'The chick said you were on the Internet but you weren't there…hi,' he adds arriving at the table and giving Zoja a look over.

'Umm, Zoja, this is Zac,' I can't hide my annoyance at his interruption.

'Hello, Zac.' She extends her ring-covered fingers to him. 'Welcome to Prague.'

'Yeah, hi.' He gives two quick shakes of her hand and me a quick look of…*who is she?*

'We met in the computer room and she helped with something.'

'Can I get you a beer?' asks Zoja. I'm sure she sensed my change of mood with his arrival.

64

'Bloody oath!' He's so fucking rude.

She goes to get him a beer and without hesitation Zac slides onto her seat and looks around the garden, giving out the occasional 'Cool.'

Shit, I really don't want him around right now.

Zoja returns with his beer.

'I was just going to suggest to Briney some places you shouldn't miss while you are here in Prague.'

'Yeah, so what's on tonight?' Shit, he's just picked up the beer and taken a swig without any thank you.

'Is there anywhere special you want to go to?'

'Yeah.' He takes another long drink from the bottle, plonks it loudly onto the table and lets out an embarrassing burp. 'Yeah a pub. Like, some place wild.'

Zoja looks at me as if trying to read my mind, or maybe my mood. 'There's a place just down the road from here. They have a local band playing tonight.' She looks back at Zac. 'That's why I'm here. I know them and can introduce you if you like?'

'Cool,' says Zac, gulping down the rest of his beer.

'You okay with that, Briney?'

Yeah, right, thanks for asking. Shit, I gotta snap out of this, she's just being friendly.

'Yeah, sure that sounds cool,' I hope that sounded convincing and I make an attempt at changing the subject. 'Are you staying here at the hostel?'

'Me? Oh no, I live in the Old Town. I know some of the people who work here so it's somewhere I can hang out until I go and see the band.' She looks back at Zac. 'I was checking my emails, Zac, and fortunately met your lovely friend.'

There go those sparks darting through me again.

Zac just grunts and walks off to look around the garden. 'Fuck, look at all this shit. This is so unreal,' he yells back attracting the attention of the others sitting around.

Zoja leans forward and whispers. 'You don't mind me telling Zac about the band do you, Briney. I don't want to interfere if you had other plans.'

'No, no that's fine,' I reply, giving her a slight smile to show she's done nothing wrong and at the same time trying to hide being pissed off at the yobbo way Zac's acting.

'It's only down the road a little, so if you don't like it you can come back here.'

I smile, knowing that's quite on the cards.

'Now Briney, I have something I need to do, so if I meet you here at seven and then we go to the pub, okay?'

'Yeah…um, sure.' I feel a twinge of disappointment at her sudden departure.

She calls out to Zac, 'See you here at seven, Zac. Nice to meet you.' Then turns to me with those smiling deep green eyes. 'And very nice to meet *you* Briney.'

Our eyes lock for a moment then she turns and disappears down the steps at the side of the building.

'She's a bit of a spunk for a Goth.' says Zac, returning to the table.

I don't answer and throw down the last of my beer.

'Zac, I need to talk to you about some money.' I'm trying to stay calm and rational. 'I know I agreed to the arrangement that you pay for everything and that's cool, but, like, I need some money to go somewhere tomorrow.'

'No probs, I'll go with ya.'

I was dreading he'd say that.

'Look, this thing tomorrow. I need to do it on my own and I need some bus fare and some spending money. I'll just be gone for the day.'

'Yeah, well, where ya going?'

I know he won't give me any money without knowing. 'It's a place called Terezín. I…I got a message.'

He's looking around at the others sitting on nearby tables and seemingly disinterested in what I'm saying.

'So, like what did it say?'

'Just to meet at this place tomorrow, that's all.'

I take the note out and show him.

'Fuck, is that all the message?'

I nod.

'Ya fuckin' crazy, Bri. That's not a message from ya old lady.'

I don't respond but he's become interested.

'Jeez, ya being conned. Fucked if ya know who or what's gunna be waiting for ya there.'

'Yeah, well you may be right, Zac, but I still reckon it's got something to do with her, and it's the only way I'll find out, right?'

'Yeah, well, whatever. But, tonight it's you and me, right? Like, I mean together, right?'

I know damn fucking well what he means. And I also know I've got no bloody option. 'Yeah, okay. But Zac, it's not gunna change anything about the way I feel, ya know. I mean if I could've got the money you wouldn't be here with me, right?'

That seemed to piss him off a bit, but fuck him. He knows I've no trouble surviving on my own. I mean I reckon I could get a job here at the hostel where I can stay and maybe even earn a bit extra. But there's no time for that now so I'm stuffed.

'Yeah, well only as much as ya really need, aye?' he says without any attempt at getting money outta his pocket. 'I mean all I got has to last until we go back, right?'

I've no idea how much he's got after all the bloody money he spent on the plane coming over. But there's one thing I know. It's when *he* goes back, not *we*! I've got this feeling I'm gunna be here a lot longer than I imagined.

CHAPTER 12

Every day for the last five days, Evzen Kravitz has sat by his beloved Ruza's bed holding her limp, frail hand, hoping for a sign, the slightest movement that she is aware of his presence. There's been no physical sign and all he can do is believe that somewhere, deep inside her comatose body, she knows.

Since allowing him to visit, the nurses have granted him time to be alone with her so he can talk freely, cry, pause, contemplate and cry some more. This open display of love, the doctors feel, is keeping their patient alive much longer than they expected.

The day after she slipped into a coma, the day after Evzen had received the message that confirmed Ruza had found her daughter, was the day he told her that her daughter was coming to see her. But there was no reaction. Not the slightest flinch of a finger or a blink of an eye, nothing. But, Evzen trusted her soul to hear him and now four days later he firmly held the belief she was listening and managing to hold on in the hope she may feel the touch of her daughter's hand on hers, to sense her presence, to hear her voice, to die knowing.

'Tomorrow,' Evzen says in the soft, quiet tone he has adopted at her bedside. 'I will meet your daughter tomorrow and bring her to your side.' His eyes widen and he looks around for a nurse, but they are alone. He was sure there was something, not a twitch of the hand, not a blink of an eye, but a smile. His hand moves from her arm to gently touch her lips. They have warmed and softened. He's positive there was a momentary relaxing from the tension of limbo and she had smiled. It was the slightest hint of life being restored. He is now convinced she recognises his presence and his words are not wasted. But because of the torment, anguish and unwelcome responsibility of meeting and befriending this girl, he must be careful in what he says. He removes his hands from her for fear that she may sense his inner trauma.

A nurse comes to check on all the attached monitors and notices a change in one of the readings.

'I'm sorry, Mr Kravitz, but you must leave now.'

Evzen is shocked and panics. 'What…what have I done?'

'Come back tomorrow.'

'Yes…tomorrow…yes, you must keep her alive until tomorrow.'

The nurse is no longer listening to him but concentrating on other monitors and drips and motions to another nurse to get the doctor.

Evzen is hastily ushered out.

What have I done, he thinks, she can read my thoughts, what have I done? He feels a tightening in his chest. He must get out of the hospital. Tomorrow he has a meeting and a promise he must keep and he cannot afford to be seen to be having an attack or they will not allow him to leave.

On the bus back to Terezín, his mind is awash with guilt and betrayal. He now sees the wrong in asking this girl to meet him at the Museum instead of telling her of her mother's condition and to meet at the Hospital. But try as he may, he cannot come at changing what has been planned, for there is another reason, a selfish reason for staying with the planned meeting at the Museum. He needs to see this girl first. Study her, watch how she moves and acts. To look for identifiable features passed on from her mother before confronting her. Yes, the Museum is right. He needs to find out what she knows of the Goose before seeing her mother as it may be his only chance. Yes, he silently nods, confident he has made the right decision.

The bus driver calls out. Evzen has not noticed they have stopped and the driver is waiting for him to disembark.

Standing on the pavement, Evzen looks around at his familiar town to decide the best way to secretly watch the girl's arrival at this very same place. The walk back to his apartment becomes a meandering journey as he plans his tactics.

CHAPTER 13

If I said I wasn't hanging out to see Zoja again, I'd be lying. After she left, I couldn't stop thinking about her for the rest of the afternoon. I mean, shit, how good was that, meeting someone like her on the first day. Someone I can ask about things here and who is more than happy to tell me more than I expect. Yeah, all that, but there's something else that has me sitting here in the beer garden since way before seven, something absolutely and totally out of the blue, a feeling I've never felt before—well not with such intensity—a strong attraction. But, it's well after seven now and she's not here. Did I read things wrong? I mean, who am I kidding? I'm way outta her league with her expensive gear, hair and make-up, And fuck, look at me in tatty second-hand crap—no offence Sarge—but jeez I now feel so fucking stupid to ever think she'd have any interest in me.

'Sorry I'm late, Briney, what I had to do took a bit longer.'

Shit, I was so into my thoughts I didn't notice her arrive. 'No problem,' I manage to get out between the pleasure of seeing her and eating the words spinning around in my mind.

'Where's your friend?' she says looking around.

I wonder why she didn't use his name, maybe forgotten it, or him —wish I could. We didn't have a great time after she left us this afternoon. He wanted to continue drinking but I told him to stay sober for tonight. That didn't go down well so he sat around, sulked for a bit then went back to bed. He wouldn't even go for a walk with me to have a look around, so I decided to stay here and read all the brochures. The only ones that mentioned Terezín were bus tours, and except for what Zoja said about the place, that was about it.

'Yeah, well I reckon he'd be busting for a beer so he won't be long.' There wasn't much excitement in my voice. Then, as if on cue:

'Hi! Shit I'm so ready for a fuckin' beer.'

I cringe. Zoja politely smiles. 'Well, will we have a drink here first?'

'Yeah…' Zac eagerly answers.

'No!' I interrupt. 'Let's go now. I haven't been out all day.' The last bit directed at Zac.

'Yes, well, bigger range of beers at the pub.' She's no fool.

'Cool!' He gives me the 'up you' eye.

We leave the beer garden and follow Zoja down the steps to street level. Even though the sun's gone done, the lights showing the way seem brighter than when we arrived and I can now clearly make out the graffiti covering the wall all the way down.

'How cool's this,' says Zac, taking in the scope of the work. 'You should do something, Bri.'

'You paint?' Zoja stops and turns to me.

'Man, she's fuckin' famous back home, ya know?' Jeez he exaggerates.

'Really?' Is she surprised or is she asking me?

I don't answer as I feel the wall drawing me in. I look at Zoja watching me three steps below and take a step down trying to act as if nothing's happening while struggling against the urge to reach out and touch the wall.

'Are you all right, Briney?' she asks, stepping up beside me and placing a hand on my shoulder. I'm instantly released from the wall's attraction.

'Yeah...fine...I'm fine. Just felt a bit faint that's all. Must be jet lag I reckon.'

I plunge both hands into the pockets of my jacket and look down to concentrate on the steps until I'm out on the street.

Zac's waiting for us, fidgety and eager to get to the pub. 'Which way?'

Zoja nods to the right and off he goes.

We follow and I'm just starting to calm down when we come to an iron railway overpass just as a train rumbles overhead. My hands tighten into a grip deep inside my jacket pockets as all the horror I witnessed under the train back in Melbourne flash in front of my eyes. I freeze.

'Briney, is everything okay?' asks a concerned Zoja.

Zac turns around, annoyed at another delay. 'Shit, come on. It's just the bloody train, that's all.'

The sound of the train overhead seems never-ending as Zoja slides her arm in mine. I'm sure she must feel me trembling. Finally the train and its noise fade into the distance. I stop shaking and give Zoja an embarrassed smile as I slide my arm away from hers. 'Bloody jet lag!' I say and quickly rush under the overpass, ears primed for the sound of another train.

We catch up with Zac at the entrance to the Kain Rock Club, its solid exterior walls painted a colour that's a warm reminder of the red earth of central Australia.

'This it?' he says eagerly opening the front door.

'Yes,' replies Zoja, but I know she's still wondering what the hell happened back there.

We step through the door into more earthy colours of red brick and ochre walls. Through the mist of cigarette smoke I see guitars, drums and other rock instruments scattered around the walls. Prominently protruding into the small space, like an altar to the rock scene, is a heavily timber-framed bar. Sitting on bar stools and talking to the barman are a couple of ageing bikers, their long white hair tied into ponytails and their leather sleeveless jackets revealing heavily tattooed arms. They all glance our way, the barman nods to Zoja and they go back to their conversation. Opposite the bar an equally leather-clad tattooed couple sit smoking and downing large pots of beer. Through an opening in the wall I see another area with tables and chairs and a small mezzanine floor, all empty. But there's enough noise and background music coming from somewhere below to suck us into the atmosphere. Zoja directs us through the bar and down steep stone steps towards the music. From the rather small bar spaces above, we enter into a much larger dungeon-like room with a much larger bar. We follow Zoja into the main area with tables and chairs around a dance floor facing the stage with drums, mikes, speakers, amps and other gear all set up and waiting. Unlike upstairs, this is crowded, all primed on beer and recorded music before the main event. Zoja steers us to a table that I'm sure she must have reserved, cuz it's got a great view of the stage and easy access to the bar.

I tug on Zac's arm before sitting. 'Zac, I think you should buy Zoja a drink.' He's not one for considering others or spending on anyone and does nothing to hide his annoyance at the suggestion.

'Why, thank you Zac, that would be lovely,' says Zoja taking off her leather jacket. I catch her cheeky glance. 'I'll go with you as their English is not good. Are you having a beer, Briney?'

I nod and sit. The warmth of the room is starting to relax me and I watch the girl behind the bar eagerly welcome Zoja—she sure is well known and popular. After introducing Zac, she looks back pointing at me. The girl waves, I smile and wave back.

While Zoja is giving Zac a lesson in Czech pub culture it gives me a chance to zone in on her without her knowing. She's got a knockout figure under a tight-fitting black T and tight black jeans. Seeing them together and comparing them, my attraction to her is even stronger.

It's like something's been released in me for the first time. I mean, I've made friends with girls before, but shit, this is definitely sexual.

They return with beers in hand and sit. I smile as if my mind's pure of thought.

'Na zdraví,' says Zoja, raising her mug of beer. Bloody Zac, never one for formality, has already downed half.

'Na zdraví,' I cheerfully respond clinking her mug.

'Very good. You have the accent perfect.'

Zac mumbles as he turns to look around the room. 'Yeah, well she's bloody Czech ain't she!'

Zoja puts her mug down in surprise. 'You're Czech? But I thought you said you were Australian.'

I'm pissed off with Zac for saying that. I reckon he's gunna go on like this all night and I give him an evil glance.

'Yeah, well, sorta. I mean I was born in Australia but my old lady was Czech.'

'Yeah, *was* is right,' Zac mumbles, still looking away from the table.

I glare at him again and I reckon Zoja's getting a fairly good picture of what's going on between us.

'Are you Australian, Zac?' She edges around in her chair to face him. I stay out of it and sip my beer.

Zac keeps his back to us. 'Yeah,' is all he has to offer in reply, shutting the door on any further discussion about him. There's a silent, tense moment.

'The band will be out soon. I'll take you to meet them after the first set if you like?' What a great mediator. I wonder if it's a Czech thing?

'Yeah, cool,' he replies, holding himself back from sounding too eager.

'Do you play anything, Zac?' I give a silent laugh at her question.

'Nah, not really. Tried guitar but gave it the flick.'

'Pity, you could have sat in later, they do that here.' She turns to me. 'You play anything, Briney?'

There's so many reasons why, but I just give the short answer. 'Umm, no, never had the chance.'

'Well, we can just sit back and listen, then.' I reckon she feels her efforts are going nowhere. 'Look, the band's coming out now,' she says with a tinge of relief. 'I'll go and get some more beer before they start.'

I watch and wait till she's out of earshot then slam a hand down on the table to get Zac's attention.

'Stop being so fucking rude, Zac! She's going out of her way to be nice and all you can do is sit there with your fucking back to her and grump.'

'Yeah, well she's a fucking stuck-up bitch anyway. Ya can see she's worth a bob or two. Nice arse though'

'What the fuck's that got to do with anything? How the fuck do you know what people are like here and how they live?'

He turns back to look around the room. 'Look, they're all fuckin' poonces here except for those three over there.'

I look to where he's nodded. At a table on the other side of the dungeon sit two guys and a girl. All three have lots of tatts and studs poking out of eyebrows, chins and through noses and unlike the others in the room with long hair, their heads are closely cropped, almost shaven. Yeah, that'd be right, just like Twig and his grotty mates back home.

'You're the poonce, Zac! A real fucking shit you are!' I'm totally fed up with him and no matter how hard it'll be I gotta find a way to get out of this reliance on him.

'Are you going to give me some money for tomorrow or not, cuz I'm going back to the Elf.' I push the chair back from the table.

'You're not going, are you?' says Zoja. I hadn't noticed her returning.

I don't know how much she'd heard. 'Sorry, Zoja. Look, thanks heaps for everything, but I gotta get up early.'

'Oh, can't you stay to finish your beer and hear one number at least?'

Zac's grabbed the fresh beer with his back still to us again. I look back at Zoja and see the disappointment in her eyes. I'm really pissed off that she's been dragged into this. She places a 'stay here' hand on my shoulder. That's the tipping point, it's all too much, I stand up, knocking the table and spilling the beers.

'I gotta go to the toilet.'

'I'll show you where it is,' she offers.

I'm all tense and flushed with rage when we get to the toilet and turn to Zoja with a hand up. She takes a step back. I turn and close the door behind me as the band starts up. It helps hide the sound of me crying.

The band is into their second number when there's tapping on the door to the cubicle.

'Briney, are you all right in there?'

I rustle some tissues, flush the un-used toilet and open the door. Zoja can't help but notice my red eyes and flushed face. 'Come, let me freshen you up.' I accept her offer. She takes a paper towel from the dispenser, dampens it and dabs at my eyes and cheeks. The cold water feels good and I attempt an embarrassed smile.

'Some shit your guy is, hey? Why are you putting up with him?'

I can't answer for fear of becoming a slobbering mess again.

'Sorry, it's none of my business.'

Oh, if only she knew how much I want it to be her business. I cough down the lump in my throat. 'No, no, I'm the one who's sorry. I should've said no to your invitation once Zac was there.' I try to lighten the mood. 'He really has some problems, and I suppose I'm one of them.'

From the dungeon below, the sound of the band is getting louder.

'Do you want to go back down?'

'Look Zoja, I'd really like to, but, I don't know if I can handle Zac much more tonight.'

'Okay, then why don't I tell Zac that you've gone back to the Elf. I'll keep him here, get him to meet the band, introduce him around and give you a chance to pull yourself together and get ready for your trip tomorrow, all right?'

'Don't know if I can go now.'

'Why not? Nothing to do with him is it?'

I'm not sure what to tell her. But if it wasn't for her I'd be totally alone, and right now, I really need someone to talk to.

'Zoja, I think I need another drink. But not down here.'

She smiles and I feel myself melt into her inviting green eyes.

'Yes, let's go upstairs where it's a bit quieter and less crowded.'

I follow her up the steps to the altar bar like a little lost lamb. Then it hits me.

'Look Zoja, maybe I should just go back to the Elf. I…I don't have any money.'

Without hesitation, she ignores me and orders two beers then motions to the mezzanine floor that's empty.

Up in the near privacy of the raised platform, I'm stumped for words. I really shouldn't burden her with my problems. I mean, it's my fault I'm in this position knowing it would turn out like this, so why start whining?

'Does Zac have control over the money?'

Shit! That's coming straight to the bloody point.

'Well, sort of…I mean…Yeah. Anyway, like, it's his money.'

'And that's what he's got over you?'

I remain silent.

'Look, Briney, if you don't want to talk about it, fine, I understand, but if there's anything I can do to help.' She reaches out and touches my arm. The sensation darts through me and I loosen up.

'Look, he got the money to come here cuz there was no way I could've unless I pinched it, so I'm sorta cornered, if you know what I mean?'

'And if you kick him out, you're stuck here alone without any money, right?'

'Well, I do have a return ticket to Melbourne, so I suppose I'll have to go back as soon as I can. I thought maybe I could get a job at the Elf.'

'You can cash in your ticket, can't you?'

'Don't know. Suppose, but if I can't get a job then I'll be stuck here.' I reach out with my free hand to touch her arm. 'I'm not saying it wouldn't be nice, but, you know, the language and all that.'

'Well, it's not going to solve your problem for tomorrow, anyway, is it?'

I feel her grip tighten and there's a moment of awkward silence. 'Let me loan you some money.'

I shake my head. 'No, no really, thanks heaps but I can't…I'll go and tell Zac I'm going back to the Elf and ask again for some money.'

There's a hesitation before she slides her hand from my arm.

'I'll wait here for you.'

I'm as nervous as hell heading down the steps. It's crowded, the air is dense with smoke, the music's heavy rock, the lights dim and the sound is up. I can't see Zac at the table we left him at. Weaving and squeezing through the dancing bodies I spot him sitting at the table with the two guys and girl with the shaved heads. The way they're slapping him on the back and laughing, they seem to be entertained by him. Yeah, that'd be right. He's in his element mixing with the worst kind. I'm not sure if I want to go up to him or try and attract his attention to get him to come to me. But I certainly was attracting attention, standing like a fucking idiot in the middle of the dance floor with everyone dancing around me. Then one of the guys with Zac spots me and makes a comment to the others. Zac turns around, sees me, then turns back saying something that has them laughing and looking at me. He's put me down for sure, the prick. Anyway, at least he's coming over.

'Look, I'm gunna hang out with these guys, so why don't ya piss off back to the Elf and I'll catch ya later, hey?'

He starts to turn back but I grab his arm and yell out above the music. 'Zac! I want some money!' That stops him as those around look at us. I lower my voice. 'Just so I can go to this place tomorrow and then I won't ask for any more, promise.'

He looks back to the table with his new 'friends' watching with great interest. I can feel his mind ticking over. Finally, he digs into his pocket, peels off some notes and slaps them into my hand, then, to my surprise, he kisses me on the cheek before heading back to his mates. I bet he's winking at them with a fucking great big smirk on his face. After all, the big macho prick has just paid off his chicky-babe and now he's in like Flynn with the grottiest bunch I've ever seen. Yeah, there they go, thumbs up, slap on the back, beer mugs crashing together. Fuck you Zac and fucking good riddance.

At the bottom of the steps I come face-to-face with Zoja.

'Everything all right?' she asks.

I glance back and see Zac at his table. I'm pretty sure she would have seen everything. 'Yeah, Yeah, it's okay,' I reply, heading back up the stairs and into the quieter space.

'Look, I don't know how much I've got or how far it'll go, but if it's enough to get me to Terezín and back with some to spare, I'd like to buy you that beer now.'

I show her the notes. 'You have enough, but I think you should keep it all just in case?'

'No, please I insist.' I feel I've a lot to thank her for.

She shakes her head. 'No…I insist. Another time maybe.'

Back at the mezzanine table there's no more talk of Zac, no more crying, no more anxiety or stress and the beer tastes different all of a sudden.

'Briney, when you return from your day trip I'd like to show you around Prague, if you'll allow me.

After what's just happened, I couldn't think of anything better than to be shown around Prague by someone who lives here, and by someone I'm totally attracted to.

'Yeah, I'd like that.'

She smiles and I feel myself melting at the thought of just the two of us together. Then, suddenly, her expression turns serious.

'And whatever we do or wherever we go, it will be my treat and you are not to pay for anything, right?' She insists with one black nail-polished finger pointing rigidly into the tabletop.

'No, I can't let you do that. I'm sure I'll have something left.'

'I insist. And when a Czech insists, you do not argue.'

I can't help but accept her insistence with an uneasy smile. 'Thanks Zoja, you're too bloody kind to a stranger you just met a few hours ago. I really don't deserve it after all the shit I dragged you into.'

She leans forward and places a hand on mine.

'I want to see you tomorrow.'

The way she said it and her touch has my heart racing.

'Tomorrow? I'd love to, but I'm not sure what's gunna happen or how long I'll be there.' Instantly, everything about tomorrow, the cryptic messages, the meeting, the strange place, everything comes rushing back. 'Look, I can't go into it, but it's all so bloody weird and I've no idea what's gunna happen.'

'I'd go with you but I've something to do. If it's so weird, are you sure you'll be all right on your own?'

'Yeah, thanks, but it's, like, sorta personal.'

'Oh!'

The way she said it I feel she's on the wrong track.

'Look, it's nothing to do with a guy or anything, it's…'

Her finger to the lips stops me.

'That's all I need to know.'

Our eyes lock in mutual understanding.

'Why don't we meet the day after tomorrow, if you can that is?' She pauses for a moment. 'Zac doesn't need to know, does he?'

'Fuck Zac!' I snap back and add with a slight grin. 'Not anymore!'

'Do you have a cell phone?'

'A what? Oh, you mean a mobile, nah, never had one, never had a reason.'

'Oh, really?' she says, unable to hide her surprise. 'Then here, take this.' She passes me a card she takes from her jacket pocket. 'If you can't make it, call me.'

Shit, I don't think I've ever been given a personal card before. Especially not like this. All black—what else—a phone number, email and what I figure is her address in grey and Zoja in red—what else. But the way she's tagged her name makes me smile. The Gothic style's there, a free-flowing form with the 'Z' joining the tail of the 'J' to be circled by the 'O' as if indicating a direction of entry, then all followed insignificantly by the lower case 'a'. I figure the slash through the 'J' hints at the Gothic cross. I smile.

'Cool card, thanks.'

I finish my beer. It's done its job and now I feel calm but really tired.

'Look Zoja, thanks for everything but I really do need some more sleep.'

'Of course,' she agrees and we both get up from the table and head down the steps to the front door.

There's a moments hesitation as we stand facing each other.

'With a bit of luck, till the day after tomorrow then,' she says and kisses me on both cheeks. The warmth of her lips, her perfume and the hush of her breath is enough to take mine away.

'With a bit of luck,' I say, fighting the urge to kiss her on the lips.

CHAPTER 14

Shit, I hope I'm on the right bus. This is the first time alone with people who don't speak a bloody word of English. Thankfully, the girl at the Elf gave me the drum on how to get a bus ticket and stuff. She said it'll take a bit more than an hour to get to Terezín so I thought it best to get the nine o'clock bus even though I don't need to be there until noon. She said I could take in some of the suburbs of Prague and the countryside on the way. Yeah right, all I can think about is what's gunna to happen when I get there.

By the time we're out of the city and in the country the bus is almost empty but for a few who look like tourists. I guess no one goes to Terezín to work.

Anyway, now we're out of the city I'm starting to relax slightly. I haven't travelled much in Australia, but I can tell the countryside's different. Like, you know, colours and stuff. It's sorta got this softness about the place with wispy trees just starting to show signs of spring and everything's so bloody green.

I reckon it most be an hour at least since we left and I'm looking for this Ghetto, but shit, what does a Ghetto look like? Then I start to hear weird noises. I look out both sides of the bus. There's nothing but peaceful country yet the sounds are getting louder and I'm tensing up again. We round a bend in the road and there, on the right-hand side is a long, low, red brick wall looking totally out of place in the peaceful countryside. Shit, what is it? Looks like a fortress or something. It's where the noises are coming from and they're getting louder, so loud

I'm forced to put my hands over my ears, but it doesn't help. I take my hands away and the noises are the same. Shit, they're in my head. What is it? What am I hearing? I can't stand it. It sounds like torture. I close my eyes in the hope it'll shut out whatever it is, but horrible images appear in the darkness. No! No! Not again, please, not again. I open my eyes and look out to the other side of the bus. Farmland, soft and green, but the sounds are still in my head. I try to resist them, but they only get louder.

Suddenly the bus comes to a shuddering, wheezing halt. The remaining passengers start to get off. Is this Terezín? No way I'm getting off if it is. I don't move. But then I hear a voice breaking through the mix of sounds in my head.

'Small fortress!'

What? I look to the front and the driver's looking back at me.

'Small Fortress, paní?' he calls louder, nodding towards the exit.

We've stopped in a large car park and the few tourists that were on the bus are walking away down a tree-lined and cobble-stoned avenue. At the end is an arched gateway edged in black and white. I look back to the driver who's still nodding towards the avenue.

I fumble with my bag and stuff and head down the aisle to show him the map the girl at the Elf gave me and point to the place she'd circled.

Without hesitation, the driver clunks the bus into gear, releases the brake and slams his foot on the accelerator. The lurching of the bus nearly knocks me over and I just manage to get into the nearest seat. As we drive away I turn and look back. What did he say, Small Fortress? The sounds fade the further away from it we go. I shudder and vow never, ever to go inside that place.

Within a few minutes we come to another wall. This one is a lot larger and we drive through an entrance and stop beside a large open space surrounded by old buildings and a couple of cars parked in the street. Again I start hearing noises but they're different, more a confusion of sounds and voices. But I see no people, I mean no one. The place looks like a bloody ghost town. I look at the driver. He's staring at me in his mirror. There's no other passengers left on the bus and no one waiting to get on so I presume this is where I get off. I give the driver a smile as I pass him. He doesn't return the gesture but continues to stare sternly ahead. I'm not sure where to go and I'm not about to ask him.

I'm barely on the footpath when the bus accelerates down the street, turns a corner and is out of sight. I'm absolutely alone except for this constant droning confusion of sounds all around me. At least they're not as horrid as those I heard back at the other place.

I heave my bag higher on my shoulder. It's heavy cuz not knowing what may happen, I've got everything with me. I look up from the map in my hand to the surrounding buildings and back to the map. I'm not good at reading them so I start walking.

At the first corner, I come across a white building on the other side of the road. A sign fastened to a black wrought iron fence in front reads 'MUZEUM GHETTA'. I know it's early, but is that where I'm supposed to go?

I look up and down the road before crossing like all good girls should, but what's the point, there's no bloody traffic. Shit where is everyone?

As I climb the steps to the museum I hear voices behind me and eagerly turn around expecting to see I've got company…but no one's there. I look up and down the street and not a sign of anyone, yet the voices are still with me. I step back down the steps to look up into the windows of the neighbouring buildings expecting to see people looking out at me, but again, no one. In fact some of the buildings look empty and bloody run-down with cracked plaster, peeling paint and broken downpipes. This place is starting to give me the creeps.

Nervously, I climb back up the steps and enter the museum, instantly feeling the environment close in on me. An old lady is sitting expressionless behind a desk. I take out the piece of paper with Magdeburg Barracks written down and approach her. 'Um, is this…' I half ask, showing her the note. She nods, still expressionless, and takes a small booklet from a pile on the counter and opens it to a foldout map of the town and points with a slight grunt. I look at where she's pointing. There's a red dot with the number 25 in white. 'Da,

Magdeburg Barracks Museum,' she says. 'You buy ticket here for both museums.'

I'm confused. Why two museums in a relatively small town? 'Yeah, okay, umm, how much?'

'You take?' she asks looking down at the open booklet. I guess I'd better. I nod. '240 Koruna.'

'Thanks' I say handing over all my money and clumsily add, 'Um, sorry, no speak Czech.' Unsurprised she hands back the change and points to a side archway leading to a display area.

Should I go in here or go to the other museum where I'm supposed to be at midday? I rummage through the bag for my clock. I've plenty of time so may as well.

Once inside the display area it doesn't take long to realise that this was a place of suffering. A shiver darts through me as I feel pain and death all around. I'm not religious at all and I don't believe in all that shit about spirits and stuff, but I can't help hearing the cries coming from the walls and the deeper I go into the museum, the more I hear and the more pressure I feel crushing in on me. I want to run out, but something keeps me going.

It only takes a couple of displays to get a picture of what happened in this place and the incredible number of people who died at the hands of the Nazis during the Second World War. This is all part of history I never learnt and I'm angry at the years of education I missed out on. But what I'm seeing and reading is too ghastly to believe it actually happened. Then I come to a cabinet containing a random stack of open identity cards with a photo of each person attached and the reality is numbing. These were real people with a name, families, friends and a life, but now, no more than a reminder on display. I can't stop myself from reading every identity card while looking into the faces in the cracked and faded photographs and sense their voices still crying out for answers.

If there's other visitors around I don't notice them as I'm drawn deeper and deeper into the museum and deeper into another world, a horrible world. I'm confused with so many voices, young and old, echoing in my head. I feel they've waited all these years for someone like me to listen. I feel odd. The walls are closing in on me. I can't breathe. I gotta get out. Where do I go? When did I come up those stairs? I don't remember. I rush down them and see the door to the street. The woman behind the desk watches expressionless as I rush past her and out into the open air.

The cool air feels good and I take in a deep breath. What have I just learnt? Terrible things, ugly things, sad things, but most of all I've learnt that I'm not here by accident; I'm here for a reason…but what? Shit! The meeting! The time! I fumble through my bag and look at the clock. Shit, shit, shit, it's way past twelve.

I look around in confusion. Where do I go again? The map, what did she point to? There, number 25. It takes a moment to figure out which way to go and I run. With each frantic stride I feel some sort of vacuum is pulling me into each building I pass. But I'm late. Shit, I hope I haven't fucked up.

Flustered and short of breath I come to the Magdeburg Museum. You wouldn't know it if not for the sandwich-board sign on the kerb. Only one of the solid wood double doors into the neatly restored building is open. Its freshly painted, soft orange walls and bright white windowsills stand out from the neighbouring grimy grey and weathered brick buildings.

I'm about to enter when a tourist bus arrives and unloads a bunch of chatty tourists. I rush in before being swamped by the tightly packed group, but a disturbing thought crosses my mind. Seeing the mix of ages, weight and appearance of the tourists, who will I look for? Even if I could remember her face, she would've changed bloody heaps since I last saw her. Then, of course, the other question is: will she recognise me? I don't have a photo on MySpace. In fact I don't think I've ever had a photo taken of me except by the fucking family police and for my passport. I'm a username only, an ID without an identity, shit, I'm my own greatest secret!

Regardless of my efforts, I do get caught up in the gaggle from the bus as they push their way along a cobblestone passage and into the museum bookshop and the ticket counter. I follow what the others are doing and show my ticket to another grim-faced woman then start looking at everyone as they check out the books and other reproduced memorabilia on show in the hope of some indication, a sign, a look or something from someone. Then I spot the clock on the wall. It's after one. I bet she's gone, sick of waiting and gone. The message was clear, 'midday' it said. I've stuffed up. No, can't be, I'm sure she'd wait. Like, it's not as if it's unimportant is it? I mean I've come half way around the bloody world to be here, surely she'd allow me some slack and wait a bit?

I follow the group back out into the passage towards a sign pointing to stairs and the exhibition spaces on the next level. Then I hear footsteps behind me. Maybe? I spin around as a group of young students, probably on a school excursion enter the building. Shit, from a deserted ghost town, this place has suddenly become crowded. The boys are doing the typical roughhouse shit while the girls are whispering together, probably social gossip and arguing who's the spunkiest guy. Even though I can't understand a word, I'm getting bombarded with all their secrets and it's getting in the way of concentrating on my immediate problem. I turn away from them and follow the adults heading up the stairs, turn left along a passage overlooking the internal courtyard to a room at the end and enter a replica of the living conditions in the Ghetto. The people around me go silent for a moment at the sight of stacked shelves that slept people side by side with only the barest of personal belongings hanging from the wooden frames or stowed in old brown travel cases. I start getting the same crushing vibes of sadness and despair I did in the other museum. I'm being drawn back into the past but I need to keep focussed on today and I follow some of the others into a brighter room displaying artwork done by the inmates of the Ghetto. Before I have a chance to check out everyone in the room, the school kids enter and spread themselves along the stretch of the gallery. A moment later the rest of the tour group arrive and the space is filled.

Then I sense it. Someone is watching me, just waiting and watching. But why, why not just come up to me? I look around and note at least four or five girls who could be confused for me. That's it; she needs to decide which of these girls is her daughter. I start walking through the long gallery of artwork, deliberately brushing against each person in the hope this new-found sensing skill I seem to have will work, and bugger me if I don't get a hint of secret thoughts from each person I touch. It seems language is no barrier for it's the notion I'm getting. I brush against a middle-aged man, one of the tourists. I pause. He's looks at me, embarrassed and quickly turns away. I reckon he knows I've caught him out perving on the schoolgirls. Next I brush past an old couple. They're both reliving memories of a painful past. Then, a young man bumps into me without any concern or apology. I feel sorry for him cuz I sense he's going through the same sort of violent upbringing I did. But the messages I'm getting are becoming uncontrollable. Voices start echoing through my head. The images in the artwork become real. I feel I've opened a door for everyone else in the room to bombard me with their secrets. The room begins to spin and the heavy thumping of my heartbeat joins in the chorus of confusion. Sweat is sticking the clothes to my body as I gasp for clear air. I feel stomach acid rising and eating into my throat. I'm gunna vomit and quickly place a hand over my mouth. I desperately need to find a toilet and rush through the crowd, out into the empty passage and through my watery eyes I see the sign for the toilets and make a dash. Just as I'm about to enter, a surge of awareness hits me and I gulp back the rising vomit and turn around. There, blurred through tears, I can just make out an old man reaching out to me. It's him. I'm convinced it's him. His presence overwhelms me, but so does the nausea and I vomit into my hand, rush into the toilet, slide onto my knees in a cubicle and throw up violently into the toilet bowl. The resulting sight and smell bring on another bout, and another, until they finally subside and I'm left dry reaching and drenched in sweat.

It takes some minutes before I have the strength to stand, get out of the cubicle and splash cold water over my face. With hands on each side of the washbasin and arms locked to support me I lean forward to look into the mirror. I see a pale face, red eyes and a runny nose. Then the image of the old man appears in the mirror. I spin around, expecting to see him standing behind me, but nothing. I look back into the mirror; his image is gone but at least I now have a face to search for. I rush back into the gallery, but the more I search the more I'm sure the old man has left and taken the force of his presence with him. For the first time the atmosphere around me is calm. The school group and tourists are leaving and I wait for them to go until there is no one else around except for the few staff, Thinking I belong to the parting groups they show me the way out. A respectful quiet returns to the museum.

Out in the street I look up and down in a last desperate attempt at catching sight of him, but nothing. A look back into the building in case someone has following me out but there's no one, I feel at a loss, disappointed that I've completely stuffed things up.

I check on the time. Nearly four. The last bus to Prague isn't for a while, so I'll have a walk around...never know I might spot him.

It doesn't take long before I start feeling an empathy with the place, an unnerving and unexplained sense of belonging and connection with each building I pass. I've got the museum book open at the map and legend describing each building and what it was used for during the Ghetto days. The building I'm passing was a shop that sold confiscated clothes back to their original owners or unknowing descendants and somewhere deep inside I hear the notes of a long-ago band playing. On the opposite corner, one of the few restored buildings was a home for girls and the sound of music and girlish giggles rings in my ears. Further down the street, past a hotel that's surprisingly open for business, I'm chilled by the screams of torture coming from what's now a bland, sombre bank. I hurry across the road and into the large central park. The sound of workers and the smell of oil and grease from heavy machinery surround me. On the other side of the park, around a corner and past more decayed and vacant buildings I come upon a restaurant open for business. Further down the street is another park softened by a haze that's drifted in and through the mist I can just make out a domed rotunda. But the atmosphere here is different. I hear the sounds of drunken laughter and music confused with a sense of loneliness. Going by the legend, I've entered an area that was off limits to the Jews and set aside as the living and recreational quarters for the SS. A hotel facing the park catered for their needs and accommodation and is still there and open. The thought of a beer to drown my frustration is tempting, but could I enjoy such comforts in a building that once offered the same and more to the SS? It's unsettling, but I'm tempted as a test of this growing understanding of the past, and enter.

The warm colour of the spacious bar and the peaceful paintings on the walls are not what I expected. A blue bicycle is resting on its strut just inside the door. At a table by a window sit two men smoking and drinking beer; I presume because there's no other customers one must be the owner of the bike. The room's wide and angled like an L-shape around a solid timber bar almost hiding the barman who's bending down restocking the fridge. I sit at a table by a window so I can look out over the park. It's warm inside so I take off my jacket and put it on the back of a chair. The sound of pulling out the chair to sit alerts the barman. In a flash he's beside me, says something in Czech with a nod and flicks a crumb from the tabletop.

'Hello.' I reply, presuming it was a form of welcome.

His face takes on a grim expression as he realises I'm a foreigner. 'What you have?' He looks around and adds, 'Alone?'

'Yeah,' I reply, noting the two men at the other table watching. 'A beer, thanks.'

He hesitates and I figure I need to be a bit more specific. Spotting the beer coaster on the table I point. 'That one,' He nods, takes one step back, turns briskly and heads to the bar. His military-like action makes me wonder if that's how the SS were served.

The two men go back to their conversation as the barman returns and places a beer on its branded coaster, scribbles the price on a slip of paper and slides it partially under another coaster. He again takes one step back and without any further expression returns to stocking the fridge.

I sit back, raise the large heavy glass of beer and take a long and welcome drink. The man facing me at the other table looks at me. Figuring I'm the topic of their conversation, I smile a froth-outlined smile. He quickly turns his attention back to his companion.

Looking out the window to the park opposite I try to imagine what it would have been like back then. With all the imagination I can muster and using all these recently discovered skills, I quickly realise it's impossible. As the old saying goes, 'you had to be there'.

The beer's going down well, calming, and I settle back into the chair to go over the day's disastrous outcome. That old man, who can he be and why him and not my old lady? I take another sip of beer. Then all the messages I got from Prague flash before me. I always felt there was something not right and they weren't coming from her. But only she could know about the clock and the name on it. So there's gotta be some sort of connection between the two of them. I'm sure it was him who sent the messages and it was him I was to meet. So why did he go away? I made eye contact with him, and unless I'm totally wrong, he looked like he was reaching out to me. So, why then didn't he stay until I came out of the toilet? I mean, shit, I'm sure he could see I was in bloody trouble with spew dribbling through my fingers.

I take another drink. The puzzle seems to be breaking into smaller pieces rather than falling into place. Even if this old man and my old lady know each other, why wasn't she with him? I'm bloody sure I'd have sensed it if she was. This is all very strange, but then again, so is this whole bloody town.

Shit, I better go or I'll miss the bus. I down the last of the beer and look at the order slip. The barman's there in an instant, probably been keeping an eye on me all this time. I'm bloody glad I met Zoja and she told me about the procedure and I give him what I think is the nearest amount and enough for a tip. 'Thanks,' I say with a wave of the hand for him to keep the change.

He nods, slides the money off the table leaving the slip behind and retreats to the bar with the empty glass.

I put on my jacket and gather up the bag and head to the door, smiling at the two men as I pass. They don't smile back. Shit is everyone in this town as depressing as its history?

The breeze is now a lot colder as darkness falls and the thickening mist adds to the eeriness of this ghostly town. I head back to where I got off the bus and just as I turn a corner a bus heading back to Prague passes me. Confused by the traffic driving on the other side of the road to back home, I run hoping I haven't missed the stop and relieved to see it pull up ahead. I board, pay and settle into a seat at the back.

Not far from the Ghetto town the bus passes the Small Fortress again. With what I've come to understand from the displays at the museums, I now recognise the noises I heard this morning were the screams of tortured, the moans of the sick and the whimpering of the starving as they reach out to me again. I tense up, but this time I don't fight it and allow the sensation to sweep over me as I try to understand better this strange ability I seem to have in sensing the unseen.

CHAPTER 15

Evzen had visited the hospital earlier than usual so he could be back in time to wait and watch from a distance the last two buses arriving from Prague before midday. Ruza was still heavily sedated and only just hanging onto life. He desperately wanted to reach out and hold her hand but feared she would sense his increasing anxiety about meeting the girl.

Arriving back in Terezín in time to observe from a distance the arrival of the two buses before noon, Evzen becomes worried as the only passengers to get off were elderly or couples. He wonders if the girl had changed her mind and was not coming. But just in case she had caught an earlier bus or arrived by car, he makes his way to the Magdeburg Museum to wait and watch each person entering. After paying for his ticket, he walks through the second level exhibition and gallery rooms, careful not to stare too obviously at the few visitors scattered about. But no one he sees fits her age, let alone the image of her in his mind. Aware tour buses arrive after midday, he returns to the bookshop and ticket counter in case she had joined a tour and finds a spot out of sight to wait and watch, positive he'll recognise something of Ruza in the girl, for his memory of her at a similar age has never left him.

As the time approaches one-o'clock, Evzen is concerned that the woman behind the ticket counter has taken an interest in him loitering in the background. But before she can do anything a busload of tourists arrive and her attention turns to serving them. Evzen becomes confused by the sudden influx of talkative foreigners and finds it difficult to isolate each person, especially after a large group of boisterous students add to the confusion and push him further into the background.

The tour group start making their way to the upstairs galleries giving Evzen a clearer look at the students. They could be around the age of Ruza's daughter, but they're Czech, so why are they holding his attention? They aren't, it's the girl following the tour group. He can feel it. Even from a distance, he knows deep in his twisted gut that she's the one he's been waiting for. The features are there. This has to be Ruza's daughter. A wave of selfish anger washes over him. This is someone else's daughter, not his as it should have been, but an illegitimate daughter and does he really want anything to do with her even though he made a promise to his dying Ruza? Then, clouding his vision is the image of the Goose. Can he possibly pass up what could be the very last opportunity to know? His anger and the lingering acidic memory of the distant past compel him through the mob of students as they also head towards the upper galleries.

He has always found crowds intimidating, but more so crowds of young people. Their disrespect in this place of serious contemplation riles him, and this daughter of Ruza is not much older. He watches her closely, looking for all the faults he can find. She is tall, slim and attractive just like Ruza was at that age, but her light brown hair is from another gene and her tanned skin reminds him of a Roma peasant, and that alone is repugnant enough. Her clothes are designed to promote sexual attraction and the way she walks, the way she carries herself, the way she's looking around the room, obviously confused by the surroundings, all increase his dislike of her.

From a distance he follows the crowd up the stairs, to the replica of a Ghetto dormitory then into the gallery of art, all the time keeping a critical eye on her as she walks around, lost and searching. Searching, yes of course, for she's expecting to be met by her mother. He was careful not to reveal himself in any of his messages, so why should he hide from her? Convinced of his anonymity he moves closer and sees her dreamlike trance. The people and artwork she passes seem to be having a strange effect on her. She is disorientated, confused and her tanned complexion has become ashen. Accepting the inevitable, Evzen plucks up the courage to finally confront her, but she starts frantically looking around then rushes back through the crowd. He struggles to keep up with her until they both reach the empty corridor. Suddenly she stops and turns to face him. Their eyes meet and Evzen is looking into the eyes of his young Ruza. He reaches out to touch her, not the girl but the Ruza he knew back in the late sixties before she fled her homeland and the Soviet occupation. This time he will not let her go. But she turns, her hand pressed tightly over her mouth, and rushes into the women's toilet.

He can only stand in silence, glued to the spot. Once again Ruza has slipped from his grasp. A group of students bump into him as they rush past and snap him out of his dream. He looks at the closed toilet door. Should he wait for her to come out? The corridor is empty again; he feels uncomfortable standing outside the ladies' toilet and walks back into the main gallery. The brief foray into the past has left him confused. What should he do? If only she had not rushed away.

The decision comes, as blunt as it is rapid. The pain of reliving Ruza's sudden departure is too much to bear. He's convinced she has heard him in her sleeping state and is holding onto life by the thinnest of threads just to see her daughter. And he's equally convinced that once that happens that thread will snap, her last wish fulfilled, and she'll die. He cannot let that happen. He turns towards the stairs, down to the entrance and out of the building.

After turning down several streets, stressed and weary, Evzen feels his chest tighten and he needs to sit. He crosses the street to the central park and finds an empty bench. As the pain in his chest and the ache in his joints subside, his breathing returns to normal and his mind clears. He contemplates his actions once again. *Was it my selfish desire to keep Ruza alive…or did I just lose my nerve? I told her to come, she came and I lost my nerve. I must go back and find her.*

By the time he makes it back to the Museum, it's closed. He had missed her. He had let his beloved Ruza down. But there was one last chance. He would go to the bus stop and hope that she was not already on her way back to Prague.

As evening approaches and daylight fades, Evzen quickens his pace to reach the other side of the park before the last bus to Prague arrives. With metres to go and in sight of the bus stop, his breathing heavy, his legs pained and swollen, he sees the bus turn into the street and a figure run to catch it. It's the girl, and he can only watch as she boards and is taken away.

CHAPTER 16

It's cold and dark by the time I get off the bus at the Florenc terminal and I'm bloody miserable and hungry. Everything's fallen through and buggered if I know what's gunna happen now. With almost no money, I guess the only thing I can do is go back to Oz and back on the street cuz there's no way I'll get the pad back. Jeez, I've fucked up big time.

A food stall at the terminal is open and after eating something I didn't recognised but tasted okay, I can't put off the inevitable any longer and head back to the Elf to face Zac and tell him he was right all along. I hope he's not pissed, but I'd be bloody surprised if he isn't.

The night shift guy at reception gives me a cheery welcome and says my boyfriend—I cringe—is up in the room. Handing over the key, he also informs me that we're now in a room with a double bed. This makes me cringe even more. If he's pissed he'll probably want a root and that's something I don't want to even think about right now.

'And this is for you,' he adds, reaching back to grab an envelope. 'It came with special instructions not to give it to your guy.' I get a rush of blood. Is it something to do with today's stuff up? Nah, can't be cuz no one knows I'm staying here. I thank him and go into the lounge just off the reception to read the message. It's from Zoja. She'll meet me at the Florenc Metro at ten in the morning and to call her if I can't make it. Bloody oath I'll make it.

Before putting the key into the lock of our new room I press an ear against the door to listen if there's any activity going on inside. I wouldn't put it past Zac to have a girl with him. Thankfully, the only thing I can hear is the sound of snoring. As quiet as I can I open the door and in the dim light I can just make him out on the double bed, still dressed, alone and stinking of beer. I hope he's had a skinful and stays passed out until late in the morning. I place my bag on the floor near the door, undress to my T-shirt and knickers and slide into the bed as quietly as I can.

I'm woken by Zac's heavy arm flopping over me. Daylight has half-filled the room as I struggle to clear my head and eyes after a solid sleep. He's still snoring, but his arm's a sign that something else is stirring and I'm well aware that soon he'll wake up with a stiff cock and a hang-over and I'm, like, totally not ready for it.

Shit, what's the time! The clock's in the bag by the door and I carefully slide out from under his groping arm, but it tightens around me. Fuck it, I need to know the time now and fling his arm away and jump out of the bed.

'Bri,' he snorts, his eyes still closed, his hand still groping.

'Gotta go Zac,' I say reaching in the bag. Shit, I've less than an hour to wash, dress and get to the Metro.

He snorts and sniffs a solid nose-full of snot down his throat then a cough to help it down further. 'What? Where ya going now? Ya not goin' back to that…that place, whatever it's called, are ya?'

'No, I'm not, look I gotta go, I'm running late,' and I rush out to the bathroom down the hall.

The shower's hot and refreshing but there's no time to indulge. A quick towel down, a brush of the teeth and I'm back to the room to finish dressing. Zac is sitting on the edge of the bed.

'So, I'll come with ya.'

I've no time to stand and argue with him cuz I know how stubborn he can be.

'Look, I'm meeting Zoja and she's showing me around Prague and you pissed her off the other night so, no, okay?'

'Yeah, well, how ya gunna pay? Fucked if I'm giving you any more if I'm not coming with ya.'

'She's offered to pay.'

'So, it's got to that stage has it? The fucking rich dyke has won ya over with a wave of the wad.'

'Yeah, well it's not gunna work with you, is it, tight arse?' That felt good and it seems he's stumped for a smart-arse comeback.

'Look, I'm not in the mood to argue. We agreed to go our own way and right now I'm going mine!'

'Well, fuck you then. Ya can get ya money from her from now on.'

'I won't need your money now anyway. As soon as I can get on a flight I'm heading back to Oz, so there!'

That's stunned him.

'So, like, what, nothing happened yesterday? It was all a load of crap, those messages and shit about ya old lady?'

I didn't want to go into detail of what happened.

'Yeah, well anyway, I learnt a lot about other things. I mean this Terezín is a real strange place with a real dark past, you know, during the war and Nazis and stuff.'

'Nazis?' he questions, showing some excitement.

'Yeah, they made the whole place a Ghetto, you know, like a concentration camp for Jews. And I sensed some really horrible things there. And then there was this old man…' Shit, fuck it, why did I mention him?

'Jeez ya still not on about this sense thing are ya? And what fuckin' old guy?'

Damn it, why's it taking so long to get dressed?

'I think he's the one who sent the messages.'

'What? Ya think? Didn't ya ask him?'

'Well, no, I mean, I was crook and about to throw up when he appeared and I just had to go and chuck. When I came back he'd gone.'

'What, just because ya see this old guy and don't say a fuckin' word to him, ya think he sent the messages? Geez, Bri!'

'I just knew it was him. I just knew it, okay?'

'Yeah, whatever,' he says in his usual brush-off manner.

I don't want to go on about it any more and finally get to pull on my boots.

'So, where'd *you* go yesterday?' I ask, making sure everything's in my bag.

'Met up with the guys at the pub and we got into the piss.'

'Yeah, so, who are these guys? I mean shit, they look bloody scary to me.'

'Yeah, well I'm their little Aussie mate now, aren't I? Language is a bit of a problem with the two guys, but the chick speaks okay English and she translates. They're cool.'

I didn't want to know any more cuz I really wasn't interested and I was running late.

'Yeah, well, see ya.' I open the door. 'I'll let you know my plans tonight.'

CHAPTER 17

I wasn't the only one to notice her. Everyone walking in or out of the Metro couldn't help but be distracted. It didn't seem to faze Zoja in the least, casually leaning against the entrance smoking with one leg cocked up against the wall. I'm not sure if it was cuz of the way she was dressed in a jet black ankle length leather coat with dots of blood red buttons down the front and a cluster of chains hanging from her shoulder, or the streak of emerald green in her spiky white hair. She's so totally Gothic and so totally sexy. Spotting me, she takes a final drag on her cigarette, drops it to the ground and grinds it to death with a heavy, black and red-studded laced-up boot.

'Hi Zoja, sorry I'm late,' I say, uncomfortably aware of how dowdy I look beside her.

'You're lucky; usually I'm the one who's late. How are you, Briney?'

She places both hands on my arms, draws me close and kisses me on each cheek.

'Now, I hope you have all day free?'

'I guess so.' Shit, why did I say it like that?

'That doesn't sound convincing. Have you something else to do?'

'Oh no, really, it's just, yesterday didn't turn out as I expected and I'm a bit down.' Hell, that's not a great start to the day.

'Oh, I'm sorry to hear.' Her excited expression drops then instantly returns. 'But, Briney, I will endeavour to snap you up from your down. I have so much to show you but first we start with the only good coffee in Prague and some cake, ya?'

'Sounds great, but…'

She stops me with a raised hand.

'And I pay for the day remember!'

She takes my arm and steers me into the Metro.

After a long, steep ride down into the depth of the earth on an escalator that gives me a touch of vertigo, then a walk through what seems like bloody miles of tunnels. I'm starting to think they don't have trains in Prague and you're expected to walk to wherever you're going. But we do reach a platform just as a train pulls in. After only a couple of stops, we repeat the long trek through tunnels and ride the escalator back to the Earth's surface and I find myself looking down a wide avenue sloping into the misty distance.

'This is Wenceslas Square, Briney, and behind us is the Museum'

I look around and find I'm standing by a towering monument with a statue of a horse and rider in front of a huge old grey building.

We head off down the centre plantation and pass a small circular garden with a plaque resting on a bed of stones and headed by a cross. The faces of two young men: Jan Palach and Jan Zajic are etched into the plaque, both dead in 1969 and both not quite twenty. A shiver bristles through me as I sense the smell of burning flesh, death and the earth trembling to the rumble of tanks. Zoja's walked ahead and I rush to catch up to her. I don't want to ask her about what terrible thing happened here, I had enough of that yesterday. I want today to be a happy one.

I'm steered down a side street and into the amazing art deco Lucerna arcade. The rich warm colours of the marbled walls are cheering me up. But nothing surprises me more than being confronted by this amazing life-size bronze horse hanging upside-down from a domed ceiling and a soldier, helmet, cape and all, sitting astride the animal's stomach.

'David Cerný's weird sense of humour,' says Zoja, taking a step back to join me in looking up. 'His version of the statue of St Wenceslas you saw at the top of the square. You like it?'

'Fucking amazing. I mean I've never seen anything so in your face and especially in a public place like this.'

'Come, we have a closer look up stairs.'

I follow her to the top of a wide staircase where she sweeps aside a heavy scarlet curtain for me to enter. The large art deco café I step into is way too luxurious for my standards, and I'm hit with the smell of fresh coffee and ever-present cigarette smoke. I follow Zoja past tables occupied by what I reckon are business people doing what business people do, I guess, eating, drinking, smoking and plotting the direction the world will take. Zoja stops at an empty table by the window and pulls out a chair for me to sit so I can look down at the arcade and the arse end of the horse.

'I come here almost every day,' she says taking off her coat and hanging it on the back of her chair. 'It's the only place in Prague I know that makes a reasonable coffee.'

I hear her but I'm fixed on the sight of the horse up close and very personal.

'How do you like yours?'

Confused, I look around. A waitress is standing over me.

'Your coffee, how do you like it?' Zoja repeats.

'Um, a strong long black, thanks.'

'And what cake?'

I shrug my shoulders, 'Oh, whatever. Never one to fuss over food.'

She orders whatever in Czech while I look around the room.

'I'm not used to being in a place as swish as this,' I confess.

She smiles at me then half turns to hunt for her cigarettes in the pockets of her coat. Her tight black top is buttoned up by a single red button at the neck then gapes open to reveal a hint of cleavage before closing again by a matching red zip at the waist. The more she turns back, the more I get a glimpse of her small, firm breasts.

'You smoke?' she asks, nearly catching me perving.

'Umm, no thanks. Don't smoke those.'

She gives me a wicked smile.

'You smoke the other then? I can fix that later if you like.'

Yeah, bet she can. I reckon she'd have all the right connections here in Prague.

I watch as she lights her cigarette. The sleeves of her black top cover her arms and extend over her hands. A red leather strap is wrapped around each wrist. All the red elements match her dark red lipstick. And even her haunting green eyes are heavily made up with a mix of black mascara and a matching dark red shade that screams out against her porcelain skin and white hair with the emerald green streak. Shit, I feel so out of place here in my T-shirt, jeans, hoody and Sarge's old weathered jacket, which I quickly take off and hang behind me on the chair with my bag.

She finishes lighting her cigarette and takes in a deep lung-full.

'It's strange seeing people still smoking in restaurants and pubs. Can't do that anymore in Melbourne.'

'Humph,' she replies blowing the smoke away from me. 'Anyone who tried to stop that here would find themselves thrown from a castle window like in the old days.'

She taps a small amount of ash into the ashtray. 'Now tell me, how was your visit to Terezín?' she asks, settling back into her chair, one arm bent holding the cigarette to her mouth and allowing smoke to slowly curl from between her red lips. I'm sure I've seen that pose in an old spy movie once.

Before I have a chance to answer, the waitress returns with some water, cutlery and one plate that Zoja directs to be placed in front of me.

'Now, yesterday?' she asks again after the waitress had gone.

'Oh, I don't know,' I mumble, realising how stupid that sounded. 'I mean, it all turned out different to what I thought, that's all.'

She remains silent, rejecting the lack of detail.

'I mean, that place threw me. Like, I had absolutely no idea of the shit that happened there, what with the Nazis and all! I mean, I don't know, maybe it's because Australia's so bloody far away or something.'

She remains silently leaning back in her chair, studying me with her arm still cocked holding her cigarette to her mouth. I feel her expression has hardened and again I'm reminded of an old black and white spy film and the interrogation. She's wanting more.

'And your friend?' she finally asks, disturbing the curl of smoke.

'Friend?' The image of the old man comes to mind.

The waitress interrupts arriving with the coffee for two and a thick slice of what I think is black forest cake that she places in front of me.

'You're not having any cake?' I ask.

'I don't eat cake,' she replies, stubbing out her cigarette.

'Oh.' Shit now I feel embarrassed to be eating in front of her.

'You eat.' She senses the hesitation.

I don't need much encouragement and fork off a large mouthful of cake and cream. Zoja's gives a single stir of the crème into her short black before raising it to her lips.

'Did you meet your friend?'

I put down the fork, stir two teaspoons of sugar into my long black and take a sip while thinking how to answer.

'Sort of.' Shit what a piss weak answer. 'Look, Zoja. I don't mean to be secretive or anything but I'm going through something that's sorta personal, and, like, well it's kinda strange at the same time, so if you don't mind I'd rather not talk about it right now.'

'Quite, right,' She takes another sip of her coffee. 'There I go again prying. I'm sorry, it's none of my business.' She places her coffee back onto the saucer and looks up at me. 'But listen, if there's anything at all I can help you with. I mean, if you need to know anything about Prague, how to get somewhere, places to go, anything like that. I want to know that you won't hesitate to ask me, ya?'

'Yeah, of course I will, thanks, but there's really nothing to tell at the moment, okay?' I scoop up another mouthful of cake hoping she won't pressure me for more. She doesn't.

'What do you want to see in Prague? There's so much of my lovely city I want to show you, I'd like to know what your interests are.'

I tilt my head toward the window. 'I must admit, that horse out there makes me want to see more art.'

That brings a broad smile to her face and she leans forward. 'That's easy, Briney,' she says tapping the table with her red fingernail. 'This whole city is an art gallery.' Then leans back into her chair again. 'Is what Zac said true? That you're an artist?'

I blush. 'Not really, Zac tends to bullshit a lot.'

'I don't believe you. The first time you noticed that horse out there, I could see you were seeing it through an artist's eye. Now tell me the truth, what do you do?'

I look around to see if anyone else is listening and lean forward. 'Look, it's not really art. I mean not like in the, you know, traditional sense.'

'Tell me.'

'Well, it's only graffiti, that's all,' I answer averting my eyes.

'Street art?'

'Well, not really, more beside train lines, actually.'

'Cool. Have you heard of Lennon's Wall?'

I look back at her, 'No.'

'We'll go there.'

'What is it?'

'John Lennon, you've heard of him of course.'

'Yeah, of course.'

'There's a wall of graffiti dedicated to him.'

'Shit, really? Jeez, I mean, all I seem to be doing here is coming across monuments to death and stuff and now there's one for another dead guy.'

Her smile fades. 'Briney, this place has seen so much death, it's almost as if all of Prague is one big monument to the dead.'

I see the seriousness in her eyes. 'Look I didn't mean any disrespect or anything. Fuck, I'm just a naïve Aussie from a country that's about as interesting as melting butter.'

She smiles.

I scoop up the last of the cake and cream.

'Look Zoja, I should have asked before, but I hope I'm not keeping you away from your work or whatever?'

She smiles and lights up another cigarette. 'I'm not a slave to work.'

101

'Well, what do you do? I mean you must do something to afford those clothes.' I figure what's she wearing would cost more than I'd ever see in a year.

She gives a little smirk. 'I'm a spoilt little brat.'

I'm surprised at her directness and let out a questioning laugh.

'Yeah, but you do work, don't you?'

She stubs out her just lit cigarette. 'Let's just say I have my means.'

I'm now too inquisitive to just let it go without any further explanation. She's obviously rich, but not having much experience with rich people, I can't see how they can spend so much money and yet not work.

'Sorry,' I say, not really meaning it. 'All I've done is talk about me and I know nothing about you.'

She leans back with her arms crossed and exposing more cleavage. 'Okay,' she says in a come-and-get-me tone. 'What do you want to know?'

I wasn't really expecting it to be quite this way, more of a general conversation rather than an interview. 'Well, um, where did you go to school?' I begin.

'I started here in Prague then went to boarding school in America.'

Her abrupt, rather unemotional answer has me a bit uneasy, but I continue. 'Boarding school? Shit, what was that like?'

'Boring.'

For a moment I feel there's nothing more coming, but then she seems to relax and it becomes more of a chat.

'I had a different way of seeing things at a very young age, you know, Goth and all, and the school was full of nerds. You know what a nerd is, don't you?'

'Shit yeah, there's loads in Melbourne, along with dorks, dills and bogans.'

'Well, as I was obviously different, I became someone of interest, and, well, when you capture a person's interest, you also have them by the balls.'

I smile. Yeah, she's definitely spoilt, but at least she has a fun side to her.

'So, like, your parents must be rich to send you to boarding school?'

Her face tightens. 'My father…my mother died not long after I was born.'

'Oh shit, sorry.' I say, while getting a flash of wonder at my own old lady's fate.

'And yes,' she continues. 'My father is a very rich property lawyer and he does spoil me rotten.'

That's it, there's no way I can have a conversation about wealth and stuff. I figure this could be a good time to stop.

'Okay, well, I suppose we should start the tour of Prague, hey?'

She unwraps her arms and her blouse closes.

I stand and grab my jacket and bag. 'Look, Zoja, I still have a little money left…'

'Nonsense! We had a deal remember?'

The waitress returns with the account, Zoja gives it a quick scan before signing and handing it back with a few words in Czech.

She turns to me with a wicked smile. 'Daddy has an account here and that's on him.'

Daddy! Shit, the only daddy I know is a sugar daddy. I try not to show any reaction, but could she? Could he be?

CHAPTER 18

I'm still to see any of the really old medieval buildings I was expecting. But as the number 22 tram crosses over the Vitava, I recognise—thanks to Google—Charles Bridge a little further up the river and a castle on top of a hill overlooking everything.

'Is that Prague Castle,' I ask to confirm.

'Yes, but you need a day to go over it so some other time, ya?'

Will there be another time, I wonder?

'Come, now we walk,' she says, jumping from her seat and I follow her off the tram. Finally, I'm standing in the Prague I'd imagined. 'This is the Little Quarter, Briney, and what you see hasn't changed since the eighteenth century.'

The cobble-stoned lanes and alleyways feed off the main street lined with churches and buildings with ornate doorways and frontages. Over each entrance there's an amazing variety of house signs; animals, violins, crests, keys, you name it. Pubs and art galleries are everywhere and tiny shops selling the most amazing wooden puppets.

We turn down one of the lanes. It's peacefully quiet with no shops or tourists.

'A lot of artists live here.' I'm told, understanding why with so much inspiration just outside your window.

After a few minutes we turn a corner and facing us is a wide stretch of wall topped with corrugated tiles. Maybe around fifty metres long and about four metres high, and on it, to a reachable height, literally every centimetre covered in dense graffiti.

So this is Lennon's wall. With so much on it, it's hard to make out anything, and if I can, the words are mostly foreign. There's a scattering of faces and cartoon images but overall most are tags. After getting over the initial impact, I reckon the graffiti isn't that crash hot. Well, no, I shouldn't say that, cuz it's obviously not done by graffiti artists as such, more likely the average dude and tourist who wants to either leave a mark of respect to Lennon, or just to say, 'we was here'. So in one way, I guess it's probably more honest.

I step closer to look at some of the smaller pieces and I feel it again. Even though the pull isn't that strong, I'm sensing that all is not right with this wall somehow.

'He's down there,' says Zoja, grabbing back my attention and I follow to where she's pointing. Just beyond a reachable height is the head of John Lennon protruding out from the wall, painted black with a bronze patch on his forehead and some spots of red and yellow paint on his top lip. His dreamy sombre stare through the wire-rimmed glasses is stilted somewhat by his frozen expression, but it's unmistakably Lennon.

'So, like, why's there a monument to Lennon here?' I ask.

104

'He was seen as the prophet of peace by young Czechs during the Soviet repression.'

Soviet repression in the days of the Beatles! Shit my education is definitely lacking. I'm about to ask her about it but I stagger a little as the wall starts to pull me in.

'Briney, what's up?' Her hand on my shoulder triggers an instant release and I slump back away from the wall. I give her an embarrassed smile. She smiles back but I can see her concern.

'Yeah, Yeah, I'm fine. Must be the lingering memory of sniffing paint fumes and the high you get, hey?' Bloody lame excuse but I hope it works.

I walk off further down the wall as if nothing happened. She doesn't follow and I glance back to see her sniffing the wall, shit, maybe my lame excuse was believable after all. All of a sudden a swarm of Japanese tourists turn into the street. For the next ten to fifteen minutes we watch as they take their photos, pose against the wall, giggle at the few Japanese entries they come across, add some of their own and walk away as fast as they arrived, I guess another item on their sightseeing list has been ticked off.

Peace returns as we gather back at Lennon's head.

'Well, Briney, what does the expert think?'

'I'm sorta disappointed,' I reply looking up to Lennon hovering above us. 'With some of the crap surrounding him, I'm not sure if he'd be to thrilled. You know, all this so-and-so loves so-and-so and fucking Tom, Dick or Harry was here. Just doesn't hit me as showing a great deal of respect actually.' Well, at least I'm honest. 'Look, Zoja, it's not that I don't appreciate you showing me, it's just that, well, this isn't the original, is it? I mean there's no political messages, no radical statements, nothing but crap, basically.'

She gives me a look like she's impressed or something. 'Very good, Briney, you're absolutely right. For years the secret police kept painting over those kinds of messages, poetry, things like that, only to have new messages appear the next day. Then as things calmed down in Prague, they gave up painting over them.'

'And then the flood came,' Shit where did that come from?

'You know about that?' she asks, surprised.

'Umm, must have heard about it somewhere,' I hastily reply, knowing it was the wall that just told me.

'Well, you're right. There was one hell of a flood in 2002, worst for two hundred years they said. I'd just returned to Prague from America, so I remember it well. Anyway all this area was about three metres under water and the wall was ruined.'

'So all this is pretty recent?' I ask, already aware of the answer.

'Including that head of Lennon.'

'Thought so.'

'You sensed it, didn't you?' she inquires. 'I could see it when you were against the wall.'

I feel cornered. 'Look it's nothing, right. It's just that I've got this sexy thing going with walls, that's all. Look, can we go somewhere else now?'

She's looking at me disbelievingly. 'Okay, but before we go, why don't you do something on the wall, you know, just to…' she laughs. 'Just to say, you woz here.'

I see the humour and smile but hold back on laughing. 'Yeah, why not.'

'Here,' she says reaching into her coat pocket. 'I brought a marker with permanent ink, you know, just in case.'

This does make me laugh, not out loud, but enough to lighten the mood. I take the pen and turn to the wall to find a space to put my mark on.

'There,' she says, pointing to a small area about the size of tennis ball.

I hover over the space and begin to hear voices again.

'It doesn't matter what it is, Briney, just something that I can come here years from now and be reminded of your visit.'

All I can think of is my tag. Seems appropriate somehow. So with a flourish, *MyRuza08* is now part of Lennon's wall.

I hand her back the pen. 'There, can we go now?'

I wait while she takes a close look.

'Rose?' she says and gives me a quizzical look.

I don't say anything and turn to walk away.

She comes to my side and takes me by the hand. 'Come, we walk back over the bridge to the Town Square. I could do with a drink and we can watch our famous clock strike the hour.'

CHAPTER 19

Zoja has gone into tour guide mode and starts describing the towering statues on each side of the Charles Bridge. I'm trying to show interest, but after only three I'm wondering who are all these saints anyway? Then a smile stretches her dark red lipstick as we come to a statue of lions climbing rocks to a figure on top offering a bare leg. 'This reminds me of Zac,' she says pointing up. I'm intrigued. 'This is the statue of Saint Vitus, the patron saint of dancers. I'm sure you've heard of Saint Vitus Dance, you know the uncontrollable twitch?' I catch her drift.

We continue on and it quickly becomes obvious I'm showing signs of saint-fatigue. Zoja notices and the descriptions become briefer and by the time we're halfway across the bridge I've become more interested in the range of tourist offerings. There's musicians, stalls selling replicas of the bridge and other Prague landmarks and lots of portrait artists that seem to have plenty of willing sitters. This is more my thing and I can't help lingering behind the various artists watching their interpretations evolve on paper.

Zoja pulls me away from one artist with a very engaging cartoon style to the other side of the bridge and another saint statue that looks rather less interesting than some of the others with only a lone figure and no lions or anything.

'This is the statue of Saint John Nepomuk,' she informs me pulling me closer. On each side of the base are two panels with a different scene in relief. On the left, as the story is told to me, is the wife of King Wenceslas IV, the Queen—looking more like a soldier in armour—is patting a dog that looks a lot like a greyhound. The scene on the right-hand panel shows the Queen watching the Saint, who, refusing to divulge her confession to the king, was tortured and thrown from the bridge. But the striking thing about both dull, grey, weathered bronze panels is the highly polished dog on the left and the figure of the Saint being thrown from the bridge on the right. This is explained by the line of tourists rubbing the dog, the Saint, or both.

'It's said that if you rub the Saint you'll return to Prague,' hints Zoja wedging me between two disgruntled German tourists.

I hesitate at the invitation, unsure if I want to since nothing has convinced me otherwise. But I can't disappoint Zoja, so on reaching the panel on the right, I lean forward and run a finger over the shiny falling figure. I wasn't expecting the jolt I got and gingerly try again. This time there's no spark from the past, just a magnetic pull to rub harder. Whether I return to Prague is not the message I'm getting, it's the possibility I may never leave.

By the time we get to the Old Town Square and the medieval, fairytale Prague I was expecting, a large crowd is gathering around the ultra-weird Town Hall clock.

'Let's have a drink and watch the hour change. It's actually quite Gothic,' she says with a wink and a nod to a row of outdoor restaurants offering front row seats.

I take in the awesome sight in front of me as we wait for our drinks and get this walloping sense of the past coming up through my feet. Shit, they're resting on the same ground that's had so much history trample over it and I wonder if all these other people hanging around feel what I'm feeling?

The noise of the crowd softens to a murmur as all eyes look up to the Dr Who-style timepiece. Then silence as the minute hand jerks to the top. To the right, a figure of a skeleton pulls on a rope with one hand and inverts an hourglass with the other. Above, twelve figures appear through an open window as the hour is chimed. Another figure beside the skeleton shakes its head and two other figures on the left of the clock do their thing. The show is over until the next hour and our drinks have been delivered without me noticing.

'Cool,' I remark, as the crowd thins out. 'I mean the whole place is just so fucking amazing, it's like walking through a fairy-tale picture book.'

'Yes, and like all fairy-tales there's always witches and evil around.'

'Yeah, I'm learning more and more about that.'

'Do you think I'm a Gothic witch?'

She looks serious but I take it as a joke.

'Na.' But she's not smiling. 'Well, Gothic, sure,' I add, trying to read her expression. Then I get this quiver. 'Are you?'

She's staring so sternly it's beginning to give me the creeps. Nah, she couldn't, but nothing would surprise me in this Gothic city.

'You're not, are you?' I ask again, trying to not be too serious.

She continues staring until finally breaking into a smile and raises her hands with her blood red-tipped fingers spread, hooked and ready to pounce. From the depth of her throat she growls. 'If I was, I would have cast a spell over you by now.'

I let out a forced laugh with the growing awareness that she may very well have already succeeded.

'Enough of this,' she says, relaxing her hands. 'Finish your drink. There's more to see.'

For the next hour or two we walk the breezy, almost claustrophobic laneways and alleys, constantly coming up against tight groups of sightseers with cameras aimed and arms pointing up and around while they follow wiggling coloured flags in an audible haze of foreign languages. We catch the lift to the top of the Town Hall tower that allows a 360-degree view over Prague. The narrow streets, alleys and laneways we had just navigated seem to merge as if being sucked down a giant plughole. Then back down and out into the open space of the Old Town Square. Zoja once again slides her arm in mine. I like this physical contact with her, though I'd never be the one to slide an arm into hers. As we pass each of the buildings surrounding the square, she tells me their history, who lived there and whether it's Romanesque, Baroque or Gothic in style. It's bloody amazing and far too much for an uneducated girl like me to grasp, but with each step, past each building, I once again sense the confusion of history closing in on me.

There's so much of it, so much turmoil, so many conflicts, so much killing. I begin to stagger.

'Briney, you look ill.' She tightens her grip of my arm in support. 'You're not eating well are you?'

She's right; all I've eaten in more than two days was something last night at the bus terminal and the slice of cake this morning.

'We should've stopped for lunch, I'm sorry. Now we go and have an early dinner.'

'Look, Zoja, you're really kind, but, I don't know, I…'

'Nonsense! You need food and so do I. We eat.'

Her grip makes it hard to refuse and she steers me back through the Square, past the Town Hall, across another smaller square into the arched entrance to Karlova 25 arcade. I'm not sure if it's the punk/Goth gear in the small shops, the tattooist or the large carved, wooden alien-looking stature hanging on the wall staring down the dungeon steps to the Comix Gallery Bar with its yellow taxi door hanging above that deters the tourists, but the place is relatively empty. Shopkeepers wave and call to Zoja as we walk past tables, chairs and benches under the late afternoon light reaching us through the narrow roofless space. She returns their greeting, each by name. If I wasn't feeling so weak, I'd be impressed and maybe a bit jealous of her popularity.

'Here,' she says, stopping at a small café. On a blackboard outside, under the brand of a local beer, the daily specials are hand-written, but the word INTERNET is what grabs my attention most and I have an urgent need to check MySpace.

Again, Zoja is greeted by a guy wiping down a table and by a couple sitting at the window. All dressed like they belong to a heavy metal band with long hair, tatts, leather and studs.

'Will we start with a beer?' she asks.

'I think I need something stronger.' I confess.

'Ah, Moravian Sunshine it is,' she says, getting a nod from the guy wiping tables.

I'm discovering that every place you enter in Prague is, thankfully, well heated, and I join Zoja in stripping out of our coat and jacket before sitting opposite each other at a table near the rear of the café as our two shot glasses of plum-coloured liquid arrive. While he's writing out the slip, Zoja talks to our waiter in Czech. I figure she's ordering food as he adds this to the paper strip, places it on the table, nods at me, I nod back and he's gone.

'Na zdraví,' we say touching glasses. I take a sip. The strength of the spirit slams into the back of my throat. 'Whoa!' I barely get out, struggling to regain my breath. Zoja smiles and in one swig, downs all, holds her breath then slams the glass back down on the table. Quick to see my mistake I throw down the rest. My throat rebels against the fire as I struggle to swallow and forces me to cough through my nose. I quickly wipe away anything that may have snorted out as the liquor finally burns its way into my stomach.

'Another?' she asks with a smile on her face.

I'm still waiting to regain some air, but nod. That felt fucking good. She gestures for two more.

'Zoja, I see they have Internet here and before I have another I need to check on something. Can I use my laptop in here?'

'There's no WiFi but you can use one of those.' She points to a couple of vacant computers against a nearby wall. 'Come, you can use my account.'

She picks the first one, enters her password and moves aside for me to take over. I login and go directly to the inbox. There's one unread message and the fire in my stomach started by the Moravian Sunshine is re-kindled. Nervously I open it.

Forgive me. Yesterday not good. You come back tomorrow. L3BIV on museum map. You look like your mother. Evzen

It's the mention that I look like *her* that's rocked me more than anything and sent me back in the chair. All I can do is sit staring at the screen unsure of how I feel. Is this the proof that all is real?

'What is it? Is it bad news?' asks a concerned Zoja, putting her arm around my shoulder.

'No, no it's fine,' I say, unsure if it is or not.

Her arm slides away from my shoulder. I want it to stay.

'Zoja, what does Evzen mean?'

Her arm slides back as she leans forward to read the message.

'It's a name, a man's name. Is this who you met yesterday?'

I'm still staring at the message and *his* name. 'I think so…well not really…I mean, we didn't actually meet…I mean, shit, I don't know what I mean anymore. I need that drink now.'

'Are you going to reply?'

I shake my head and log out. I need to think about it first.

The second Slivovitz feels a lot smoother and calming this time.

Zoja is toying with her still-full glass. I can sense her mind ticking over now she's had some insight into my secretive behaviour.

'So, you're going back tomorrow?'

I know I must.

'I guess so, but this L3BIV, what is it?'

She downs her Slivovitz. 'If only you had a map of Terezín.'

Without hesitation, I search through my bag for the booklet with the map and open it out on the table. She comes around to my side and leans over my shoulder. I can feel her cheek close to mine and the smell of her intoxicating perfume is teaming up with the hit I'm getting from the Slivovitz.

'There,' she says. I follow her finger as it traces one of the streets to the edge of the map. 'You see, the Germans gave the streets in the Ghetto a number instead of a name. The letter L is for streets running north to south and the letter Q east to west. The numbers are the order of the streets from bottom to top and right to left.' Her finger has stopped at L3 and the outline of the building shows the bold letters BIV in its centre. 'There, L3BIV.'

Above the letters BIV is the number 26 in a red circle. 'I was next to it yesterday. Look, number 25 is just across the road. That's the Museum I went to.'

She turns the pages of the map legend to number 26 and its description.

'It says here it was Hannover Barracks where working men were housed.' She turns to look at me. Her face so close I can feel her warm breath. 'Does that make any sense to you?'

It doesn't, nothing does, except I feel I'm drifting away from the map, from yesterday and Terezín and being hopelessly swept up into the deep green current of her eyes. She moves closer, her lips parting slightly releasing a whisper of breath. I melt back into her shoulder and we kiss. The taste of her lipstick is followed by the invasion of her tongue, I hesitate, is this what I want? It is.

The kiss is short, but long on substance. She moves to stand, pressing herself against me until a breast is against the side of my face. I feel its firmness and a strong urge to kiss her nipple.

The arrival of our food and two beers puts a stop to it going any further and she returns to her seat opposite. I notice a blush on her porcelain white cheeks then the rich appetising smell coming up from the hearty meal in front of me.

'That's our national dish of roast pork, dumplings and sauerkraut —potato dumplings of course, not the other ones. That will bring back your energy.'

I'm smiling. Well, stupidly grinning more like it, as the effect of the Slivovitz has well and truly hit.

'You start,' she adds, turning to search through the pockets of her coat then takes out a small black case. Shit, I would never have thought she wore glasses. But they weren't glasses she takes out, but a long thin metal cylinder. I watch as she pulls the cap off one end with her teeth and holds it in her mouth as she turns a dial on the other end of the tube. As I'm wondering what the hell she's doing, she pulls up her black blouse and injects herself in the lower stomach. All the time it takes to transfer whatever it is from the tube into her body, she doesn't look up, but I'm nervously looking around to see if anyone's watching and relieved to find there's no interest in what she's doing at all. After removing the fine needle from her flesh, she replaces the cap from between her teeth, puts the tube back in its case and the case back in her coat then looks up to see me staring with mouth wide open. I lean forward and whisper, 'is that okay to do openly in Prague?'

She looks at me confused. 'What?'

'You know,' I say, nodding down at her stomach then look around the room again, 'drugs!'

She smiles. 'Oh yes,' she says mischievously. 'I do it all the time.'

'Fuck!'

Not wanting to tease me any more, she leans forward. 'It's insulin, darling. I'm a diabetic.'

'A what?'

'A diabetic.'

I don't know what to say.

'You do know what that is, don't you?'

I feel the Slivovitz weighing heavy on my brain. 'I've never known anyone who's, you know, that.'

With a sympathetic smile she explains. 'I need to inject insulin before a meal to help regulate my sugar balance.' She looks for a reaction and sees confusion instead. 'You really don't know anything about diabetes, do you?'

A twinge of rage sparks through me. I get it whenever I'm drunk and when I think I'm being put down because of a lack of upbringing and education, and I snap.

'Look! I know how to survive on nothing. I know the rules of street life. I know how to handle the shits I meet and I fucking well know how to give them what they want so I can have a decent meal now and again. That's what I know and that's all I fucking well know!'

The outburst results in silence. Zoja is stunned. I dive into the food. Hungry for it and the wall it's created for me to hide behind.

Zoja picks at her smaller meal, then puts her fork down and slides her hand across the table to touch mine. I start to stubbornly move away, but stop as the reality of our difference shows in our hands. She has delicate unblemished skin, manicured and painted nails with designer rings on three of her perfectly long fingers. Mine are unadorned except for a single, plain plastic amber ring, chewed nails showing a hint of dirt under them and calloused skin that's already showing signs of ageing. The difference is overwhelming and I put down the fork and slide my hand under hers in an attempt to conceal its ugliness while imagining her hand is mine and that life has been very different.

'I'm sorry, Zoja, I didn't mean to snap at you like that,' I offer, keeping my eyes lowered.

She tightens her grip.

'I want to watch you eat,' she says, sliding her hand away.

I look up at her. Shit, is she serious? I hate anyone looking at me at any time, but to watch me eat, fuck! But strangely I've a rush of excitement. It's Zoja who's watching, and that feels very erotic.

Without a conscious effort to act differently, I eat. Silence surrounds us except for the sounds of knife and fork on plate and the moist chewing as I savour the rich flavours of the food and relax into the totally foreign experience of exposing myself—a sort of culinary nakedness.

Zoja continues to watch with great interest as I reveal a lack of etiquette and a primeval handling of the tools. As I lift an overladen fork to my mouth, a spot of gravy drops on the outside of my lower lip and ever so slowly crawls to my chin. I feel Zoja itching to inform me of this spot of gravy but, teasingly, I insert another mouthful of food. I'm taunting her. Her breathing is becoming heavier. Then, ever so slowly, I lick at the dribble of gravy as far as my tongue can reach. This has Zoja thrusting her hands beneath the tabletop, and due to the slight movement of her arms, I can only imagine that she's massaging herself.

All the pork's eaten, the sauerkraut has gone and the remaining dumpling is left to soak up what's left of the gravy. Zoja is still massaging herself under the table but now her eyes have closed slightly. I place the knife and fork on the plate and with one hand, break off a piece of dumpling and glide it around the gravy while the other hand slides off the table to rest between parted legs. I raise the piece of dumpling to my mouth but a spot of gravy drips onto my chest. I look down, finish chewing the dumpling, lick my fingers and slide one under the spot of gravy and over a hard nipple. Zoja's mouth is slightly open as she licks her dark red lips. Aware of her approaching climax, I sense my own surfacing. I'm turning on another female, something I've thought about but only in the privacy of my imagination. Her orgasm is silent so as not to attract attention, her jerking movements hardly noticeable. I have a strong urge to follow in my own release but deliberately suppress it, well aware that I would never be able to climax quietly, and happy just to revel in the experience.

For what seems an eternity, we remain silently frozen in our final moment of mutual pleasure. Then, surprising both of us, I uncontrollably break out into laughter. To avoid seeing Zoja's embarrassment, I cover my mouth and look coyly down at the plate. But deep inside I'm feeling satisfied that I've finally experienced something I've questioned about myself for some time. However, Zoja deserves an explanation.

'Look sorry, Zoja, but that's the first time I've done anything like that and I wasn't sure how to act.'

She leans forward placing both hands on the table. 'You did just fine…just fine. You turned me on and all I can hope for is that I had the same effect on you.'

'Yeah, Zoja. Yeah, it had an effect on me, a really nice effect in fact.' Nice! Shit why did I use that word?

I'm coming down from the high, the booze has eased up fucking around with my head, the meal has satisfied the hunger pains and I'm returning to the world I've created. I need to think. Not just about Zoja, though I wish it was, but about this old guy, Evzen. I was prepared to walk away and go back to Oz, but this new message is nudging the recent and more favourable thoughts out of my mind.

'Look, Zoja, I really do appreciate you taking me out today and showing me a good time and everything, but I reckon I need to get back to the Elf and sort out what I'm to do about this new message and tomorrow.'

She slides her hands off the table as if cutting any bond that may have formed. 'Yes,' she says. I sense her disappointment. 'I am taking up too much of your time, I'm sorry.'

'No, no!' I try to assure her. 'Look, I want I see you again, I really do. And I promise I'll tell you all that's happening after I find out myself.'

Her understanding smile is welcome.

'Briney, as I told you before, if there's anything I can do to help, I mean it. If you do go back to Terezín, do you want me to come with you?'

'Thanks, but I need to do this on me own.'

'If you say so,' she places her hand over mine. 'But I'll hold you to your promise.'

'I promise, Zoja. I want us to be friends.'

We both smile knowing there's more than just friendship in the wind.

'I'll arrange a taxi to take you back.'

'No, really you've spent too much on me already.'

'I insist,' she snaps back. 'You have money for tomorrow?'

I'm not sure how much I've got left or if it's enough, but I don't want to accept any money from her. 'Yeah, I'll manage.'

'You still have my card?'

I nod and we get up to leave.

It's getting dark as I approach the Elf and pass Zac in the streetlight, staggering up the road from the pub. Shit, he's pissed to the eyeballs. By the time I get out of the taxi he's there.

'Where the fuck ya been? With ya fuckin' dyke, hey?' he spits out.

The taxi driver looks out the window. I nod to let him know it's okay to drive off and wait until he's turned and heading back to the centre of town.

'We need to talk, Zac. I just wish you weren't so bloody pissed.'

He's riled and angry and pushes me through the gateway and roughly against the wall. I've seen Zac pissed and angry lots before, but this time he's frightening me.

'Come on Bri. I know ya like cock better than cunt,' he sputters, saliva hitting me in the eye.

'I told you it's fucking over between us, Zac, now let me go.' I'm preparing to knee him in the balls if he gets any rougher.

'Bullshit. Ya not turning queer on me, are ya?'

'You'd make anyone turn queer you're so fucking pathetic.'

He pushes away with his outstretched arms still pinning me against the wall.

'That fuckin' dyke bitch…I learnt a few things about her today.'

I'm suddenly interested. 'Who from?' I ask without lowering my guard. 'Those skinhead pricks?'

'Yeah, well, you're not the only fuckin' one to have new mates.'

'They didn't look like mates to me.'

'What the fuck do you know, they're cool and I reckon I can do a bit of business with 'em.'

That worries me.

'Fuck Zac, you're not gunna spend all your money on a deal are you? I need some to get back to Terezín tomorrow.' I grab his arms. 'You do remember why I'm here, right?'

'Shit, that's all fuckin' bullshit and ya know it.' His mood's changed and he rests his forehead on mine. 'Listen, I got ya here okay, but it wasn't because of your fuckin' goose thing. I just wanted to get away with ya and have a good time, right? So come on Bri, why don't ya drop this bloody weird thing you're on and we have some fun, hey?'

His beery breath and tooth decay is overpowering as he closes in for a kiss. I tense my leg ready to lift it into his balls, but the strangest thing comes over me. Even though it's fucking obvious at this point, I now have the opportunity to compare, or more likely convince me once and for all where my true sexual feelings lie. And then, of course, there's the chance I might be able to get some money out of him. So I lower my knee and allow myself to be kissed.

'That's fuckin' better,' he says, easing back from me just enough to get the words out then back for another kiss, this time firmer in an effort to force his tongue between tightly closed lips. I can feel his hard-on as he presses his body against me while one hand slides down to my tits. The touch sends sparks all through me and I press against his hand and his crotch. Needing release from the sexual tension built up with Zoja, I accept his advance.

'Not here,' I say, with the street only a metre away.

He looks blearily at me with a drunken, conquering smirk and leads me up the steps to the hostel and to our room.

CHAPTER 20

The sound of early morning arrivals dropping their packs and chatting in the hallway wakens me. Unfortunately, the first thing I notice is the smell coming from the wastepaper basket in the corner where Zac threw up as soon as we got to our room. He then collapsed, leaving me sexually and financially unfulfilled. He's still out to it with some crusty dribble sticking his face to the pillow, so I gently turn him and the pillow over to face the other way. The only response I get back is a mumble and a fart. That's enough to get me outta bed to be rid of him.

Sitting on the floor, I search through my bag for a clean pair of knickers then grab my jeans and take out what's left of my money. There's not enough to get to Terezín and back and still have some extra for whatever else. After a quick check on Zac to make sure he's still out to it, I slide across the floor, grab his jeans and go through the pockets. He never carries a wallet so diving into each pocket I manage to find some money and a crumpled note. I'm surprised at how little there is and hope he's got more somewhere else. Out of the 3750 Koruna I find, I take 500, hoping he lost count of how much he spent yesterday on booze, and put the rest back in his pockets. I check him out again before unfolding the note. What I guess are names and a phone number written down mean nothing to me, but I get an uneasy feeling. I study the names, Deratz, Stik and Dasha. Nothing registers, I figure they must be his new skinheads mates.

With legs crossed in a sorta yoga position and his jeans on my lap, I look around the room with the realisation that all I own is as sparse as my options.

I indulge myself under what could be the last hot shower until whenever, towel down and go back to the room to dress. After making sure everything I own is stuffed in my bag, I scribble a note and leave it on the vacant pillow beside the totally out to it Zac. He's such a child,

I think with a twinge of sadness. Shit, we've had our moments together, some good ones, but now it's time to follow my gut feeling and accept whatever comes without worrying about anyone else. I put on Sarge's jacket and swing his bag over my shoulder and head out the door.

There's a new girl at the reception desk, probably just starting the morning shift. I nod hello and head to the computer room for one last check if any new message had come in from *R. Vesely*—or should I be saying Evzen from now on? Apart from several complaints about no graffiti secrets for some time, there's nothing else. I open yesterday's message to once again read... *You look like your mother.*

Before leaving the Elf I go to where the free breakfast is being laid out and grab some bread, sliced ham and cheese, then head for the bus terminal.

CHAPTER 21

The thick, dark clouds and icy wind have given this one-time Ghetto town a gloomier, more deserted and even more depressing air than when last here. I shiver against the cold and everything about this place, pull the hood up over my head and start walking against the wind in the direction of the Magdeburg Barracks Museum and this building L3BIV.

I noticed it last time, but only because of the stark comparison between the freshly restored Museum, and a building that is severely weathered and left to decay. Chunks of plaster render have fallen off the walls revealing old, unevenly laid bricks and cracked mortar. The downpipes are all rusted with gaping holes, the eaves and guttering droop from rot and the weight of plant life that's taken root. Thinking this can't be the place cuz it looks condemned and deserted, I look at the map again. But it is and I feel a shiver down my spine. The wall facing the Museum has no entrance so I walk to the far corner facing the outer wall of the fortress. The weather's been less kind to this side of the building with even more decay and even more grime. This doesn't help my nerves at all. I mean, sure, I've shacked up in places just as bad, but everything about this town makes it worse. I look up into each of the dark, empty windows hoping someone will see me and come out to meet me. I wait, but nothing.

The double doors at the arched entrance are open, revealing a dim arcade leading to an internal courtyard and still no sign of life. Taking a deep breath I enter, tentatively treading on solid worn paving stones. Through my feet I sense the movement of transport that once travelled through here, while the walls on each side echo with the march of heavy boots.

The sounds in the tunnel fade as I enter the courtyard. The eerie silence is giving me goose bumps. There's not even the sound of a bird. It's as if death has squatted and repelled all life. Weeds outline the paving stones that cover the courtyard, showing no sign of trampling feet or traffic for quite some time, maybe years. Rubbish is piled up in corners and against walls. More weeds coil around rusted and broken chairs, desks and tables that lie among broken glass and other rubbish. Mould is creeping up the walls from the ground, and in some areas, there's the blackened evidence of a fire above a pile of charred rubbish.

The surrounding walls begin to feel like they're closing in on me and the silence is broken by the sound of men in a confused babble of pain and hunger. Then, strangely, I also hear what sounds like drunken revelry. But all I see in each dark, blank and broken window are blurred faces in my mind's eye—faces of old men, in pain, confused and desperate. Then, young men appear in the mix, relaxed and playfully leering out at this female intruder, only to fade as fast as they appeared back into the cold shadows beyond the windows. Fade, fade, fade… except one image barely visible in a darkened window on the second level. The image is not fading, it's becoming clearer, it's the face of the old man. I rub my eyes. He's gone. Was it wishful thinking? All is quiet again except for the wind blowing through the entrance and swirling around me, and then the scrape and clunk of a metal bolt opening echoes around the courtyard. I look in the direction of the noise. A corroded red metal door is slowly opening, creaking on its rusted hinges. I swing my bag in front of me for some form of protection. The door opens and from the darkened interior the figure of the old man appears. He stops and stands just inside the entrance. After a moment to make sure he's the one I saw in the museum, I walk towards him.

'Hi, I'm Briney.' I reach out one hand while still holding the bag in front of me with the other.

Without a word he continues to stare at me. His eyes are red with weariness and sadness and I sense some anger. His lined face is stubbled and his thin grey hair ruffled. Seeming reluctant, he slowly raises his trembling hand. I take the initiative and grab it, feeling the cold, calloused skin and protruding knuckles and give a couple of stabs at shaking. But his fingers never tighten around mine. I look back into his eyes. He's studying every feature of my face and I spot a tear seep over the puffiness under an eye and down through the crevices of his weathered face.

'Ruza,' he utters, barely audible.

'Yeah, Briney Ruza,' I reply feeling his hand tighten a little.

'Ruza,' he repeats, as if to himself and shuffles back, pulling me into the cold, gloomy darkness.

As soon as I step through the door I feel the chill of others watching. I gradually grow accustomed to the faint light from the open doorway and the grimy cobweb-covered windows. The inside is dusty, bare and smells of mould. I shiver and pull my hand away. Without a word he turns and flicks a crooked finger towards stairs leading up to the next level.

Shit, I must be out of my mind to be going up those stairs with him. But the years of living on the street have taught me a lot, especially how to handle old buggers like him. Still, I tighten the grip on the bag. If anything happens, the laptop inside is the hardest thing I have to hit him with.

He flicks a finger towards the stairs again. What the hell, why not? But then I hear other voices coming from the depth of a dark corridor that runs beside the stairs. Shit, he's not alone! If I had any bloody sense I'd get outta here right now, but I'm confused between the real and the unreal. These voices are different, more like whispers, chanting, hollow and beckoning me to approach.

Again he urges me to follow him up the stairs and I get a whiff of his trailing body odour, a musty mix of stale old clothes and a body decaying from the inside. Smells that are all too familiar where I come from and a reminder of old Sarge.

At the top of the stairs, he leads the way down a hallway, limping and sliding one leg. His baggy pants are worn and hanging loosely from old leather braces over a thick flannel checked shirt. A button is missing on the back of his pants, leaving one of the tabs of his braces curled up and flapping as he wobbles along. At the third door down the hall, he stands aside for me to enter. I pause at the doorway and look in. The room is as stark and as cold as the downstairs. The air is stale and pungent. In one corner is an old mattress with two worn grey blankets crumpled on it. A small simple wooden table and a chair are against one of the stained, mouldy walls. Beside the mattress is another chair with what looks like a tattered grey coat thrown over it. All around the room, newspapers are piled up in corners with some spread out by the bed, for extra warmth I reckon going by experience. On the table is a coffee-stained chipped tin mug sitting on an equally stained and chipped tin plate, a spoon, an open pocket knife, a jar containing something unrecognisable and a single candle, thick and well dribbled. I've seen worse.

He pulls the chair out from the table for me to sit and shuffles to the other chair, throws the coat over the mattress and slides it across the bare floorboards to the table, flops himself into it and resumes his study of me without a word.

I don't know if it's youthful impatience, but I gotta start the conversation somehow.

'Who are you?' I blurt out, the words echoing through the empty building. He shakes his head and waves one trembling hand. 'Who are you?' I say again. 'Are you Evzen?'

His expression changes from a sort of dreamy, bewildered look to a more aggressive frown as if seeing me for the first time.

He mumbles something I don't understand, though I did pick up the last word, 'Ruza'.

'Yeah, Ruza, Briney Ruza,' I say, pointing to myself. Then, with a shrug, 'Me speak no Czech.' Why is it we always sound like Red Indians when we try to talk to foreigners?

He looks a bit disappointed and grumbles to himself. I feel we may have a big problem here.

'You no Ruza!' It sounded more a statement than a question, but at least it was in English, sorta.

'Yeah, I'm Briney Ruza,' I try to convince him.

He shakes his head. I'm getting confused and I think he is too.

'Umm, me,' he points to himself while shaking his head. 'Me English not so good. You no Ruza...ya momma Ruza.'

That pricked up my ears. 'You know my...*her*?' Still can't say that word for some reason.

I figure he hasn't spoken in anything other than Czech for a while and now he's struggling to translate into English what he wants to say.

'Are...you...Evzen?' I ask again slowly.

'Ya, Evzen,' he says poking his chest. 'Kravitz, Evzen.'

'Hi Evzen,' I say as politely as I can. 'Umm, how do you know her?'

'Ruza,' he replies, but I feel his mind has gone back to what he was thinking earlier.

'Is she here?' I instinctively look around the room, hoping she isn't. He doesn't reply but is staring at me with that distant look again.

'Here?' he questions.

'Here in Terezín?' I press on.

He nods but I sense there's something else.

'She's dead isn't she?' Don't know why it came out like that.

'Ruza,' he says, wiping some dribble from his nose.

'She's dead isn't she?' I repeat. Somehow, somewhere in the back of my mind I'm hoping he'll say yes.

He seems not to be hearing me. 'I first need tell you...'

'Yeah?' I interrupt, getting impatient.

He holds up a crooked finger in protest at being cut short.

'Hear what I say,' he says calmly, but I feel as if I'm being told off.

He turns and takes up the coat lying on the mattress, reaches into the inside pocket and takes out a well-worn, dog-eared photograph and slides it across the table.

'This Ruza,' he says.

I push forward and pick up the photo. I feel suddenly suspended in limbo. All I can do is stare at the photograph at arm's length. I don't know if it's the initial shock of seeing what she looked like, as my memory of her had faded long ago, or the shock of seeing myself in the photo, the similarity unbelievable. I'm overwhelmed by a tenderness I've never ever felt…never! I trace her young face with my finger, totally baffled by this strange emotion.

'Tell me your story,' I whisper to the photo, for it's her story I want to hear more than the old man's.

There's no reply. There never has been. Nor has there ever been tears shed over her, only stubborn bitterness, loneliness and survival… until now!

I don't know how long I cried for. It seemed like ages until I felt a comforting hand on my head. I imagined it was *her* hand, steady and calming as *her* fingers combed through my hair, stroking ever so gently. But his croaky voice awakens me from the dream. 'Why you leave, dear Ruza?'

I raise my head. His rough hand slides down over my face.

He's not looking at me, but through his own tears into the past.

'Tell me your story,' I ask again, sliding the photo across the table back to him.

He looks up from the photo. His expression has changed. Gone is the distant look. Gone are the tears. All replaced with a cold, steely, serious look.

'You know of Terezín…um…history, ya?'

All I've seen and learnt at both museums flashes before me and I reply with a nod.

'My family sent here when Ghetto.' Pain joins the mix of expressions in his weary eyes. 'Ruza family sent also.' There's a long pause as he swallows and sniffs back a dribble from his nose. 'Both our parents die before year pass. Ruza, Marika and me then alone… umm…orphan…but we stay together.'

'Marika?' I question.

'Ruza's sestra,' he answers.

'Sister?' I figured that's what he meant. 'You mean she had a sister?' I pause. 'Is she alive?'

'We stay together,' he continues from where he left off. 'But Ruza get typhoid…very sick…nearly die.' His hand is hovering and twitching over the photo. 'We care for Ruza…under Nazis…then Soviets…but you survive, ya!' He's staring at me but I figure his looking at *her*. 'You healthier now, ya?'

I force a smile as if I was her. Actually, I don't think I ever did see her smile.

'It hard under Soviet, ya. You can no work…and if no work… Soviet no want you. But I look after you, ya?' Then, with a shudder, his voice sharpens. 'But you leave, Ruza. Why…you no tell me?' In fresh rage he slams his hand down onto the table upsetting the mug. I steady it. This change of mood concerns me but he's raising questions I need answers to.

'Is that when she went to Australia?'

It takes a moment for him to hear the words and realign himself to where he's at…and me.

'Australia? Is that when she went to Australia?' I repeat.

His glazed eyes begin to focus on me. He grunts. He's coming back. He's hearing me.

'What year did she go to Australia?'

He shakes his head. '1968…year of *Prague Spring*. She no tell…she just go…she escape with help of Italian student.'

'Escape?'

'Ya…Soviet control…hard to leave.'

'How old was she?'

'Old?' he says shaking his head and waving his finger. 'No, young… too young.'

'But why did she leave you if you and her sister were looking after her?'

'She too ill to work…life very hard…she feel she a burden…but that no matter…I love her.'

I'm starting to get the picture of their relationship.

'Yeah, I see that. Um…did you, like, marry?'

He looks away from me and down to his lap.

'Marry? I ask many time…but all time she say no. She say she die if she no go away.' He sniffs back a tear and clears his throat. 'I say to her…that no matter…I stay with her till day she die.'

I wanted to ask more about how she got to Australia, how could she afford it back then, but I felt I knew how she earned her passage, after all I was an innocent witness to her profession. But I felt Evzen had no idea of this part of her life and it would hurt him to know.

'Did she write to you?' I ask, trying to skip over lots of what must have been painful years.

He looks back to the photograph on the table.

'Ne, never…until…maybe month or two ago.'

A month or two? Interesting.

'From where, Australia?'

'Ya, Australia. A letter came for Marika.'

'Had…umm…Marika been in touch with her before then?'

'Ne, we thought Ruza dead.'

The revelation that all this time she was alive and in Australia and never once tried to find me, leaves me rattled. Then another thought hits me. Maybe she's still back there and I've come all this way for nothing!

'But, but, I'm confused. Where is she now?'

'Ya…she home.' There's a hint of a smile on his craggy face. 'My Ruza come back to me.'

He's passed into another dream, staring down at the photo.

We both take a moment for reflection. While still confused, and seeing her only as a fleeting image in time, to this old man, she was and will always be a real person who has real problems, and someone he has carried his love for over so many years.

'Can I go see her?'

Evzen looks up. 'She resting.' It sounded defensive.

'Resting? What does that mean?' That's got me angry. 'Shit, I've come from the other side of the bloody world on some crazy whim and cryptic messages and all you can tell me is …she's resting!'

He stiffens up in his chair with a new fierce look in his eyes.

'You no understand, you young people. You…you know nothing of pain. Nothing of torture…nothing of death. You live in soft peaceful world with your…your…Internet and games. You are rude…you ignore the old.'

Shit, what's he on about all of a sudden? 'Look!' I say with equal force, determined to show he's not intimidating me. 'Don't start again with your bloody cryptic bullshit.' Then it hits me. 'When you say she's resting…do you mean she's…at rest…dead? '

He looks stunned by my outburst. I keep pressing.

'And if she is dead, then why didn't you bloody well tell me so I wouldn't waste my time coming here?

That got a reaction. He leans forward with an intense look in his eyes. This time I do feel intimidated and lean back away from him.

'You here.' He pauses, waving a crooked finger at me. 'You here because of your power.'

'What power?' I ask, though I reckon I know what he's talking about. 'Look, so I get these flashes of things from walls, okay. But I wouldn't call it a power. I mean, shit, it's more an annoying embarrassment actually.'

He's waiting for more. Baiting me with his stare.

'I mean, shit, so sometimes I reckon the walls are talking to me… but it's crazy, right?'

His hand closes to a fist and his knuckles turn white as he deliberately utters each word. 'You…see…Goose.'

'Yeah, right, the fucking Goose…'

His fist slams down onto the table rattling the tin cup in the plate. 'You no use such words!'

That's it. Now he's got me really pissed off.

'Fuck you old man. What's with you and this Goose and what the hell's it got to do with my…with her?'

Every time I refer to *her*, he seems to go into another space, but I need him to stay with me on this.

'Anyway, this Goose is all in your head, cuz no one else saw anything like a Goose or duck and I'm not sure I saw it either. It's a game, right! My graffs are done so anyone can see whatever they want…it's just a game.'

I push the chair back and stand, furious at the realisation, and wave a pointed finger at him.

'You bloody tricked me, didn't you? You bloody tricked me to come all the way here, using her as an excuse, just so you can ask me about a fucking Goose?'

He shakes his head, but I reckon I've hit the spot.

'Look, the way I figure it is that she came back, told you things about me and that's how you knew about the name on my clock. But what I don't understand is how an old guy like you found me through MySpace?'

'Ruza tell me.'

'Bullshit! How would she know?'

'She say in letter to Marika.'

'This letter, do you have it? Show me.' I demand, still to be convinced.

His eyes look down at the photo on the table. It's as if he's talking to it, asking her what to do. Then he turns back to his coat and takes out a small envelope and slides it across the table. So the letter is real, and looking down at it I'm suddenly unsure of what to do. The top is tattered where it was hurriedly ripped open. The blue 'Airmail' sticker neatly placed on the top left corner has deflected the tear to run around its edge. On the right are four fifty-cent stamps placed neatly in rows two-by-two. Each of the four stamps show a single red rose with three leaves growing from the stem. It was all the proof I needed to confirm the letter was from her, for the choice of this particular stamp was made with me in mind. The rose, Ruza, her name and the tag I adopted…and, what's even weirder, the rose on the stamp is the same design as the tattoo I have. This is the first physical contact I've had with her in more than three quarters of my life and all I can do is hold the envelope and study the hand-written address…

Marika Veselý
C/- Post Office
411 55 Terezín
Czech Republic

Her writing style is similar to mine. The tense grip on the pen nervously digging black letters into the paper, a trait I hate, yet when I paint, my hand is light and fluid.

I look closer at the postmark. Dated 5 February 2008, the location, PRAHRAN! She was in my own neighbourhood when she posted this letter! Did she live there? I snatch up the envelope to turn it over. No return address. But now, holding the envelope, I'm sensing the energy within. So much has been revealed on the surface of this envelope yet so much still remains unanswered, but still I'm finding it difficult to take out the letter. I'm torn between the desire to know and the urge to keep a lid on the past.

I feel Evzen's eyes burning into me, waiting. I give a slight nervous cough and take out the letter—noticing the cheap notepaper—and slowly unfold it, careful not to add to the tears where the folds have weakened. Two pages with the same handwriting but with a different pen, blue this time, presumably written in a private place, no doubt.

There's no return address on the letter either and that disappoints me. I take a quick glance up at Evzen. He's staring at the letter. I look back down and silently begin to read.

'You read out,' he snaps loudly.

I glance up and see the expectation in his eyes and reckon that as the letter is written in English, he's probably only heard it translated to Czech. I clear my throat and begin to read.

'*My dearest sister Marika, I trust this letter finds you well.*'

I need to clear my throat again as I'm all tensed up at seeing her words. I sniff and continue.

'*I start by asking your forgiveness and your understanding and the patience of a lifetime for me to write you. I can only offer an unworthy apology. If you wish to throw this letter away now I understand, but I beg you to hear my final words as I am dying.*' I hear Evzen cough but I dare not look up. '*My reason to leave Prague may seem to you selfish, but I could no longer be a burden to you or my darling Evzen who I loved so much and who I have never stopped loving.*'

This time I grab a quick glance up at him before continuing, repeating the last few words for his benefit.

'*...my darling Evzen who I loved so much and who I have never stopped loving. You may be pleased to learn that my life has seen much punishment for my leaving, more than you can imagine, but I now have come to my end and I have only one request that you see in your heart to accept me back so I can die in the arms of kin and in my place of birth.*

If you are still reading this letter, I have something to tell you, something that I have shamefully kept from you, but never from my heart. I have a daughter.'

I cough to clear the rising lump in my throat.

'*I have a daughter. Or to be more precise, I did have a daughter for I abandoned her, just as I abandoned you and Evzen. And as I have forever loved you both, I have forever loved my daughter but my shame stopped me from facing her as it has from facing you.*'

Shit, I can feel tears building up and I don't want to cry again.

'*Though I abandoned my daughter at the age of seven, I never abandoned my love for her.*'

Anguish rises from some deep dark crevice that had been crusted over by the many years of unhealed rejection. I need to clear my throat again.

'*I lost contact when she was taken from me and her name was changed, but I have spent all my remaining years searching for her. Thinking I see her one day but never again, then another day and never again, this for many years. Even though my last memory of her is as a small child, I feel I would still recognise her now.*

Then, during one of my many hospital stays, I heard a group of nurses talking about a graffiti game. I immediately knew they were talking about my daughter when one mentioned the name RUZA, my name, I was certain it was her. My heart lifted after all these years of searching as I now had something I could connect to her.

I asked the nurses for more information and was given a website. Every day I would go to the library and look at this website for her latest painting. But I am getting too weak to continue my search. I now must use what energy I have left to see my country and my sister for one last time and to hopefully see Evzen again if this is possible.

I will send details of my flight and arrival. If you are not there to meet me I will understand.
Your eternal sister,
Ruza.'

There's silence as both of us are lost in our own thoughts. I'm staring at her signature. The similarity to my own is clear. All the energy has been drained from me, leaving a hollow shell echoing with hollow words. If she loved me all this time, then why was I rejected? What started off filling me with hope has now made me angry.

'Where is she? Where is Marika…and why you?'

He takes a grubby handkerchief from his pants pocket, wipes his eyes and blows his nose.

'Marika die six year ago. She never see letter.'

'And…?' I want *all* my questions answered.

'First, you must tell me what you know of Goose…then you will have answer.'

'What? That's fucking bullshit.'

My language annoys him. Fuck him, I don't care.

'I told you. I don't know anything about this fucking Goose!' I say, waving my arms in the air.

He's just staring at me. This is so fucking crazy.

'Look, I had this accident, right? After I did the graff you supposedly saw a Goose in, we did a train trick and, well, I slipped and fell under the train. After that I put a hand on the wall, on the wet paint, and since then weird things have happened. But I've got no idea about this bloody Goose, right!'

He's taken back the letter and is smoothing out the creases. Silly old bastard. Then his mood changes again and his knobbly hands tense up and press firmer down on the open pages. Shit, he's a bloody angry old bugger as well. His pushing down so hard his hands start to scrunch the paper that he was only just smoothing out so tenderly.

'Train? You say you under train?'

'Yeah…so?'

'What you see?'

132

'What? What'd I see? What do you think, the bottom of a train for fuck's sake!' I didn't want to tell him what I thought I saw.

My crude, sarcastic answer was obviously not what he wanted to hear as he slams his fist down in rage, but quickly realises that he's slammed it down on the letter. Immediately he smoothes out the pages then carefully folds them, making sure to follow the previous creases, and places the letter back in its envelope and back into his coat pocket. Instead of throwing the coat back down onto the mattress, he stands and puts it on.

'You come,' he says, passing me, expecting me to follow. I do. Maybe now I'll finally get all the answers.

We head down the stairs and out the red door and into the courtyard. Even though the light is dull through the heavy clouds, I squint and follow a step or two behind him as we walk through the entrance tunnel and into the deserted street. A distant car noise hardly breaks the silence as we cross the road, pass three statues of elegantly dressed ladies in front of a building set into the fortress wall, pass an entrance into the wall that is closed off and topped with a covering of weeds, then come to a corner where a road leaves the town. Evzen has stopped ahead of me, his arms hanging and his shoulders hunched as he stares down at the ground. By the time I reach him a sort of trance is coming over me and I continue past him towards a distant sound that is becoming familiar. I leave the road and walk on the grass beside it. As the surface becomes uneven I look down. The grass has thinned and I'm walking over stones, familiar stones. My eyes glaze over and I start sweating despite the cold wind I'm walking into. I shiver—is it cold or nerves? The sound ahead is closing in on me as I step over timber embedded in the stony ground. I feel I've turned to steel and the weight buckles the legs under me. Slumping to my knees I make out what I was beginning to dread and reach out in the direction of the approaching sound of metal wheels running over the joins in the steel tracks on each side of me. I lower myself until I'm lying prostrate on the ground as if giving myself to some higher being. But no, I'm giving myself to the train as it passes over me. The noise surrounds me, deafening and menacing, then the screech of brakes, the hiss of steam and the cries, the cries, oh shit no, the cries. I smell the metal and feel the vibration as the train passes over. I hear the rattle of the spikes and the nestling of the ballast. Now the cries turn to screams, those horrible screams. With arms stretched out in front of me I feel warm sticky blood flowing around me, under my arms, touching my face, seeping into my clothes. I dig my fingers into the compacting stone ballast; splitting nails and cutting flesh so my own blood merges with the crimson flood I'm drowning in. I scream, but no one hears me. Then, all is silent.

Light starts creeping into caked eyes. There is no train. There is no blood. There are no bodies. All I see disappearing into the distance is a set of rusted tracks and overgrown weeds covering the remnants of timber sleepers. I'm breathless and lost in a haze of fear and confusion. A shadow moves over me and I turn to look up. Standing there is the stooped figure of Evzen. I struggle to stand without any offer of assistance. He's just standing there with a terrified look on his face as if it was him who'd seen a ghost.

'That...all this.' I wave my arms towards the overgrown tracks. 'It's got something to do with you, hasn't it?'

'Ya,' he finally mouths as I watch his eyes go cold.

'You know what I saw, right? Like bodies and stuff?'

His silence is confirmation.

'Shit, it was them wasn't it? It was your parents I saw under that train.'

This is really so weird it's just impossible to believe. How? Why? I'm looking around for answers, at the tracks, at Evzen, back to the tracks and then all around. It's when I look back to Evzen that I get one hell of a jolt. The tears in his eyes and the horror on his face is unmistakable. Nah, couldn't be, could it?

'I saw it the way you did, didn't I?'

I watch him falter and rush to hold him up, still struggling with the weakness in my own legs. I can feel his trembling frailty and at the same time an unexpected connection.

We head back to the old building.

CHAPTER 22

Evzen can go no further than just inside the red door. Hunched over and wheezing, he rests against the wall. What just happened has sapped the energy from both of us and I wander down the corridor a little way to make some space between us so I can think. I no longer doubt I have some sort of power, but it only raises more questions. Why me? Is it inherited? Is it only coming out now that she's found me? Or was it the train running over me that's connected all three of us? Whatever the why, what's its purpose? And more importantly, do I have any control over it? From further down the dimly lit corridor I can still hear the murmur of voices I noticed the first time I walked into this place. I now know they're not from the living, so it's as good a time as any to give these powers a workout. I glance back at Evzen. His breathing has eased and he's not as hunched over…and he's looking at me with interest as if he knows what I'm about to do. I face the wall, and, after a second of hesitation, place a hand on the cold, grimy plaster. Instantly I feel a strong force. I look back at Evzen again. His wheezing has stopped. He's holding his breath watching in hope and expectation.

'Okay, so, like, what am I supposed to look for?'

Aware that I understand the situation, Evzen takes a much-needed breath and the wheezing returns.

'It find you,' he says with an air of accomplishment.

I'm now certain that everything that's happened is about him, the reason I'm here, this power he knew I had, everything is because of this wiry old man.

Without conscious effort I begin to trace a deep crack along the wall with both hands. Loose crumbs of mortar and fragments of plaster are dislodged until I reach the end of the corridor. I turn and face the wall coming off at right angles—the dead end. I close my eyes, trying to understand the jumbled murmur of whispered chants coming from within. I sweep a hand across its surface, back and forth, up and down.

I feel a stronger pull than from the other wall and place both hands against the peeling, grime-covered surface. The texture feels different, then, as happened the morning after we got to the Elf, I'm slammed up against the wall as if a strong magnet on the other side is suddenly turned on. I feel the full weight of my body as if I was lying on a floor. In the darkness of my mind, shapes and colours begin to flicker, slowly at first, then gradually faster and faster. I can't make out anything from the shapes, but the colours are becoming more defined, not bright colours but subdued. My head starts to spin, then, as if being spat out, I'm pushed from the wall and stumble back and into Evzen who's followed me down the corridor. All has gone quiet. The voices, the whispered murmurs have gone. I look around at the walls each side and they too are silent. But I know where they've gone...they've found their way into me and I'm overcome with an intense urge. I turn to Evzen. He's calmly waiting for more, his eyes the clearest I've seen and showing a hint of self-satisfaction. I can only look into them as I weigh up the consequences of what I must do. It's not as if I have a choice, the choice has been made for me, for whatever it is, I've been found.

In a calm, almost robotic voice I say, 'I need paints.'

There's no change to his expression. It's as if he knew.

'Come. We rest upstairs,' he says, turning and heading back down the corridor.

Settling into a chair in his smelly little room, I look around with a new understanding of what I can sense.

'You don't live here, do you?'

'Sometimes,' he says, sitting across the table from me. 'Marika has a place I stay.'

'So, like, why do you stay here at all?' Though I don't know what the other place is like. I mean, shit, walking around this town, they could all look like this.

'I try what you have power to do...search for secrets.'

'And?'

'No understand.'

'And what secrets have you found?'

He shakes his head. 'None. Um, I find some things...but of no interest. Soviet army use as barrack after Nazis go…so most things of value gone.'

That explains the drunken revelry I sensed earlier.

'Does the Goose thing have anything to do with what you've been looking for?'

It seems any mention of the Goose gives him a jolt and a spark of rage flashes in his eyes. For a moment I feel he's not going to answer.

'I nine year old…with mamma and poppa. We wait for train…I find later…to Auschwitz. Poppa try get guard for me to stay…to work.' He gives a sniff as his eyes begin to water. 'But Kapo see poppa pass me his ring…he grab it then beat into poppa. Mamma and I try stop him… but they go under train.' He looks down at his closed fists. 'I try to join them…I want die with them…but train go over me.' He leans towards me. 'You see what I see…they…' He coughs and needs a moment before continuing. I don't interrupt as the horrid images appear again. 'Ruza and Marika…they also wait for train with their mamma and poppa…they see all.' He rubs a hand across his stubble to hide a quivering chin. 'When they drag me from under train…commandant order they stay and take me…so…you can say I save their lives.' He pauses to look at me, to make sure I understand what his saying. I give a slight nod. 'But…in only one month…your grandpappa and grandmamma both dead…Ruza, Marika and me…we all orphans. It then we make vow to care for each other…forever.'

I've just stepped into this part of history and already everything's spilling over itself. I no longer see what happened here as just exhibits in a museum. Those people in the pictures are no longer strangers. They're now connected to me. I need time to take this in. But he continues.

'My poppa's ring…it very special. He a very good tailor…had ring made special for him…you know of Goose neck?'

Shit, I may look stupid but before I can answer he assumes I don't and goes on.

'Goose Neck is shape of handle on iron use by tailor.' Okay, so I didn't know that. 'Poppa design ring of two goose heads crossing over.' He unsuccessfully tries to illustrate with his stiff knuckle hands. 'One have beak slightly open to cut thread while he work…it very valuable… made of platinum and gold.'

He pauses to make sure I'm still listening and his expression stiffens.

'Kapo who take ring…he kill your grandpappa.'

Shit! When will this connection end? But I was ignorant of another thing.

'What's a Kapo, anyway?'

He gives out a deep groan.

'Kamp-Polizei! Vermin! They prisoner too…but SS use as guard. Many bad criminals…murderers before Ghetto days. This one like power…he very cruel.' He pauses to calm himself. 'When Ruza come back to Terezín…she say when in Australia she hear of a Ghetto guard who flee there…to escape War Crime Tribunal. For many year she look for him…and she believe she close to find him.'

'Did she think he was the same, um, Kapo?'

'Ya.'

'Did she do anything about it? You know, tell anyone or anything?'

'Ne…she too ill.'

He leans forward a little more and points a trembling finger at me. 'But you…'

'What?' I start to protest then slump back in the chair as *the purpose* of my power becomes clear. 'Fuck! So this is what it's all about. You want me to use this…this power to find this Kapo?'

He shakes his head. 'Your power can go only so far. He old man now…much older than me if still alive.'

I kinda get his point.

'So it's the ring you've been searching for?'

'Ya…Kapo had quarters here.'

Shit! All I came here for was to find my old lady…dead or alive… and not to go around feeling up walls in search of a fucking goose ring.

'Look…this is bullshit. I…'

His fist hitting the table stops me.

'You find something down stairs, ya?' he snaps back.

'What? That was bloody voices…and they definitely didn't sound like fucking Geese!'

He's getting angry, and I don't think it's because of the swearing.

'You not know what you find…until you paint.'

I give out a puff of laughter. 'What?'

'I see goose in painting that you not see.'

'But that was in Melbourne. On the other side of the bloody world!'

We stare at each other, my mind in a whirl.

'Okay then. So let me get this clear. You reckon this Kapo guy's in Melbourne and you see a goose in a painting I did in Melbourne and then get me to come all the fucking way over here, right? So…if what you say is true…then the ring is beside a fucking train tunnel in Prahran. There! So now tell me about…Ruza, so I can see her and go home. Mission complete, okay?'

'Ring not in Melbourne,' he says calmly.

'Okay. If you're so bloody sure then you must know where it is, right?'

'Ring not in Melbourne. Ring still in Czech Republic.'

'Shit, what do you want me to do then, go around and paint on every fucking wall until a goose pops up?'

This is becoming ridiculous and I reckon he's gone senile.

'You find something down stairs…do you not want to know what?'

He knows he's got me. After all I've discovered today, how could I not?

Again we sit staring at each other, just like the old guys I've seen in the park playing chess. One's about to declare Check Mate and the other's not accepting the game's lost.

'Where can I get spray cans around here?'

I don't think he knows what I'm talking about.

'You know, spray paint. Spray paint in a can.' I've got my hand up and finger pressing down on an imaginary button. 'Hiss, hiss, hiss!'

'Litoměřice.' He nods with the slightest hint of a smile. 'We go tomorrow…now I take you to apartment.'

He starts to get up, but I stay put.

'Evzen, is she…is Ruza dead?' It's the one question I need resolved before our deal is sealed.

His shoulders slump as he turns to pick up his coat.

'Evzen! Is she dead?' I repeat abruptly.

'Ne,' he says under his breath. His coat is half on as he walks towards the door.

'Ne? Is that no?' I call out, jumping up from the chair and following him out of the room. Then I remember my bag, rush back, grab it and catch up with him halfway down the stairs.

'You mean she's alive? Then where is she?'

'Litoměřice Hospital…we go tomorrow…but she may not see you.'

We reach the bottom of the stairs and I stop him from going any further.

'Not see me, why?'

'She in coma.'

He starts to walk around me.

'A coma? Shit, what does that mean?'

I follow him out into the courtyard and grab his arm.

'Evzen, what does that mean?'

He doesn't look at me but continues to stare down at the ground. 'My Ruza…dying.'

I let go his arm and he walks on through the entrance arcade with his head bowed low. I don't follow for a moment. It's bloody strange, but now, knowing she's alive, and only hours away from seeing her, I don't know if I can handle it…or even if I want to.

CHAPTER 23

I'm still confused, but I feel I have a better understanding of this so-called *gift* I seem to possess. I'm totally consumed by it whether I like it or not, and following Evzen back to where he really lives, it's hard to work out what's real and what's not. I don't know if the voices I'm hearing are confused thoughts or coming from the walls I pass. This one building I've come to is sending me stronger vibes. I brush a hand over exposed bricks where the plaster has fallen away. A cold shiver rips through me and I let out a loud gasp. I look to Evzen. He's stopped, but just stands watching as if waiting for more to happen. It does. The chill I'm feeling is now coming from under my feet. I look down at the worn paving and place a hand over my mouth to smother another gasp.

'Someone was killed here,' I manage to get out. Each word vibrates down the length of my body as if shaking me free from the confines of flesh and bone and I find myself hovering above like cigarette smoke in a café. Below, are three ghostly images. Two adult men and a boy but their faces are blurred. Transfixed, I can only witness from above the brutal murder of the older man. In a flash I'm back in my body, rigid with the horror of the brutality and stunned by the other image that appeared…my old clock!

I look up to Evzen. He hasn't moved, just watching me.

'Kapo,' I mumble. Then before I can say more of what I witnessed, he comes up to me and takes my arm.

'Come…we move from here.'

I'm pulled away from the spot to the other side of the road. I look back as he drags me further away until we turn a corner and the scene of the murder is out of sight. I want to stop and tell him what I saw but he continues around yet another corner. Midway down a short street he stops at an old building that's been fixed up a bit and painted, though some time ago by the looks of it. I wait as he unlatches the door. A rusting rubbish bin beside me smells as if it's been waiting far too long to be emptied.

I follow him into a small passage that leads to an inner courtyard. On the right, just before the end of the passage, is a staircase. I follow Evzen up the red painted steps, the toe of his right shoe catches the lip of each step as he drags his gammy leg. The higher we climb the air becomes warmer and dryer compared to the cold, damp mustiness at ground level. At the top of the steps, Evzen struggles to insert a key then pushes open the door of his apartment. I follow him into a surprisingly warm, but still musty, living room. To my relief it's nothing like his other room at the barracks. The walls are timber panelled, dark and rich in colour and a relief from the cold greyness that blankets the whole town. On the left is a door to a small kitchen and a short hallway facing. Two windows on the right are draped with lacy curtains that I figure look out over the street.

Evzen's walks down the hallway and points to the right. 'You sleep there.'

I close the door and drop my bag where I'm standing.

'Evzen,' I call to him. 'Tell me what I came across back there. It had something else to do with you, didn't it?'

He drops his hand, his shoulders slump and with a slight shake of his head, says, 'you see enough today.'

I take a step forward.

'If you want me to help find your Goose ring, you gotta tell me what I came across back there. I need to know to make some sense of it.'

He walks towards me with his eyes lowered.

'What you see here will never make sense…no matter what I tell.'

He passes, takes off his coat and eases himself into an old leather armchair with a sigh as the weight is taken off his weary legs. 'You will see things…inhuman things…impossible to understand. You come from peaceful country. But…if you wish to understand the things you sense…you must expect to share in the pain.'

He waits for an answer I don't have. Then, almost like an aftertaste, I get a hit of something else I sensed back there. I pull a chair out from the table in the middle of the room and sit facing him.

'You don't want to tell me, do you? I sensed another of your many secrets just then and this one you don't want me to know about.' I pause for a reaction. There's is none. 'Look, whatever happened back there, I reckon it involved my grandfather.' Sensing my old clock—his clock —convinced me of that. 'If you don't tell me, the family I never knew will always be a secret.' I lean forward. 'And so will the ring.'

Our eyes are locked together. A standoff, but I feel I may have the upper hand.

'You saw me,' he whispers.

The three ghostly images have not left me—two adults and a boy.

'I…I think so. I mean I didn't recognise your face or anything, but I knew it was you. How do you explain that?'

I try to picture him as a young boy but the years of suffering are too deeply etched in his weathered face. It's as if his youth was erased by the premature need to be an adult.

His hands start to shake more than usual as he studies me carefully, offering me a chance to change my mind and leave it at that. I swallow nervously and give a nod to continue. He removes the crumpled handkerchief from his pants pocket and wipes his eyes and nose.

'You only sense secrets…you do not unlock them.'

'But…but I'm sure the one killed was my grandfather. It was him, wasn't it?'

'Ya,' he says without hesitation.

'And you were the reason my grandfather was killed, weren't you?' Shit, why did I say that?

He shows no surprise, only sadness.

'Ya,' he replies, taking in a deep breath of resignation. 'That Kapo…he a brutal homosexual…sick…depraved. Ever since I orphan he never stop…' He takes a moment to control his growing anger. 'I die if he touch me one more time. Your grandpappa…he find out what he do to me…and over there.' He nods in the direction of the killing. 'Kapo grab me in front of your grandpappa…he start to take me in building. Your grandpappa try stop him…this Kapo not a man but a diseased animal and he…'

'Enough,' I interrupt him. There's no need to tell me what happened, as the brutal attack is still very clear. 'Enough,' I repeat softly.

I study him for some time. His head is bowed, his face paler and the painful memory has him trembling. We sit in silence.

I wait until I can no longer hold back my curiosity.

'Did *she*…Ruza, know what was happening to you?'

His head snaps up, his eyes wide and glaring at me.

'Ne…ne…never,' he spits out.

I understand.

'Then it stays your secret.'

143

His glare softens but I sense his unease. He looks away and struggles to his feet.

'It late…I make meal.'

I accept his need to walk away from any further emotional embarrassment. I'm now the guardian of two secrets, Ruza's past and Evzen's past…both sexual…but both without the sensual.

We eat in silence something that looks at lot like some of the stews they hand out at the homeless shelters, but a hell of a lot tastier.

'Has Marika had this place a long time?' I ask, wanting to lighten the mood.

'Ne.' I wait while he finishes chewing. 'Only nine year.' He breaks off some bread to soak up the gravy. 'No one live in Terezín after war… only Soviet army.' He loudly sucks on the soaked bread. 'They leave nineteen year ago…after Velvet Revolution kick them out.'

'So, like, where did you go after the war then? I mean the three of you stayed together, right?'

He stops chewing and wipes his mouth.

'It very hard…Ruza in hospital with typhoid for long time…after that we all together again.'

'How did you survive? I mean you must have been still young, right?'

'I lie about age to work in Prague factory. I find shelter and we care for Ruza…she so weak…she never recover right.'

That's one of the few memories I have of her, she was always ill, but I don't want to touch on the other thing, her secret life, and the chat goes cold.

We finish off with a strong black coffee, and I mean strong. Coffee making is something that needs a lot of work in this country.

I help clear the table and wash up, all done without another word. I can see Evzen is very tired, breathing heavily at the slightest exertion.

'I go to my room now,' he says, as soon as the last plate's put away. 'We go early to Litoměřice.'

The day has taken a lot out of me and I head to the bathroom to brush my teeth and have a wash. I turn the light out in the living room then slide into my new bed. I've never slept in one so soft with blankets so thick. That's all that's needed to shut my mind down and I turn over, turn out the bedside lamp and not even the snoring coming from Evzen's room can stop me falling asleep.

CHAPTER 24

I'm so bloody nervous I knock back the offer of breakfast. Evzen's shuffling around trying to avoid me so I guess we both don't want to talk about visiting the hospital. I even consider giving it a miss. I mean, what'll I say to her if she's awake and outta this coma? *Hi mum, whatcha been doing all these years since turfing me outta your life.* Shit, do I really need this?

'We get bus now.'

At the bus stop, Evzen pays for both tickets without a word to me and on the short ride into Litoměřice we sit next to each other but facing in opposite directions.

The country looks so different outside the Fortress. The sun's out and everything's brighter and cheerier. Jeez, I don't know how anyone can live in that place. Reckon they should pull it down and start again. Evzen gives me a quick, harsh glance. Shit, can he read my mind? Nah, he can't...can he?

After only a few minutes we cross a bridge and arrive at the Litoměřice bus terminal where we change buses. The closer to the hospital the more I'm trembling. Then, there it is, the Městká Nemocnice v Litoměřicích.

Evzen's up from his seat and heading for the bus exit like I'm not there...and I'm so wishing I wasn't. I hang back for a moment checking out the place through the bus window. It's not as gloomy or threatening as I was expecting. In fact the reflection pool in front of the entrance, with a bronze female torso perched over it, eases the butterflies in my stomach enough to give me the courage to follow.

But as soon as I enter the reception area, the atmosphere of disinfectant, germicide, bactericide, or whatever, makes me feel sick. On top of frazzled nerves, it can't get much worse. I stay a few steps behind Evzen who hasn't once looked back to see if I'm there. We go up a level and down a long corridor to a smaller reception area. There's a conversation with one of the nurses. I don't understand a word they're saying, but it seems to cheer him up. Shit, I bet she's out of the coma! The nurse points down the corridor and he waddles off as if I wasn't there.

Evzen has stopped at a ward and is looking through the window of the closed door. I join him on shaky legs wondering if he's going in or not.

'You okay?' I ask with a dry throat.

'She out of coma,' he says without turning. Why isn't he going in? Is it because I'm here? Again, as if reading my mind, he turns to me. 'But she sedated…maybe asleep.'

He turns back to the door, opens it and enters. I take one step and stop in the doorway. I'm frozen to the spot as the atmosphere closes in on me. There's six beds, three on each side separated by screens. Evzen pauses at the first two beds, then the next two until stopping at the last bed on the left. I take a deep breath, swallow what little saliva there is, and step into the ward. The first two beds are empty. My heart's pounding and I feel the blood pulsating inside my head. The next bed on the left is empty but the one opposite has someone asleep. I shiver at the sight of a pale face—half buried in a pillow—with a tube up her nose. If it's oxygen, I sure could use some right now. A screen is partially hiding the last bed where Evzen has stopped. All I see is the shape of legs and feet under a blanket. This is definitely not my scene. Evzen turns his head slightly towards me. He doesn't look at me, just turns enough to see I've followed him in. He hasn't said anything and there's no movement under the blanket. If she's out to it, then I don't have to talk to her. I can just take that one last step, look at her and leave. Yeah, at least I can do that. I step forward. It's like a curtain parting in a theatre for the opening act, and there she is, silently lying there all connected up to a mess of wires and beeping gadgets. There's a tube up her nose like the other body. A plastic bottle is hanging above her and a clear liquid is drip-fed onto an arm so thin and so pale except for blue veins that look like they're on top rather than below the skin.

I hover behind Evzen, hiding myself from her view even though her eyes are closed. I want to leave. I've seen her now and I want to leave. This is a stranger to me. Someone old and dying I have no memory of. I look harder to try to awaken something deep in my memory, but nothing. Everything is different, the hair is thin and grey, not peroxide blonde. There's no heavy red lipstick to make her lips fuller, just pale wrinkled skin. No thick mascara and long eyelashes, just closed, sunken eyes. No, I don't recognise this person. I want to get out of here before she wakes.

'Ruza?' whispers Evzen, stepping to the side of the bed to take her hand and easing himself into a chair beside her. Shit, he'll wake her and now I'm clearly in view. That's it! I can't bear it any longer.

'Evzen…I can't…I just can't. I'll wait for you outside the hospital.' I'm gone before he has a chance to say anything. Down the long corridor, down the flight of stairs and out into the fresh air.

I turn back to face the entrance feeling a real coward, but stubbornly sure that I don't want to start up a relationship with that person lying there. She's not the mother I'd hoped to see, to meet— though damned if I know *what* I was expecting. All I know is that I've seen her and now I want to get on a plane back to Melbourne as fast as I can and put all this shit behind me. No more fucking walls that talk to me, no more trains, no more bodies, no more old man, no more history lessons. I just don't want to know about this place anymore.

I sit on the low concrete wall of the rippling pool. Beside me, the contrasting brilliance of the white marble against the dark bronze torso reflects the difference between that withered figure I've just seen and my image of her. I rest my head in my hands. What the hell was I expecting anyway? Was I hoping for something totally unrealistic like the picture postcard image of a family united? Shit, what a fucking joke. For years I cried out for her and now it's all too bloody late. I don't need her now. I'm hardened to the life she forced me to live. And if that's all she's done for me, I'll give her credit for that. But now there's nothing to keep me here. I've been tricked by some crotchety old bugger, and for what, to find his fucking Goose ring? No, I'm outta here today!

The sun felt good and the blue sky has me thinking of returning to Oz and to the life I know. Not the greatest of options, but, I've never had much choice anyway.

I must have drifted off until the shadow of someone passing makes me look up. Shit, Evzen's walked right past without a word. Yeah, well, I kinda don't blame him being pissed off. I catch up to him.

'Evzen, look sorry but I...that wasn't my...shit, what did you expect?'

He stops and turns to me. 'Nothing,' he says with a trembling glare. 'Ruza not know you there...maybe that good...ya?' He turns and continues on in his quick shuffle.

I catch up to him again. 'Look, I'll get my gear and get outta your life. You don't want me around anyway. I mean, except for this Goose thing, but shit, I reckon there's nothing I can do about it anyway.'

We arrive back in Terezín without a further word.

CHAPTER 25

With all I own hanging from my shoulder once again, I open the front door of the apartment and look back at Evzen sunk into his old leather armchair like a deflated rubber figure and staring off into the distance. I sorta feel sorry for him. I mean, what I've learnt about him in only a one day is that everyone in his life seems to have died, is dying or has left him—and now it's me.

'Look, Evzen, I'm really sorry, but...'

He raises a shaky hand. 'You not of this world,' he says calmly while continuing to stare ahead. 'Go back to peaceful life where you belong... you have given all you can.'

I don't know what he means by that last bit, but the first bit is spot on. I'm not of this world and I don't want to be.

'Look, I'll write you, okay. You know, to see how you're going and stuff, okay?' I don't want to go into news of her condition or death. Probably don't deserve to be told anyway.

His head's nodding but I'm not sure if he really means it or is just hurrying me out.

I'm reminded of old Sarge. He sat looking into the distance like that. But I never got a chance to say goodbye to him. He just disappeared.

'Yeah, well…umm…take care then.'

I pause for a last response but none comes so I gently close the door behind me and tread softly down the stairs. I don't know what my feelings are. It's as if they've all drained outta me.

At the bus stop I keep looking back towards the apartment. I can't see it but I look in that direction anyway. I don't know why, but I feel I'm leaving something of myself here. No, bugger it! I've made up my mind. I gave it a shot and it didn't turn out as I hoped—whatever that was. Shit, where's that fucking bus, I need to break away from all these voices calling me.

I settle into a seat at the back and refuse to look out the windows as we drive out of the fortress. I close my eyes in an attempt get myself back to the Briney I'm meant to be, a simple and probably very stupid street kid.

The bus hasn't gone far before I'm once again invaded by the frightening screams coming from the Small Fortress. We pull into the car park to collect some tourists waiting to go back to Prague. I look into their faces as they board, all showing shock, sadness and disbelief. Now the voices from outside become unbearable. I try to shut them out, but it's no use. I want to scream to drown them out, but I can't. Then, as if I've lost all will, I'm out of my seat, and with bag flapping, I hurry down the centre aisle and rudely push through the last of those boarding and out into the car park. Without hesitation, the door closes behind me and the bus, kicking gravel up in its wake, takes off for Prague.

Immediately, as if this was not the first time being here, I know exactly where to go as I run down the tree-lined avenue towards the red brick rampart and the arched entrance framed in bold black-and-white. To the left a timber guard tower watches over a grassy moat in a settling mist, or maybe it's a permanent mist, it looks so right. As soon as I buy a ticket to enter the prison, the voices and screams close in on me…devouring me…I'm completely under their control.

What I'm about to tell you is what I recalled later, for I lost total control of myself and was consumed by the lingering residue of the past inmates. I was, you might say, taken on the most terrifying ride of their lives!

The first thing I remember is my bag and everything I own taken from me. I'm pushed forward, falling over and grazing my knees as I'm dragged into a small office. Here I join others crowded against a counter that divides the room in two. Behind the counter, sitting at a writing desk and a small table, are two SS administrators. I wait and wait until I present my ticket. The ticket is now a number. I'm no longer Briney Ruza; I'm just a number in a register, stripped of my identity along with all my belongings. I'm taken into another room and the final denuding of who I was is carried out as I stand shivering, exposed and naked as the day I was born…and I'm now beginning to wish I never was.

I remember shuddering violently like I was being belted from the inside. I'm now a man, a young, reasonably healthy man. I'm in a group and a guard has stopped us at the entrance to another courtyard. Above, a sign reads ARBEIT MACHT FREI; 'work makes you free' a guard translates. We all know we never will be. We're marched under the sign and across a broad courtyard. With every step I take I feel days and months pass by. I'm gasping for breath, for clear air, doubling over with stomach cramps while my hair falls out and the festering wounds from the brutal beatings spread their septic poison. I'm dying in a dark corner of an overcrowded cellblock I share with 72 others. I feel life deserting me. I feel I'm one of the lucky ones.

Next to enter this naive hollow shell of mine, is fleeting glimpses of the chaotic inhuman activities that no one should ever endure. I'm a girl of about the same age as I am, awake and aware of the degrading abuse and torturous mutilation I'm undergoing on the operating table. I'm an old man pushing a cart collecting wretched, deformed bodies, no, more like skeletons. I've become desensitised to those I cart, knowing that before long it will be my turn to be wheeled away. I change into a worker in a dark and airless mine. Weak from lack of food, I collapse, dragged out of the pit and beaten to a pulp. Now I'm a figure running through a long tunnel in an attempt to escape, but I'm caught, beaten and dragged semiconscious to a mound against a wall in an open grassy area away from the main prison. I'm doused with water to recover and propped up against the wall. With eyes cleared of the blood, I see a line of guards aiming their rifles at me. I turn to the left and catch the eyes of a man stepping up to a noose that hangs from a simple wooden gallows. We look at each other with an unspoken promise that we will meet in another realm very soon. I become both of the condemned. First, jolted by the bullets bursting into me. Gushing blood, I slump to the ground. Then, on the gallows, the large knot under my ear cracks my neck. With bodies jerking and legs treading air, we're already dead.

It's then, that I, Briney Ruza return. I find myself sitting on the grass in front of the execution mound with the weathered frame of the gallows still standing to my right. Passing tourists ignore me, I figure out of respect to allow anyone to ponder what happened here in their own way. The voices, screams and groans are fading. Those poor individuals who entered me have all gone. I feel empty as if scraped clean of useless and selfish matter. All my senseless fears and fabricated worries have been exposed as trivial and petty in comparison to those who entered my consciousness. They have shown me the unimaginable truth of real hardship, torment and torture. They have shown me the real reason that brought me here.

I decide to walk back to Terezín. I needed time to think. But as I pass the thousands of graves in the cemetery outside the wall, I realise however utterly daunting the experiences I had shared with a handful of prisoners, it's obvious I've hardly scratched the surface of the suffering that took place here.

I feel no remorse, no doubt and no embarrassment as I knock on the door to the apartment. It opens before I finish knocking as if my return was expected. His rigid, almost smug expression, gives me the eerie feeling that it was. He blocks the entry, takes the bag from my shoulder and places it just inside the door and steps forward, forcing me to step back while he closes the door behind him. We both know what needs to be done.

'We go back to Litoměřice for your spray paint now, ya?' he says.

CHAPTER 26

There wasn't a great range of colours to choose from but I managed to match those that came to me from that wall at the end of the corridor. What I do with them, I reckon, is something for the wall itself to sort out.

'How you get painting on…um…Inter…Internet?' Evzen surprises me with his question on the way back in the bus. The Internet? Not really what I had in mind. I mean, like, the graffs I did for MySpace were part of game, a bit of cheeky fun, but there's definitely nothing funny about this morbid place.

'You're not serious?' I ask. 'That's just a bloody game.'

'What I see in your last painting…not a game.'

'What, the Goose? Yeah, well, you saw what you wanted to see cuz no one else saw it.'

'Is that not the purpose of your game?'

'Yeah, but I followed a formula. I filled in the same word every time —and I sure don't see me painting SECRETSINCITY across that wall… it's…it's just not what I pictured.'

'You paint what you see…not worry about word…but you put on Internet.'

I feel uneasy about this. I know there's a secret in that wall and it fits in with what I was doing, but, like, I've come to respect all those who suffered and died here in the Ghetto days, so, if I do put it up, for the first time I'll really feel like a vandal.

'You sure?' I ask as if wanting someone else to share the blame if it upsets anyone.

All I get is a nod as the bus arrives back at Terezín.

'I need to get my camera then.'

There's a change in the weather by the time we get back to the apartment and the winds cold as ice. The only gear I have sure isn't suitable for anything this fucking cold, and by the time I get to the door, I'm shivering like crazy.

I grab the bag from where Evzen dropped it by the front door and take out the laptop and any clothes. I check the camera is still there and put in all the paint cans. Evzen has rummaging through the wardrobe in the room I slept in and hands me a thick woollen beanie and scarf. Back out in the freezing cold wind, the extra warmth makes it almost bearable.

At the barracks I put my bag down on the floor just inside the red door and look down the corridor to the wall I'm to paint. Unlike all the other times, I sense nothing. Shit, have I lost the connection? Where are the voices, the murmurs and the chanting? All I hear is the sound of the wind creaking, groaning and banging things loose throughout the building.

Evzen picks up the bag and starts to take it to the end of the corridor. Shit, he's anxious for me to start but I can't. I've lost it. I need time to concentrate and hope I can make the connection again.

'Look, um, leave the paints, Evzen. I can't start just like that. I…I need time to…' To do what? Whatever it is I sure as hell can't do it with him hanging around. Then a thought crosses my mind.

'Is there a phone outlet in Marika's place?' I ask, having not noticing a phone anywhere.

'Phone? Na, no phone,' he replies.

'Look, if you want me to put whatever I do on the Internet, I need to find a place that has WiFi. You know what that is?'

His blank look is the answer.

'If there's none, I can't do it…understand?'

'Information Centre at Litoměřice,' he says with some delight.

153

'They have computer. Young man there...he speak English good.'

'I don't want to upload the image on some other computer. I need to use mine.'

He shakes his head, confused. I figured technology hasn't caught up with him yet.

'If there's WiFi or a modem I can plug into, fine, but I need to know. If they don't, then maybe a hotel might. Is there a hotel here?'

'Ya...but what...what this why fly?'

'WiFi...wireless connection...um...no wires...signal in the air.'

Waving arms around is only making him more confused.

'Look, I'll write down what I need and get you to go to a hotel and just show them the note, okay? I'm sure someone will understand English there.'

I always keep my notebook in the front pocket of the bag along with my passport and plane ticket, and after writing down as clearly as I can what I need, I hand him the torn-out page.

'It's important you find this, okay, otherwise no graff on the Internet. You understand?'

I knew it was bullshit. If there's nothing here, then there's sure to be a place in Litoměřice, but I need to get rid of him so I can be alone to concentrate.

He shakes his head and shrugs his shoulders at the note in his hand, but the importance of the task and the fact I'm relying on him changes his expression. He becomes less confused and straightens his shoulders. Is it because others have relied on him for most of his life? I don't know, but with a nod he shuffles off with an air of purpose.

I'm now alone with the noises the wind is creating in this hollow, empty place. I gotta get used to these distractions before I can do anything so, leaving my gear, I walk around the whole of the ground floor trying to separate the physical from the non-physical sounds.

It takes a while before I feel I'm gaining some control over what I sense. But I'm yet to get any inspiration to pick up a can and I'm starting to doubt if I ever will. I'd allowed myself to be consumed by the discovery of this new power, and now when it's time to convert it into art, I'm failing. I sit down on the dusty floor with my back resting against the dead end wall. Who am I kidding anyway? I bury my face in Marika's scarf, taking in its soft warmth, and the surprise hint of sweet pepper from the perfume she must have splashed on when she went out. The scent has faded over the years since her death, but what I can smell is becoming more and more pronounced. I close my eyes for one more effort of concentration and press back against the wall, willing the cold structure to connect, to tell me what I need to know, to accept this power I have and trust in me to reveal its secret.

Minutes pass and nothing. It's useless. I may as well grab the paints and go find Evzen before he wastes any more of his time. I try to stand but can't disconnect from the wall. I begin to feel I'm coming under its control and entering another space. The perfume in the scarf is now more intense and I'm hearing the voices and chanting I heard yesterday. Suddenly I slump forward, released from the wall's pull but not from its sounds. Something's on the other side of this wall but how do I get there? When I walked around I found nothing that led to the other side of this wall. There's a room off the corridor a little way down, but I looked in there...though I didn't go in. I get to my feet and walk to the open doorway. The door is lying on the floor as if blown off its hinges. I step over it. It's an internal room sandwiched between the stairs and the corridor so no windows and I need a moment to get used to the semi-darkness. A single light bulb hangs from the ceiling. I try the switch even knowing there's no electricity. I slide a hand over the surface of the wall searching for some other doorway, but nothing. I look at the floor, hoping to find a trapdoor: nothing there either. I'm now against the far wall that should be in line with the dead end wall in the corridor. But it seems further away from the entrance. I measure how many steps to the door...twelve. Back in the corridor I walk to its end...seven steps. The corridor is shorter than it should be and knowing there was no other external door other than the red one, I get a rush of excitement and cautiously place both hands on the wall. All I get is a slight tremor and struggle to keep my eyes open. I lean forward in total darkness to embrace the cold, hard surface of chipped plaster and patches of bare bricks and crumbling mortar and there's a sudden rush of colours and shapes. But I feel something else...a difference...

a big difference…this wall is now mine. I step back, reaching out for the paints with eyes still closed so I don't lose the vision. With the bag of spray paint in hand I open my eyes and pause for a moment, the vision is still there, as is the urge, and I walk up to my new canvas.

The hand on my shoulder startles me. I'm sitting in the middle of the corridor facing the end wall. The scarf is still wrapped around my nose and mouth to keep out the paint fumes as well as allowing the scent of the perfume to be a barrier against the smell. I raise a hand to point to the wall and look up at Evzen. He looks to where I'm pointing and as his eyes grow accustomed to the dim light, he steps back stunned. After a moment he walks up to the wall for a closer look. The surface is completely covered in abstract shapes of red, pale yellow and a touch of black. After a moment of study he turns and looks down at me still pointing at the wall. He scratches his scruffy hair then turns back for a closer look.

I lower my arm so it rests back on the floor.

'Hotel Memorial,' he says, still facing the wall and totally confusing me. Has he seen something?

'What?'

'I find you…um…why-fly. I find it.'

'What?' I say again before realising what he's talking about. I get to my feet and point back to the wall.

'Thanks, but it's all a bloody waste of time. I thought I felt something, but look at it, nothing, it's all crap except something that sorta looks like candles.'

'You have photograph?' he says with some insistence.

I shake my head. 'What's the bloody point?'

'You take photograph!' he orders.

His abrupt tone surprises me and I reach into the bag for the camera. He steps aside while I aim it at the confused mess and take three shots with the flash and three without. He gives me a short, sharp nod then turns and walks to the door.

'Come, we eat.'

I pack up the paints, swing the bag over my shoulder and follow, pausing at the door for one last look at the wall, the abstract shapes barely visible now in the enclosing darkness. A dozen cans of paint wasted. As far as I'm concerned, the wall's secret is till intact—whatever it was.

CHAPTER 27

During the meal of leftover goulash and thick slabs of hard dark bread I ask Evzen if he saw anything in the graff. I thought from his reaction he may have. But he just waves a crooked finger at the plate for me to shut up and eat. I guess he's run around more than he's used to and when he gets tired he gets crankier. I even tell him I'll wash up so he can sit and relax, but he ignores me and makes it pretty obvious he wants me out of the kitchen. So I figure it's a good time to unpack the laptop and upload the photos. As soon as I try to boot-up, the bloody thing gives a blink and then nothing. Shit, the battery's dead. I plug the power pack into the laptop and look around for a power point. There's a dark wood-stained side table next to his old armchair with a reading lamp so there most be a plug nearby. On hands and knees I reach under the table, pull out the plug for the lamp and then discover I've got a problem.

'Shit, you got different plugs here.'

He comes into the lounge room and I show him the useless plug.

'Ruza had other plug that fit that…you need now?'

'Yeah, like my laptop's dead so I can't upload the photos.'

He walks away mumbling something about it being in a storage space then returns with a key. I get up off the floor and follow him out the front door, down the stairs, into the chest-high pool of cold damp air constantly clinging to the ground, turn into the dark inner courtyard barely lit by light coming from a couple of windows above. I'm wishing I'd worn my jacket, beanie and scarf; it's so bloody cold.

He turns on a cobweb-covered light fixed high up on the outside wall. The light barely reaches the ground, but it's enough to make out all the plumbing for the building, some bins, an old chair and some solid doors next to grille-covered windows.

Evzen goes to a door that's below our kitchen window and after a bit of a struggle with the key, opens it. The door's certainly seen better days and is patched up with whatever's been lying around. It's also warped and difficult to open so I help him push it inwards to the scream of rusted hinges and the jarring of timber on timber.

The air that rushes out from the dark space cuts right through me. I retreat from the door shaking, not with cold, but with alarm.

Evzen reaches into the dark room and turns on a single dust-covered globe hanging from the ceiling. Again, there's very little impact on the darkness.

'Come…you help find,' he says from inside the cramped space.

'There…there's something in there,' I mumble, shivering. There's no way I'm going in!

'Not much,' he replies. 'All that was damaged is gone…come look.'

I take a couple of hesitant steps toward the partly open door and peer in with a hand on the doorframe. Unexpectedly, I feel heat coming from the door—impossible in this freezing cold. I quickly take my hand away and step back as ill-defined images shudder through me.

'This what you need?' Evzen asks, appearing in the doorway holding an extension lead with an adaptor on one end. 'It not?' he adds, seeing the look of dismay on my face.

'She…she…died in there didn't she.' Shit, why did I say that?

Without any response, he turns out the light, closes the door and turns the key in the lock. When he turns around, I see, even in the dim light, his bottom jaw is trembling.

'Marika died there, didn't she?' I repeat, staring at the locked door.

'Upstairs…we talk.' His words are as shaky as his jaw.

Once inside the apartment, shaking and wheezing, he plops himself down into his armchair. I pull the chair out from the table and sit opposite him, concerned at the way he looks, but also eager to confirm what I've sensed.

'She drowned, didn't she?' I say, without giving him time to relax.

'Big flood…very bad.'

He gives a cough and takes out his handkerchief to wipe his eyes and blow his nose. I need to know more.

'How? I mean, she drowned in that storage room, didn't she?'

'Ya! Flood rise so fast…no one ready.'

'But why, I mean, why go down there when she would have been safe up here?'

He pauses and looks at me with teary eyes. 'I not here to save her… I go help others outside.' I sense the look of guilt on his eyes. 'I tell her… you no leave… she promise she stay.'

'She didn't break her promise to you, Evzen.' I pause as other images swirling in my head become clearer. 'I think she was forced to go down there.'

His eyes widen and his head shakes in disbelief.

'Look, I felt something strange down there.' I look down at my hands. The heat from the door still lingering Will I say it? I look back into his eyes. I need to. 'I don't believe Marika drowned by accident.'

Waving a finger at me, he mumbles, 'Ne, ne, impossible, impossible.' He tries to stand, to walk away from what I'm suggesting, but falls back into the chair, tense and pale and gasping for breath, his eyes wide and glazing over as they lock onto mine and now his hand starts to frantically tap his chest.

'You okay?' I ask with growing concern.

He continues tapping his chest while trying to speak but his gasping for air won't let the words out. Shit, what'll I do? What's happening to him? I get up from the chair and touch where he's now pointing and feel something hard under the frayed old grey cardigan he wears when in the apartment. Inside the breast pocket of his flannel shirt I find a small pillbox. In my panic I struggle to open it and it falls onto his lap. I look from the box to his face. He's no longer pale, but flushed with red. His mouth's wide open as he gasps for air, his tongue protruding and turning blue. I look back down at the box sitting on his crotch, gulp and try to gently grasp it but my shaking hands only push the box deeper down between his legs. Another gulp as he lets out a sharp gasp of pain and I dive my hand deep under the box, trying not to feel anything else. I take out one small white tablet and offer it to him.

159

What do I do? His mouth's wide open and he's tongue's sticking up and out. With one hand beckoning me to feed him the tablet, the other is grabbing at his chest. I feel his cold lips, the dribble of saliva and the space where a couple of bottom teeth are missing as I place the tablet under his tongue. He immediately closes his mouth and drops his hand. His heavy breathing is now rasping through his nose and forcing out bubbles. I place a hand on his chest, alarmed at the erratic beat of his heart and the tightness of the skin over his ribs. As the tablet dissolves his breathing relaxes a little and his body becomes less rigid and he sinks back into the padded chair. All I can do now is sit back down to watch and hope he recovers.

After around twenty minutes he appears more relaxed and the redness in his face has faded back to the ghostly grey. His chest spasms have gone and his breathing is almost regular. His eyes are still closed. He starts to snore…he's asleep.

For near on half an hour, I dare not take my eyes off him. Jumping at every snort and twitch. I can't help comparing him to old Sarge back in the laneways of Melbourne. Both are grisly old buggers, and both have the ability to drive me up a bloody wall. But with Evzen, whether it's out of desperation, hope or something else, I'm looking at him as the closest thing to a relative I'll probably ever have. Not that he'd see it that way, I bet.

There's a mumble, a loud snort and a cough and he's looking around as if he doesn't know where he is.

'You okay?' I ask leaning forward.

He blinks at me and mouths something but built-up phlegm in his throat blocks his voice and he coughs again to try and clear it.

'I'll get you some water.'

He nods and again mouths something I can't hear.

I fetch the water. He sips and sighs as he's eased back to relative normality.

'Dík,' he says, his throat cleared but his voice still weak.

I take the glass and place it on the side table next to him.

'Shit, ya gave me a bloody fright. Was that a heart attack?'

He shakes his head while tapping his chest. 'I no time get tablet.'

'No probs, but you scared the fucking shit outta me.'

He shakes a finger at me. 'You must stop using such word.'

Yeah, I reckon he's feeling better.

'Look, sorry if I caused it, but I had to tell you what I sensed down there, right?' I check he's breathing just in case bringing it up again starts off another attack.

'Marika drown by accident!' he insists, gaining more energy. 'You wrong to say other.'

I know I'm not.

'Look, I know you don't want to believe it, but something violent happened to Marika and it wasn't *just* the drowning.' I take a deep breath. 'What I'm saying is that she didn't drown by accident…she was deliberately drowned.'

'Ne, ne, you wrong…no one harm Marika…all like her…you wrong,' he says, shaking his head.

'Yeah, right, I wish I was, but the sense I had was stronger than anything I've felt before. I can still feel her struggling against strong hands. I know I'm right. I'm positive she…she was…' I figured best not to say *the word*.

His breathing is becoming erratic again.

'Oh, shit, I've made you have another attack.' I reach for the pillbox

'Ne, ne, I all right.' But he takes a sip of water anyway. 'I no believe anyone do that to Marika. Not gentle Marika.'

'Look, tell me, was there anything going on before the flood.' I drag my chair closer to him.

'Before…ne…nothing.' His head wobbles from side to side as he gives a slight shrug of the shoulders.

'Think. There must have been something.'

He's staring at me, searching his memory. I wait.

'There is lot you still not know.'

'Yeah, and a lot I've discovered without you telling me, right?'

'You only learn small part of days in Ghetto under Nazis.' He pauses, studying me. 'You not know what happen after…under Soviets.'

161

He's got me there.

'No one own property anymore…all belong to State.'

Now I'm seriously confused.

He looks around the room. 'This building…your grandpappa once own.' He waits for a reaction.

It takes a while to sink in. I look around the room. 'You're fucking kidding?'

He gives a sigh at his failure to stop me swearing.

'What? The whole fu…the whole building?'

'Ya, when Nazis come…Jews forced to give up all assets…all property.' He takes a deep breath. I think any mention of the Nazis gets him upset. 'They say this…Terezín Ghetto…new life…*New Paradise*.' He gives a snort of contempt. 'But this Ghetto…no paradise…no care… no food…nothing but suffering till *Final Solution*…death to all Jews.'

That word is bouncing around in my head.

'Jewish? You're…you're saying my grandfather was Jewish?'

This seems to surprise him.

'Ya…and your grandmamma, Marika, Ruza and me…and you.'

'But I don't give a shit about religion. I mean, I don't even reckon there's a God, cuz if there is, he or she's sure doing a pretty lousy job going by what I've seen on the street and all the things I've learnt about this place.'

'If you born of Jew…then you Jew no matter what you think.'

'Fuck!'

He slams his fist down on the arm of the chair. 'Please…you no swear when talk of religion.'

I'm stumped. But, hey, I don't believe in religion, so what the hell… right? I drop it.

'Yeah, well, anyway, what's all that got to do with what happened before the flood?'

He shrugs his shoulders. 'As it turn out…none.'

I'm confused. So why did he bring it up? But I gotta go for a piss.

When I return, he's staring at the photograph of Ruza in his hands.

'All could be different…if Ruza here to help,' he says without raising his eyes.

'What? What do ya mean? What are ya talking about?'

'Marika very bright, but as she get old...she confuse easy. I...I think she prefer when under Soviets. Without parents...Soviet control gave her feeling of protection. She miss Ruza so much after she leave... and I no talk to her as a sister.' He looks up from the photo as if asking for forgiveness. 'I try help...as I have since Ghetto days...but much changed and she start ignoring what I say.'

'Um, sorry, but I'm not sure I understand.'

'After Soviets go and we become Republic...it agreed that all Czechs...not only Jews...could claim for property lost to Nazis and Soviets.' He places the photo of Ruza on the side table, propped up against the water glass to face him. 'By then...I think Marika forget her parents once own this building. After Ruza go...I stay with Marika. We move much to find work.' A distant memory interrupts him briefly. 'We come back here...to Terezín in 1998. This apartment vacant...so we move in...only then she say she once live here...that it once owned by her parents.'

'So, like, this claim thing, did she make one?'

'In English, it called Restitution Law. We talk about it but she confused...I think she think it all too complicated.'

He picks up the photo and holds it close to his face. 'Ruza younger...understood modern ways. She would have seen things clearer.'

'See what things clearer?'

He looks up from the photo. 'Deadlines...two deadlines. First... make submission by May of 2001. Second...end of December to lodge claim.' He shrugs his shoulders and places the photo into his shirt pocket. 'But to make claim...proof of ownership needed. As many original owners dead, descendants able to claim...but proof not easy to find.'

'What do you mean?'

'All documents seized by Nazis...then many disappear under Soviet rule...all property then belong to State...not people.'

'So...you're saying she never made a claim?'

'Not first...her mind clear one day...confused another. Then, one

163

day she say she go to Prague, to Katastrílní úřad...it Property Register Office. But deadline for submission passed...deadline to lodge all papers of proof was near.'

'And...did she find anything?'

'I not know.'

'What do you mean, didn't she tell you?'

'I want go with her...but she say no. She confused when she return...it like she never went to Prague. I ask if she find proof but she not answer. I think she not find proof.' He takes up the crumpled handkerchief from his lap and wipes his eyes and nose again. 'It different if Ruza here...she not strong like Marika...but she clever... I sure she would find proof...if there any.'

This is all getting too bureaucratic for me and if there's one thing I hate it's the fucking government. But something else has crossed my mind.

'Evzen, if there was no contact with Ruza since she left in '68, how did she know where to write that letter to?'

There's no immediate answer. It's like he's never thought about that before and he rubs his fingers through his stubbled chin.

'Hmm, I not know.' He scratches his head. 'Maybe she also has your power?'

Nah, no way...but what if...nah, she would've found me earlier if she did...that is unless she wasn't ready to find me. Now, I'm the one slipping back into the past.

Evzen pushes himself up off his chair. 'I tired...I go to bed.'

I watch him drag his hunched body off to his bedroom and I realise how tired I am. It's been one heck of a long day. So much has happened and so much has been discovered. The hospital, seeing her, me doing a dummy spit and walking out, the Small Fortress—I don't want to think about that again—then the painting and now what I reckon happened to Marika down stairs. Shit, what'll I do about that? No one's gunna believe me. Evzen doesn't so why should the police? Shit, I can just imagine me walking into the police station to report an aunt was murdered because the walls told me. Jeez, I'd be locked up in the funny farm so fast and after load of tests for drugs.

On the floor beside Evzen's chair, I see my laptop waiting to be charged up. I'm still pretty sure that putting today's graff up on MySpace is a bloody waste of time, but what the hell, may as well plug it in.

CHAPTER 28

I'm up before Evzen and eager to get on the computer. There's something comforting about having it working again. It's a kinda connection to back home, seeing all my old graffs and stuff. I've upload yesterday's pics and they're totally not like anything I've done before. Except for what could be candles, I still can't make out anything. I wonder if my SECRETSINCITY followers will accept this as a new challenge. Anyway, I'm sure I'll find out if I can get a pic uploaded to my website at this hotel Evzen found.

I intended to make some breakfast before the old bugger gets up but I'm having trouble finding things. Then I hear him awake and coughing.

'I go see Ruza,' he says, coming into the kitchen and pushing me aside to cut some bread. I guess he assumes I won't be going with him.

'Look, I...'

He stops me in my attempt to explain.

'*I* see *my* Ruza,' he stresses.

Shit, he's really pissed off this morning.

'Yeah, well I'll just go to the hotel and put the graff online, okay?'

He just gives a grunt.

'I mean, that's what you want, isn't it?'

He grunts again. 'You do as you must.'

The Memorial Hotel faces the main park, but it never registered as a hotel until now. They're even setting up tables and chairs outside because the the sun's out killing off some of the cold. Sort of surprising to see alfresco dining in this creepy town.

I wasn't fazed about coming here on my own after Evzen told me the manager spoke good English, and he was right, but he didn't mention that he was the junior manager and not much older than me. As soon as I walked in he was all over me. It seems Evzen stretched the truth a bit by describing me as a famous artist from Australia who needed to send images of my latest paintings back to a gallery and for security reasons I couldn't use any computer but my own. Shit, I wish! So I was treated like bloody royalty even though I knew this guy was coming on to me big time. I've got pretty good at using this situation to get what I want while keeping up their hopes of getting what *they* want. So after I'm shown to a table in the smallish dining room next to the reception and told how to log into their WiFi, I thank him with a big smile and a little flutter of the eyes.

After booting up the laptop and looking over the comments asking why no new graffs, I notice I have a new message in the linked Yahoo account I rarely use. It's from Zoja. I feel a twinge of excitement, and after reading a couple lines I reckon I'll read the rest in private and save it as a PDF. So, sorry my friendly junior manager, my sexy bits have been tweaked by another.

With the chosen photo uploaded and filling the screen I reckon I need to write something to explain why it's has been a while since the last graff, but what? I slump back into the chair to think then feel someone hovering behind.

'Is that your new painting?' It's the junior manager. Shit, what happened to fucking privacy?

'Excuse me?' I say, looking up at him and ready to give him a serve.

'Sorry, I don't mean to be rude, but your interpretation of a synagogue is very abstract. I like it.'

I look back to the screen with renewed interest. A synagogue? Where? Some candles maybe, but damned if I can make out anything like a synagogue. But, shit, I've never been in one so how the hell would I know? Not wanting to get into a conversation about something I don't know or can't see, best I make out it's exactly what I intended to paint.

'Yeah, umm, glad you like it?'

'I don't know what a Rabbi would say, but I can see you know what you are doing.'

I look deeper into the painting, still nothing.

'Look, I'm sorry, but I need to write something and it's, you know, sorta personal, do you mind?'

He takes the hint with a look of disappointment and goes back to his duties, whatever they are?

A synagogue? Nah, no way! But I'm now intrigued to see if anyone else hits on it. I decide to treat it as I would any other SECRETSINCITY graff and key in that I'm now in Prague. I hit the send button and the supposed abstract synagogue is now out there for comment and I pack away the computer to leave.

'Thanks,' I call out to the junior manager standing behind the reception desk.

'So soon,' he says with a look of disappointment. 'Will you be back?'

'If that's okay with you?'

'Of course, but only when I'm here. The WiFi really is only for hotel guests, you understand, and others may not agree to you using it.'

Yeah, right! I give him a big cheesy smile and shake his hand.

I'm eager to read Zoja's message before Evzen gets back from the hospital so I use the spare key he's given me to open the door. After checking he's not here, I quickly open up the laptop.

Hi Brightlight. Hope you don't mind me calling you that but that's what you do—brighten up my life. I miss you. I miss looking at you. I miss hearing your way of speaking that so excites me. I'm touching myself as I write and hope you do the same while reading this. I think of your hand between my legs, damp and pressing. I feel your hot breath on my nipple and your teeth teasing me to shiver. I desperately want to slide my hand between your thighs and enter you where it's wet and hot. I want to kiss you and press my tongue deep between your lips. Both sets of lips. I want to feel you tense up as I tense up. I want to feel you jerk with spasms as you climax, to feel your erect clit retreat from my touch. I'll

167

hold you tight until you have calmed, until you are ready for more and you do the same to me, and we go on like that, over and over and over until we can go on no longer and we lie side by side covered in each other's sweat and juices. Please come see me soon my Brightlight or I shall have to come visit you.

Zoja xxxx

Shit, that's got my sexy bits telling me I gotta go and see her real soon. I slowly read her words again while leaning back in the chair, touching myself and allowing all the sensual feelings to take their course until I double over in delicious ecstasy.

I have to reply, but I'm bloody hopeless with words. Anyway I can't send it unless I go back to the hotel. I'll do it later.

As my mind calms I begin focusing on the surroundings. The dark wood of the wall panels gives the apartment a warm feeling, in contrast to the exterior. I reckon because this building isn't very big, it was never used as a barracks like the other place. Most likely guards' or officers' quarters as a wild guess. The few pictures hanging on the walls are cheap, simple prints of countryside scenes. On the mantle above an old oil heater, where you'd expect to see photos of people, there's some books in Czech that have no meaning to me. Beside the books is a small white vase with flowers painted on it. A few dried-up flowers hang over the side—probably left to wilt since Ruza went to hospital. Above is another picture of green fields and trees on a distant hill. In the entire room there's not one picture of a person.

I go to Marika's bedroom, and again, just one simple scene facing the bed. It's like all images have been deliberately chosen to show fresh, green, simple open countryside. I reckon all the horrible memories from her childhood, and all the struggles since, could only be eased by scenes of open country and freedom.

I'm further intrigued and go to the front door to listen for any footsteps coming up the stairs before going into Evzen's bedroom. The curtains are half drawn and the old man smell is strong. The room is as sparse as the other, except on one wall is a small round mirror with a shelf below holding a woman's hairbrush and some bottles of medicine. I pick up the hairbrush…it's hers. I touch the mirror and can sense her image stored in its reflection. I look at the bed and hesitate, unsure if I should invade someone's privacy, but the temptation is far too great and I run my hand over the bed-head, over the pillows, over the sheet and quilt, all senses are of her and Evzen. They'd made love here. I rush out into the living room feeling ashamed at the intrusion.

I casually edge around the room—acting innocent if Evzen walked in—and come to the old side table next to Evzen's chair. I've never had a good look at it until now. It's the usual four legs and a top with a drawer below. The wood has been stained a dark, almost black colour, showing off the scratches and wear in greater contrast. On top is a stained but delicate lace doily. Something I imagine Marika could have made over many months. The reading lamp sits on top, its heavy cast-iron base decorated with delicate leaves and flowers in relief and delicately reflected in the painted glass shade. Both the lamp and the table give the impression of being the only pieces saved as mementos of another time and another place. Unlike Evzen's armchair that looks like it was reclaimed from a dump somewhere…or maybe it was among the discarded furniture in the courtyard of the old barracks. I resist the urge not to, but I'm compelled to lower myself into to it. There's no leather smell, just mustiness and fart smells. Yeah, I reckon Evzen found this for himself. I slide my hands over the worn leather arms that are burnished by many hands over many years but I only sense the hands of Evzen. Suddenly I tense up and grip the arms of the chair tight as I feel them folding around me. I'm held by the presence of another, a man, not homely or hospitable but something else, something I felt only recently. I try to concentrate. Shit, why can't I see faces?

Releasing myself from the chair, I rush out of the apartment, down the stairs, out to the rear courtyard and stop facing the door to the storage space. What I sensed yesterday is back and stronger. Now, in daylight, I can see where the plaster has been eroded away to the height of the flood line exposing the bricks beneath. The water would have been up to my chest. I reach out and gingerly grasp the door handle. I feel the hand of the man who had sat in Evzen's chair. My grip becomes tighter on the handle as once again I'm overcome by the images of Marika drowning, fighting for her life as his hand, coarse and large, pushes her down, down under the water until she can no longer struggle. I feel giddy and reach out to steady myself against the door. Everything that took place in the darkness beyond is revealing itself to me. I see images like I've never sensed before. Real images, real people, real danger…and real murder! I pull my hand away from the handle and rush back into the building, up the stairs, into the apartment and grab my paint cans.

'Briney?' I hear Evzen call out as he comes into the courtyard.

I'm on my knees with a can in each paint-smeared hand. I hear him but can't look away from the wall and door of the storage space.

'Are you al…' He stops in mid sentence, frozen by what he sees.

The painting is unlike anything I've ever done, clear and frighteningly realistic.

'My God! What…what have you done?' he calls out behind me.

In front of him is a simple but clear, precise painting of bluish water to the flood line and above that, painted over a threatening red background, is the black figure of a man, hunched over, his arms and lower body merging into the water. Below him, barely noticeable, is the shape of a woman scratched out of the blue of the water, the man's hands firmly on her shoulders, pushing down, drowning her. Only the back of the man is seen, but the submerged figure has enough detail for Evzen to recognise Marika.

'I'm sorry, Evzen, but I had to do it.' I look up to him. 'There's something else.'

He looks back to the wall.

I look up at him while pointing to the painting. 'That is the same man who visited Ruza recently. Tell me, was she attacked? Is that why she's in hospital?'

He suddenly looks older and greyer than before.

'Ne, ne, you must be wrong,' he says, shaking his head and backing away from me. Or is he backing away from the painting? He looks from the wall to me, desperation in his glaring eyes.

'What have I done?' he says, grabbing me by the arm. 'You must stop this now…you must!'

'I can't. You got me here. You got me involved.' I point to the wall I've just painted. 'See, it's too late…there's no way you can stop me now.'

I reach down into my bag and take out the camera.

'No, please…you no use this…please.'

I ignore him.

Back in the apartment, he's making every excuse to do anything but sit down and talk. I stubbornly follow him around like a cat wanting some cream. His shaking is getting worse and he's constantly wiping his eyes and nose with his handkerchief.

'Evzen, sit,' I insist. 'I'll make some coffee.'

He looks defeated and flops down into his chair and I wait till he's settled before quickly making a mug of coffee for both of us.

I set down the steaming mug on the soiled doily beside him and sit opposite with my mug and wait. After a while, he brings the coffee to his lips; his hands are still shaking and some spills down the front of his pullover. While his attention is on placing the mug back onto the table and brushing off the spilt coffee, I break the silence.

'Who was the man who visited?'

'I…I know of no visitor,' he abruptly answers without looking up.

'Maybe you were out. But she had a visitor, right?'

'She no tell of visitor.' He takes a moment to think then looks up. 'How you know?'

'He sat in your chair.'

He looks down at the padded arms of the chair with a squirm.

'I felt his presence.' I pause. 'Look, I know you don't want to hear this, but I believe whoever sat in that chair was also responsible for Marika drowning.'

He struggles up from the chair and waves a crooked finger at me. 'You…you take this power too far…you not right about this.'

If what I'm sensing is real, then both Marika and Ruza have kept him in the dark. I try to settle him down before he gets too upset.

'Okay, okay I believe you don't know anything about this visitor, so sit down and finish your coffee.' He looks back at the chair as if trying to sense what I have, then, with a slight shake of the head, slowly eases back into the worn upholstery.

I pull my chair up closer to him.

'Evzen, why did she need to go to hospital?'

He points to the floor where I'm sitting. 'I find her…lying there.'

I move the chair back immediately. Why didn't I feel that?

'I thought she dead…she make noise…I go to neighbour for help.' He's eyes widen, pleading, as if asking me for forgiveness.

'Has she been in a coma since then?'

He shakes his head. 'Not first…just before you come.'

'So, you had a chance to ask her what happened?'

He doesn't respond straight away, just staring at me.

'You ask her, ya?' he mumbles softly.

I shake my head. 'What?'

'I look for tell you…Ruza awake today…she want to see you.'

CHAPTER 29

He needs to dig deep into his sparse reserve of willpower not to show how much he's hurting. His skinny frame means less flesh to dull the pain of the needle but he's determined to hide his agony from Dasha. Unlike Zac, she reclines next to him totally relaxed and enjoying every bite of the tattooists' needle. She's used to it, already displaying tattoos on her upper arms, back, and as he found out only the night before, a provocative little icon on her lower stomach—way lower—of a frighteningly real-looking spider crawling out from her pubic hairs that have been clipped and shaved to resemble the spider's web. This freaked him out when he first spied it, but that was its purpose and a regular source of entertainment for her.

She's getting extra colour added to an intricate tattoo on her shoulder of a flying skull with wings protruding from each side and wrapping around her taut muscled arm.

This being his first tat, Zac feels rather naked, exposing his bare pallid flesh, as unadorned and pristine as the day he was born but for some random curls of body hair that have yet to make an impression, a few small moles, a scattering of freckles and two pale nipples doing absolutely nothing to enhance his masculinity. Except, inserted into one nipple is his only body adornment to date, a Zircon gold nipple ring with a titanium ball attached. Something he has no memory of having done, as he was so high at the time.

Having a tattoo was something he constantly boasted he'd do, but never had, until now. And now was not the time to procrastinate any longer. His new 'gang' and his new 'sheila'—a term they found amusing—all have tattoos as if it was a condition of membership and he wanted desperately to belong. There's one common icon they all proudly display, a simple design that Zac had thought looked pretty mild compared to the other ornate illustrations of skulls, wings, daggers dripping blood and other deadly symbols. It's a wolfsangel, a mirrored capital 'N' with a vertical stroke down the middle. It means nothing to him but he assumes it's their tag, so as it's a small, simple design, and therefore quicker and less painful to tattoo, he had offered to have the wolfsangel as his first tat. He was, however, sternly warned that he was not eligible. So now he's manfully hiding his agony as the beefy, totally illustrated bald tattooist with pins, bolts and studs protruding from various parts of his face, works on a simple cobweb on his skinny elbow.

He hadn't understood the joke when he chose this design. After all, Stik and Deratz had one and a few of the guys they knocked around with had them as well, so it didn't seem to be a tag, it was just a cobweb. But unbeknownst to him, it was generally accepted that only those who'd been in prison could wear the jailhouse tattoo and every rung of the web represented a year spent behind bars. Zac, who is having five rungs, has not been told about the 'jailhouse tattoo' legend; it was the 'gang's' private joke, for Zac had become their little mascot from Australia, a harmless source of comic relief and very manipulable.

While Dasha is no one's exclusive screw in the group, she's had, at various times over her year or so with them, shared sexual favours with each. Now there's a new face on the scene, skinny, funny, totally unworthy of belonging to the group, but a trophy nevertheless—especially now because of his link with Zoja's latest 'mate'. Zoja is known to the mob, as she is in all social quarters, and fancied by many. She's in no way part of this scene but her fame has made her a challenge to be conquered—a bragging prize for the first male to plant himself inside her and successfully make her climax. Of course many have sworn it would be easy, but rape was out, it had to be consensual. None have succeeded. As Dasha is the only regular girl in the group, those who Zoja rejected take out their sexual frustrations on her. This wasn't a problem, as being available to all is her membership ticket. But the fact of being a consolation to a known lesbian makes her mad. So Zac is a minor form of get back, distant and indirect, but enough for her to give the finger to Zoja and his ex—the girl she saw at the Kain Club.

The whir of the needle as it pricks holes in his thin skin seems to be endless. He's beginning to wonder how long he can contain his agony when finally the whirring stops. He's cleaned up. The artist inspects his handiwork and shows Zac the result in a mirror. The relief of no more pain makes the design extremely acceptable. After his new tatt is covered in cling-wrap film, he gingerly puts his shirt back on, wipes the sweat from his brow and sits to watch Dasha. She's naked from the waist up, showing off her firm sculptured breasts. She's very athletic and sexy in a rough sort of a way, and now, after suffering the pain of his own adornment, Zac has a surge of masculinity and is unable to hide his thoughts. She notices, suggesting his cock be tattooed while he's here. This has an immediate reaction and she smiles at his deflating bulge. But it will soon be resurrected as she has promised to celebrate his initiation into the world of tattoo.

Even though the group looks on Zac as a puny boaster, a name-dropper and exaggerator, actually they have underestimated his street cred and it has only taken him a couple of days for him to talk Dasha into taking him in. She shares a place with Deratz and Stik not far from

174

the Elf Hostel in an old building marked for demolition as the construction of a new overpass gets closer. Each has a separate bedroom but it isn't unusual for them to gather into one for a drunken, drugged orgy. But Dasha wants to have the new mascot to herself so on returning from the tattooist, she closes her bedroom door and pushes a chair under the handle so they won't be interrupted.

The room's nothing special, but it's warm, the bed's big and comfortable and Dasha is his prize. There isn't a lot of furniture and clothes are scattered over the floor and hanging from a makeshift frame in one corner. The smell of the place is comfortably familiar to Zac: unwashed linen, stale air and the aroma of sex and drugs.

He's hardly sat on the edge of the bed when Dasha is on top of him. She ignores his aching arm as she roughly pulls his shirt off and rips away the cling-wrap. It hurts but he manages to hide his grimace as she begins to perform a rather clumsy striptease to some heavy metal music. The sight of her undressing eliminates his pain and heightens his erection. Finally naked, she turns her attention to ridding Zac of his jeans. He lies back to allow her the freedom of his body. After all, this is all part of his initiation.

The build-up to this point is too much for Zac. Having endured the agony of the needle, excited by the sight of Dasha enjoying her pain, ogled at her teasing strip, devoured, and now feeling himself slide inside her, he climaxes immediately.

'You fucking came! No, you are not to come yet. I want more,' she calls out continuing to ride his deflated manhood.

He's still in spasm mode. 'Yeah, Yeah, okay, just give me a minute will ya?'

'Humph, that's what you get from fucking a lesbian, yah?'

'Oh, come on Dasha, just give me a minute. No need to bring her into it.'

She looks down. 'See, that's what happens, no need of cock for a dyke.'

Zac has to defend himself.

'Look, I didn't know she was a fuckin' dyke until we came to Prague, okay! Maybe I should blame this place?'

'Maybe you should blame the bitch Zoja. Seems she's got more balls than you.'

'Oh, fuck, Dasha, give me a break. Ya so fuckin' horny, I just couldn't hold it back any longer.'

This appeals to her ego.

'Okay, then I wait till you get hard again.' She leans forward, her breasts resting on his chest, and then slides herself up until she straddles his face. 'Now, give me your tongue while I wait.'

She manages to climax three times and Zac once again after regaining his erection. The long, exhausting encounter has them drenched in sweat as she lies with her head resting on his chest while she fingers his nipple ring.

'Why you come here with her?'

'What?'

'Why? It look like you two had split when I first saw you.'

'Yeah, well, we had, sorta.'

'Then why?'

He thinks about it for a moment.

'It's a long fuckin' story. You wouldn't be interested.'

'Well, I am. When you first came to the Kain with her and Zoja and they left, all you could do was talk about her and how she was supposed to be some great graff artist or something.'

'Yeah, well it wasn't just her, ya know, we worked as a team, right.'

'Is that why you split? It wasn't just because she was a secret dyke but because she wanted to break up the team?'

'No, it wasn't like that, and leave the dyke thing out of it, it was a fuckin' surprise to me too. No, she had this, this strange thing with the last graff she did in Melbourne. I didn't know what the fuck she was talking about, but for some reason she had to get over here.'

'What did it have to do with Prague?'

'Fucked if I know. Something about her old lady, I think.'

'She Czech?'

'Who, her old lady?'

'Your dyke bitch.'

'Nah, she told me she was born in Australia.'

'So, tell me about this great team you once had.'

Zac proceeds to explain their SECRETSINCITY project with exaggerated emphasis on his own involvement.

'Can I see this site?'

'Ya got a computer?'

She jumps out of bed, removes the chair from under the door handle and goes to the next room naked while Zac rushes to pull his jeans on and follow.

Stik and Deratz are on the computer, logged into a German porn site, and ignore Dasha's nakedness. She tells them she wants to see Zac's graffiti, with no mention of Briney; such was Zac's skewed description. That interests them enough for them to leave the golden shower orgy on the screen and move aside for her to take over. She pauses a moment to study the scene before logging out then pats the seat space beside her for Zac to sit while she logs in to her MySpace page.

'What's the page name?'

Zac hesitates, knowing this will give away the fact that it's not his site, but Briney's.

'Zac?'

'Yeah, um, MyRuza.'

'Who is this Ruza,' she asks.

Zac shrugs his shoulders. 'It's just the tag, that's all.'

The page opens and to Zac's surprise, the latest image appears. He leans forward for a closer look with Stik and Deratz peering over his shoulder. Stik utters something in Czech. Dasha glances back at him with a shrug and turns back to Zac.

'What the fuck is it?' she asks.

'Fucked if I know,' replies a genuinely puzzled Zac. 'Ain't seen that before, looks like she's done one on her own.'

He scrolls down to another of the graffiti images.

'There,' says Zac pointing. 'I worked on that one.'

On the screen is the graffiti done the day of the train incident, and what, as far as he was concerned, should have been the latest.

Deratz leans towards Dasha and whispers to her in Czech. She looks closer at the image, and after a moment, points to the screen.

'What's with the goose?'

'What?' he replies, with a startled look at Dasha then up at the two bulky figures standing over him.

'There's something there that looks like a goose,' she says with a nod of her head towards the image.

Zac still can't see any goose but needs to cover up for his minor involvement in the painting.

'Umm, Yeah well, that wasn't planned, ya know. It just like sorta happened when she fell against the wall and messed it up.'

'Who she?' asks Deratz, this time in strained English.

'His dyke girlfriend, the one you saw with Zoja at the Kain.' With a cheeky smile to Zac, she takes over the mouse and scrolls back to the first image. 'Seems she's gone out on her own now, hey?'

Deratz leans closer to Dasha and in Czech whispers, 'Find out all you can. I'm off.' He nudges Stik to follow and they both leave.

'What's that about?' asks Zac as the front door slams shut.

'Nothing,' says Dasha looking over the gallery of past graffiti. 'So tell me, how does this little game work again?'

Zac describes the whole process, finishing off with the list of non-answers Briney posts that cancels out any suggestions that come in.

'Sounds like it's all her idea. So what, all you did was carry her paints, or something.'

'No, fuck, Dasha, I had lots of input.'

'But it's her site, her new piece that's a surprise to you, and I don't see anything about you there.'

'Yeah, well, I wasn't that fuckin' interested in all the online shit.'

'What were you interested in? Just a fuck, then?'

He dismisses her remark.

'Look all I know is that after this last piece in Melbourne, she went all strange and said something about a message from someone called… umm…Veselý I think. They saw the goose and that led to her coming here to Prague. Fucked if I know why, but the way she acted you'd think it was some bloody life or death thing.'

'Veselý?' Dasha repeats quietly to herself.

He wipes his nose with the back of his hand. 'Got a feeling it had something to do with her old lady.'

'But you said she was born in Australia, so why the rush to come to Prague?'

'Yeah, well, your guess is as good as mine. I just thought it'd be a fuckin' hoot to come here, so I arranged some…umm…finances, you might say.'

'How'd you do that?' she asks with a new interest.

He laughs and is about to tell her then decides against it.

'Let's just say I was owed some.'

She's studying him carefully, fully aware there's far more behind what he's prepared to tell her.

'This new one she's done, why's it so different to the others?'

'Fucked if I know, it's just a load of strokes and shit. Told you I had a lot of input into the others.'

'Why don't you send her a message?'

'Why, she's got fuck all to do with me any more.'

'Prove it,' she says, sliding her hand down inside his pants.

He feels excited and threatened at the same time, but she has a defiant look in her eyes and her hand is fast diluting the threat.

'I don't know, what'll I say?'

'Just tell the little dyke that she can't paint for shit and that you're the real thing. Something like that.'

Knowing it's far from the truth, he stalls for time to think what to say. As a distraction, he clicks on the image of the supposed 'goose' graff and scrolls down the comments for a clue on what to say. The last message from R.Veselý comes up.

Dasha senses his hesitation. 'I won't look at what you say, promise. I'll be busy down here.' She says, unzipping his fly.

He quickly reads the message… *Today not good. Sorry. Please come back next day. L3BIV on museum map. You look as your mother. Evzen*

He reads it again, committing the words to his visual memory before returning to the latest graff. Dasha's skilful handling and the release of his erection from the confines of his jeans is sending his mind into a spin but he manages to quickly type a message in the comment box before she blocks his view. He's forced to push the chair back a little to give her room to sit on his lap with her back to him. He closes his eyes and reaches around to fondle her breasts and kiss her new tattoo. Her timing is spot on. He'd not yet pushed the send button, giving her a chance to read his message.

CHAPTER 30

'Evzen, I'm going to the hotel first. I'll meet you at the bus stop.' I left it at that—a statement not to be questioned. The fact that I'd meet him at the bus stop did change his mood a bit cuz it meant I was going to the hospital.

'I go with you.'

That surprises me. Does he want to stop me putting up the graff of Marika? There'll be a bloody scene in the hotel foyer if he tries.

'No, I'm fine, I'll meet you at the bus stop, really.'

'I go with you.' He insists, struggling into his coat.

What the hell, nothing he tries will stop me.

The junior manager's glad to see me but disappointed I'm with Evzen. At least it'll put him off hovering around and looking over my shoulder.

We sit down and within a minute I have the MySpace page open and notice there's quite a few comments on yesterday's upload. A quick scan shows they're mostly from the regulars, all saying roughly the same thing that they're glad to see I'm still alive after so long, but surprised at the change of style. Then I come to one in a language other than English, Czech I think, so I'll get Evzen look at it after I read more comments. Then, shit! There's one from Zac. It's under another username so I have to read it twice to make sure. I slump back into the chair frowning.

'Is problem?' asks Evzen.

'Um, no, no it's just bloody strange, that's all.'

'Strange! What you mean, strange?'

'Um, nothing really, but can you tell me if this is Czech?' I scroll back to the foreign message and turn the screen a bit towards him. '

He leans forward to read the first few words. 'It Czech…I read, ya?'

I think for a moment before giving him the nod.

He mumbles as he reads to himself and then turns to me with a worried look.

'This not good message,' he says waving a finger at the screen. 'This not good for you to see.'

'Why? What do you mean? What does it say?'

He leans forward and whispers while looking around the room. 'You know what is anti-Semitic, ya?'

I also look around the room, for what I don't know, then shrug my shoulders and whisper back, 'Not really. Anti? Against something, I guess?'

He leans closer and whispers so quietly that I can barely hear. 'Against Jews.'

I look at him unmoved.

'The writer of this message…much hate…make threat to you.'

'Me?' I say out loud, attracting the attention of hotel guests having breakfast in the dining room. He hushes me with a finger to his lips. 'Me, why?' I repeat in a whisper.

'This person…they no like what they see.' He pauses and I see a hint of fear and rage in his eyes. 'I no like this message…I think you stop this painting on walls.'

'What? Why?'

'Many still hate the Jew. This…this…is one.'

'But I know nothing about Jews.' Then I remember. 'I mean, shit, I didn't know I could be a Jew until you told me—and I still think you're wrong—so how can I be hated as a Jew?'

He's just staring at me. I look around the room. It feels like everyone else is staring at me as well. Shit, do I look like a Jew?

'It's bullshit,' I continue to whisper. 'Anyway, what did they see in the graff that's pissed them off?'

'You show words in painting. Words used in synagogue.'

I'm stunned. 'What? But I don't know any words used in a synagogue. I've never set foot in one'

He looks around to make sure everyone had gone back to whatever they were doing.

'I saw it myself…images used in synagogue. Your painting show what behind wall…secret synagogue of the Ghetto.'

I'm trying to grasp what he's saying. After a moment, I lean forward to check out the sender's tag…Deratizátor…shit, weird name.

'Does that mean anything?' I ask, pointing at the sender's name.

As he always does to stress a point, he wiggles his crooked finger at the screen. 'Deratizátor. It mean…exterminator!'

'Exterminator? Shit, sounds like an Arnie Schwarzenegger movie.'

He obviously doesn't get the joke or doesn't understand who or what I'm talking about.

'This no joke.' He looks around the room again. 'We talk outside.'

I'm still not sure what he's on about but I can see he's genuinely worried.

'Yeah, okay, but I want to upload my graff first.'

'No,' he snaps, placing his hand nervously on mine as I begin to work the track pad. 'You no show.'

As far as I'm concerned this exterminator crap has nothing to do with me. I brush his hand aside and prepare to upload. Evzen angrily pushes his chair back, almost toppling over as he stands and hobbles out of the hotel. I watch him leave but my mind's made up. I give the image a once-over. It's so different from anything I've ever done that I reckon it's even got some artistic merit. I hit the upload button, wait for the file to be sent, check the page to make sure it's there, then shut down the computer and rush to the front door to catch up with him.

'When you next come back?' says the junior manager from behind the reception counter. Shit, forgot about him.

'Sorry! In a bit of a rush, but thanks again.' I say, giving him a friendly wave and hurry out into the street.

Evzen's already well into the park opposite, staggering and hunched over on his way to the bus stop.

'Evzen, slow down will ya,' I call out. 'You'll have another bloody attack.'

He ignores me, so I walk silently beside him until we reach the other side of the park and the bus stop. He's out of breath so I suggest we sit on a bench until the bus comes. He's in no condition to refuse.

I wait a few minutes for him to calm down.

'Okay, so what's with this...exterminator?'

He turns to me, and, even though there's no one around, he continues to whisper, 'There is strong anti-Semitic movement here... they no worry about using violence.'

'But it's just a graff, I mean, shit, I didn't even know what I was painting.'

He shakes his crooked finger at me. 'They use such thing to make threats in Prague. I have seen. They use the power of this...how you say...graff. You now compete from other side. They no like that.'

It takes me a moment to understand.

'Okay. Okay, if you're right, that could be just a one-off. What about my last one of the...' I don't want to say *the murder*. 'The one I just loaded. Do you see anything Jewish in that?'

He pauses, then with a shake of his head, says, 'Maybe no.'

I want to know more, but the bus arrives, and I immediately switch into panic mode at the thought of meeting her.

CHAPTER 31

I can't stop shaking as I follow Evzen down the hospital corridor. He keeps looking back to see if I'm still with him. I am...just.

She's been moved to a general ward and it's busier. Again, I hesitate entering until a nurse comes up behind me and I'm forced inside. Slowly, step-by-step, I pass each bed, all occupied by old women— some asleep, some trying to sleep and some groaning in pain or despair...or just groaning. Evzen has stopped at the end of the ward, only two more beds away. I stiffen up, my feet heavy as lead and my breathing's just as heavy. I'd sooner turn and run out again but something's urging me on. I stand behind Evzen shielding me from her sight. Then, nervously, I look over his shoulder. She's just laying there, her head turned to face the window. I'm not even sure if she's awake. Wires and tubes are still linking her to whatever. Then Evzen moves to the side of the bed facing the window leaving me exposed. He bends down, casting his shadow over her, and kisses her gently on the forehead. Her only reaction is a twitch of a hand resting on her flattened stomach. He pulls a chair by the wall closer to the bed, sits and places his hand over hers and whispers something to her. In one slow continuous motion she turns her head, taking in Evzen, then locks her eyes on me. I gasp and feel I've been caught out spying, then see something in her eyes. Something I remember those many years ago when I tried to understand. Tears.

Her free hand rises, shaking from weakness, to point at me. She mouths something, but no sound comes out. She licks her lips and swallows, a dry swallow, and then attempts to speak again. This time there's a sound, weak and barely audible, but I can just make it out. 'My Ruza.'

Evzen turns to look at me. They're both looking at me and I react in a way I never thought I would…I cry.

I feel a hand on my shoulder and allow a nurse to ease me into a chair she'd moved from the next bed, then leaves as silently as she appeared.

Moments pass. I dare not look up as tears fall unhindered until I'm forced to wipe the dribble from my nose with the back of one hand. I've no idea what the other two are doing. I just can't allow myself to go any further and have visual or physical contact.

I sense of movement forces me to look up. Evzen is shifting in his chair because the way he was sitting was giving him some pain. It's all that's needed to break the impasse, but silence remains. Maybe no one knows what to say. I sure as hell don't.

Then, from a very weak croaky voice she says, 'You are beautiful.'

I'm still unable to speak.

'I leave for moment?' says Evzen, stirring to get up from his chair.

'No!' I call out pleadingly and waving a hand for him to remain where he is. 'No, stay, please!'

He settles himself back down.

I look back down. 'I named myself Briney,' I mumble. 'I use Ruza as a last name.'

'A lovely name,' I hear her say.

There's another moment of uneasy silence.

'Would you pass me some water, please?'

I look up and around to see a jug of water and a glass on the side table beside me, damn! I fumble in my seat and pass her the glass of water trying to avoid looking into her eyes.

'Thank you, Briney,' she says, as I place the glass into her frail hand. The slight touch of her cold flesh sends a shiver through me.

She struggles to raise the glass to her lips and Evzen moves to assist, but her trembling upsets some water onto the blanket. I'm confused by the emotion of the moment and unsure of what to do. The space of a lifetime has come to this, the inability to talk, to ask, to tell, to express anything. Where to start after so much time and so much blame?

It's Evzen who breaks the silence as he raises the glass to her lips. 'You think of what I say yesterday, ya?'

I can feel her eyes have not left me as he hands the glass to me to place on the side table.

'I always knew you would find a gift.' The sip of water has made her voice clearer and a little stronger, but I'm not sure what she's talking about. 'Since seeing the first…I would travel for hours on trains all around Melbourne…looking for your paintings. I knew they were the work of my daughter.'

I flinch at the word *daughter*. A deep-held resentment surfaces, together with the lump in my throat. I swallow hard, trying to clear it. She notices.

'Yes, you do not see me as a mother…I understand.' She pauses. I feel uncomfortable. 'There is no way of changing what I did to you. I have lived knowing of the…the…hatred you must have of me.' She coughs as her breathing falters. I look up as Evzen places a caring hand

185

on her shoulder. 'I cannot apologise. I know it would be worthless so I will not even try or explain. All I can do is to ask for the past to stay in the past…we only talk of today and of the future.'

I look back down as an unexpected calm come over me. What had lingered corrosively deep inside me just waiting to explode in an outburst of hate has gone. It's clear, there's nothing that would come anywhere near smoothing over the past and her suggestion of not even going there suits me fine. I lift my head with a look of resigned acceptance and the slightest smile of relief. She studies me for a moment to make sure of our mutual understanding; once convinced, she relaxes back into her pillows.

'Yes, Evzen,' she says to him, but keeping her glazed eyes on me. 'I have thought about what you told me.'

She lifts her hand, inviting me to hold it. I hesitate, then nervously reach out to take her hand. The cold, dry, pale, tissue paper flesh sends another chill through me.

'Yesterday, Evzen told me everything. About his messages to you, and you thinking they were from me.' She squeezes my hand a little. 'I would have, but I fell ill.' She takes in a deep breath and I hear the oxygen machine hiss. 'I was surprised when Evzen told me you had come to Prague. I did not expect that…but I'm glad.'

I feel another lump building in my throat but swallow it away.

'And he has told me of your new power.'

I look to Evzen who hasn't taken his eyes from her. I don't know what he's told her but I figure I should tell it my way.

'Look, I really don't know what this…this power thing is all about yet. I had this sort of accident, right? Like, with a train, right, and, well…' I glance back to Evzen. 'I sorta saw Evzen's parents.' I look back to Ruza. 'Then this strange thing came over me and the next thing I know I'm getting this weird message saying, umm…*the goose will reveal all*…and well, the rest is history, here I am.'

They're both studying me as if that's not all they want to hear…and it isn't.

'Now Evzen has just told me you believe my sister, Marika, did not drown by accident?' She asks in a more serious tone.

I'm surprised this has come out so soon. Not that I didn't want to talk about it, I did, but, just coming out with it like that is a real shock.

'I…I think she was murdered.' Shit, now it's me. I guess I could've been a bit more sensitive. 'I mean, like I'm still coming to grips with this…this thing I sorta have, and well, I could be totally wrong.'

Evzen leans close to her and whispers to her again. She studies him for a moment before refocusing her attention on me.

'You have new painting of Marika?'

Instinctively I grab my shoulder bag carrying the laptop.

'And a man? I must see the painting!'

Evzen whispers to her again while glancing down at the bag I'm now holding to my chest.

'You have a photo of the painting on your computer? You must show me!'

This is all happening far too fast. In an instant, she's dismissed the past as if irrelevant or never happened and now I'm just a messenger. I'm brought back to the harsh reality of our separation and the cold hard fact that it will forever stay that way. I suddenly feel I'm being used and if I hadn't had that thing under the train I'd still be back on the streets in Melbourne living my crappy life. But hey, what was I expecting? Fuck all, really. My life was set out a long time ago and that's just the way the cards fall. I'm here, I've met her, I'm involved in something I don't understand, so what the hell.

I look at them both and then around the ward.

'Can I turn the computer on in here?' Thinking I may stuff up someone's monitor or pacemaker or something.

I can see Evzen's nervous, but Ruza nods.

I take out the laptop, turn it on and navigate through the process of opening up the photo of the painting of Marika and the dark stranger. I hesitate before turning the computer around to face her. She needs to be raised up on the pillows and indicates with a movement of her head for me to get her glasses from the side table while Evzen helps with her pillows. All this is done with slowness and clumsiness on everyone's part. I wait until she's manoeuvred, has her glasses on and Evzen has settled back in his chair. Shit, it was an effort just watching them.

I hold the laptop for her to see the screen, taking up the weight for fear it might crush her frail body. Her eyes roam around the screen, confused for a moment before the image registers. Her eyes widen, her body tenses up and her breathing falters as her spindly finger points at the computer.

'He...' The only word she can get out before coughing up a glob of phlegm from her chest. She wipes it away with a tissue. 'He...' She coughs again. I lean forward to hear her better and get a nose full of strange odours.

'He visited you didn't he?' I help out.

She glances at Evzen then back to me, indicating with a slight nod towards the water. I pass her the glass. She sips and coughs again as the water catches in her throat.

Evzen is suggesting she rest but she closes her eyes and shakes her head. He gives in but looks around to make sure a nurse is nearby.

The water is finally dislodged. She takes a deep breath before continuing.

'You know the property where you are staying...once belonged to my father?'

'Yeah, Evzen told me. But that's...'

She interrupts. That's all she wanted to hear.

'In Australia, I knew nothing of this new law to reclaim lost property. Then when I came back to Terezín and heard about it, I was surprised when Evzen told me Marika had not made a claim. If I had known earlier, I would have come back to help her. You see, that property should be yours now. It was the only thing I felt I could leave you.'

There's a hushed moment as we study each other, knowing full well that apart from the property, there is absolutely nothing either of us can give the other...absolutely nothing!

She continues, but I can see she's failing. 'I could not believe Marika did not try, so I did my own investigation. I knew that it was many years since the claim deadline and nothing could be done, but I needed to believe that Marika had made an effort to find the proof.'

She pauses for breath.

'Rest, have some water,' suggests Evzen. She closes her eyes in acceptance.

I figure she doesn't want to see the painting anymore so I shut down the computer and pack it away.

I hand Evzen the water and watch as he fusses over her, raising the glass to her lips, wiping the dribble from her chin and stroking her forehead. The display of tenderness has me feeling sorry for him. It's clear he's carried his love for her through all the years they were apart, and now, finally together, all he can do is wipe away her dribble.

'I went to Prague.' Her sudden burst of revived energy surprises both of us, but she's struggling to keep her eyes open. 'There *was* proof…and Marika *had* found it.'

This is a surprise to Evzen more than to me.

'But all the documents now belong to the new legal owner. They refused to see me…then I…Briney…I am so sorry it has turned out this way.'

I'm not sure what to think. I'd never considered inheriting anything so I feel no loss, but I needed to know one more thing.

'Did you have a man visit you?'

There's no answer. Her eyes glaze over with fatigue and close, shutting out the world and squeezing out a tear. Her breathing is erratic with fluid bubbling in her lungs as she lapses into deep sleep.

'We must leave now,' says Evzen as he kisses her forehead and brushes a hand over her cold cheek. I figure we both realise her time is fast running out.

CHAPTER 32

Sitting across the aisle from us on the bus back to Terezín are three old ladies with parcels of food and other stuff piled on their laps after a morning's shopping in Litoměřice. They're chatting and laughing over their successful outing—unlike the two of us, sitting silently facing in opposite directions. I don't know what's going through Evzen's head, but I feel I'm in some sort of limbo. I've met her, I've spoken to her and yet there's no emotional connection. She remains just as much a stranger as ever. Is it me? Am I a cold hard bitch? I don't know, but the hatred that lingered for all these years has gone, so I suppose that's one positive thing that's come out of today.

Before long, the passing scenery of gentle hills and fields of early spring flowers morph into the dull grey of Terezín.

We follow the three chatty ladies off the bus, their happy mood bringing a bit of much-needed life to the quiet stillness. But it's short-lived as they walk away in another direction. I wonder what makes them laugh and enjoy themselves and not Evzen. Maybe they haven't lived the hardship he did, or is it because they have company in each other?

'I'm going to the hotel to go online again.' I say as we get to the junction of paths in the centre of the park. I want to reply to Zoja's message and have another look at what Zac was on about.

'If you must,' he mumbles back, taking the path back to the apartment.

'Yeah, well, see you later then, okay?'

Without another word he shuffles off, head bowed, wiping his nose on his sleeve. I watch this sad, lonely old man until he reaches the edge of the park and I wonder how different things could have been if Ruza was well and they, too, could laugh together after a shopping spree.

A breeze has sprung up as I walk to the other side of the park and for the first time I smell life in this place, not the usual stale decay and death stuff, but everyday life stuff. Food cooking, fresh leaves in the trees and a hint of exhaust fumes. I look around. The place looks the same. The buildings are still a mix of repaired and untouched, the streets wide and deserted and the colours of the day now feel familiar. I know I don't fit in, but I feel a sense of belonging. Has today, with all its fears and disappointments, made me realise something that I thought impossible, that I have a family connection to this place?

The mild weather has people sitting at tables and chairs under two large white umbrellas on the pavement in front of the hotel. A tour bus turns the corner and stops, blocking their view of the park. I rush to get inside and grab a table before the new arrivals crowd the foyer. It's still busy and I wait for the junior manager to notice me.

'Good afternoon, madam,' he says with a formal smile.

'Hi,' I reply, accepting the madam shit was for the benefit of the many guests and other staff hanging around. 'Umm, I'm hoping to use my laptop again if that's okay?'

He looks around as the group from the bus start to enter. 'It's very busy, will you be long?'

I can see the rowdy new arrivals are demanding his attention, but I reckon he'd like to have me hang around until they check in and things calm down.

'No, I promise. But I'll have a coffee and some cake if that'll help pay for the time?'

'Of course, take that table over there and I'll send over a waitress, but please excuse me while I tend to the new quests.' I get a rigid official nod before he spins around, leaving me to set up the laptop. He is kinda cute.

I'm just about to read Zac's message when the waitress arrives. I quickly scroll his message off the screen and give her my order. She says nothing and leaves. With Evzen around earlier, I could only glance over his message, but it was enough to get a feeling he was definitely pissed off. Now I have the time to read it fully.

hey see ya on the page again with a bloody fuckin useless piece of crap. thought ya was top shit did ya well I can now see what ya can do without me or should that be cant do. me mates STIK and EX here think so to especially me special mate DASHA. now she really knows how to fuck. by the way hows ya dyke mate goin. hope ya like suckin rubber from now on. ZAC(of)

Yeah, he's really pissed off with me. But even for him, it's a bit out of character. He can be crude and weakly threatening when he's pissed, but this was cutting and nasty. I mean, I can tell he wasn't drunk cuz I've seen his spelling when he's pissed and this was relatively good.

191

I read it over a few more times. There's something more to it than I can figure out. Not so much in the wording or even reading between the lines, but it's giving me the same feeling when I sense things in walls. I shrug my shoulders, oh well, fuck him.

The waitress returns and I rearrange myself to make room for the coffee and cake and make sure the screen's facing away from anyone passing. I thank her but she's already gone. I sugar the coffee and take a sip while reading Zoja's message and I'm instantly reminded of better coffee and better company. I feel my face blush as I think of what to say in reply cuz so much has happened since getting her message I haven't had time to prepare anything.

In the end it's a short reply, nothing of great detail despite what I've been through the past couple of days. I feel uncomfortable telling her and it seems too personal or something. I mention uploading a new graff without any description; I want her to see it without any prompting from me.

I knew I wasn't saying all I wanted to and how much I missed her, so I let myself go and added exactly how I felt and how desperately I want to see her again and that I'll come back to Prague real soon. I could have sent it off then, but something she told me has given me another reason —other than lust—to come to Prague. I reworded the message to sound like a request. It wasn't a false request, but one I'd thought of asking as soon as I learnt about the property claim going haywire. She told me her father was a property lawyer, so I asked if I could meet him. I didn't go into any great detail, just saying I wanted some clarification of property ownership that my aunt was involved with before she died.

After packing up the laptop I look at the order slip on the table for how much I owe. It's some time since I looked at how much money I've got left and for a moment I thought I might come up short, but after searching in every pocket I managed to come up with enough that included a tip, but just.

Shit, I've no bloody money left!

This has thrown me into a big fucking spin. Jeez, how can I get to Prague? I wonder if I can get any work somewhere? Maybe here at the hotel now I know the junior manager? Yeah, fine, but even if I can, it won't get me instant money. Shit, I guess there's only one person I know around here I can ask!

He's still hiding in his silent shell so I try to keep things light and ask him to teach me how to cook whatever it is he's cooking. I don't think he really believes I want to know, but he plays along and gets me to peel some potatoes. After cutting them up and putting them in the pot for boiling, all I can do is stand back and watch as he does the rest. He hasn't told me what it is he's cooking, and I showed no interest in asking. I'm too preoccupied wondering how to start talking about money. I've always had a problem talking about that subject. But bugger it; I'll do it in a cowardly roundabout way.

'Evzen, I might go to Prague tomorrow.'

'You no come with me to hospital?' he asks, continuing to concentrate on his cooking.

I knew he'd bloody ask me that and I did wonder if going to Prague wasn't just an excuse not to go and see her again. I also didn't want to tell him about Zoja or her father. I mean, it all could be a waste of time and I don't want anyone getting excited about me making any property enquires.

'Um, no, look, tell her I'll come the day after. Anyway I think she could do with a rest after what she went through today.' That sounds reasonable, even to me. Anyway, somehow I feel he'd be happier if I didn't go.

'Look, um, there's something I need to ask you and I hope you don't take this the wrong way.'

I wait for some response, but all he does is throw some salt over the meat.

'I um, I sorta don't have any money left.'

He places the pan into the oven and wipes his hands on the floral apron that was obviously Marika's.

'Look I wasn't gunna bring this up but, well, I gotta tell you something.'

He now throws some salt in with the potatoes, seemingly without interest in what I'm saying.

'You see, the only way I could come all this way from Australia was if I let this guy pay and come with me. There was no way I could have ever got the money myself, so, like, he sorta had me over a barrel if you know what I mean?'

He brushes the salt from his hands onto the apron and gives the potatoes a stir.

'And like, as soon as we got here we sorta had a bit of row and, well, because he wouldn't give me any money for myself…I…like…had to nick some.'

His expression remains totally deadpan as he continues to stir the pot.

'So, like, I can't go and ask him for any money after stealing from him now, can I? So, um, until I can sorta find some work I…'

He stops stirring, wipes his hands and takes down an old flour container that's sitting on a shelf beside the oven. From it, he takes out a wad of money.

'You take,' he says, waving the money at me.

I wasn't sure about this. I mean it looks like a lot of money for someone who doesn't seem to have much. I feel lousy taking it but it's offered, I need it, so what else can I do.

'Look, I'm really sorry, but I promise to pay you back some day, I promise.'

'This not my money,' he says. 'Ruza leave for you…is not enough?'

CHAPTER 33

The friendly junior manager was having his day off. It was something I hadn't considered, so I had to deal with this bitchy woman who was not at all happy about the arrangement I had with him. She told me in no uncertain terms that the use of the WiFi was for guests only. And not only that, she kept looking down at my tatty clothes. Bitch! Anyway I managed to convince her that it was a matter of life or death that I go online. I'm sure she didn't believe me but it was a busy morning with people arriving and leaving so she gave up arguing.

I was so eager to see if Zoja had replied, but the only new messages were from SECRETSINCITY subscribers saying they aren't that impressed with the latest effort. It's more like a painting than a cryptic graff, they said, and there was no challenge to find any secrets—if only they knew. Also, there are no threatening messages from the likes of Exterminator. Obviously it wasn't Jewish enough for them.

The bitch is giving me the evil eye, so I'm just about to pack up and let her have her way when the laptop clunks. A new message has come in and it's from Zoja. Unlike her other one, this is short and to the point.

Hi Brightlight. Great to hear you're coming back to civilisation. Had to wait till this morning to talk to daddy. He would love to meet you for lunch today, so there, you have a date. Things are a bit frantic this morning so can I ask you to meet us in front of the Town Hall Clock at one. I'll book a table at the restaurant opposite. You have my number if you can't make it, but I'll be disappointed. Zoja xxx

It's so good to be back among people again, lots of people, and lots of young people. With my new wealth I reckon I need some new clothes to wear when I meet Zoja's old man. But it didn't take long to learn that the money I have isn't going to get me much, not in the shops around Wenceslas Square anyway. I check out a couple of shops away from the main drag and while they're cheaper nothing grabs my eye. It's now well after midday and I'm starting to get desperate so the next shop will have to do. As soon as I walk in, the girl greets me in English —funny how they know—and starts off by asking me about my T-shirt and where I got it. The 'back home in Australia' story erupts into a full conversation about her desire to travel. She seems nice and I feel she likes me and starts showing me clothes that look okay and that I could afford. After trying on a few different outfits, I decided on a simple red top with a neckline that shows just enough cleavage and long tightly fitting sleeves that reach over the hands just like Zoja wore once. The rest of the new outfit is a pair of black straight leg jeans and a black jacket of some lightweight fabric that reaches to just above my knees. After checking what I look like in the full-length mirror and ruffling up my hair, even if it wasn't as Gothic as I'd hoped, I'll do. I explain to the girl that I need to wear the clothes now and she happily packs the old gear in the store carry bag and tells me how to get to the Old Town Square.

It's almost one o'clock on arriving at the Town Hall Clock and I have to push through the growing crowd in search of Zoja. A tap on my shoulder makes me turn expecting to see her, but it's a tourist telling me that I'm facing in the wrong direction and the clock's about to strike the hour. I smile and walk away, ignoring his kind advice.

It's almost twenty minutes after one by the time I look back at the clock. The crowd's thinned out and I'm left wandering around in circles until another tap on the shoulder.

She's in a pair of faded blue denim jeans, a black T-shirt with a dagger piercing a bright red heart on her left breast and an equally faded blue denim jacket. I immediately feel a little foolish and a bit overdressed.

'Brightlight, you look great.' I think she actually meant it. 'Look, daddy's running a bit late but told me to order for him, he shouldn't be long.'

She's noticed my surprise at seeing her in un-Gothic gear.

'I've spent the morning working on a film being shot nearby in the Lesser Square and no time to change, but you look so sexy I feel pretty dowdy. Never mind, let's go eat, I'm starving.'

I feel it's all a bit of a rush and I'm a little disappointed that she didn't give me a welcome kiss. Maybe that's the way rich people act, always seeming to be in a rush, just finished working on a film, busy at the office, in a hurry to do lunch, so there's not much time to talk, or kiss. But hey, feeling stylish in my new gear, in the company of a well-known socialite *and* about to lunch in a restaurant, it's exciting being part of *the scene*.

I'm led through shaded tables packed with diners and bustling waiters that line the edge of the Square to a rather simple entrance. U

ZLATÉ KONVICE in soft lettering follows the curve of the arch above two open wooden doors, each holding a blackboard menu. Inside, there's just a small area with a bar and a couple of tables and chairs, and a stairway leading down. We take the stairs, passing two full sets of knights' armour acting as sentries to the Prague underworld of dungeon dining.

The headwaiter greets Zoja as a regular customer and I'm introduced as her friend from Australia. He nods his welcome and leads us to a table set up for three at the rear of the long, narrow cellar. He pulls out chairs for us and is about to place menus on the table when Zoja stops him. She chats to him in Czech, he nods, packs the menus under his arm, turns to me, nods again and leaves the two of us to relax.

I'm amazed by the medieval, or is it Gothic, richness and warmth of the place. A large boar's head is leering at me from a wall above a spit, where, turning slowly over red-hot embers, a once lively member of its breed is roasting away. The enticing aroma and the thought of eating it makes my mouth water.

'It gets hot in here,' says Zoja, removing her denim jacket and placing it over the back of her chair. 'Take your jacket off and sit and relax.'

I willingly obey, relishing the feeling of being studied by her.

'Very nice top.'

I smile. 'Thanks,' I don't believe her but I accept the compliment. 'Thought I'd better get something new to meet your father.'

'Let me take you to where I shop next time. But you do look very, very tasty my darling Brightlight.'

I blush as we lock eyes for a moment.

The waiter returns with two glasses of champagne. There's another short exchange with Zoja and he leaves with a bow.

'To us,' toasts Zoja, raising her glass.

'Um, na zdraví,' I say with a smile as we clink glasses and remain fixed in a visual embrace, and drink.

Suddenly she looks past me and with a broad smile calls out, 'Hello daddy.'

I nervously jump up from the chair, knocking my glass to the floor.

'Oh, fuck,' I call out in total embarrassment. I don't know where to look first: Zoja's dad, Zoja, the dripping champagne or the broken glass. A waiter instantly ushers us away from the table as Zoja begins to laugh and her dad stands back with a bemused look on his face. Flushed, I look at Zoja for comfort while other diners just smile and return to their meals unfazed.

The headwaiter summons another to clean up the mess while he fusses over our clothes for any spilt champagne. Satisfied we're all dry, he checks that the table and chairs are the same before we sit.

'See Daddy, I told you she's exciting.' Then turns to me. 'Briney, meet my father, Doran. Daddy, I like you to meet Briney from Down Under.'

Doran offers his hand. I shake it, sensing a strong grip.

'I'm very pleased to meet you my dear,' he says with a nod and in a deep velvety mix of American and Czech accent.

I nod, still flushed with embarrassment. 'Same here.' Shit, that sounded so fucking Aussie. 'Look I'm really sorry about that, bloody clumsy me.'

'Not at all,' he replies, removing his hand and indicating we sit. 'I would have been disappointed if an Australian did not do something like that to break the ice.'

'Yeah, well I try.' I relax knowing he's taken it in good humour.

The waiter returns with two new glasses of champagne and a short glass of what looks like neat whiskey.

'Well, to you Briney and I hope you enjoy your stay in Prague.'

We touch glasses and drink.

'Where are you from in Australia?'

'Um, Melbourne…well…actually around Melbourne. Have you ever been there?'

'No, I spent some years in America.' He gives a nod to Zoja. 'Zoja did most of her schooling there.'

'Yeah, she told me. And she also said you're a, umm, property lawyer?' Oh, hell…not so quick. Why do I always do that?

'Ah, yes,' he says straightening up in his chair. 'And you wish to ask me something.' He pauses to look around the room. 'But first I should call Tibor over for a menu and order.' He looks back at me with a warm smile. 'Then we can get to know each other a little better over some classic Czech food, yes?'

'I've already ordered Daddy,' says Zoja, rattling off a list of totally unpronounceable menu items.

'Perfect,' replies Doran and then to me, 'you will like.' It sounded more like an instruction than a suggestion. 'But allow me to order the beer at least,' he adds.

The first course arrives. Three large bowls of steaming soup, rich in colour with a strong smell of garlic and thick chunks of toast floating on the surface. 'Old Bohemian garlic soup,' explained Zoja as I wait to see how the others tackle it. 'You will smell of garlic for a week,' she adds with a laugh.

The soup was hot and delicious, giving little chance for small talk. But it did allow me a glance or two at Zoja's *Daddy*. A fairly handsome man and I can see where Zoja's good looks came from. His neatly trimmed grey hair and fine wire-rimmed glasses give him a look of a judge rather than a lawyer. He has that look in his eyes of a judge as well, intense and concentrated and the lack of smile lines on his rather smooth face sorta belies his friendly attitude. But hey, I just met him. His dark steely-grey suit looks tailored and expensive and his striped shirt and silk tie have been carefully chosen. While totally opposite to his daughter's outrageous Gothic character, there seems to be a mutual understanding and acceptance between the two. You could say on first impression, he's pretty cool.

'I believe you are something of an artist?' he asks, downing a large portion of his dark beer.

'Well, I don't know if you'd call me that,' I reply timidly.

'But you paint don't you?'

'Yeah, but it's...' I hesitate, unsure if I should announce my vandalistic talents.

'Daddy, she's a famous graffiti artist,' Zoja butts in.

Doran takes another sip of his beer and wipes his mouth with a napkin. Probably considering how to talk about something he disapproves of.

'And what does a graffiti artist like you paint?' he asks showing a degree of interest. 'Political comment, maybe?'

'Oh, not really, well Yeah, sometimes. I don't know, I sort of mainly do weird stuff for people to see whatever they want to see and get their reactions.'

'Mmm, interesting concept. Have you done any graffiti here in Prague?'

'Well, not really here in Prague, um, in Terezín.'

'Terezín?' he says with a degree of surprise. 'Ah, yes, Zoja did mention that's where you're staying. Do you have family there?'

Shit, I was supposed to be asking questions of him, not the other way around. I take a sip of beer.

'It's a long story, but Yeah, I've only just found that out.'

'Interesting, so you are Czech?'

'Oh no,' I rush to say. 'I was born in Australia.'

'So your parents are Czech?'

'Well, my, um, mother was…is.'

'And your father?'

I look at Zoja who's silently listened with interest.

'Um…not sure about that.'

Before he has a chance to say anything Zoja comes to my rescues.

'That's enough, Daddy, stop being such a lawyer.'

'Yes, I apologise my dear. I do tend to become over-inquisitive sometimes. Now, what did you want to…' The waiter interrupts, removing the soup bowls while another places a red-glazed terracotta plate in front of each of us, then in the middle of the table, a large platter overflowing with roast pork, crispy crackling, a light and a dark plump sausage, some other meats that looked like they were smoked and heaps of red and white cabbage. Doran orders another round of beers.

'We share, Brightlight, you will not get a more Czech dish than this I assure you,' says Zoja, leaving me wide-eyed at the amount of food.

Doran looks at Zoja, momentarily in wonder, then, most likely because he's used to his daughter's ways, dismisses the nickname she's adopted for me.

After some minutes of relishing the tastes of the food on offer, we pause for a rest and another beer.

'Now, as I was about to say before being deliciously interrupted, you wanted to ask me something, Briney?'

'Um Yeah, but like, I really don't know much about it, but it's to do with reclaiming property.' I pause, waiting for some assistance from him.

'You mean property that was taken during the war?' he asks with some authority. Zoja leans forward and rests her chin in her hands, full of interest.

'Yeah, I guess so.'

'Can I ask if your family is Jewish?'

Why is everyone asking me that? 'Yeah, well, my old lady is, I've just found out.'

'Briney, I don't mean to sound like I'm prying, but I have represented many Jews and have been relatively successful in helping them get their rightful property back.'

He leans forward and his voice drops.

'But my dear, the time has passed and there is nothing that can be done now, if that is what you are asking.'

I half expected the answer to be as simple as that but I felt I needed more detail to take back to Ruza and Evzen. 'Yeah, like, I'm aware the deadline was some years ago, but it's just that I learnt that my aunt tried to, you know, make a claim, but she died before anything was done.' I pause to gather my words together. 'And, like, I was hoping maybe she'd started the process and that there was still something that could be done.'

He's studying me—more judge than lawyer—and I feel a bit uneasy. Then, after some thought, he asks, 'Your mother, is she living in Terezín?'

'Well, Yeah, but she's not well and in hospital in Litoměřice.'

'I'm sorry to hear that. Will she recover soon?'

I offer a slight shake of the head as a simple answer.

'You say your aunt. She is your mother's sister, yes?'

'Yeah.'

'And your mother, was she with your aunt when the claim was made?'

'No, she's only been back here since early this year.'

'Mmm,' he murmurs. 'If you give me your aunt's name, I'll see what I can find out, but, my dear, there really is nothing that can be done about the property now.' He reaches across the table and pats my hand. 'But sometimes I have managed to get some financial compensation if there is enough evidence of ownership. I'm sure this is not exactly what you are seeking, but after such a long time since the deadline, I'm afraid that is all I can suggest. Now if you would be so kind to tell me your aunt and mother's name so I can start the search.'

The feel of his warm hand on mine is comforting. It's a long shot, I know, but there may be something to come out of this after all.

'Ruza, my, um, mother's name is Ruza and Marika was my aunt.'

'And family name?' he asks, taking out a pen and a small notepad from his inside jacket pocket.

'Vesely. Look, I've written down the names and address.' I dive into my bag and tear out the page from the notepad.

He takes the note and reads it carefully. 'And how shall I contact you if I need to?'

'I'm staying in my...umm...at that address.'

'This address?' he says pointing at the paper. 'Is it leased?'

'Rented or leased, Yeah, I'm pretty sure it is cuz he told me Marika wanted to live in the place even if they couldn't own it.'

'He?' Doran questions.

'Oh, I forgot to mention that a friend of Ruza and Marika is living there too. They were all orphaned in the Ghetto. He looked after them and...well, I guess he still does.'

'Ah, yes, the Ghetto.' He hesitates for a moment. 'So this man is not a relative?'

'No, but I think he feels he's part of the family.'

'What is this man's name? You never know, it may help.'

'Um, Evzen.' Then I realise I've forgotten his last name. 'Shit, sorry that's all I remember. He did tell me once but I didn't think it was important so I didn't write it down.'

'Never mind,' he says adding Evzen's name to the paper. 'If I need to, I'll ask you to get his last name later. Now, are there any other relatives? I mean, apart from you?'

'No, I'm pretty sure I'm the last one.'

'Well, if there is anything else you can tell me or that you may uncover later, that would be very helpful as I really don't have a lot to work with.'

'Yeah, look, I realise that and, well, it's just that I thought you might find something. I mean, anything to show there was an attempt to find some proof.'

'Yes, of course my dear. I can fully understand why you would like some definite answers, seeing it would be you who would inherit this property.'

Shit, no way do I want anyone to think I'm doing this for my own greed.

'Look, up to only a few days ago I had not idea of all this, so I'm not sure how I feel.'

'No, of course not. And I trust your mother with recover and be around for a long time yet.'

I avoid a reply.

'Look, I really do thank you for seeing me and all but I don't know if I can pay you for your…'

'Nonsense, You are a friend of my daughter and that makes you a friend of mine. It will not take me long to get whatever information there is and that will be that. But you must accept that if the necessary information is not there I'm afraid there's nothing I can do, you understand that, don't you?'

I nod and feel a slight tear building.

'Good, now I'm afraid I must go back to work and leave you two to enjoy the rest of the day.'

He's about to put the note into his pocket when Zoja stops him.

'Wait, Daddy, I'll write down Briney's website so you can look at her work.'

'Of course,' he says handing her the paper. 'I will have a look back at the office. I must admit I'm very curious how you entice people to tell you what they think they see in your graffiti.' He hesitates. 'No, your art, my dear…I shall call it your art.'

He stands and comes to my side of the table. I carefully rise from the chair and he takes me by the shoulders and gives a gently shake. 'And I do not want to leave such a lovely young lady with a tear in her eye—it is not good for my image.'

I sniff back the tear. 'Thanks again for seeing me and it's great to meet you.'

He kisses me on both cheeks, leans across to Zoja and kisses her on each cheek plus one. 'You two enjoy yourselves now, yes?' He leaves.

'Well, my little Brightlight, I think that deserves a Slivovitz, don't you?' she says waving her hand at the waiter.

'Yeah, I reckon I could do with one. Look, Zoja, I'm really grateful your father agreed to see me and that he'll look into this thing.'

'Oh, Daddy's like that, always ready to help wherever property is involved. Like he said, he's managed to get some good results for those who lost property.'

'Those? You mean Jews?'

The Slivovitz arrives before Zoja can respond.

'What shall we drink to?' she asks.

'To your father.'

'And to a successful outcome for you, what ever it may be.'

We down our drinks and slam the empty glasses back down on the table with such a loud bang a passing waiter asks if another refill is required. We look at each other with a smile. That's good enough for the waiter to accept as a yes.

'Zoja? Is there a Jewish synagogue in Prague?'

She smiles. 'Brightlight, for starters, all synagogues are Jewish, and secondly, in the Jewish Quarter there's one of the oldest where you can still worship.'

'I guess you can tell I've only just found out that I'm supposedly Jewish, can't you?'

'But you don't believe in *any* religion, do you?' she asks with some seriousness.

'Me, shit no, never been in a church of any kind. Well, that's not true actually, I did go into a church in St Kilda a few times, cuz of food and clothes they hand out, you know.'

'No, I don't know,' she says with a cold, hard look that suddenly breaks into a broad smile and a laugh. 'Brightlight, I'm the model for the world's most spoilt child, didn't you know that?'

I didn't quite see the joke at laughing at her privileged upbringing when I come from a life of handouts, scavenging and dirty dives. But, not to offend, I pretend to and quickly change the subject.

'This old synagogue, where is it?'

'Oh, not far from here, but Brightlight, you're not thinking of leaving me for a synagogue are you?'

'No, no,' I quickly reply.

'Good, because we have some catching up to do,' she says as the two new drinks arrive.

The ring tone startles both of us. It sounded like Dracula getting ready to drink. Being Zoja's mobile phone, it probably is.

'Sorry, darling,' she says struggling to get her phone out of her jacket hanging over the back of her chair. She looks at who's calling her. 'Got to take this.' After a short conversation in Czech she closes her phone.

'Well, that's the end of that. Drink up Brightlight, I'm summoned back to the film location. Seems someone fucked up and they have to re-shoot a scene and they can't do it without me.' She downs her drink. 'But I'd like you to come with me and watch and wait, and wait, and wait, as that's what happens on film sets.'

'Look, thanks, Zoja, sounds interesting but I need get some things before catching the bus back to Terezín.'

'I'm really sorry I have to go, but promise me next time you stay more than a day...promise?'

'Yeah, next time, I promise.'

She calls the waiter over to settle the bill.

'Look, thanks for the meal, it was delicious and I'm so full.'

'Good, now they are waiting for me. Come.'

We climb the stairs out into daylight and into the gathering crowd, as the clock is about to strike three.

'That synagogue you mentioned. Which direction?' I ask.

'What? You really are going there?' she says with some surprise. 'If you follow this road you'll come to it. If you get lost, just ask anyone. Most of these people are tourists so they're either going, or have been.' She kisses me on each cheek. 'Brightlight, now next time you stay, right?'

'Right,' is all I have a chance to say before she rushes off and disappears into the crowd. I feel a bit let down. I was hoping to spend more time with her, but then I'm not used to being around people with busy lives.

CHAPTER 34

Synagogue…church…I wonder if they're the same just different religions? And I didn't know you had to pay to go in! But, with ticket and information sheet in hand, I follow the queue into the Pinkas Synagogue. As soon as I enter, I sense an invisible mist wrapping itself around me and once again I'm attracted by thousands of voices drawing me deeper inside until the mist retreats into the walls. I'm not sensing pain or agonising death like I usually do, this is a kind of peaceful death. Stepping into the main part of the synagogue totally stuns me. I'm confronted by the surrounding walls covered in what look like names. A glance at the brochure tells me they're the names of all the Czech Jews who perished in the Nazis extermination camps. I look back up to the walls, and riveted on an axis, I slowly rotate a full circle. The whole interior, and I mean all the walls of all the different rooms, chambers, or whatever they're called, are completely covered, not with computer-generated names, but each name carefully hand-painted. What surprises me even more, they're painted in the same colours I used on the wall of the old barracks. The emotion on the faces of the other visitors show they share my same intense reaction. I continue turning around and around to take in the enormity of this death register. Never have I seen such a thing nor understood the enormity of this part of history. Never have I seen it in such an easily understood and in-your-face-manner than just the 77,297 names of the dead. Never have I considered graffiti to have so much power and so much impact. This constant invisible force now leads me to the back wall of a smaller side chamber. The closer I get I begin to focus on two names, Lida and Josef Veselý…my grandparents.

Their names appear to pulsate in and out towards me in time with the thumping pulse in my head. I feel I'm about to fain and step back to break the connection. Their names merge back into the roll call of the dead. But, far from appearing insignificant, their names bring together the total impact of the horror of the inhumanity each and every one succumbed to. For the first time ever, I feel I'm Jewish.

For quite some time all I can do is stand and take in what's before me. But now, the voices start multiplying and crowding my mind. Each voice behind each name is calling out to me…no one else…only me. Louder and louder they ring in my head until I can no longer stand the burden of it. I need fresh air and desperately search through the fog of voices to find an exit. I finally do, but not out into the open air of today's world but into the restricted confines of the Old Jewish Cemetery. Thousands of eroded and broken grey tombstones are piled together as if washed up in a storm and unceremoniously dumped onto an inland island. Is there no end to death's display? I can hardly breath. I need to escape this connection but each path I follow leads to another pile of tombstones, then another and another, some with small pebbles balancing on them, some leaning so much they'll not stay upright for much longer. Then, finally to my relief, an exit sign. It's through another, smaller synagogue. I rush through, rudely pushing aside others as I go, until finally I step out onto the street and back into today's world.

I'm bent over with hands on knees, heart pounding and gasping for air. This first real Jewish exposure is far beyond what I expected. I'm confused. I'm bewildered. I've seen the ultimate power of what graffiti can achieve. I could never achieve such impact and I wonder what, if indeed anything, is expected of me. I now feel embarrassed at the utter crap I've produced over the years. I've now seen a truer purpose of what can be achieved from the walls that are willing to divulge their secrets.

I head back to Florenc and the bus terminal. But first, I'm sure somewhere near The Elf and all its graffiti, I'll find a place that sells spray paint.

The area seems strangely unfamiliar even though it was only about a week ago that Zac and I arrived. Yeah, Zac, shit, that's why I'm nervous, he could still be hanging around here.

I do find a paint store—well more like a store that also sells paint —and managed to find similar colours that match the painted names in the Pinkas Synagogue and what I used before. Now, with my shoulder bag and the store bag carrying my old clothes full of paint, I head for the bus back to Terezín.

I rush pass the Elf, pause at the rail overpass to check for trains, and then run down the hill.

'Well, well, looks who's fuckin' back.'

I freeze, sprung by Zac standing in the doorway of the Kain pub.

'Zac,' I fumble. 'Yeah…no…I mean…umm…so I see you're still hanging out here?'

'Free country.'

'No, I mean…'

I take a step back as he steps forward.

'Yeah, well, what's it to you now anyway?'

I can see this is not going to be pleasant but at least he isn't totally pissed yet.

'Fuck Zac, if that's the way you're gunna be, forget you saw me.'

'No point now is it? And look at you in ya new gear. How did ya get the money, hey? The money ya nicked from me wouldn't have been enough.'

Shit, I was hoping he hadn't noticed the missing money.

'I'm not that fuckin' stupid ya know,' he says, tapping a finger to his forehead.

I offer no response.

'So, did ya fuckin' dykey mate chip in, hey?'

I didn't want to go there so I thought I'd try and change the subject.

'Look, I got your message and I must say it was a bit fucking nasty.'

'Yeah, well whatcha expect, a fuckin' glowing report or something?'

Just then a group of backpackers pass and a couple of blokes come out of the Kain.

'Look, if we're gunna talk can we go somewhere else?'

'Talk about what?'

I wasn't sure, but I didn't want to have a scene on the street.

'We can go in here and you can buy me a drink with *my* fuckin' money.'

'Rather not, how about a beer at the Elf?'

'Not staying there anymore.'

I could tell he was hoping I'd ask where he was staying, but I wasn't interested.

'Look, if you don't want to talk, that's fine. I only came here to buy some stuff and head back to Terezín. So best I keep moving.'

'What stuff?'

'Paint and stuff.'

'What paint an' stuff?'

He's playing games with me and I'm loosing patience.

'Look, I got a bus to catch. Sorry I bumped into you.'

He grabs my arm as I start to walk away.

'Hey listen, how the fuck did you expect me to react? Shit, I mean ya fuckin' rob me, piss off and now ya doing ya thing without me!'

'Look, it's not like that.' I try to pull out of his grip. 'Things have got sorta weird.'

'Yeah, how?'

'Well, I've found out it's all, I don't know, it's all different.'

'What's different…and what've you found out?'

I hesitate. 'I can't tell you.'

He lets go my arm and steps back with a laugh. 'You fuckin' said ya wanted to go somewhere and talk and now you're fuckin' telling me you can't.'

'Look, Zac. A lot's happened to me in the last couple a days that's, well, sorta personal.'

'Yeah, well I thought we was fuckin' personal once.'

Another area I didn't want to get into, but I felt I owed him some sort of an explanation.

'Look, I've found out a lot about the family I didn't know I had, okay. And a lot about what happened here during the war and stuff.' I look for some sign of understanding from him, but nothing. 'There's a lot of personal stuff that I'm still trying to come to grips with, and, well, what I do is something I gotta do on my own.'

I don't know whether I explained that well or it was too much for his tiny brain to handle.

'Yeah, well what's that gotta do with goin' out on ya own and doin' a fuckin' SECRETSINCITY without me?

'Look, for a start, you don't own it. It was my idea, and now I'm on my own, that's all there is to it whether you like it or not. Anyway, you seem to be set up with this Dasha and your new mates, hey?' I didn't intend to bring that up but what the hell.

'Yeah, and they think what ya did was shit too.'

'Yeah, well I couldn't give a fuck what they think.'

'Well, at least *I* haven't turned gay.'

This was now getting nasty and I gave him a fierce glare.

'Fuck you, Zac.'

I start to walk away, but stop, dive a hand into my bag for a 500 Koruna note. 'Here's your fucking money.' I say, slapping it into his hand. 'I don't need your lack of generosity anymore. And for your information, I've just put another graff up on my site.'

I rush off fast enough so I can't hear what he's saying…and I couldn't care less anyway.

That went well, I reckon.

CHAPTER 35

Doran Rychtar leans back in his black leather executive chair impatiently waiting for his long-distance call to be answered. He looks at his Girard Perregaux watch. It's almost six o'clock and daylight is no longer streaming through the window. A manila file is spread open in front of him on his neatly organized mahogany desk in his equally organized, uncluttered and spacious office. The door is closed.

He hears a sharp 'Hello,' on the line and leans forward to pick up a sheet of paper from the open file. 'Doran here,' he says in English. 'Something's come up that I thought was well and truly sorted out.' He listens for a moment. 'No, not that…Cadastral Unit 566 in Terezín.' He places the paper back in the file as he listens, then interrupts. 'Well, it seems there's a daughter.' He picks up the page out of Briney's notepad. 'A Briney Ruza, She…' This time *he's* interrupted and listens with increasing annoyance then leans back in his chair while studying Briney's handwriting.

'No, you got it wrong then!' he snaps into the phone. 'And what may surprise you even more is that she's Australian and she's here in Prague.' A slight smile breaks the tense look on his face as he listens to the response.

'Yes, of course I'm sure, I had lunch with her today.' He listens. 'No, never mind how and why. The fact is she's making enquiries.'

He puts down the note, takes off his glasses and rubs his eyes before putting them back on, his frustration showing.

'No, she's still alive, in hospital,' he says shuffling through the documents in the file. 'Yes, Ruza Veselý.' He pauses. 'No, I don't want to hear about that…nothing has changed…it was a terrible accident, right?'

He listens for a moment.

'Well, maybe you should be worried because this girl has a website showing her graffiti to the world and her latest piece should interest you.' He turns to his desktop computer. Filling the screen is Briney's painting on the storage space. 'I'll email you the link and I expect you to take it from there…I'm not to be involved, you understand!'

He listens while hitting the 'send link' button then types in the first letter of the recipient's name and the rest is automatically added— Goddard Klein. Into the subject box he adds 'Briney Ruza [Veselý]' then hits the send button.

'It's on its way.' He listens for a moment then aggressively interrupts while flipping the file closed. 'No! I don't want to hear from you until this is taken care of…as it should have been already!'

He slams the phone back into its cradle and slumps back into his chair. Once again he removes his glasses to rub the strain from his eyes and mumbles aloud, 'Incompetent bastard!' After a moment to calm down, he leans towards the computer and scrolls down the page to look at Briney's earlier works for the umpteenth time, and then back to her latest. He studies it one last time before shutting down the computer and locking the file in a bottom drawer of his desk. With his desk clear, he smoothes his hands over the surface to rid it of any paper lint and rests forward on his elbows. With his hands together and the tips of his fingers tapping his lower lip, he contemplates this new development.

This is not the start to the day Goddard Klein expected. It's a sunny Saturday morning and already the temperature is climbing towards the high twenties with an expected top of thirty-two, fairly warm for an April day in Melbourne. Wearing khaki camouflage knee-length board shorts and a yellow sleeveless T-shirt hugging his ample stomach and showing off his tanned and tattooed broad arms, he was about to get into his new silver Mercedes-Benz SLK convertible for the drive down to his coastal retreat at Portsea to join his wife and friends for a weekend's sailing on the Bay. But the phone call has changed all that.

He opens his laptop to check his emails. There are several, but he's only interested in one and clicks on the link to MyRuza's MySpace page. The storage wall graffiti is the first to appear. After a minute or two studying the graffiti in detail, he stands and paces around his study, constantly glancing back at the screen with a puzzled, worried look on his face. Returning to the computer, he bends over it rather than sitting and scrolls down to her earlier pieces then back to the latest. Something else has taken his interest. He was well aware of both Ruza Veselý and Marika Veselý, whom he had comfortably put out of his mind until now, but this graffiti artist? He returns to the email from Doran that carried the link and her name…Briney! He fumbles in the pocket of his board shorts, takes out his mobile phone and punches in a number.

'It's me,' he says in a hushed tone even though there's no one else in the house. 'What's the latest on my so-called son?'

'Huh, huh…Yeah…well that's not fucking much is it?' His growing aggression has him stabbing a fat finger onto the desk. 'Look, can you tell me this then…what's the name of the fucking bird he was shacked up with?' He listens, his hand forming into a tight fist before slamming it down onto the desk upsetting a container of pens and pencils. 'And what was the tag this bitch used on her graffiti?' He listens then takes the phone from his ear to hold it only inches from his face and yells into it. 'Well, you useless piece of shit, I've just done your fucking work for you. They're both in fucking Prague!' He puts the phone back to his ear for a response. 'The fucking Czech Republic, that's fucking where!' He thumbs the hang up button and paces around the room tapping the phone against his chin. After a moment, he looks up the contact list in his phone and connects to an international number.

His patience is now on a short fuse, and after waiting for only a few seconds, he's about to hang up when he hears a voice and places the phone back to his ear.

'Goddard here,' he says and has a quick glance around the room before continuing to talk in German. 'There's some unfinished business and an extra job I…' He stops, stunned by the words coming back at him. 'What do you mean you were expecting me to call?' He stops pacing and listens intently. 'How come *you* saw this fucking piece of shit graffiti…you know the girl…how come…what the…what the fuck's his name?' He's about to throw the phone against the wall but controls himself. 'Listen…don't let him out of your fucking sight… understand? You lose him and you lose your fucking balls.' He listens for a moment. 'Well, if she has to fuck him until his dick falls off that'll save me cutting it off myself. Just make sure he's never out of anyone's sight, hear me? I'll get on the first flight I can and see you in a day or so.' He hangs up and slams the phone down onto the desk. 'Fuck!' he calls out and stomps over to a small bar set into a corner of his study where he pours himself a large neat Scotch and throws it down in one hit. After a quick glance at his watch, he rings Melbourne Airport for information on the earliest and fastest available flight to Prague. He pours another Scotch and paces the room until the girl comes back on the line to say a Lufthansa flight is leaving at fifteen-fifty this afternoon and arriving at nine-twenty the following morning local time, but, she adds, the only seats available are first and business class. 'Lufthansa, perfect,' he tells her, adding that he only travels first class and to book the flight with an open return date.

He looks at his car keys on the desk and makes another call.

'Darling,' he says in the most pleasant tone his rage will allow. 'Look, something urgent has come up and I need to catch a flight to Prague this afternoon. Pass on my apologies to our guests and make sure they all enjoy themselves. I should only be gone for a week at the most. And call my secretary, I know you have her number, and tell her, okay, bye.' He hangs up before his wife has a chance to say anything and heads for the bedroom to pack.

Deratz has stepped away from the phone and stands in front of Dasha's closed bedroom door with his tattooed arms crossed and his mind in overdrive. He snorts in anger as Dasha opens the door.

'Fuck Deratz, ya frightened shit outta me,' she says, surprised at seeing him just standing there.

'Where're you going?' he asks in Czech.

'Out for a fucking beer,' she snaps back at him.

Zac has stopped behind her, unable to pass or understand the conversation between the two.

'I've changed my mind,' says Dasha, turning back to him. 'We stay in tonight.'

'But I thought we were goin' for a beer?'

'I suddenly feel very horny.'

'Shit, Dasha, I could really do with a beer, and like, it's getting a bit fuckin' tender down there.'

'Well, fuck it! Looks like I'll have to find someone else.'

'Shit, come on Dash, I'm only fuckin' joking.'

'Yeah, well, get back in there and think about hardening up,' she says slamming the door in his face.

CHAPTER 36

What I miss most since being in Terezín is waking to the sound of birds in the morning. Instead I wake to retreating shadows in my imagination…or are they imagined? Does this power to sense secrets never sleep? Constantly filling my mind with discoveries that I don't recognise then mixing up those I do? I feel so out of my depth in this place, yet, here I am, unable to stop, unable to accept my own limitations and unable to decide what's fact or fiction. I notice another movement. Is it the last shadow to retreat before the room fills with daylight? No, it's a spider…I'm awake.

I can hear Evzen in the kitchen. He was about to go to bed when I arrived back late last night. I didn't want to keep him up he looked tired, so tired in fact he didn't even notice my new clothes. Or if he did, he didn't approve and just shuffled off to his bedroom. Anyway, now is a good time to tell him about meeting Zoja's old man. I stretch and swing my legs out from under the quilt.

'Morning Evzen,' I say gently so as not to startle him. He grunts and gives me a glance, then quickly look away as I stand in the doorway dressed only in a T-shirt and showing bare legs.

'You dress. I finish breakfast,' he orders.

Over toast, cheese and cold sausage I ask how Ruza was when he saw her yesterday. He just grunts that she was very tired and he didn't stay long. It makes me feel less guilty not going with him.

'Evzen,' I begin cautiously. 'I had a lunch yesterday with someone I met when I arrived in Prague.'

'Huh, ya,' he mumbles with a mouthful of toast.

'And I also met her father.'

He stops chewing and raises his head to look at me with a new interest.

'He's a property lawyer.' I wait for some comment but all I'm getting is his attention. 'I asked him about, you know, the claiming property thing.' There's still no comment. 'He said he'd helped many Jews to get their property back but because the deadline had passed years ago it's impossible to do anything now.' I pause for a reaction but still none. 'Anyway, after I explained that Marika had begun to search for proof but died before making a claim and then Ruza tried to find out if she'd found anything, he said he'd look into it. So I gave him this address and...'

He gulps down his mouthful of food and sits up in his chair with a worried look on his face.

'What? Like, you think I shouldn't have told him?'

'Ne, ne,' he says, trying unsuccessfully to lighten his expression. 'You no understand, but since Ghetto, I no trust strangers.' He lowers his eyes and cuts another mouthful of sausage. 'But...I sure you do right thing. Ignore this old man's suspicions.' He hesitates with a piece of sausage on toast at is mouth. 'You say to him Ruza in hospital?'

'Yeah, I told him she was very ill and he was sorry to hear it and hoped she'd get well soon.'

Suddenly, without any reason at all, the hospital corridor flashes in my mind with sinister shadows darting from ward to ward. I pour a coffee and push the mug across the table to Evzen. The hint to hurry doesn't go unnoticed.

'What is it?' he asks, his hand frozen around the handle of the mug. 'You hurry...you sense something wrong, ya?'

I never know what's driving me any more so I have no answer.

'No, um no, I don't think so...I...I don't know...I just feel we need to be with her until the danger's passed.'

'Danger! What you mean, danger?' he asks, sliding his hand away from the mug. 'We go now,' he says, pushing his chair back from the table.

It's way earlier than visiting hours when we arrive at the hospital. The corridors and wards are busy with the morning activities of handing out medicines, feeding, washing and changing beds. Doctors are doing their rounds while nurses are busily preparing new patients and those to be discharged. We seem to be going against the traffic of all this activity. Then I stop. Evzen's several paces ahead and he turns sensing I'm not following. Our eyes lock together for an instant before I spin around to look back down the corridor to study everyone we'd passed.

I turn back to him and see his confused and concerned expression. 'Um, it's nothing, let's go, quick!'

On entering the ward she was last in, we're both shocked to see her bed empty and a nurse changing the sheets. Evzen rushes to speak to her while I look around the ward. Evzen comes back to me with a worried look.

'She back in intensive care,' he says with a quiver in his voice while patting his chest. 'They no way to call me.'

'Ask the nurse if she had any other visitors.'

He can see I'm worried and turns back to the nurse. They talk and he comes back shaking his head and leads me out into the corridor.

'What is it?'

'Nurse say…she just come on duty…see no one.'

'I felt him pass me in the corridor. She must have seen him. Quick, we need to go to Ruza.'

At the intensive care ward we're told to wait until her doctor comes. Evzen asks if anyone else has been to see her or enquired about her condition. The answer is no, but that doesn't stop me from eyeing everyone, doctors, nurses, anyone who comes into the waiting area or walking past in the corridor. Then I feel Evzen's hand on my arm for support. His face is pale and I ease him into a seat.

'Do you need a tablet?' I ask.

He shakes his head and takes a deep breath but I can hear the effort of getting air into his lungs. At least if he's having an attack, he's in the best place.

Several moments pass before he has the energy to speak.

'Who you think...want see Ruza?' There's still a quiver in his voice.

'I've no idea, but...' Shit, am I starting to over-react to everything?

'You think...he threat to Ruza?'

'I don't know, but I did sense she had a visitor. Are you sure she saw no one after she came back from Australia?'

He shakes his head. 'Ne...I know of no one. But...I not know who she see when she go to Prague that one day.' He takes out his handkerchief to wipe his forehead. 'She different when she return.'

'Different? What do you mean?'

'She...she go through all Marika's things again.'

'Again?'

'Ya, when she first come back and learn Marika is dead...she go through all her things. I think it natural...she no see her for many year...she need find out all she can about her.' He waits till a nurse passes. 'After she return from Prague...she go through Marika's things again.' He pauses, his finger tapping his knee. 'She...she no just look through her things...more she look for something.' He looks at me to make sure I understand what he's trying to say. I nod for him to continue. 'First time, I watch her...she study each thing she find...one by one she would stroke it, put it to her face to smell and feel Marika's being...to again know her sister. But this time...I sure she look for one thing only.'

'Do you know if she found it?'

He shrugs his shoulders. 'I ask if she look for something...that I might help...but she no want me to help.'

I study him for a moment as his hands begin to shake more. I can see he's getting upset, but he continues.

'I...I think about it now...after second time she go through Marika's things...she angry...so I think she not find what she look for.'

Just then a doctor approaches us. Evzen stands and I remain seated while they talk in Czech. The doctor glances at me, obviously asking who I am. I stand and Evzen introduces me as Ruza's daughter. The conversation continues in English. We're told her condition is critical and that we should prepare for bad news. Evzen begins to wobble on his legs and grabs at his chest as his eyes widen and become glazed over. The doctor immediately calls for a nurse.

'He's got pills,' I say, finding them in his shirt pocket. The doctor reads the label, sees they're nitroglycerin tablets and places one under Evzen's tongue. The nurse returns with a wheelchair, eases him into it and immediately wheels him away. I'm about to follow but the doctor suggests I stay, saying he'll be okay once the tablet takes effect but they'll need to do some tests. He motions for me to sit and joins me on the next chair.

'I believe the hospital tried to get in touch with your father but they have no phone number on record,' he says.

I'm about to correct him that Evzen is not my father, but decide it's too much of a hassle to explain. 'No,' I reply instead. 'And I don't have a mobile.'

He looks surprised. 'Maybe you should get one and let the hospital know the number once you do.'

I nod, unsure of how to go about it but I'll work something out.

'Now, I must go and check on your mother.' He stands and starts to walk away, but stops and turns back to me. 'Your mother kept calling out your name when she was semi-conscious, I thought you should know.' He turns and is gone.

I'm left isolated in the hum and sterile odour of the hospital. The only remnants of a recently discovered family are now both patients with death hovering over one, if not both. Suddenly I feel so very much alone.

It's almost an hour before I'm told that Evzen's resting and will be kept overnight for observation, and that, if I wish, I can visit Ruza for just a moment even though she's asleep under heavy sedation. I follow the nurse into the intensive care ward. A sight that depresses me even more. She's transparently pale and the beeps and bings from the monitors attached to her are the only proof she's still alive. The nurse tells me I should stay for only a moment and allows me some space.

All I can do is stand and look at her withered old body. Is this the only memory I'll have to keep, of her lying at death's door? Other sounds become more obvious as I hear someone in another cubicle crying. Will I be doing the same soon? Can I cry over her dead body, I wonder? Then, a now-familiar feeling comes over me. I'm urged to place a hand on the white, sterile wall. Nothing! The sense is there, the sense I feel from walls, but not this wall. I look down at Ruza, the sense is strong, calling me, and then, to my shock, her hand moves. I hesitate before sliding a hand over her cold flesh and close my eyes to concentrate. What is it? What's her secret? Is she trying to pass it on to me? I hold my breath and try to ignore the pounding pulse in my head. I feel her hand move as a spark of energy passes between us. A sudden gasp for much-needed breath snaps me back to reality. From the eerie silence, the beeps and bings return and I can hear the crying from the nearby cubicle again. Fearing the worst, I look at Ruza but she is again peacefully resting, her hand now relaxed. I give it a gentle squeeze of acknowledgement—for what, I'm yet to understand.

Taking the doctor's advice, I decide to walk into the centre of Litoměřice in the hope of finding a place that sells mobile phones. I don't expect there'd be one in Terezín somehow.

I had an idea where the centre of the town was when we left the bus terminal, so I walked back along the bus route till I could see some shops. There was nothing that sold phones until I came out into a large open square surrounded by shops and cafés. On my left is the Elektro Šípek, a large electronic store with arched windows and sandwich boards either side of the entrance. One is advertising mobile phones.

Luckily the young guy serving speaks some English. He works in the shop part-time while studying International Relations and is more than happy to further his English skills and at the same time learn a bit about Australia. But all I want is to buy the cheapest phone and register the number with the hospital as quick as I can. Anyway, I weaken a little and flirt a good deal and score a lesson on how to use it. I've never used one before and everything on the box and the enclosed booklet is in Czech or Russian or both. With a number and a connection, I ask one last favour—to ring the hospital and tell them I now have a phone and to pass on the number. Of course he willingly agrees and now having my number, asks if he can call me some time. I give him a wicked smile —without the slightest interest in accepting his offer—thank him with a peck on his blushing cheek and leave.

CHAPTER 37

Before I go back to the apartment to look through Marika's things in the hope of finding a clue to what Ruza was searching for, I want to have another look around Terezín with this property claim thing in mind. I mean, it's now, what, six or so years since claims could be made and it makes me wonder why there's still so many empty, rundown buildings. Sure, I realise the town's seen as some sort of a war ghetto monument, and maybe that's why nobody wants to live here, but I just have this gut feeling all's not kosher. Shit! Where did that word come from?

As I walk through the central park looking at the surrounding buildings, I wonder if I'm wrong. Most look like they've been renovated and occupied. But, once I'm through the park and into the side streets things are different. Building after building show signs of neglect: eroded plaster, exposed bricks, boarded-up windows and rusted downpipes all the way to the fortress wall. I turn and look back down the street for a broader view, and what I hadn't noticed before becomes clear. The flood of 2002 was far more destructive than I imagined and left a line of corroded, stained and missing plaster to the height of my chest all the way down the street. No wonder people drowned. Shit, then it hit me. Could I be wrong? What if this man I imagined drowned Marika…was actually trying to save her? I shiver at the possibility and the doubt it raises. Have I become too much of a believer in my own game of tempting viewers with hidden secrets when there are none?

'Tell me something,' I say to the unflinching wall beside me. 'Give me a sign that I can control the search for secrets.'

I get no answer, but the cold drab facade has seized my attention. Why? I step back onto the road, unable to look away. There's nothing unusual, it's in as much need of repair as the others, its style is rather plain compared to some but, as I isolate each detail, a groan of realisation erupts through me. What I'm seeing on this wall is material graffiti: doors, windows, eaves, downpipes and numbers.

Numbers! The white house number stencilled on a small blue plaque above the door, that's what's attracting my attention. I get out my notebook and a pen and write down the number, then the number above the next door and the next each side of the road until I reach the corner. There's another blue sign with the name of the street, DLOUHÁ. I refer to the map of the ghetto I got at the museum. There's no Dlouhá Street but I remember Zoja telling me the street names on the map were the German names. I decide to make my own map by tracing the basic street layout and adding all the current street names and the building numbers of the whole town.

It's late in the afternoon before I get back to Marika's apartment. I add the street name, ŘEZNICKÁ ULICE, the building number and take a photo as I've done with all the others. As I zoom in and the camera automatically focuses, something catches my eye in the LCD screen. I peer over the camera but it's too high to make out anything clear so I look back into the LCD screen and zoom in closer. It's very hard to make out, but above the numbered blue plaque there's something red showing through the fading paint. I need a closer look and after a look around to see if anyone's watching, I gingerly stand on the rubbish bin hoping it won't collapse under my weight. It doesn't and I carefully scrape away the thin layer of covering paint with the door key. It's another number, but different to the one below. I write the number down on the map and take a photo of both.

With the map laid out on the dining table, I scratch my head having absolutely no idea what I'm looking for. With Evzen not around to maybe shed some light, I lean back in the chair stumped. Then I remember what I'd originally planned to do before the numbers got in the way.

I hadn't taken much notice of Marika's things before. Personal things I mean. All my clothes and stuff I keep in my bag or dumped on the floor, so I've never had reason to go into any of the drawers or the wardrobe. The bedside table is first. The top drawer is filled with her underwear and a strong smell of camphor. But I'm a bit surprised. I envisaged Marika to be neat and tidy. I mean the whole place is, so I expected she'd have her clothes folded and neatly placed, but her underwear is pretty messed up. The next drawer's the same. Someone else has been through the drawers, probably Ruza, but I would have thought she'd be a bit neater.

The wardrobe also smells of camphor but with added mustiness. Here the few dresses and coats are hung in a more orderly fashion. I separate the hangers to look over each garment and check through any pockets…nothing. One of the coats has fallen off its hanger and lies crumpled at the bottom of the wardrobe. I pick it up and her aura is still strong. I sense a kind, gentle person who hid so much sadness. A woman who liked a particular perfume because it covered up the smell of an ointment she used for a skin condition. A woman who continued to darn and repair the years of wear to her clothes rather than replace them. A woman who suffered from something that was curving her spine and who struggled under the weight of this heavy coat in winter. I brush my hand down the woollen fabric into one of the side pockets. There's nothing there, nothing material that is, but a feeling other hands have also searched for something. I close my eyes to concentrate. Ruza has been through the pocket…but she wasn't the only one. I'm getting a strong indication of a man, a big man, the same man who sat in Evzen's chair and who I still believe visited Ruza…and the man who once had his hand on the door handle of the storage room. But what's even worse, I reckon this man's hand was in the pocket very recently, even as recently as today! I shiver at the thought…the hospital! I'm sure I passed him in the corridor heading towards the exit. Shit, he was here only hours ago.

CHAPTER 38

The Lufthansa flight from Melbourne via Frankfurt touches down on a damp runway at Prague's Ruzyně Airport at the scheduled time of 09:30. Within twelve minutes the first and business class passengers are disembarking. Goddard Klein is the first passenger off and rushes to the customs counter ahead of all the other passengers. Once through, he bypasses the baggage collection carousels, as his only luggage is the carry-on cabin roller he's dragging behind him.

The hours confined in the air have frustrated him and now he's arrived, his temper is building. He rushes out of the terminal and jumps into the first cab at the rank to the outrage of those waiting in line. The driver plants his foot on the accelerator with a promised 200-Koruna tip if he gets to the destination quick smart. His attempt at a welcoming conversation to a new arrival in his country is crushed with sharp instruction to 'shut the fuck up and drive!' as Goddard checks that his mobile phone has picked up the local network and makes a call.

'I've arrived,' he says in German. He checks the rear view mirror to make sure the driver is concentrating on the road and not his conversation. 'Is my parcel still under wraps?' There's a pause as he gets the answer he's expecting. 'Take it to the factory and I'll meet you there in a couple of hours.' He's about to hang up then adds in a sterner voice, 'The parcel is still in the dark I hope.' He hangs up without waiting for an answer—it was not a question, but a threat.

In his suite at the Hotel Josef, there's no time to unpack, just a quick piss and a wash before making another call.

'Yeah, morning, Goddard Klein here, is Doran in?' he says to the secretary, straining to calm his manner and temper his impatience.

'Goddard? This is not an international call. Are you here in Prague?' says a surprised and concerned Doran.

'Yeah, just got in. I've got something I need to do for the next few hours. How about we meet at the Hotel Josef bar, say five o'clock?'

'Five o'clock…ahh…why are…'

Doran's phone goes dead. He looks at the handset before slamming it down into its cradle. 'Rude bastard,' he says out loud then leans back in his chair wondering why Goddard Klein has decided to come all this way to Prague when in the past he'd mostly stayed back in Australia with others to arrange things for him there. Now, having to meet him face-to-face is something Doran is not looking forward to.

CHAPTER 39

On top of the usual nerves and nausea that hospitals bring on, I'm bloody tired. The thought that someone had been in the apartment without forcing the door kept me awake, despite the chair I wedged under the door handle before going to bed.

Evzen's recovered and I find him sitting beside her bed. She's still out to it and looks much the same, which even to me isn't a good sign. He tries to convince me she's improved slightly, but I'm sure it's wishful thinking.

We sit watching her in silence. There are so many unanswered questions that, my feeling is, she'll take to her grave. The nurse suggests we should go as they need to change the sheets and wash her. The hospital will call if there's any change and she confirms they have my new number.

As we walk along the corridor, I ask, 'Evzen, I want to talk to you about something. Can we get a coffee somewhere?'

For a moment I think his mind is back in the ward and he hasn't heard me, but then he nods and suggests the hospital café. It's not my preferred option—wanting to get out of this depressing environment —but it will have to do.

Evzen sits while I get the coffees.

'I want to ask you about numbers,' I say after we've had a sip of the bitter and burnt coffee. 'Street numbers, you know, the white ones on blue?' He gives me a blank look. 'Well, I came across another number on a red panel that was sorta painted over on the outside of our building. What is it?' That seemed to get his interest.

'That číslo popisné…um…how you say…number to describe building.'

'So it's not a street number?'

'Ne, it Cadastral registry number.'

'So, like, what's the Cadastral registry and why paint over them?'

'It where all property is registered…red number no more used in Terezín.' He looks at me questioningly. 'I no see that number… building painted before we move in. So, how you see it?'

'Would this number still be in the registry?' I ask, skirting around his question.

'Ya, I think,' he replies, without showing any more interest

'Um, wouldn't that show who the owner of our building is, or was?'

'No point now,' he says with a slight shrug of his shoulders.

Not for him maybe, but I'm now wondering if Marika or Ruza had checked. And then I remember something Ruza had said.

'Ruza said she found the new owner but they refused to see her. Do you think she knew the number?'

'In Ghetto…she very young and keep repeating things…maybe she remember.' He takes another sip of his coffee. 'You have number?'

'Yeah, I wrote it down.'

His eyes start roaming the room. There's something churning around in his mind. Then he takes a last sip of his coffee and pushes his chair back from the table.

'Come, we go.'

'Where?'

'Cadastral Office. Is not far from here.'

It was only a short walk from the hospital, but half an hour before Evzen's called to one of the two windows. I've given him the map I made with the street names and numbers and our building with the red number circled. As I wouldn't understand a word, I stay seated.

I watch Evzen as he switches his weight from one leg to the other. His once broad shoulders are hunched, his scruffy grey hair thinning and his pants hanging low from loss of weight. He keeps looking back at me with a nod each time the woman attending to him goes to find something. As the minutes pass, I see his discomfort from standing so long until finally he hobbles back and flops into the chair beside me. Breathless and trembling, he mumbles something in Czech while shaking his head.

'They want know all about you…but tell you nothing,' he says, then, to my surprise, gives me a cheeky look. 'But I learn lot in Ghetto… and years under Soviet silence…I learn to get what they think they do not give.'

His smile broadens. I think it's the first time I've seen him smile cuz it's the first time I've noticed his stained crocked teeth and the gaps where some are missing.

'I still have charm, ya?'

'Yeah, you're real charming,' I respond, trying to hide my true thoughts.

'Company who own building…ústav Statek.'

'What? A company and not private?'

'Ya, but…I find out more…they own many other.'

'Many! Like how many?'

'Ten…twelve, maybe. I mark them down,' he replies, handing back the map.

I look over it and count those he's marked, twelve. But not just apartments…twelve buildings!

'Shit! This company owns nearly a quarter of Terezín?'

'Ya, maybe, but,' he says waving a crooked finger at me. 'It seem some buildings they own…are…um…in negotiation for sale.' he pauses to take a breath. 'I think I know who they negotiate with.'

'What? I don't understand. They're negotiating with only *one*?'

He nods then shakes his head. 'Um…maybe once, ya…not now. There was talk Terezín become town of education…um…place of learning. It was intended University take over town.'

'So, it's the University they want to sell to?'

'Ya, but since flood, University cannot afford…too much repair needed.'

'So?'

'So it now hoped different institutions…from all over…buy a building…one for art, one for medicine and so on…there already school of music.'

'And you reckon this company has bought all these properties knowing this?'

'Ya, I certain,' he says and places a hand on my knee. 'This company, ústav Statek…I think in English it mean Institute Estate.'

I lean back in the seat to think for a moment.

'You didn't get a chance to find out when they took ownership of our building, did you?'

His expression changes from a satisfied look of a job well done to one of serious concern. 'Ya…final day of claim deadline.'

I'm staring at him, bewildered. 'But how? I mean how could they if they didn't have proof of ownership when it belonged to Marika and Ruza?'

He shrugs his hunched shoulders. 'That…I not know,' he says and then raises his finger at me like a teacher about to correct a student. 'But, we still no have proof of ownership. Number on building is only part of document number. They can only tell of current owner. Full certificate number needed before they tell who past owner. If that known…it would have been enough to make claim.'

'So, what? You're telling me that Marika and Ruza both thought they owned the building but it could all be a dream?'

'Ne, ne,' he says eagerly. 'I saw document…'

'You what?' I shout, attracting the attention of others in the room. I lean closer and in a quieter voice, 'Then why the fuck haven't you said where it is?'

He taps his finger to his mouth in protest at my language.

'I say I see it…not have.'

I'm trying to understand what he's telling me.

'I see your grandfather show Marika and Ruza. Then he hide it.'

'The old barracks?'

'Ya, it last place he could hide document before he…you see what happen to him in street.'

'So, you've been looking for the document, as well as the ring, all this time?'

He shakes his head. 'I look for ring first. It only after property claim law came in that I also look for document. But I sure…after so many years…it now rotted away or eaten by rats.'

Together we sit speechless for some time. I figure we're each considering our failed expectations. Then, quietly and under his breath, I hear him mumble, 'But, at least Ruza save something to remember her mamma and pappa…that why I no stop searching for *my* pappa's ring.'

'What? Sorry, what did you just say?'

He doesn't answer immediately, his mind swimming in the past. 'A clock…I remember Ruza save her pappa's clock…I only see it once before she hide it.' He pauses, noticing a change in my expression. 'Is something wrong?'

'I have it. I have the clock.'

He's stunned. 'You?'

I fish around in my bag and take it out. His eyes widen, his shaking hands reach out. I hand it to him. At first touch, I can see he's jolted back to the dark past.

'How you get this?'

'I took it. When I was being taken from her, I…I just took it that's all.' I didn't want to go into detail.

He immediately hands it back. 'You must never let this out of your sight! You not know how much this is worth…in memory alone.'

I'm about to take it but see sadness and fresh tears in his eyes. 'You hold it for a minute.'

His hands stop shaking as he cradles the clock in its leather case. Then, as if blind, he delicately strokes the outer casing until he finds the latch and opens it. He closes his eyes and places the flat of his hand on the clock face while the tips of his fingers rest on the inside of the cover.

I watch his display of sensitivity and sadness and in a moment of sympathy, I place a hand on his. I feel his hand tense up and his eyes open wide.

'What is it?' I ask.

'I now know what you feel,' he says, placing the clock in my hand.

'What do you mean?'

'Your touch…I feel it.'

'What? I don't understand.'

'Your touch…you pass your power…in clock…I feel it.'

'What're you talking about? Feel what?'

'In clock…something of property.'

I look closely at the clock, turning it this way and that, looking into all the joins and frayed stitching of the case to see if anything looks altered.

'I don't see anything.'

'I sense it…like you…I sense it…but it is you who must find it.'

'It? What's it? What am I supposed to be looking for? I can't see anywhere a document can be hidden.'

'Not document…it something else…what you last sense?'

I look at him confused. I think he's bloody serious.

'Well, nothing today.'

'Ya, yesterday then…what you do yesterday?'

'Yesterday?' I don't want to tell him I was searching through everyone's things or that I wasn't the only one. So, I decide to skip that.

'Well, it was the number that was painted over. The old red building number.'

He nods.

I see a hint in his nod. 'The numbers?'

He nods again.

I look down at the clock, turning it over and over and holding it at an angle to the light to see if there's any invisible inscription that may have left an indent or something. But I see nothing.

'All I see are the instructions, but they're in Czech.' I say, showing him.

He nods again without offering any assistance.

I close my eyes and concentrate on what we've just learnt. The numbers, the property, the company that now owns the building and anything related that comes to mind. I feel a tingle of energy at my fingertips. There's something, but what is it? I hand the open case back to Evzen.

'The instructions…' I take in a deep breath. 'Read them.'

Before taking the clock he reaches into his coat pocket for a pair of glasses I never knew he had. They're old, as cloudy as the clock face, the arms are loose and the wire frame, broken at the bridge, is held together with tape. He sits them on the tip of his nose, focuses onto the fine print and reads the instructions silently before translating. There's nothing in the instructions that have any connection at all. He lifts the clock closer to his eyes, adjusts his glasses and with a shake of his head, hands back the clock.

'On bottom…under name of maker…very small…I cannot read.'

I hold the clock up close. On the bottom, below the instructions is the name of the manufacturer, *Mauthe*. Under that is what looks like a product serial number. I read it out, 'VOOR430772/566'.

'The map…you give,' he asks. It's still on my lap and I hand it over. He looks over the top of his glasses. 'Say number again.' I repeat the number. He mumbles to himself then gives a triumphant nod.

'That no product number,' he says with a strong sense of certainty. 'VOOR…I believe that initials for…Vlastnictví osvědčení o registraci.'

I look at him blankly.

'Property Ownership Registration Certificate…the last three numbers…they are same as number on building…this number of ownership document.'

I look again at the instructions adhered to the inside of the clock's case. 'But this is printed, not handwritten?'

He snorts with a slight grin. 'Humph! Your grandpappa…he work in Ghetto print shop.'

'What? You're saying he had this instruction printed and stuck it over where the original was?'

He gives no response.

'So, like, what does that mean?'

'It mean…copy of certificate at Cadastral…now we have number…we can ask see copy.'

'Can you go back to the counter and see?' I eagerly suggest.

He shakes his head. 'We need go Prague…central office…old documents only kept there.'

I look back at the clock for the time. 'Do you know where the office is? Can we go there now?'

There's a lack of enthusiasm on his face.

'Look Evzen, I know this is tiring for you. I'd go myself but I can't speak the language.' I look back at the time again. 'Look if we catch the next bus, I'm sure you can be back home before dark.'

Seeing the importance of it and, I guess, thinking it's the least he can do for Ruza and Marika, he agrees.

CHAPTER 40

Zac is woken from a deep sleep by a sharp slap to the side of his face. Startled, he heaves himself up on one elbow, shakes the echo out of his head, rubs his stinging cheek and sees Dasha standing over him.

'Fuck! What was that for?'

'You stink,' she says.

'Your fault.'

'Get yourself clean and dressed. We go out…now!'

He rubs his eyes, sniffs and asks, 'Out! Shit, I need more sleep. What's the fuckin' time?'

'Better hurry…Stik and Deratz no like waiting.' She walks out of the bedroom leaving the door wide open.

Zac peers into the lounge room and sees the two men sitting watching him with grim expressions on their faces. 'Shit!' he mumbles and flings his legs over the side of the bed, grabs some clothes and heads to the bathroom.

Dressed and with his long hair still wet and bedraggled, he's roughly ushered outside and into the back seat of a red 1998 Škoda Felicia. Dasha follows him in as Stik enters from the opposite side. Zac is now tightly sandwiched between them in the cramped back seat. Without a moments delay Deratz throws the car into gear and plants his heavy foot on the accelerator. The oil-starved engine obeys, but with a protesting cough of thick black exhaust.

Unnerved and confused at this rough treatment, Zac attempts to lighten the mood and add some of his trademark Aussie humour.

'Hey guys, loosen up. I feel like I'm in a fuckin' gangster movie and being *taken for a ride*.' But no one responds or even bothers to look in his direction.

After several minutes they pass the Florenc bus terminal and drive under the railway overpass then turn sharply into a small car park where two elevated rail overpasses converge. Zac hunches down to look out the front window at a squalid factory wedged beneath a two-tiered signal box. The many years of oil, grime and metal dust have masked out whatever colour there was, turning the whole scene into a dark, blackened set suitable for a horror movie.

Stik is first out of the car, dragging Zac with him by the arm.

'Yeah, Yeah, I'm coming,' he protests. 'Watch the tat, man. No need to be so bloody rough, hey?' Stik smiles and tightens his grip on the fresh, tender tattoo.

There's a double door to the left of the single-story factory that shows just a hint of the original brown paint. Three thick wire-meshed windows are evenly spaced between the door and a small protruding outhouse. A sign on one of the double doors reads PŘÍSNĚ ŽÁDNA POLOŽKA, *STRICTLY NO ENTRY*. The other door is slightly ajar and Deratz pushes it open halfway, allowing a thin sliver of light into the dark interior. The windows grimed over long ago allow just enough light to pick up the floating dust. Zac is shoved into the darkness, trips over something and tumbles to the floor. Their sudden violent attitude towards him is starting to make him seriously apprehensive. He looks back. Deratz and Dasha are standing just inside the doorway, silhouetted against the grey light from outside.

The smell of grease, grime and metal shavings adds to the stale air.

From deep in the factory gloom, Zac hears a sound and turns his head in the direction it came from. He hears it again, a hollow, metallic click then a flash of light before a hollow clunk extinguishes the glow. This is repeated again and again and with each flash of light, a little more detail of a figure is revealed. Another click and a flash, but this time there's no extinguishing the flickering flame from a Zippo cigarette lighter as it sheds a faint light on an approaching face. Zac is roughly hoisted back onto his feet, his arms held tight behind him. The large figure looming out of the darkness is now close enough to recognise. Zac's eyes widen in disbelief—it's impossible, it can't be— whack! The heavy hand loosens a tooth and draws blood. He'd be back on the ground if it weren't for Stik holding him up. Another whack. This time a large gold ring on the assailant's stubby finger gouges a strip of skin from under Zac's chin. There's no immediate pain as his head is still numb from the first blow, but his vision has cleared and he stiffens in fear as he recognises his father.

The hand that hit him twice is now wrapped tightly around his throat as the other holds the lighter, its flame long and fierce only inches in front of his eyes and illuminating both faces, one showing sweat and fear, the other sweat and rage.

Goddard's grip on his son's throat tightens, while the heat from the flame begins to sting. Zac tries to push back, but the brick wall of Stik behind him is immovable. He's unable to speak, even if he wanted to, but what was there to say anyway? It's left to his old man.

'You, fucking scum,' yells Goddard, spitting into his son's face and tightening his grip even more. Zac starts to feel faint from lack of oxygen and fear. 'You have no fucking idea of the shit you left for me to clean up. And you've no fucking idea of the deep shit you're in now.'

With a shove he releases his grip on Zac's throat. 'I...I...don't know...what...what ya talking about.' he stutters gasping for breath,

'Shut the fuck up,' yells Goddard. 'You never were too fucking bright, were you? You and your fucking little slut think you can just get on a plane and that's the end of it. Well, you pathetic little piece of shit, you're both going to pay big time.'

There's a moment of eerie silence before Goddard steps back, lights a cigarette and blows a cloud of smoke into Zac's face. He's well aware of his father's violent capabilities, having witnessed many times his strong-arm control over his construction site workers. He's also well aware that his father is not one to play games with, and now is not the time to make matters worse, but to own up and admit his mistake.

'Look,' says Zac, searching into the depths of his street cunning for an excuse. 'I probably did you a favour, right? I mean the car was insured, right? And like, you always want the latest model, right?'

'Fuck the car, you little dumb shit. I'd already sold the fucking thing and it was waiting to be picked up.' He grabs his son by the shirt, popping some buttons and ripping out some of his sparse chest hair. 'You put a lot of people under the spotlight with the fucking limp-brain deal you had with your fucking street scum.'

Zac now realises how deep is the shit he's in. The deal he had with his street mates was that in return for them knocking off his old man's car and splitting with him what they got for it, he'd introduce them to his drug supplier—the same dealer his old man has used for years to keep his construction workers happy.

'You see, dumb little pricks like you don't see beyond their fucking noses,' says Goddard, pressing his stubby finger onto Zac's nose. 'I spent years setting up this dealer network to keep my workers happy and I knew you were using it for you regular pissy little deals. But, being such a fucking good father, I thought that's the least I can do for my dope-head shit of a son, who, with a bit of luck, would fucking overdose and die.' He lets go of Zac's shirt and gives him another backhander under the chin, opening up a deeper gash, then steps back into the shadows. 'That little fucking deal you struck with your street scum has caused a lot of people a lot of grief. You exposed my supplier cuz those grimy little shits couldn't keep their fucking mouths shut and they spread the word all over bloody Melbourne. And for what…the price of a fucking old Merc, just so you and your street slut could go on a fucking holiday.'

By now Zac's eyes are getting used to the dim light and he begins to make out remnants of some of the old machinery that once turned, rumbled and spat out whatever they spat out.

'You know what's about to happen to this place?' asks Goddard, his back now to Zac while he taps an upturned crate with his foot. 'In a few months all this'll be bulldozed for a new development and my friends here will no longer have their headquarters.' He turns back to Zac. 'Sad, hey?' He doesn't expect or wait for an answer. 'But I doubt you really know much about your new friends here, do you? You just sort of ran into them, got friendly with them and got pissed with them.' He glances to the door where Dasha is still standing. 'And got fucked by them too, hey?' He reaches down and carries the crate over to Zac. 'Well, sit down, my dumb-ass son and I'll tell you a little story before I decide what the fuck I'm going to do with you.'

Zac's roughly pushed down onto the crate as Goddard strolls around, turning over rubble with his feet and kicking empty beer bottles out of the way until he's at the far wall, still in darkness. He squats on his haunches at some rubbish and flicks open his lighter to ignite a discarded Pizza box. As the flame slowly spreads so does the light onto the wall. Hanging there is a large flag, a red flag, and in its centre a white circle carrying the symbol of the Nazis party, the Swastika. Zac shudders at the sight and looks around at Deratz and Dasha at the door then back to the flag. He knew a lot about his father and his underworld dealings but not about this.

Standing beside the flag, Goddard has one hand behind his back and the other holding the cigarette to his lips, a pose that seemed choreographed for the occasion but for the lack of an SS uniform. 'You remember your grandfather, don't you?' he says, his voice echoing through the hollow space.

Zac is too stunned to speak, but he has a strong memory of his grandfather. Old, stocky, grey and with a steely look that always frightened him as a small boy. He never spoke much but whenever Zac met him, the old man would just stare into his eyes, one hand, that never seemed to have any strength, rested trembling in his lap, while the other, which did have movement, would squeeze his leg, high, so high Zac would feel the freckled old hand tighten as it reached and nestled against his cock. Yes, he remembers him well.

'Your grandfather should be living the life of a hero here in Prague. He was a true warrior. He single-handedly removed more Jewish scum from the Ghetto than anyone else. He knew his role and he took it very, very seriously.' Goddard steps away from the flag. 'Now, it has come to my attention that your Jewish girlfriend is stirring up some shit here and sticking her fucking nose in where it's not fucking wanted.'

Briney being Jewish surprises Zac and he mumbles 'No!'

'What?' Goddard asks, approaching. 'What was that you were trying to say?'

'Look I don't see her anymore, right. We split as soon as we got here.'

Goddard grabs Zac's shirt once again and lifts him up from the crate to hold him nose-to-nose. 'Well, I have news for you, you little shit.' His words send a stream of saliva over Zac's sweating and bloodied face. 'You two little lovebirds are about to link up again, see, and when you do you're gunna get her to pack up her spray cans and get the fuck back to Oz and bury herself in some fucking drain somewhere with her stupid art.' He stares deep into Zac's wide eyes to make sure his words had sunk in. 'I can't hear anything?' questions Goddard.

'I...I...don't even know where she is and...um...and...what if she doesn't want to go, anyway?'

'Well, you little shit, you find her and you make her go, or, you know what? Your friends here will do it for you and they don't fuck around. If she plays the stubborn little bitch, she's gunna get very hurt.' He leans closer. 'And I mean so very, very fucking hurt that she'll regret she was ever born to such a short life. And one more thing...you go down with her.'

Zac knows enough to take the threat seriously. At the age of about five he accompanied his father to one of his construction sites. With his hand tightly held in his father's, he was forced to watch and learn as one of his henchmen was ordered to beat a worker to within an inch of his life. Then at the end, as they walked past the crumpled, bleeding body, his old man laid a heavy steel-capped boot into the victim's chest. Ever since, Zac has never been able to get the sound out of his mind of ribs cracking and the hiss of escaping air from punctured lungs.

'Now, I've got things to do so I'll leave you in the loving care of your new friends,' says Goddard, shoving Zac back into the strong arms of Stik. With his arms wrenched behind him, Zac's shirt is torn further, baring his heaving chest and exposing his nipple ring that catches the light. 'Well, what the fuck is this, hey?' says Goddard ripping the shirt wide. 'What fucking poofter thing is this then?' He runs a finger down Zac's trembling sweaty and blood-smeared chest to his left nipple and the ring hanging from it. His large fat hand squeezes down over the nipple and in one swift motion rips the ring away together with the pierced flesh. Zac's scream is stifled by Stik's hand coming from behind to clamp tightly over his mouth leaving bubbles of snot from his nose as the only indication of his agony.

'That's a reminder to show your little Jew darling that we mean business.' He looks down at the ring in his bloodied hand. 'And this I'll keep as a reminder of the son I never had.' He walks to the door and whispers to Deratz in German, 'I don't want him dead hear me. He still has some use.' Deratz nods his understanding and shows an eagerness to get on with the beating. 'And cut that fucking hair of his off!' he adds. Dasha remains in the doorway, forcing Goddard to squeeze past her. He gives her a salacious glance. She pushes out her ample bosom against the half unbuttoned leather waistcoat she always wears and seductively gives a tilt of the head. Goddard gives her a faint smile then disappears into the car park; his smile broadening as he hears behind him muffled yells of pain following the meaty thud of skin on skin.

CHAPTER 41

The main Cadastral at Kobylisy is a twenty minute tram ride from Florenc. Unlike the small, simple office in Litoměřice, this is huge. Seven floors, sorta modern with a curve that follows the road and painted an insipid washy green. I reckon straight outta the stock government department design manual...and totally intimidating poor old Evzen. His fear of government institutions will never leave him and I thought I'd never get him through the revolving entrance. But a hand on his arm helped coaxed him in.

Once inside it wasn't just Evzen who was intimidated, shit, so was I! A bloody large foyer and a great big staircase facing the entrance with corridors running off to the left and right. I reckon I felt the same as Evzen, that if you went down either corridor, there was a chance you'd never come out.

There's two small info booths on each side of the entrance. Inside each a glum-looking public servant sits behind a glass window just waiting to show off their superior officialdom to any lowly peasant brave enough to ask directions.

Preferring to bypass such put-down, we take a chance on a direction screen beside the stairs. To my surprise, he figures it out where to go and pushes a button that spits out a slip with a number on it. After looking at the room numbers above the entrance to each corridor, he decides to take the right hand one.

On each side of the corridor has a row closed doors with frosted glass panels. Chairs line the corridor where you sit and wait for a buzzer to announce your number and the room number to go enter.

We watch as others waiting respond to their call and disappear into the nominated cell. None have come out in the time it takes for our number to come up, which is a bit of a worry and does nothing to calm our nerves.

Inside our allotted room is another room with another glass window and a space at the bottom to hand any documents through. Thankfully there's a chair in front of the window so Evzen can sit. Once again I'll be in the dark with the language so I stay back and lean against the opposite wall watching.

From what I can gather, the conversation between the guy behind the counter and Evzen is strained, to say the least. The guy is raising his voice and keeps pointing to a sheet of paper that I assume is some sort of list of procedures, protocols, rules and regulations. Fucking bureaucracy! He's the typical weedy, smelly little runt with far too much power, and he keeps giving me a suspicious leer while filling in some sort of form. After some time, he slides a piece of paper through the gap below the window and turns to punch in the number of the next customer. Evzen looks uncertain at what he's been given but gets up and we leave the room. I get a look at the paper in Evzen's hand and it sure doesn't look like a certificate.

'What was all that about?' I ask as soon as we're back in the corridor. 'That's not it, is it?'

His shaking head and flushed face show signs of anger and frustration and he takes a moment to calm before answering.

'They need to search...I must come back tomorrow with this receipt.'

'Is that all? What was all that finger pointing and arguing about?'

'He need know if I a relative...and who you are.'

'And what did you tell him?'

'I...never mind.'

I look at him closely as we step onto the street. It's taken a lot out of him and he's shaking and breathing heavy. 'I think you better sit and rest for a bit. Do you feel like a coffee?'

He stops and looks around. On a nearby corner is a small restaurant with a now familiar Pilsner Urquell sign over the door.

'A pivo,' he says. 'I need beer.'

The first beer hardly touched the sides. We both needed it. For me it was a sort of celebration that I'm possibly one step away from actually getting the proof of ownership. Evzen, on the other hand, needed it to calm his nerves after his confrontation with authority. I guess the scars of his past will never heal. He's slumped in the chair, head bowed and looking spent and sad. I'm getting to understand his moods a bit now and reckon his mind's back in the dark days of the Ghetto.

'Another?' I ask, hoping to break him out of his bubble of darkness.

It takes a moment to register, and when he does look up, it's as if he's looking at someone, somewhere else. His eyes are puffed and moist and there's the ever-present dribble running from his nose.

'One for the road?' I say again in a more cheery fashion.

His face changes as he enters the present and his eyes focus.

'Or we can go now if you want?'

He shakes his head and the slightest smile squeezes a tear from his eyes.

'Ne, ne…we drink,' he says and wipes his nose with the back of his hand while I order two more beers with the universal two fingers and a nod.

The beers arrive. We lift our large glasses and nod to our wishes and drink.

'Evzen, do you come to Prague much?' I ask out of interest, for I feel he's somehow still a prisoner of Terezín.

'Last time…when Ruza comeback from your country, before then…not for year…two maybe.'

'Do you have any friends here?'

He looks at me as if wondering why I ask.

'Like, you know, you spent years here with Marika before going back to Terezín, right. You must have made some friends.'

I'm not sure how to read his look.

'No friends…no trust anyone but Marika.'

Yeah, I think I felt the same way living on the street.

'What of *your* friend?' he asks, catching me off guard.

'Mine?'

He nods.

Friend? Is he talking about Zac or Zoja? Nah, can't be Zac, shit, I've just wiped him off that list. But oddly, I'm getting this feeling thing's aren't right with him. Nah, he's a little weasel and can wiggle himself out of any trouble…and anyway why should I give a fuck about him? But Zoja?

'Thanks for reminding me. I should call her…oh, I told you I got a phone, didn't I?'

Evzen is blankly interested as I take out me new toy.

'Got it yesterday in Litoměřice. The hospital suggested I get one if they needed to…' I didn't want to go any further with the why. 'They have the number and I'd better give it to you, you know, just in case.'

I tear a page out of my notepad, write down the number and hand it to him. He stares at it as if he's never seen a mobile number before, and probably hasn't.

When I tore out the page, Zoja's card fell onto the table. I punch in her number and place the phone to me ear under Evzen's watchful eyes.

She answers the phone and it's a while before I realise I'm listening to a recorded message. It's in Czech, but her voice still gives me a tingling feeling. I wait for her message to finish and the beeps to sound.

'Hi, Zoja, It's me…um…Brightlight.' I look up at Evzen and give him a slight smile of embarrassment. His expression is unchanged as he witnesses modern technology at work and I hope he thinks that everyone needs a code word for mobile phones. I continue. 'Look, I have some news, and yes, I do have my own phone now so you can call me back on this. Anyway, look, I've located the original ownership certificate for this property I told your father about, and like, I was hoping I could, you know, like, maybe see him tomorrow…late…cuz I don't get it till tomorrow. So…umm…call me back…bye.'

I click the red hang-up button and place the phone back in my bag.

'We go now, ya?' says Evzen.

'Yeah, um let me pay for this.'

'Ne, I pay…I go to bathroom first.'

'Okay, I'll wait for you outside then.'

A few minutes later he joins me in the street and we catch the number 24 tram back to Florenc and the bus terminal.

———————

CHAPTER 42

Doran thought that after the special police unit established to review all property claims was disbanded a few years back, there would be no further contact with his insider. Getting the second of two calls from him in the last couple of months was very disturbing.

This particular ex-special police unit member—now working

behind the counter at the city Cadastral office in Kobylisy—had been a very valuable and rather costly source for Doran and his scheme. This new information will undoubtedly cost him again.

His services should have ceased the day before the property reclamation deadline in 2002 when he'd inform Doran of the properties that were still to have a claim made on them. This would then allow the company he and Goddard Klein had set up to claim under the pretence that they were acting on behalf of the owners, or in most cases their descendants. Those, who were now living overseas and aware of the Reclamation Bill and had proof of ownership had been cleverly, and in some cases legitimately, convinced that their property was a distant financial burden. Through Doran's legal firm, they were able to transfer the property for a negotiated price and the company would then take over the claim. It was costly, but considered a profitable future investment as the amounts negotiated fell well short of the properties' true value. It worked well and everyone had something to gain. At the same time, Doran was acting on behalf of the many Jews who *did* make successful claims—all good public relations.

But now this Australian girl is making unwelcome enquires with the help of some old man, and somehow, heaven only knows how, they have come across the registration number. Of course, there's nothing he can do to stop them getting a copy of the original certificate of ownership, and even though time is well past making a claim, he's still deeply concerned and annoyed, especially now that his distant *partner* has arrived in Prague and he is about to meet him. A meeting he's definitely not looking forward to, but at the same time he is eager to know why Goddard needed to be here. After all, this wasn't a major problem and he would normally leave it to his contacts in Prague to *take care of things*. Doran had no idea who Goddard's contacts were, nor did he want to know—or what those *things* were. There was no love lost between him and Goddard…in fact he dislikes him intensely. If it hadn't been for ties that reached back to the Ghetto, ties that have bound him tightly for sixty-odd years, he would have preferred to go it alone.

He leans back in his chair, two fingers pressed together at his lips while he considers the likely ramifications of this latest news. He can now expect a call from his daughter to say her friend would like to meet him again as she has something to show. He'll act suitably surprised at her discovery and show false disappointment that it wasn't found in time to make a claim. He'll then remind her of his promise to try for some financial compensation now she has a copy of the certificate and that she can expect with a degree of certainty some payment. Yes, he believes that should do it. Costly for him, but that should put an end to this rather drawn-out saga. He'll need to pay out of his own pocket of course, but that's how it will have to be unfortunately. He leans forward, happy with his appraisal of the situation, and starts to jot down some figures on a pad. How much is it worth to end this thorny problem? He writes down a number, crossing out one figure and then another. Australian, hmm, she won't have much of an idea of property values in Terezín, so he puts down a lower figure, then pauses. She's a friend of Zoja's so maybe a little more to make him appear generous, yes, that should do, and he finally settles on an amount.

CHAPTER 43

Despite six years having passed since their last face-to-face, Doran immediately spots Goddard seated at a small glass-topped table at the rear of the Hotel Josef ground floor lounge. He's involved in a conversation on his mobile phone and hasn't noticed Doran enter. The expensive designer clothes and flashy gold jewellery cannot disguise the thug element, nor can his swarthy features disguise his heritage. Doran looks around the modern, minimalist, off-white interior of the boutique hotel and wonders who else in the lounge bar is aware a Roma has invaded their space and that he, Doran, will be judged as an acquaintance, not something he wants.

As Doran approaches, Goddard looks up, interrupts his call, nods to Doran, then to the bar.

'Get me a Scotch on the rocks and whatever you want,' he orders and goes back to his call.

Doran feels his skin crawl at being ordered about by a Roma, but obeys. While waiting for the drinks, he leans on the bar and studies his business partner—a distant partner he wished had stayed distant. *Why is he here? He's aged a bit and looks more like his father.* Again he feels his skin crawl and silently curses his own father for doing a deal with Goddard's all those years ago.

Doran sets the Scotch and his honey-flavoured beer down on the small table and sits waiting for Goddard to finish his call.

'So how're they hanging?' asks Goddard, closing his phone and grabbing his Scotch. 'Let's talk English in here, hey? My Czech's a bit rusty and I know you don't like to speak German.' He gives Doran a cruel grin as he takes a sip.

Ignoring Goddard's interest in his privates, he nods agreement to the English. 'Did you have a good flight?' he asks, not really interested but wanting to start with a pleasantry.

'Yeah, the hostesses are better looking in first class.'

Doran can only imagine the demands and treatment they would have endured for all those hours in flight. But he was there to talk business and get it over and done with as quickly as possible.

'You know, there was no reason for you to come all this way. I have the matter under control and I could have kept you informed by phone.'

'Yeah, well I felt like freshening up old acquaintances.' He leans back in his chair with an air of distrust. 'I mean, I have a fucking lot at stake here, right?'

Doran looks around at the increasing number of people filling the lobby bar. 'Do you think we could talk somewhere else?'

'Why? You're the lawyer, and everything's fucking legit, right?'

Doran can't help but notice the threat in that implied question and feels sweat on his brow. Goddard notices.

'Look, Doran, I trust you, hey? If you say you have the problem under control, I believe you.'

Doran cannot help but notice the sarcasm.

'Look,' says Goddard leaning forward and lowering his voice. 'I thought we'd got rid of all the problems back in 2001, then 2002 and now, six years later, this problem seems to have popped up again, not just once but twice.' He starts tapping the glass tabletop with his thick, stumpy fingers. 'And not only that, but it seems all the plans to sell to the University have hit a fucking brick wall as well.'

Doran feels he needs to defend himself.

'Yes, I agree that has been stalled somewhat, but no one could have foreseen the amount of damage done by the flood. And as far as this particular property goes, it was you who insisted on sorting it out yourself.'

Goddard reacts with a fierce glare.

'There was no claim made by the deadline, right? So I did fucking take care of it, didn't I?'

'And now?' asks Doran, nervous but determined to hold up his side of the argument.

'Yeah, well, the fucking sister turning up was a surprise for both of us, right?' replies Goddard softening his tone a fraction. 'Anyway, she's dying in hospital and I didn't see the point in increasing the odds of bringing unnecessary pressure on us, okay?'

'And now?'

'Another unexpected intrusion—but that's being taken care of.'

That worries Doran.

'Look, Goddard, I said I had this under control. I've seen the girl and I'm sure she'll accept whatever financial offer I put on the table.'

'Yeah, you do, do you? Well, we'll see.'

'She's been to the Cadastral with the property certificate number and made a request to get a copy of the certificate, so let's solve this nice and simple, okay?'

This is news to Goddard and he shows it.

'Number? How the fuck did she find the number. I thought you said you were one hundred percent sure the number couldn't be found by anyone else, and now, this shitty little street kid from Melbourne comes over here and within a few days turns up with the number?'

'I can't answer that, but apparently there's an old man helping her.'

'Old man? What fucking old man? Shit, how many fucking others are gunna turn up outta the fucking blue? Jeez!'

'I'm getting more details about him…' Doran pauses as something Goddard said hits him. 'How did you know the girl's from Melbourne? I only mentioned she was from Australia.'

That seems to shut Goddard up for a moment and he takes a drink before answering. 'Her graffiti shit, that's what I mean.' His attempt at brushing aside the question sounds weak even to him and he continues, hoping his slip will be forgotten. 'So, what's the score if this kid turns up with the certificate then?'

'If she does, all the better, there's nothing she can do now to reclaim any property, but with the certificate I can tell her she's justified in getting some compensation from the Endowment Fund, pay her, and that should be the end of it.'

'But that Fund also had a deadline and ended long ago.'

'Yes, but I doubt she'll know about that. I seem to have her trust that I'm giving her the right advice.'

'Well you sure seem to be doing more than you need to, why?'

There's no way Doran wants to bring his daughter into this and he sees a way of reversing the interrogation.

'I could ask you the same question. You seem to know more about this girl than I've told you.' He pauses to take a deep breath. 'Why are you really here? Is there something I should know?'

Goddard stares at Doran intensely. He hates being questioned.

'My father worked fucking hard to build up his construction company, and now that I'm in charge, I don't want to see all that hard work come unstuck because you can't seem to finalise the remaining sales. There's more at stake than just the money my company gets to restructure Terezín for the University, you know.'

Doran didn't know, but it added fuel to his belief there was something else going on.

'Yes, well I'm working very hard on finalising the remaining sales, but since the University pulled out as the only buyer, you need to be patient. There's some solid interest and I believe the remaining buildings will be sold by the end of the year.' He looks around the room and leans forward so he can lower his voice. 'And you need not worry about your company being the sole tenderer for the rebuilding, it's firmly in the contract as a condition of sale.'

He looks at Goddard, knowing that all this has been gone over many times since the University pulled out, and until all the sales go through there's nothing for him to be involved with, so there has to be another reason why he's in Prague and he decides to confront him again.

'If there's anything else I should know that could have legal consequences for our arrangement, I think you should tell me.'

Worse than being questioned is being threatened and Goddard shows it by slamming his fist down on the table. 'When I decide you should fucking know anything, I'll tell you, but until then…mind your own fucking business!'

The two stare at each other for a moment in strained silence.

'Now,' says Goddard leaning back and locking his fingers together on his extended stomach. 'Unless you have something fucking good to tell me, I'm going out to eat.'

Doran is now more worried about the real reason for Goddard's visit. His role in this partnership—keeping everything to appear legal and above board—is threatened with such a bloated hothead let loose in *his* town. He's forever suspicious of Goddard's tactics, and of those who secretly work for him in Prague, but has managed to keep that at considerable arms length so nothing could possibly be traced back to him. But there's something different going on and it involves this girl Briney, and that's reason to worry.

As Goddard defiantly waits for him to go, Doran accepts that it's pointless to press the issue and leaves without another word. As soon as he's outside the hotel, his phone rings. It's Zoja telling him that Briney has located the property certificate and that she'd like to see him late tomorrow if possible. If so, and as she's invited Briney to stay the night, why not meet at her apartment. Doran looks back to make sure Goddard is nowhere around. Satisfied, he accepts the invitation and heads back to his office.

CHAPTER 44

It's been a long and stressful day for Evzen and I'm desperate to get him back to Terezín and into his own bed for a long rest. He fell asleep on the tram back to Florenc and it was an effort to wake him for the walk to the terminal. The bus to Terezín is waiting with motor idling. Not wanting to miss it as it'll be dark by the time the next bus arrives I hurry him up. He's wheezing and short of breath as I take some of his weight to help him into the bus. That's when I get the strangest feeling. It's like somebody has tapped me on the shoulder. I turn around but see nobody, just the road beside the terminal that runs under a rail overpass. Evzen stumbles and I turn back to help him on board and into a seat at the rear so he can sleep uninterrupted on the journey home. He's gone pale and is gasping so I undo the top button of his shirt to make him as comfortable as I can and check his shirt pocket to make sure he has his pills with him. He starts to doze off so I figure he doesn't need a pill just yet and I sit down beside him. But I can't help looking out the window towards the overpass. Whatever this feeling is, it's getting stronger and stronger to the point I can't ignore it any longer.

'Evzen,' I rouse him. 'There's something I have to do. I'm staying in Prague a couple of nights, so give me the receipt and I'll collect the certificate tomorrow and save you the hassle, okay?'

His eyes are partly open and he gives the slightest of nods as if he couldn't give a shit what I do as long as he can rest. I take the receipt from his coat pocket and watch his eyes close again, relieved to hear his breathing is less raspy.

'I'll tell the driver to make sure you get off at Terezín, okay? You'll be fine after a bit of a rest. I'll call the hospital tomorrow and see how things are, and if you need to call me, you now have my phone number, okay?' The only response I get is snoring.

I hear a hiss as the bus's hydraulic brakes are released and rush down the centre aisle to the driver. After some frantic arm waving and pointing to the back of the bus where Evzen is snoozing, I can only hope I got my message across before jumping out onto the kerb. As the bus drives off I peer into the passing windows and catch a glimpse of Evzen sound asleep. He'll sleep all the way I'm sure.

I follow the bus under the rail overpass until it's out of sight then stop as if on command. Everything seems to have gone silent and my attention is drawn to a dingy, grime-covered factory set back from the road where two rail overpasses merge and in the shadow of a signal box towering above. This is not a good place, I feel, yet I continue over the empty cracked and uneven concrete car park until I reach the closed, greasy, hand-stained double doors. I feel sweat trickling down my back. This is crazy. What am I doing here? I should turn and walk away, but I know it's not gunna happen, I'm utterly trapped.

I look around to see if I'm alone. A bus and a couple of cars pass… that's all. A dark cloud overhead adds to the gloom of the fading daylight as I grip the door latch. Instantly, I sense whoever recently entered were not all strangers to me. With thumping heart, I slide the rusted bolt from its home, push open the door and enter the darkness with its sickening smell of fear and blood.

'Zac!' I call out for some reason and stumbling over unseen rubble lying on the ground. 'Zac?' I call out again. I can smell him. I can smell his fear. But there's no answer. I'm alone again in the cold company of dark secrets.

I come to a wall and feel the heat of its energy. Besides the factory stench of dust, metal and grease, I smell cigarette smoke and the strong cologne. I brush a hand across the grimy brick surface until touching the softness of fabric. The force within the material intensifies as my hand passes over something different sewn onto the base material. An explosion of all the sounds of hatred, brutality and torture that I've come across since arriving in this country sends me reeling backwards in shock until I trip over a crate or something in the evil gloom. More screaming enters my head. I'm scared and confused by the forces surrounding me. Zac's his pain is now my pain. Then, as suddenly as the sounds exploded inside me, an eerie silence takes over and I hear the echo of my own racing pulse. I scramble to my feet, wait a moment for my head to stop spinning, then calmly and deliberately walk out of the factory, into the gloom of early evening and yield to what is required of me.

I've no idea how much time has passed or why I'm sitting in the dark in the middle of the car park in front of the factory. All I know is that both hands are covered in paint and I'm holding my camera. There's a vague recollection of buying paints but it's like I was a hovering onlooker. I feel weird. Like I've been released from a nightmare, but when I look down at my hands, they tingle with unfinished business. I struggle to my feet, surprised at how weak I feel, and walk away without a backwards glance.

The girl behind the counter at the Elf recognises me and is about to give me a cheery welcome back when she sees the state I'm in.

'Been busy, aye?' she says with a smile, obviously used to seeing paint-splattered graffers in this part of town.

'Can I have a room for the night?' I ask.

'Sure...you with your boyfriend?'

'Um, no, just me,' I reply, though he's never left my mind tonight.

'Can't give you the same room but I can give you one that's next to a bathroom.' I get the hint.

'Yeah, thanks...and I better have one of your Elf T-shirts while the paint dries on this one.'

I sign in and head straight to the bathroom to wash the paint off my hands and put on the new T-shirt. There's only a little paint on my jeans and none on my jacket. I must have taken it off. I've no memory of anything. Maybe what's on the camera will give me some answers. After wiping the paint off the LCD screen, I flick back though the latest images. The detail on the small screen is a bit hard to make out, so I head to my room, unpack the laptop and plug in the camera. Thumbnails of the photos taking from inside the factory fill the screen. I double-click on one for a full view. Centred on a freshly painted blue wall is a large red flag with a white circle and a swastika screaming out. Around the flag are words and numbers that have a vague familiarity about them and I get out the map I drew. The numbers are the same as

251

those Evzen marked and the words spell out the name of the company that owns eight of the buildings, *ústav Statek*. But what of the eighth number, the number on a red background that I scraped the paint from? Then I see it just below the swastika, still on a red background, but this time it's the red flag.

I've no idea what all this means, but then...why not? I look around the freshly painted orange walls of the room where prints of a sad-looking cow, a fish's tail in negative and a pair of large black scissors on a grey background with white dots hang. Why not? I consider again. Why not let others work it out for me. I head down to the computer room and plug one of the unused computer's Ethernet cable into my laptop. As I look over the thumbnails for the clearest image to upload I delete those that are too dark. This brings other images onto the screen that I hadn't seen—images of the factory exterior with the single word KAPOVILLE sprayed across the windows, the door and covering the entire length of the factory front. That's two images I need to upload.

Just then my phone rings, scaring the shit outta me. I'm not used to it and look around, embarrassed at interrupting the others in the room while fumbling through my bag for the phone. I manage to get it to my ear then realise I have to push a button to answer it, bloody thing! Finally I hear the click of a connection.

'Hello?' I answer inquisitively.

'Well, Brightlight, I though I'd never get in touch with you. I've called you three times over the last couple of hours and no answer.'

She most have called during the time I've no memory of, so I try explaining it away with my ignorance of mobile phones.

'Oh hi, Zoja, sorry, not used to this new gadget and didn't hear you ring. Anyway, I guess you got my message, right?'

'Yes, and I talked to Daddy and he can see you tomorrow night. You are coming to stay with me, right, because I've arrange for him to meet you here at my apartment.'

'Yeah, sure, that's fine...but...' As I begin to gain control over my mind, I realise I won't be going back to Terezín to change into new clothes. 'Um, listen...I won't bore you with the details, but I hope you don't mind if I'm...you know, a bit scruffy?'

'I like scruffy, Brightlight. Anyway, Daddy won't be here until eight, so why don't you come earlier and you can go through my wardrobe and pick out whatever you want to wear. How does that sound?'

'Yeah, sounds cool.'

'Okay, then. My place at, say, seven o'clock? You still have my card don't you?'

'Your card? Yeah, it's here in my…' I flip through the notepad and nothing falls out. I flip through again, nothing. Shit, where is it? 'Listen, it must be somewhere at the bottom of my bag and you know what that means. Best you give me the address again.' I write it down. 'Okay got it. See you tomorrow at seven then.'

I wait for her to hang up, do the same and look around the room as all eyes are darting back to their screens and I go back to mine. This interruption, though welcome, has left me wondering what I was doing. Then, as if I'm falling under the spell again, I mechanically open up MySpace and upload two photos.

CHAPTER 45

Goddard can't believe his eyes. His anger erupts like an unplugged volcano and he has a desperate need to kick and trash something. His first instinct is to heave the open laptop against a wall, but he'll need it. His mobile phone is saved from being stomping on, as he'll need that as well. He flings the chair back from the writing desk, letting it crash backwards to the floor and stumps around the hotel room looking for something else to hit, kick or throw but, to his growing frustration, can only settle on magazines and the hotel compendium. 'Fuck, fuck, fuck!' he yells, slamming his clenched fist onto the desk and bouncing the laptop perilously close to the edge. He watches it teetering, in two minds whether to let it fall or to slide it back to safety. He snorts and gives it a nudge, just enough to stop it falling, then picks up his phone. Rage has him shaking so much he can hardly punch the keys. The first attempt is a wrong number and he gives the innocent on the other end a furious outburst before slamming the phone shut. After a deep breath, he manages to key in the correct number.

'It's me,' he yells in German. 'You seen this bitch's fucking latest?' He waits for an answer. 'Now! Just fucking now! I've been going over her past shit and then, fuck me if two new ones don't suddenly pop up.' He holds his mobile away from his face, sneers at it before placing it back to his ear, and in a jumble of German and English, unleashes a tirade of threats and abuse, not just at the listener, but also at this infuriating, interfering girl and her intolerable desecration of the Nazis flag and his shrine.

'I want the fucking bitch gone, hear! Gone and never to fucking surface from whatever fucking hole you plant her in. And if you have to use that fucking scum of a son of mine, do it. I don't want to fucking see or hear anything about them ever again…and I fucking mean never…period!'

He points his phone towards the computer screen while triggering the hang-up button as if firing a gun. As far as he's concerned she's now dead meat. He snorts out a final expression of fury. His death warrant will have to do, even though he'd much prefer to do the deed himself.

The rage has him in need of a stiff drink, even if it's only seven-thirty in the morning. In only his underpants, which are almost hidden by his wobbling, bulbous stomach, he walks to the bar fridge, takes out the last mini bottle of whiskey, unscrews the cap and drains the contents in one take, following it up with a loud belch. He pats his naked stomach and gives his privates a scratch. Catching a glimpse of his figure in the full-length mirror on the opposite wall, he sucks in his stomach, with minimal effect, and clenches his fists to extend his biceps, triceps and pectoral muscles—full of admiration for his tattooed masculinity and his power over life or death.

But this feeling is briefly interrupted by the fact that he has also condemned his son. With a shake of his head to rid it of any invading doubt, he further tenses up his bodybuilding pose to reaffirm his inherited power. *Doing the weak prick a bloody favour*, he thinks, walking away from the mirror and flopping down on the edge the bed.

Unlike his brother, he missed out on those unique genes passed down through me from my old man. He swings his legs onto the bed and lies back in contemplation of his father. *He'd bloody well have done the same to me if I'd turned out like him, no question. Wouldn't fucking worry him in the least…not after all he did during the war. Shit, he knew how to serve out punishment. He knew how to use people. He knew how to survive. He had a license to kill and he used it.* He looks down at his growing erection pushing against his jockey shorts. The indelible images of his father's description of the death and brutality he inflicted on the Jews in the Theresienstadt Ghetto, and the fact that he now carries on his father's legacy, never fails to get him excited. The immediacy of his need makes it impossible to get a girl over in time. He runs his hand over his stomach and under the elastic waistband of his underpants and accomplishes the final act of relief himself.

After a shower, and wrapped in a towel, Goddard picks up his mobile phone. The one thing left unresolved is what to tell Doran. He begins to make the call then pauses. *Why should I tell Doran anything? He's weak and would only get in the way. This girl could just disappear and never get back to him and that would be the end of it. She simply gave up and went back to Australia or somewhere else. So what if he thinks I had something to do with her disappearance? The problem is gone, he saves money and that's the end of it. No, there's no point in telling him anything.*

He puts the phone down, finishes dressing and heads to the restaurant for a hearty breakfast.

CHAPTER 46

Slumped in the bath like a discarded pile of soiled old clothes, Zac is jolted out of his unconsciousness by the shock of cold water from the shower head above. As awareness kicks in so does the pain spread through his battered body. The overall sting of the cold water has yet to isolate the worst damage and he tilts his head back hoping the cascade will clear his mind. The image of his old man is frighteningly clear but the rest is a painful blur. As the blanket of pain is gradually washed away to expose individual sites of damage, it's the cold sensation on his skull that makes him painfully lift an arm and run a hand over the crude stubble of hair. But the sharp pain of lifting his arm compels him to look down as his torn, blood-soaked shirt is washed aside revealing the jagged tear where his left nipple once was…and he passes out again.

Coming to, Zac finds himself on Dasha's bed, naked but for a crude bandage wrapped around his chest. The pain has eased slightly, but looking around he finds it difficult to believe that on this very same bed, no more than a day ago, he was having so much sex and pleasurable pain. But now his agony is deeply physical and mental. To have a beating from his father was not unusual, and to have a severe beating was sort of expected after what he'd done. But, the revelation that his father was somehow behind this gang of neo-Nazis and that his grandfather had been involved in the extermination of Jews during the war, only added to his feeling of nausea.

The bedroom door is unlocked and Dasha enters with a plate of food and a beer.

'Can't have you fucking dying of starvation, can we?' she says with a smirk of sadistic pleasure. 'And I don't want you getting an infection either, especially in my bed,' she adds, pouring some beer onto the bandage wrapped around his chest. The alcohol stings, forcing him to grimace, but he holds back any sound.

Suddenly, from the lounge room, Deratz yells out a German expletive. Dasha thrusts the beer bottle into Zac's hand and rushes out of the bedroom leaving the door open. Zac listens to the conversation but can only understand the anger in their voices, then tenses up in fear of another beating as three figures fill the doorway.

'Ya dyke girlfriend's still fucking active,' says an angry Dasha, stepping aside to allow Deratz and Stik to enter.

Zac is pulled from the bed, aggravating all his injures, and half dragged out into the main room where he's pushed onto the chair facing the computer and forced to look at the screen. He wipes his bruised and swollen eyes to make out the wall at the scene of his beating. The flag and the swastika are now covered with numbers. Confused, he attempts to look back at his captors, but his head is forced to face the screen. Deratz leans over his shoulder and scrolls to the other image of the factory frontage with the large letters 'KAPOVILLE' painted across it.

Zac shakes his head. 'I…I don't understand…I…'

'You no understand!' says Deratz spinning the chair around so they face each other, nose to nose and in German adds, 'Understand this, ya! No one…fucking no one…does that to our flag and to our headquarters and gets away with it, understand!'

Zac looks at him blankly.

Dasha translates. 'Ya dyke girlfriend will soon be a dead dyke… and we make it look like you do it.'

'Take him back,' instructs Deratz pulling him up from the chair. 'We get girl.'

Stik roughly jostles Zac back into the bedroom and thrusts him back onto the bed. As he's about to close and lock the door, Stik turns back, takes out his flick knife and with a click releases the deadly glistening blade then licks along the serrated edge while his beady eyes sparkle with eagerly anticipated blood lust.

Inside the locked bedroom, Zac listens to muffled instructions, a shuffling of feet then the slamming of the front door. All is silent. He waits, listening intently for any other sound…none. All have left?

He pushes himself up to rest against the wall and try to piece together what's just happened. His breathing is heavy yet the pain in his chest is masked. Anger can do that. 'Fuck you, Briney. Fuck you…fuck you!' he calls out, slamming his clenched fist down on the bed with each word. Talking out loud, regardless of a swollen split lip, helps to see the situation clearer, and it's not looking good. 'Fuck! Why did ya have to go and do such a stupid fuckin' thing? Jeez you're so in deep shit.' He wipes blood from his chin onto the back of his hand and looks at it for a moment. 'Well, fucked if I can do anything…and fucked if I want to. You're on ya own now and it's all because of this fuckin' talking to wall bullshit…nothing but…and now this…fuck!' He looks around the room. It's bare and depressing and he feels the same. 'Get ya self fuckin' killed, I don't care.' Then, after a moment's thought, he nods and thinks to himself, *and while that's happening it gives me a chance to get outta this shit hole and go where no one'll ever fuckin' find me.*

With renewed energy, he struggles off the bed and rummages through his bag for some bloodless clothes to put on. Dressing is painful, but his determination wins out. Slapping his jeans pockets, he finds some money and takes it out. Not much, but finds more in his bag.

Making sure all he owns is in his bag—except for his torn blood-stained clothes—he tries the door handle but it won't turn. He looks around for something to prise the door open, but there's nothing strong enough. On his knees, he starts pulling out everything from under the bed until he sees a box set well back against the wall. Stretching his arm is agony and fresh blood seeps through the makeshift bandage as he manages to get the tip of one finger onto the edge of the box, then two fingers and just enough to move it closer so he can grab the rim and drag it out. Sitting on the floor with his back against the bed, he pulls the box between his legs and opens it. Among the porn and pleasure toys, he pulls out a fierce-looking knuckleduster. He puts it on and imagines what he could do to those who hurt him, but it won't open the door. He dives back into the box and this time finds something that will, a nasty-looking flick knife. Not as big as the one Stik carries but it will have to do.

Wedging the hardened steel of the blade in beside the lock tumbler, it takes all his strength to finally pop the door open.

After a quick glance out the window to check no one's standing guard, he opens the front door just enough to look up and down the street. Seeing it's all clear, he hurries out, slamming the door behind him, and runs as fast as his broken, bruised and bloodied body will allow.

With no idea of where he's heading, Zac can only think of getting far away and as fast as possible. He runs down street after street, turning into every side laneway and alley to shake off anyone who may be following, until the intense pain and difficulty in breathing forces him to stop and rest before he collapses. He turns one more corner and comes upon line after line of buses. He's at the bus terminal.

The return ticket back to Australia is with is passport, but the airport would be the first place they'd look for him, and anyway, his old man would find him without much problem back there, so that's out of the question. So, anywhere else and wherever the bus goes will do and he'll take it from there. He picks the first one that's not airport-or city-bound, and goes to board, but something catches his eye and he looks back at the destination sign beside the bus. Has his escape been thwarted by fate? On the list of stops, is the only place, other than Prague, he's heard of in this country. No way! He'll pick another bus. But something stops him from taking that one step back onto the pavement. 'Fuck!' he yells to the surprise of the driver and others around. 'Yeah, man, fuck!' says a young guy passing behind him. Zac looks around and watches as a mirrored image of himself walks away —skinny with a tattered bag slung over the shoulder, hair dirty and matted, but more importantly, free to wander. It could be…no bugger it…*should* be him walking away. 'Fuck!' he says again and looks up at the waiting driver. *No, fuck you, Briney! You got yourself into this mess and you can get yourself out of it.*

Then the words he had forgotten come back loud and clear…*we make sure it look like you do it!*

His heart is pounding and his mind is in turmoil, but as the bus door begins to close he steps forward, hands some money to the driver and mumbles the word he blames for all that has happened, 'Terezín'.

Slumping into a window seat, he looks out as the bus drives under the rail overpass, then with a rush of blood and fearful memory, past the old factory and the scene of his beating. There, blazoned across the full width of the frontage is the word 'KAPOVILLE'. He cowers down in his seat in case any of the skinheads are around and stays down until the bus is well past.

From an adjoining unit, Deratz, Stik and Dasha wait, wondering why it was taking so long—after all, the door never did lock properly.

259

When finally Zac makes his escape, they follow at a distance, watching as he turns down laneways and roads then easily pick him up again as he emerges, such is their better knowledge of the streets of Prague. And now, peering out from behind a fast food outlet at the bus terminal, they watch the Terezín bus disappear under the overpass. Deratz grabs Stik by the arm and orders him to get the car and meet him at the factory then tells Dasha to go back to the pad and wait.

CHAPTER 47

I'm running, bewildered and disorientated, through a maze of solid brick walls with no doors or windows—one hand never leaving the cold, hard, craggy surface. Turning corner after corner, right, left, right again. Where's this maze taking me? Then abruptly, I'm at a dead end, out of breath with both hands resting on the wall…and it moves…moving in on me, or am I moving into it? The voices within are calling louder and louder until the sound is deafening and I'm unable to move. It's as if I'm turning into bricks and mortar and becoming another wall of the maze and there's nothing I can do about it. Is this it? Have I gone too far?

'Help!' I call out, pushing myself up from the pillow and frantically look around the room, but these walls are still and silent. Evenly plastered, freshly painted and silent. *Where am I?* I shake my head to clear the remnants of sleep. It was a dream, a nightmare. But why am I here? This is not Marika's bedroom. I look around and spot the safety sign stuck on the door and the Elf logo. On the floor is my bag, jeans, jacket, Elf T-shirt—where did that come from?—and another covered in paint—why? I look at my hands and see paint under my fingernails. 'What have I done?' I call out, my eyes wide open searching the blank walls for an answer, but these walls remain silent.

I jump out of bed and quickly dress. All the time trying to recall why I'm here and what did I do after…Evzen…Yeah, I remember putting him on the bus back to Terezín, but everything after that's a blur. I grab my bag and head to the computer room. Whatever I've done, I have this strong feeling it'll be there on MySpace…and shit…for everyone to see!

It seems to take forever for MySpace page to open…and there they are, two graffs I've no memory of doing. I study each in detail. The numbers, the flag, the swastika and on the second photo, the word KAPOVILLE painted across some old factory wall. All completely new to me. The thought crosses my mind that someone's hacked into my site and planted them, but no, there's a recognisable style. I most have done them! I look up over the screen and stare at the wall facing me. Posters of Prague, festivals and concerts cover every inch, but I know that behind those posters and the plaster and paint, there are secrets. I didn't paint the walls of the factory, the walls did. I was only the means.

I look back at the screen and scroll down the page till I come to the list of comments. There's more than I've ever had…much more. Looking over the names I can only recognise a handful of regular subscribers. A quick read and they're still less than impressed with my new style. But the comments from those who are new to the site tell a different story.

After reading all the ones I can understand, I'm sweating with fear at the extent of hate and racism expressed. While only a handful support what I've done to the Nazi symbol, the rest, to my horror, are threatening me with all sorts of violence and death. Shit, is it only those with so much hatred who have the urge to comment, while those who agree are happy to stand back and allow the graffs alone to speak of their beliefs? Or are they just too bloody scared to come out into the open?

I suddenly feel I'm a pawn in a game of growing anti-Semitism. This is not me, this is not what I want to be. Despite being told I'm Jewish just because I was born to a Jew, I have no time for religion. I have no time for racism. I have no time for hatred. I have no time for any of this. I just want to go back to Melbourne and disappear back into my hole and close my eyes and ears to the world around me. I hit the logout button.

The sun's shining outside and I'm in desperate need of some warm comfort so I grab a beer from the fridge and head out to the open fresh air and the brightness of the beer garden.

Two girls are sitting, smoking and drinking coffee at the first table from the door. They smile at me and I smile back but ignore their invitation to join them and head to a table in a far corner. The bright yellow table against a backdrop of colourful red, yellow, orange and green shapes is a pleasant change from what I've just seen. I sit and take a sip of beer, its coldness cuts through the tension and I let out a sigh.

The surroundings make me think back to the first day in Prague… the mounting tension between me and Zac…then Zoja happening on the scene…shit, it seems so long ago. I had no idea then of what was to happen. I mean, shit, I had no idea of anything then. I take another sip of beer, put the bottle down on the table and gently rotate it as my mind turns over the past week or so. Evzen, Ruza and all the stuff I've learnt about Terezín, the property thing and now I'm up to my neck in a fucking skinhead, anti-Semitic war.

So what do I do now?

I look across the field of graffiti-covered walls, furniture and sculptured objects decorating the beer garden. Pleasant, bright, colourful signs left by happy travellers. I don't understand the foreign words on the walls but I sense they're friendly. I look over the row of fence pickets; each hand painted with the name of the country the artist came from. I feel a twinge of homesickness spotting the picket AUSTRALIA wedged between CZECH and MEXICO. I smile at the irony of the Czech and Australian pickets together, knowing I've Czech blood in me…and, shit, not only that, but Czech-Jewish blood! Does that have any bearing on what I do now? No! All I want to do is wrap things up here and piss off back to Melbourne.

Wrap things up, shit! I dive into my jacket pockets and come out with the receipt. The department! I need to get to the department and pick up the copy of the certificate to show Zoja's old man. Did she call? I don't remember. Maybe I should call her now. I grab the phone and my notebook where I put her card between the pages, but it's not there. I flip through the pages again to check and spot her address and the time of seven o'clock tonight written down. She must have called, or did I call her, I've no recollection at all. So that's it then, tonight I give the certificate to her old man and find out if there's anything he can do.

Which, I reckon is probably zero, but what the fuck, that's life. Then tomorrow I'll…I find myself lingering on the thought of a whole night with Zoja…what if I stayed here? Could we get into some sort of relationship? Na…who am I kidding…I'm probably just a bit a fun… a casual diversion from her many other pickings. We live in different worlds and it wouldn't last…but what the hell…I intend to make the most of it tonight.

CHAPTER 48

Getting off the bus at Terezín was difficult for Zac. Sitting immobile for over an hour has tightened up all his injuries and the congealed blood has stuck the bandage to his chest wound, making any twist or turn painful.

Hunched over to lessen the pain, he looks around the empty streets and old grey buildings with no idea of what to do or where to go. *This is fuckin' hopeless*, he thinks to himself. *Unless Briney pops out of a fuckin' building and says, 'Hi', there's no way I'm gunna find her.* But that's all he has to work with and limps off down the street and around the first corner.

At the same time a red Škoda Felicia had come to a halt on the other side of the rampart entrance to the fortress town. The driver and passenger watch Zac stumble from the bus, pause for a moment then limp off around a corner. The Škoda moves slowly through the entrance to follow at a distance.

Rounding a corner, Zac spots the words, MUZEUM GHETTA on a large white sign attached to a spear-pointed wrought-iron fence on the other side of the road. *Museum…something about a museum?* His mind grasps at this sniff of a clue. *But what was it?* He knew during his limited school years how hopeless he was at learning and remembering what the teacher said. Back then it was all background mumbling as his mind drifted off imagining a life uncontrolled and free, but even if what the teachers said didn't sink in, he had a strong visual memory for images, words and numbers. *What was Briney's last message from her old lady or whoever?* He closes his eyes to concentrate. *A map...the museum map and something about meeting at a building marked on it.* He crosses the road.

The old lady behind the desk looks up, surprised and shocked at seeing a bruised and bloodied skinhead entering.

'Map! I need a map?' Zac asks abruptly.

Fearful of what skinheads stand for and in this sanctuary dedicated to the ill treatment of Jews, she pushes a Ghetto brochure across the desk and quickly moves back.

Without a word, Zac snatches up the brochure and leaves. He studies the map out on the street, hoping to see something that'll jog his memory. There's numbers in black circles, but that didn't seem right. He studies the letters within the outline of each building. 'V', he says aloud. *There was a V, but what else, there's a lot of buildings with a V.* He closes his eyes to try and picture the message in his mind, and through the pain, it begins to appear. *Something about being sorry and to come back, Yeah okay, what else, um, Yeah it's coming, L, Yeah starts with L. Then there was a number, three, I see a three. It's getting clearer now, L3...um...then B. I'm pretty sure it was B. There's four letters and one number. V...I'm sure it ends in V. What have I got? L3B something V. I! That's it! L3BIV!*

He looks over the map and finds a BIV but no L3 with it. Then he notices a row of Ls down the left-hand side of the map, each with a number and a line down the length of each street. He follows the line for L3 and it leads to building BIV. 'That's gotta be it,' he says aloud, then looks around to get his bearings.

The Škoda turns into the road Zac is heading down and pulls into the kerb. Deratz and Stik are content to sit and watch but ready to move on if he turns another corner.

Zac is still in a lot of pain and his breathing is restricted by the damage to his ribs and the bandage around his chest. At the end of the road he leans forward to ease the pressure and rests a hand against the decayed, old grey building. The wall is cold and damp and he wipes his hand on his pants, surprised at being at all worried about such a thing. But it wasn't just the cold dampness that he felt. He looks up and places his hand back on the bricks and crumbling plaster and lets out a painful cough as his body is jolted by the wall's connection. *This is it.*

He sees no entrance and lurches to the corner. This side of the building faces the fortress wall and halfway down is the entrance.

The Škoda pulls out from the kerb as Zac disappears around the corner. At the end of the road Deratz and Stik lean forward, their heads almost touching the windscreen, and catch sight of him entering the building. They back up and park the car, get out, look up and down the road to make sure no one's watching, then creep around the corner.

A stumble on the uneven cobblestones of the entrance arcade has Zac clutching his chest again and he stops a moment for the pain to ease. Ahead he sees a courtyard, overgrown and cluttered with rubbish. He shakes his head. *Something's wrong, no one lives here.* As the pain eases a little, he continues on into the courtyard and turns a full circle to take in all four internal walls and windows, most broken, all dark. To his left is a large, red, half-open door and he limps towards it.

Deratz and Stik peer into the entrance arcade in time to catch a fleeting glimpse of Zac walking across the courtyard and out of sight.

'This is the place…we have her now,' Stik whispers in German and starts to enter the arcade.

Deratz pulls him back with some force, slamming him back against the wall. 'Wait! We'll make sure she's here first.'

They quietly make their way through the arcade just as Zac enters the building, then sidle around the corner into the open courtyard, their backs flat against the wall so as not to be visible from the windows above. They remain still for a moment, and then Deratz nudges Stik to follow and takes one step but feels a hand on his shoulder. He turns. Stik is shaking his head and still pressed hard up against the wall. Deratz gives him an exasperated look and once again tilts his head towards the door. But all Stik can do is shake his head. 'The wall,' he whispers.

Deratz looks over the wall and sees nothing unusual. 'Come!' He orders with another flick of his head. But Stik remains frozen. Deratz's patience is short and he pulls Stik towards him and immediately a large piece of plaster crumbles to the ground, shattering a broken window pane lying on the ground. They press themselves back against the wall, dislodging more plaster, and wait for any reaction from within the building.

Once inside the building, Zac pauses to get accustomed to the dim light then steps deeper into the gloom. The floorboards groan and creek with each step muffling the plaster crashing outside.

A shiver of fear runs through him, for he'll forever be wary of such places after his brutal beating.

He comes to a stairway leading to the next level. After mouthing the words with no sound coming out, he swallows to moisten his dry throat and quietly coughs. 'Hi…um, anyone there?' But his voice is still soft. He coughs a little stronger and louder and a sharp pain shoots through his chest. 'Anyone there? Bri, you here?' He listens for a reply but all he hears is his words echoing through the hollow building. He slowly climbs the stairs, each tread offering a unique grind, groan or squeal. The pain of carrying his weight up each riser forces him to pause halfway and rest. He grasps the handrail, further loosening it at the wall fixtures as small crumbs of plaster fall and bounce down the steps. 'Fuck, Bri! It's me, Zac…ya there or not?' he calls out, disturbing a pigeon above.

He continues to the top of the stairs. There's more light coming from the windows and he steps into the corridor and again calls out, 'Bri? Shit, where the fuck are ya?' After a moment peering into the descending gloom of the corridor through puffy, blood-shot eyes and straining to hear some response, he accepts it a waste of time and turns back to the stairs.

'Fuck!' he yells out, coming face to face with what looks like a ghost —pale, grey, scruffy, old and bloody scary. 'Fffuck,' he whimpers as the ghost raises its spindly hand and taps one knuckled finger to its mouth indicating the need for silence.

'Wha…what the fuck are you?' he utters in trembling words.

'You young people swear too much,' the ghost replies.

Zac realises he's not speaking to a ghost, but someone possibly human. 'Yeah, well you'd fuckin swear too if ya had the shit scared outta ya.' Then his mind clears a little. 'You, umm, ezz...somebody?'

'Evzen Kravitz...ya...and you are boy who leave Briney with no money.'

Zac is insulted at the suggestion. 'What ya fuckin' mean, she robbed me, the bitch! Don't know what she's told ya, but I bet it's all bullshit. Is she here?'

'Ne.'

'D'ya know where she is?'

'Why?'

'She's in fuckin' danger, that's why!'

'Danger?'

'Yeah, look long story...d'ya know where she is?'

'Why danger?'

'Look...all I can say is that she could be seriously hurt...even worse...right!'

Evzen takes a step closer to Zac, his stale smell coming with him, and looks over his damaged body. 'Who do this? You tell me all.'

Zac shakes his head, the resulting pain making him wish he hadn't.

'It's all because of her fuckin' graffs...all this thing with fuckin' walls and shit...and that's where it's got me...and her...in real deep shit.'

He sees Evzen is confused.

'Skinheads...you know...neo-nazis stuff.' That gets a reaction. 'Yeah, well she fuckin' painted shit all over their fuckin' headquarters and the stupid bitch goes and puts the pictures up on her site doesn't she...and...'

Evzen raises his finger to stop him.

'What she paint?' he asks pressing his finger against Zac's chest and making him wince.

'I don't know...fuckin' numbers and shit.'

'Numbers?'

'Yeah, she painted the wall blue with fuckin' white numbers all over it. But what really pissed them off was she painted a number over their fuckin' flag.

'Flag?'

'Yeah, you know…red flag with the Nazis swastika on it.

'The number…you know number?'

'The number? I don't know, it was just a fuckin' number that's all.'

Evzen remains silent, his watery eyes grim at the flippant answer.

'What…ya really want to know?'

The rigid response from the human ghost is all that's required.

'Jeez, it was five something. That's all I remember. And there was some words with it.'

'Words?'

'Yeah, fucked if I know what they meant…you know…being fuckin' foreign and all'

'You think hard, ya…what words?'

Zac closes his eyes and tries to picture the words in his mind. 'Um…I think the first word started with 'U'…'

'And the next word start with 'S' ya?' interrupts Evzen.

Zac opens his eyes. 'Yeah, 'S'…how the fuck did you…'

'Ustav Statek…and the number is five-six-six!' interrupts Evzen under his breath.

'Yeah, Fuck, how'd ya…anyway, that's not all she fuckin' did.'

'What you mean?'

Zac gives out a brief laugh, but is pulled up instantly by the pain it causes.

'She painted this great big fuckin' word across the outside of the place…K…A…P…O…V…I…L…L…E!'

Evzen's eyes widen showing a pattern of red veins. 'You make mistake…ya?'

'No…no fuckin' way…it was so fuckin' cool…Yeah, definitely KAPOVILLE…right across the whole front of the place for everyone in the street to see.'

'You tell me all you know,' says Evzen, shaking a crooked finger at Zac's face.

'Know? Shit, fucked if I know what I know. What the fuck does KAPOVILLE mean anyway?'

Evzen's eyes wander. Under his breath, he utters. 'End of search.'

Suddenly, the pigeon that had resettled flutters back into the air. Evzen snaps out of his contemplation and places a finger to his lips for silence. Both turn towards the stairs to listen as the creaking steps announce they have company. Evzen turns to Zac and points down the corridor and they hurriedly limp and stagger away from the stairs as fast as their frail, damaged bodies will allow.

Reaching the top of the stairs, Deratz and Stik see the two figures hurrying away. Being sprung, there's no need to creep around any more, and they run after them as the old man grabs Zac and pull him into one of the rooms on the left. Deratz smiles at their stupidity.

The two huge figures block the doorway to the small room with a single window in the facing wall that looks out over the courtyard. It's broken, but an iron grille has imprisoned Evzen and Zac as they press themselves hard up against wall with the window between them. Deratz takes a step into the room followed by Stik, the shiny steel of his open flick-knife reflecting the light from the window.

'Where is she?' Deratz directs his question to Zac.

'I…I…don't know…honest…I thought she'd be here,' he replies, fearful of another beating.

Deratz turns his attention to the old man and in Czech asks the same thing.

To everyone's surprise, Evzen calls out in clear English as loud as his croaky voice can muster, 'GET FUCKED!'

This is not what Deratz wanted to hear. 'What you say…you fucking Jew?'

Zac looks at Evzen, pleading with his eyes not to anger them more. But Evzen is defiant. 'Fucking Nazis scum,' he adds, daring them on.

Zac shakes his head. 'What the fuck ya doing? They'll kill ya.'

'Smart,' says Deratz as Stik steps up beside his leader slapping the blade of his knife against the palm of his hand. 'We kill you…if you no tell where she is!'

'I know…but I no tell you bastards,' Evzen calls out.

'We will see, ya,' threatens Deratz, fuming.

Zac, wide-eyed and trembling, presses hard up against the wall as the two heavies step menacingly forward. The floorboards creak under their bulk, but their minds are on the pleasure of forcing an answer out of the Jew. In the centre of the room, the combined weight of the two is more than the floor can bear and it collapses, sending them plummeting into the dark cavity below. Evzen and Zac stay pressed against the wall as the floor around the edges of the room remains relatively stable. A thick plume of dust rises from the gaping hole as the crashing timber and falling bodies reach the bottom. Not until the last of the loosened struts and boards have fallen does all become quiet again.

Evzen and Zac stand transfixed. There's a groan from below and Evzen leans forward to peer down, but the darkness and dust make it difficult to see. With a nod and a tilt of his head, he motions for Zac to sidle around the wall while he does the same on his side of the room.

At the doorway, the old man dares another look down into the floor cavity just as the sun breaks through a cloud and reflects light off the walls into the space below. The dust is beginning to settle and he can just make out the two twisted bodies lying among the pile of broken flooring and a glint of light catching on the steel of the knife half-embedded into Stik's chest. But something else catches his eye. He smiles to himself, nods and turns to follow Zac down the stairs and out into the courtyard.

Zac drops to his knees and wraps his arms around his painful chest. 'Go tell Bri she needs to get outta this country quick and hide,' he says breathlessly, but there's no answer. He looks around to see Evzen slumped and doubling over against the open doorway with one hand pressed against his chest and the other fumbling in his pocket for his pills.

'What's up? You okay?' asks Zac crawling over to him.

Evzen lifts a shaking hand, dropping his pills, and points to the door. "I need rest…you go,' he says in a quivering, breathless voice.

Seeing the old man is incapable of anything for the time being, Zac realises it's up to him to find Briney.

'Where is she, where's Briney?' he asks.

Evzen points to his jacket pocket. Zac reaches in and takes out Zoja's card that Briney had left on the pub table. With heavy eyes and a flicking of his finger, Evzen utters between gasps, 'You go…I see they no follow…I come later.'

Zac is well aware that even if Deratz and Stik don't follow, Goddard will not let up and will continue to hunt him and Briney down. He looks back, picks up the pillbox Evzen dropped and places it into his damp hand, nods, heaves himself up with some difficulty and limps out into the street.

Evzen feels his heart rhythm stabilising, the pain in his chest is subsiding and his breathing is no longer laboured. But his energy has been sapped and he remains sitting, limp and motionless by the open door.

Then he hears the sound.

Not a sound he's accustomed to and certainly out of place in this old deserted barracks. He looks back into the darkened interior then around the courtyard, but sees no one. He pushes himself back into the building, but the sound has stopped and all he hears are the normal noises he's become used to. Then, it starts again and this time Evzen realises it's coming from the end of the corridor to his left. Struggling to his feet, he walks cautiously and unsteadily down to the dead end and face-to-face with Briney's graffiti. The sound is coming from within. He presses an ear to the painted wall. The sound reminds him of something he heard once on the bus to Litoměřice. It stops again. He presses his ear harder against the wall. Nothing. All is quiet. He steps back, trying to recall what it was he heard on the bus. Then, the sound starts again and jogs his memory. It's the annoying sound this young man's mobile phone made before he answered the call. He's not aware of the correct name for it, not at all interested, but this rap music ring tone is much the same. He takes another step back, looks over Briney's graffiti and smiles. What caught his eye, when he looked down into the gaping hole the skinheads had fallen into, was more graffiti. The seemingly abstract strokes Briney painted are the reverse of the Hebrew words painted on the other side of the wall, where now, dead or dying, the two thugs are imprisoned in a secret synagogue that she'd unknowingly discovered. The collapsed floor must have been weakened by the only access, a well-disguised trapdoor, its underside rotted by years of damp in the enclosed space. After all his years searching through this building, Evzen is sure there is no way out and he walks away, smiling at the irony of where the neo-nazis, anti-Semitic thugs, finally lie. He leaves the building as the ring tone once again echoes within the sacred walls.

CHAPTER 49

For the fifth time Goddard cancels his unanswered call. Seething with rage he paces around the hotel room wondering why they aren't answering or why they haven't called in with an update? He looks at his watch again. All they had to do was follow his son to the girl. If she's not stopped soon, she'll meet with Doran and tell him about his skinhead connection. It's also possible that Doran will see the photos of the desecration to his temple and what was painted on the flag. He must be stopped before doing anything hasty that could jeopardise all that he and his father had planned just when it was so close to coming together. Confronting Doran face-to-face would give him the chance to test his reaction, and if need be, take whatever course is required. He makes the call.

The receptionist greets him with the warmth her personality was hired for. But her welcome is cut short by Goddard's abruptness.

'Goddard for Doran,' he snaps in English.

There's silence on the line as the receptionist puts him on hold to inform her boss.

'Goddard…I was expecting your call,' answers Doran, in a cold, angry tone.

The angry tone answers Goddard's question…he's seen the latest images.

'I take it you've seen that fucking bitch's latest…we need to talk.'

Doran had gone to Briney's MySpace page only moments before to learn as much as possible about this girl before meeting her with his final payoff. The photos that immediately came up took him a while to work out. The sight of the Nazis flag in the first image sent a chill down his spine. The second image of the factory frontage had a different response and, after the initial surprise brought a wry smile to his face. He knew Goddard owned the factory, having done some of the legal work for the purchase, but that was two years ago and he was surprised it was still standing. It was his understanding that Goddard intended to demolish the factory for a new development, then, without an explanation he terminated Doran's involvement in the deal. Now, seeing the word painted across the factory front and the Nazis flag displayed on a wall inside, all his suspicions are confirmed.

'Yes, I think we need to,' agrees Doran, his mind ticking over the possible consequences all this may bring.

Goddard wants to divert Doran's attention away from the neo-Nazi movement to their business dealings.

'The fucking numbers and the company name! How the fuck did she know all this?'

Being so startled by the Nazi flag and the word KAPOVILLE, Doran had not noticed what was painted on the flag or on the wall behind.

'Doran?' Goddard calls out impatiently.

Doran is studying the numbers and the name. *How did she know all this?*

'Doran, you said she found only one number, so what the…'

Doran cuts him short. 'Not here…not on the phone…where are you?'

'In the hotel,' Goddard replies.

'I'll meet you in the car park in ten minutes.'

Goddard hangs up without another word.

Doran sits back in his chair, tapping his lips in thought. The numbers and the company name are not a problem; anyone who really wanted to find this out could through the Cadastral records. But the factory front with KAPOVILLE painted across it brought back the violent images permanently etched into his memory from his childhood in the Ghetto. He slams his finger onto the exit button and closes down his computer. He has come to a decision, one that he should have come to many years ago, and now is the time to face Goddard with it.

Doran sees the rage in Goddard's eyes as he approaches. *This is not going to be easy.*

'Goddard, listen…' he says in a controlled voice, but his words are cut short.

'No! You fucking listen,' snaps Goddard; stomping on a cigarette he's dropped to the concrete floor. 'You were always too fucking soft, and now this little slut has been allowed to paint our secrets all over a fucking wall and put it online for the whole fucking world to see.' He steps up to Doran and grabs the lapel of his coat. 'Over the years I've taken care of any problem that sprang up. Even some you didn't fucking know about. And in less than two weeks, all those years of planning and work have been exposed by some shitty little street kid from Melbourne.'

Determined, yet inwardly trembling, Doran pushes Goddard's hand away from his lapel and smoothes down the expensive woollen blend.

'I've had enough of your crude and vulgar shit and now I'll tell you what the situation is and what's to happen from here on.'

Goddard is stunned by Doran's unexpected defiance.

He leans back against a concrete pillar, his arms crossed and a mocking smile on his face.

Surprised at how easily he's allowed to speak, Doran continues.

'Ever since the Ghetto days I've detested the relationship between your father and mine. When my father died and I took over running the business I found out I'd also inherited the scheme our fathers had set up. And what's even worse, I had to deal with you after you took over from your father. But today it ends.'

He pauses for some reaction, but there is none, just the smug sneer on Goddard's face.

'But let me remind you,' he continues. 'It was my father who had the brains to set up the scheme to cheat the Gestapo out of some of the property taken from the Jews. It was my father who had the skill to know which assets and which property were suitable to hold back without attracting attention, and it was he who created the cover in case they did become suspicious. But it was your father who could have wrecked the whole scheme because of his ruthless brutality, intimidation and, may I add…murder.'

This wipes the smile from Goddard's face and he pushes himself away from the pillar and again grabs Doran by the lapel.

'Don't you speak of my father like that,' he spits out. 'He controlled the pathetic Jews with an iron fist and it was your father who accepted his protection and, may I add, all the extras that came with the arrangement.'

'Yes, *the arrangement*?' Doran questions. He looks down at Goddard's hand until it's removed from his coat. 'That *arrangement* was based on fear and survival. We were all to be exterminated. My mother was Jewish, and because your father was the Kapo who decided who was to be transported, my father set up this arrangement to save us.'

'And so he did,' scoffs Goddard.

'Yes, but she died in the mental institution she was sent to.'

Goddard gives a disinterested humph.

'But don't forget, your father was expendable too. A Roma Kapo who would also have been killed by the Gestapo if it hadn't been for the opportunity the *arrangement* created and the possibility of bribing the guards with promises of deeds to confiscated property. This was all because of my father's skill.' He hesitates a moment before revealing what he has known for some time. 'And I have a hunch your father is still alive in Australia…and still wanted for war crimes that would lead to certain hanging.'

This surprises Goddard, as he was sure no one, least of all Doran, knew his father was still alive.

'He's dead,' Goddard insists.

Doran looks at him disbelievingly. 'Maybe…but he has taught you well, hasn't he?'

'What do you mean?'

'That building the girl painted. That wall and the Nazis flag. Why that building? Why KAPOVILLE? Why has this got you so stirred up?'

'The numbers...the numbers and the company name...that's what!'

Doran knows his lying.

'I can handle any problem that may arise from the revelation of the company owning all those buildings. But that's not it, is it?'

It's rare for Goddard to be cornered, but he knows that Doran holds the legal reins to their main project and he manages to restrain the urge to lash out with a closed fist.

'My father was a true believer in the Nazi cause and I've proudly carried on his work,' says Goddard. His massive shoulders hunch up as he releases venom into Doran's face. 'Without you knowing, I've financed the neo-nazi movement since the early nineties and we will again be in power and not you nor anyone else can do a fucking thing about it.' He smiles. 'In fact, you...you son of a Jew...have been providing the finance for my chapter to grow through all your so-called expertise in the reclamation scheme. So how the fuck do you feel about that?'

Doran is sickened by the thought. The scheme to siphon off small parcels of property that the Gestapo had confiscated from the Jews on entering the Terezín Ghetto was one thing. Securing ownership of property that was not claimed during the restitution period that ended in 2001 was another. But to hear income from the sale or development of these properties was financing the rise in the neo-Nazis' anti-Semitic movement is too much to contemplate.

'Tell me, Goddard, how many of those who failed to make a claim for lost property did you have murdered?' Doran asks, his rage building.

Goddard has now returned to his comfort zone...in control. He arrogantly leans back against the pillar with crossed arms once again.

'Look, this girl...' Doran is searching for words. 'There's no need for any harm to come to her. I said I'd pay her out of my own pocket. She understands there's nothing more can be done and she'll be back to Australia and out of the equation in no time.'

Goddard has not moved, nor has his expression.

'When are you seeing her?'

'Tonight...look...' he dives a hand into the inside pocket of his coat and pulls out an envelope. 'See…I've got her cheque with me now. It's over, so let her go.'

'She's a friend of your daughter…a dyke?'

'Leave my daughter out of this. She knows nothing!'

Goddard stays silent.

'I mean it!' says Doran, trying to sound threatening. 'You hurt my daughter in any way and I'll spill everything. I've kept a dossier on you and your father as security in case something like this came up. You are aware Romas are still a despised race, aren't you? And even though you were born in Australia, you are a Roma in every sense of the meaning. And of course there's the matter of a warrant still out for your father's arrest for war crimes.' He puts the envelope back in his pocket, brushes his lapels and takes a step back. 'I have it all down in the dossier, so I suggest you pack up and return to your father's side and let me wind up the company.' He nods and turns towards the car park entrance. 'You'll get your full share of the wind-up, but I'll make damn sure none of it can be used to finance your hateful club.' His words trail off as he walks away. Goddard, his eyes red with rage, watches him…a dead man walking.

CHAPTER 50

I thought catching the tram to the Cadastral office at Kobylisy around midday would give me plenty of time to get the certificate and then make my way back into the Old Town to find Zoja's place. I mean, shit, all I had to do was hand over the receipt. Well, how wrong was I? Not only has it taken over an hour for my number to be called, but who do you reckon is there on the other side of the window, the same creepy guy that gave Evzen the run-around yesterday. Now it's my turn to get the run-around. After handing over the receipt he went on about something in Czech while giving me the up-and-down look of suspicion. After finally convincing him I didn't speak Czech and I have no idea what he's talking about, I then had to wait while he makes a bloody phone call. Fucked if I know what that was about because it ended up the bloody certificate was sitting in the box beside him all the time. I had to sign something before he gave it to me. All I understood was it showed a number that ended in 566, so I just had to accept it was the right one. Shit, government offices are fucking depressing.

By the time I get the tram back to within walking distance of the Old Town, the bloody weather's turned real cold, wet and windy. Even though I don't have as much time as I thought I would, I figured I can still check out a couple of shops. You never know, I might see some cool gear I can buy later if I get some money from Zoja's old man. Not that it's mine mind you, but I think I've earned a little of it.

I'm still not used to this shopping for gear caper. While I've seen some great stuff, I can't get my head around the bloody prices. I guess it's not just buying clothes I'm not used to, but also having the money to do it.

In the fourth shop my bloody phone rings. Shit, another thing I'm not used to. In a panic I rifle through my bag to find the bloody thing and shut it up.

'Hello' I say in a serious tone, thinking it could be the hospital.

'Hi...um...Brightlight?'

I reckon my serious voice made her think she rang the wrong number.

'Zoja, hi...um...I wasn't expecting you to call, is everything still okay for tonight?'

'That's the reason for my call, darling.'

My shoulders sag at expected disappointment.

'Look, this storm has put a stop to filming and it's a wrap for today, so, if you want, you can come to the apartment as soon as you're able.'

'Yeah, Yeah, sure,' I reply with renewed excitement. 'Um...look I'm just in a shop at the moment...I don't think I'm far from the Town Square...where do I go?'

'Head to the Town Square and go behind the old church, you know, the one you think looks like Disneyland. On your left, set back a little, is a Gallery and beside it you'll see a two-storey building with a skylight set into a sloping red-tiled roof. My apartment is on the top floor. There's an intercom at the entrance, just press. I'll let you in then go to the top of the stairs…got it?'

'Yeah, I think so…hey…um…I can't wait to see you.'

'Me too…I'll wait for your buzz, bye.'

'Yeah…bye.'

I fiddle with the phone to hang up and put it back in my bag with an embarrassed look around the shop. Shit, I've always hated hearing people talk on their mobiles and now I'm doing it.

It's weird, but somehow I never thought anyone actually lived in these old medieval Gothic buildings? They all seem like museum pieces. I mean, there's Zoja's place with its skylight, a curved wall with little upside-down keyhole windows scattered around and right in the historic centre of Prague. Shit, she must be rolling in it. And here I am, just standing here looking at the bloody intercom and not pressing her button. I'm so not used to visiting people in such high places and I'm nervous as hell. Nah, who am I kidding? I'm bloody nervous at the thought of being with her in private. Jeez, I don't think I've ever felt like this over anyone…ever…especially with another female. Shit, I hope I know what to do. She's gunna need to teach me. Hmm…that could be fun.

'You going to stand there forever or are you going to push my button?'

Shit, I'm sprung. She's right behind me and I spin around.

'I was just getting a bottle of champagne from the restaurant here and I noticed you hovering. You having a change of heart?'

Shit, if she only knew.

'Um…hi…no, Zoja…um, you surprised me.'

Her lips are instantly on my cheek and I get a hit of her perfume that sends tingling messages right through me.

'Well, come up to my parlour, then,' she says with a look in her eyes that I know the rest. I'm more than happy to be her fly.

She leads the way up the stairs and I follow, unable to take my eyes off her firm arse, tightly wrapped in stretchy designer jeans, the bottle of champagne swinging from her hand adding to the seductive image. I desperately want to reach out and cup my hands over her bum and feel her muscles tighten as she climbs each step.

At the second landing she unlocks a solid dark wooden door and ushers me into a small entrance room with another set of stairs facing. The decor is totally different, totally Gothic and totally unbelievable. There's one large delicately patterned lead-light window above the stairs. The walls are covered in a red and black pattern that mirrors the shape of the tapered window. The handrail and post of the stairs are a heavy pinkish stone of some sort. Under the handrail is more of the same stone—carved into swirling shapes of dragons fighting. The red of the walls is reflected all around and I feel I've just entered my own living fairytale.

She points to the short flight of stairs for me to go first. As I climb, I wonder if she's looking at my arse the way I looked at hers. I hope so.

At the top, the room opens up to more red and black. The ceiling is vaulted, just like in a church, only here, hanging from the centre, is a huge heavy black iron chandelier that looks like it once belonged in a bloody torture chamber. Under each of the six flame-shaped globes, that I guess would have once been candles, a threatening spear or arrowhead points downward. Directly under the chandelier is a large heavy wooden table with four solid legs set in from each corner and joined to a centre frame filled with Gothic arches. The other furniture in the sprawling room is similar, all solid dark wood and ornately carved with cool scenes of dragons and mythical beasts. Where does she get this stuff…or has it always been here since the real Gothic days?

At the far end of the room, under more church windows, a large, thickly padded black leather couch and two matching armchairs are the only modern touch.

'Make yourself comfortable, Brightlight, while I open up this bottle. You will have a drink, won't you?'

I'm snapped out of my mouth-gaping awe. 'Um…Yeah, Yeah, sure, thanks,' I stammer.

'Put on some music if you like,' she calls out from one of three rooms off to one side which I figure to be the kitchen..

'Um, no, I'll wait for you.' No way was I going to touch anything in case I break or scratch it. Anyway, I couldn't see any bloody CD player. Must be hidden away somewhere I reckon.

I hear the pop of a cork and a moment later she returns with the open bottle and two tall flutes filled with bubbling champagne.

'Come sit over here,' she says walking past me to the leather couch. I follow.

Before we sit, she hands me a glass of champagne and I instantly lock eyes onto the lines of bubbles endlessly rising from some hidden magic.

'To us,' she says, raising her glass.

'Yeah, um…to us.'

She smiles. We touch glasses and drink. The bubbles tickle my nose and I let out a schoolgirl giggle.

'Sit, my little Brightlight, and tell me what you've been up to.'

I sit, but I'm unsure of what to say, or what *not* to say, so much has happened. She sits down beside me, crosses her long legs and swings an arm over the back of the couch behind me, giving me another whiff of her perfume.

'I told you I managed to get a copy of the property certificate to show your old man…sorry, I mean your father…that was something.'

'Certainly was,' she says taking another sip of champagne then putting her glass down beside the bottle on another piece of Gothic furniture. 'But Daddy did make it clear that it may be of no help as so much time has passed, didn't he?'

'Oh, sure and I'm aware of that, but, well, I don't know, it just seems like I need to show it to him, that's all…sorta like…I don't know… mission accomplished I guess.'

'Well, he also said he may be able to get you some compensation, and Daddy never says anything will happen unless he's sure it will… even a maybe.'

'He's still coming tonight, is he?'

'I haven't heard from him that he isn't. But he did say he can't get here until around eight.'

She reaches over to collect her glass.

'So, we have quite a bit of time to kill until then.'

The look in her eyes sends darts of excitement all through me. She notices and quickly changes the subject.

'Well, I had a hell of a day, up before dawn setting up this shoot... I'm so glad it was an early wrap.'

'So, like, what do you do, actually?'

'Oh, a bit of this and a bit of that, but mainly dress the sets and locations.'

I don't know what that meant and I'm too bloody shy to ask.

'So, like, will you need to do it all again early in the morning?' As soon as the words are out I wondered if my one-step-ahead thought was too obvious.

They were and she gives a knowing smile.

'No, darling...I don't work on Saturdays.'

'Cool,' I say, thinking it must be a union rule or something.

'But my darling Brightlight, I do need to freshen up before we have our dress-up session, so, do you mind if I have a shower?'

I can tell there's an invitation in there somewhere, but regrettably, my inexperience holds me back.

'You can start looking through my wardrobe and see what you'd like to try on. The bedroom is just in here.' She gets up, grabs the bottle of champagne, and I follow her.

The bedroom is as I expected, totally Gothic with a huge four-poster bed in the middle of the room. Above is a similar chandelier to the one in the main room, its spearheads pointing down. Shit, I hope it's bloody well secured to the ceiling.

On a wall is one of the weirdest lights I've seen. It looks like melted iron or some other dark metal, that's been dribbled into an erratic mixture of shapes and curves against the red and black patterned wall. Then there's this square chest of drawers made of embossed burnished steel that seems out of place amongst the old wooden furniture. On top sits a candelabrum made of the same metal. It's shaped a bit like an Arabian sword I guess, curved with the pointy end highest and along the curve are five thick candles set into five gold sculptured cups. Something about it is strangely familiar.

Zoja has gone into the bathroom directly off the bedroom and I hear the shower start as I step up to the wardrobe. I run my hands over the chunky engraved dragons in each of the four door panels. The cool, lacquered wood gives me a tingle, not the same sensation I feel from touching walls—this feels gentle and pleasant. I open a door and, shit, I'm faced with my reflection in a full-length mirror. After getting over the initial shock, I step back and take a good look at myself. Shit, there's no bloody way I'm gunna look good in any of her gear. I open the other door and run a hand over all the hanging garments. The feel of velvet is rare to me and I carefully take out a long, caped dress. Black, of course, like most of her clothes. I turn to the mirror with the dress against me, but the door has swung open further. I move so I can see my reflection again. The dress helps, but shit, my hair's a mess and I sweep it back, and that's when I see her reflection over my shoulder. The door to the bathroom is half open and a naked Zoja is stepping out of the shower, her body, pale, shiny, wet and in perfect proportion. I can't move or take my eyes off her.

CHAPTER 51

The violent banging at the front door startles Dasha. She opens it thinking Deratz and Stik have returned and is immediately pushed aside by a raging Goddard.

'Are they here?' he spits out, looking around the room.

'No…umm…' she looks up and down the street before closing the door. 'I thought you were them.'

'Where the fuck are they?'

'I…I don't know for sure…I left them at the bus terminal. They were following Zac.'

'Follow him where?'

'He got on a bus to Terezín.'

'Fuck' he calls out slapping a fist into his other hand. 'She's not fucking there…she's still in Prague. If that little bastard has deliberately led them away from her…I'll kill the fucking prick myself.'

He points a finger at Dasha.

'Give them another try…I need to think.'

She grabs her phone and dials. Goddard paces around the room as she listens to the ring tone. He turns to her. She hunches her shoulders and shakes her head.

'Fuck!' he yells. 'Do I have to do every fucking thing myself?'

'You…you want me to get some of the others?'

Goddard thinks for a moment.

'You know this dyke, Zoja, don't you?' he asks in a different tone, his mind working through a plan.

'Ya, sort of…not fuck mates if that's what you mean?'

Goddard gives her a look up and down knowing she'd fuck anything.

'You know where she lives?'

'Ya, Tyn Court.'

'Where the fuck's that?'

'In the Old Town behind…'

'Yeah, Yeah, okay…don't want to know the whole fucking history. That's where the fucking Aussie bitch will be tonight,' he says, wandering off around the room again.

With Deratz and Stik not around, Dasha recognises an opportunity for her to show what she's made of and a chance to climb higher up the ladder within the movement.

'I'd have no worries about scratching their fucking eyes out,' she says as threateningly as she can.

Goddard looks back at her, sizing her up. 'The last few years…were you around when the others carried out my instructions?'

She knew damn well what those instructions were.

'I can kill just as good as they can.'

Her bluntness has Goddard looking deep into her eyes and he sees the cold menace of a killer.

'No,' he says, turning away from her. 'There could be three that need taking care of. You'd need help.'

Dasha wonders why he's not including himself, or does he just order others to do his killing for him.

'The two of us can do it?' she says, testing him.

Goddard doesn't answer but recognises the challenge.

Taking advantage of his hesitation, she steps towards him, sliding her hands into each pocket of her jeans. With her elbows thrust back, her ample breasts push out against her leather vest to expose more bare tattooed flesh as the front zip eases down under the strain.

'I'm sure there's a lot we can do together.'

If it weren't for the urgency of the job in hand, he'd have no hesitation in taking up her tempting offer. She's built for many things, but is she strong enough to handle the bigger problem? He's always controlled operations from a distance and had others do his dirty work for him—they knew who held the purse strings, who his father was, and they'd sworn allegiance to the neo-Nazi cause. If it was just to get rid of the girl, sure, Dasha could easily do the job. Even if this Zoja got in the way, he was confident she could handle her as well. But Doran was his. The threat that he had a dossier of all their past activities, and his knowledge that his father is still alive, and possibly his whereabouts, was eating away at him and the only relief would be to take care of him personally.

He looks at his watch. Almost six o'clock. There was enough time to work through a plan and still take up Dasha's offer.

He reaches out and slides his broad hands down each of her illustrated arms. She steps up to him, excited and aroused by the understanding that they'll be killing—and killing time—together. She slides one hand out of a pocket and cups it over Goddard's crotch to check he's as excited about it as she is.

CHAPTER 52

The reflection in the mirror of Zoja coming out of the steamed-up bathroom wrapping herself in a large white towel has me mesmerised.

'Seen anything you like?' she asks, coming up behind me.

I'm not quite sure what 'like' she's talking about.

'This is one of my favourites,' she says, reaching in front of me. I half close my eyes at the hint of roses on her wet flesh. 'Put that one back. This'll look better on you.'

I turn around and look at her as she steps back to show off the dress —well I think it's a dress. It's got this little corset top of purple velvet with a waist so small I take in a breath. The off-the-shoulder front has been cut away and replaced with a fine black lace material that would be pretty useless at hiding what's underneath. The skirt is black, long and tight, flaring out at the bottom to show a glimpse of scarlet velvet underneath. I've never seen anything so sexy.

'Come, get rid of those clothes and try it on.'

Suddenly I feel dirty, smelly, unworthy to even touch such expensive clothes.

'Look, Zoja, I...do you mind if I have a shower first?'

'Of course darling, how rude of me not to think. I'll hang the dress up in the bathroom so you can slip it on when you're finished. The steam will do it good.'

I wonder whether to strip here in front of her or in the bathroom.

'I'll be in the kitchen rustling up some nibbles,' she says, relieving me of the dilemma. 'Help yourself to whatever, I'm a compulsive shopper of perfume and bath soap, and there's fresh towels in the cupboard.'

I wait a few seconds until I hear here tinkling about with plates and stuff then start undressing. I've never owned a bra so it's straight down to my knickers. Then I wonder if I've got a clean pair in my bag? But it's out in the other room and I don't want to be caught seen in these old things. Stuff it...I won't wear any.

The shower's hot and long. I've never been in a bathroom as luxurious, I mean, just the smell is expensive. All the fittings are Gothic, naturally: dragons, bats and naked ladies. I make the most of a good scrub and wash my hair with shampoo and conditioner…what a luxury.

The bathroom's well and truly steamed up by the time I'm finished and I need to wipe the mirror to see myself. With the image of a naked Zoja etched in my mind, I make a comparison. I'm more tanned than she is, and all wet and shiny I reckon I look pretty good. My tits are a good size and shape, I've a trim waist, my legs are long and…shit… fucking hairy!

I look around for a razor but can't see one. Nah, she probably has her legs waxed somewhere I reckon. I open the double doors to the vanity cupboard under the sink and mirror. The shelves are stacked with so much it looks like a bloody chemist shop. Creams, moisturisers, cleansers, cotton buds, shit you name it she's got it. And there it is, a razor and some shave cream, phew…and something else. Nestled in an open box, metallic and shiny, is a gold dildo. I go to take it out and have a closer look, but I reckon I better get on with the business of shaving legs and under arms.

Shaven and smooth as silk I give myself a once over in the mirror and instantly spot something glaringly obvious and in need of attention. I've trimmed it in the past, but not for a while and it's now pretty au naturale—a coyote bush, Zac called it—and it needs cutting back. No, fuck it, why not a bit of shaping as well? Or, of course, I could go all the way and have no hair at all. Nah, I think I like some down there.

First try was a heart but I couldn't get both sides equal so I tried to make it into a butterfly. By the time I'd messed around to get the shape, I was running out of hair, so I've ended up with a little landing strip. I check in the mirror and the sight of my own freshly trimmed pussy and all that fiddling down there has me feeling very randy. I look down at the dildo staring enticingly up at me. Why not a little…

'You okay in there, Brightlight?'

Shit, I'm glad I closed the door.

'Yeah, um, sorry got a bit carried away under the shower. Just got to put the dress on and I'll be right out.'

I towel my hair dry enough and grab some of the hair gel on the shelf and rough that through to get it standing up and sticking out all over the place. Something I've seen the celebs do in those mags. My hair's a little longer than Zoja's, so it doesn't look as spiky, but it'll do.

I slip the dress over my head and it falls down on me perfectly, but the back needs lacing up. I pull the front tight around me to see how my tits look through the lacy front. I'm impressed.

'Well, who's this then?' says a surprised Zoja, as I step out into the bedroom. She's holding two freshly filled glasses of champagne and wearing what could be a dressing gown, but I'd call it a sexy blood red satin thing in a style I'd imagine Robin Hood wearing, all ragged and hanging but obviously tailored to look casual. A large hoody kinda collar hangs over her shoulders and widens the neckline to show off plenty of cleavage. And there's plenty of her long legs showing with a raggedly cut hem reaching not much lower than one of my t-shirts.

'I can't do up the back,' I say, half turning my back to her.

She hands me a glass of champagne. 'Have your champagne while I tie you up.'

Now there's a thought!

I have a sip then give a little shudder as she places her cold hands on me. She keeps her hands still for a moment so I get used to her touch.

'You have such lovely tanned skin,' she whispers. I tense up as her hand slides down my spine. 'It must be nice to live in such a warm climate and not have to wear heavy clothes all the time.'

I feel her breathe on my neck as she comes closer and I tilt my head forward. She accepts the offer and kisses me. The electricity it generates would light up this whole place. I sigh and I don't care if it is loud. The laces are now ignored and I feel both her hands under the dress and around me. I hold in a breath as her hands slowly climb to the base of my tits, then pause teasingly as she kisses me again. Her lips part and I feel a gently bite that sends sparks to all my nerve ends. Her hands continue to explore. Yes, explore me, please. My nipples harden in anticipation of her touch, but her fingers linger and ever so gently stroke the sides of my breasts. I can't stand it any more and turn slightly. She knows what I want, and I feel two fingers pinch a nipple. Fuck, I'm going to come! Now her other hand does the same to the other nipple. I jerk violently, spilling the champagne, while her body presses firmly against me to the rhythm as I climax.

Her hands slide off me, creating uncontrollable spasms with each movement. She reaches around to take the glass and place it beside hers on the dresser. I hear her gown fall to the floor, followed by the dress I've only just put on. I'm completely naked and selfishly wanting more...and I'm not disappointed. I flinch as she tenderly slides her hands around each side of my waist, over my stomach and down. I feel the wetness building. I feel her naked body press against me and I lean back against her firm breasts. Her hands continue to slide down, generating another spasm as they reach the freshly shaped landing strip, following it down, down, until I let out a sigh as she slides a finger effortlessly and delicately inside me. I'm coming again and jerk violently with legs parted to allow deeper entry.

I desperately need to explore her but I must try and settle down and lower my pulse rate for a moment. I rest my hands on hers to keep them still yet remaining deep inside me. The spasms ease. She moves. She knows what I want next and I know she wants it. I turn to face her beautiful body, so pale and firm, and reach out to touch her breasts but she slides her arms around me and we kiss, long and firm, our tongues exploring.

We continue to kiss as I bring my hands up over her breasts. I sense a slight bite to my tongue as I touch her nipples and I pull away from her lips to kiss each breast, her hand, now behind my head, directing me from one breast to the other. I slide a hand down her waist and feel her legs part invitingly while she applies slight pressure to my head. I lick the scented skin of her stomach, tasting the sweetness of the rose shower soap. Out of interest I look to see what she's done with her pubes. A small tattoo of a dragon is breathing fire of blonde hair down to her slit. I lick her hair hoping I don't extinguish the flame. She sighs and her legs part a little more. I close my eyes again as I start to taste her juice, sweet and warm. I extend my tongue and feel the nob of her clit.

I feel it growing. I also feel something else. I pause. I taste metal. My tongue continues to explore. I feel shapes. I feel some points and her clit getting larger. She's moves away from me and I open my eyes as she sits on the edge of the bed and lies back, her legs open, her hands now each side of her vagina and spreading herself wide. I lean forward to gaze at the pinkness of her slit, the pale bulb of her clit…and the clit ring.

I don't know how, but I must continue with the pleasure giving without her sensing I'm in shock. I also needed to look closer at the detail of the ring. I slide a finger down her slit and slowly insert it. Her sigh convinces me she hadn't noticed any change of interest.

I'm frantically searching through my memory while concentrating on the job at hand. The image has fragmented since Evzen described it but it's coming together…two goose heads side by side, one with its beak slightly open to allow the thread to be cut. This is it…this is the goose ring that started everything! Zoja senses some hesitation and pulls me closer. I must concentrate and close my eyes so the ring is hidden from view. I lick and plunge my tongue deep inside her until I feel her tension build and she raises herself up on her elbows to watch me devour her then cries out in ecstasy.

Some minutes have passed and we lie on the bed in each other's arms. I'm resting my head on her chest listening to her heartbeat slowing, relieved it wasn't the other way around, cuz mine's still racing. What will I to do? I need to ask her about the ring. I mean, shit it could be just a similar ring. Yeah, how could she have the ring that went missing, what, around sixty years ago? Yeah, it's probably just one like it.

'Um…Zoja,' I say quietly, my head remaining on her chest while I look down her stomach to her fire-breathing dragon. 'I guess you realise all this has been…you know…new for me, don't you?'

'Mmm…I would never have guessed it, Brightlight.'

'Yeah, well, I'm sure you guessed it's the first time I've seen a clit ring…in place that is.'

'You like?'

'Yeah…sure…but I've never seen one like that…it's so unusual.' I gulp. 'Where did you get it?'

'Sorry, Brightlight, but it's a one-off. I know where you can get others just as interesting if you're thinking of having one inserted—they do add to the sensation, you know.'

It being a one-off is not what I want to hear.

'Um…so how did you get it?'

'My grandfather gave it to me when I was fairly young…oh, not to use like this though. I don't know what he'd say if he was still alive and found out.'

Shit, what does this mean? My mind's racing through all that Evzen has told me.

'Yeah, I can imagine,' I say trying to remain casual. 'But, what are they, Geese? So unusual, how'd he come across it?'

'It was a long time ago. I don't know the full story but he never wore it, so I suppose he thought it would look better on me.' She gives out a slight giggle.

'So, like, he didn't have it made especially for him then?'

'No, I don't think so. He got it during the war. Must have been when he was in the Ghetto.'

'What…what Ghetto?'

'Terezín Ghetto…isn't that a strange coincidence?'

'Terezín Ghetto?'

'Yes, my grandmother was Jewish…just like yours I guess. Maybe they knew each other? How strange would that be? But she died there before the war ended.'

My head's spinning with what I'm hearing.

'I vaguely remember when we returned from our time in the States, Daddy's new business partner—I hated him immediately and wondered why he was dealing with him—well, anyway, I heard him mention something about the ring. I was a bit worried because I'd already had it put in down there, but it made me wonder how the hell he knew about it. I mean he's younger than Daddy so he wouldn't have been in the Ghetto. And now I think about it, he was born and lives in Australia…so, that's another how weird is that, hey?'

Shit yeah, how fucking weird is right.

Just then the buzzer of the intercom goes off and Zoja bolts upright.

'Shit, talk about Daddy, that's probably him now.'

There's a mad scramble as I grab my clothes and stumble putting them on. Zoja's gone to the intercom in the nude and answers. She returns unhurried and slips on the gown she'd dropped.

'It's Daddy,' she says, unfazed.

CHAPTER 53

I don't want Zoja's old man seeing me coming out of her bedroom, so I quickly dive onto the leather couch in the main room as if I've been there, waiting for him, all the time. Of course, wet hair, blushing face, no boots on and struggling to do up my fly are all dead giveaways. Jeez I gotta calm down. I'm not sure what's got me more flustered: the sexy romp or seeing the bloody goose ring.

Zoja's gone down to the lower entrance to let him in. Shit, what did I just hear her just say, that we were playing around in the bedroom? Fuck, why'd she have to say that?

'Hello Briney,' says Doran, coming into the room and approaching with his hand outstretched.

'Hi,' I reply, standing and shaking his hand while covering my partly open fly with the other hand. 'Um, I…we…we were looking through the wardrobe…um, great clothes.' Shit, that sounds so bloody unconvincing!

'Yes, well, sorry I'm a bit late.'

Late, shit if he'd come any earlier! But I'm getting the feeling that he's as flustered as I am and not the smooth, suave, relaxed man I met the other day.

'I needed to put something together for you. Nothing important, just explaining the property reclamation process in case you still had any queries.'

He takes his coat off and hands me a USB stick he'd taken from one of the pockets. I take it with a smile, unsure of why he needed to bother.

'Yeah, thanks, and I've got something for you too.' I grab my bag beside the couch, throw in his USB stick, take out the folded certificate and hand it to him. 'I hope this is the right one?'

He just gives it a quick glance. Strange?

'Well done, it was very astute of you,' he says placing it into the inside pocket of his jacket. 'I hope you don't mind if I ask how you came upon the number?'

'Sure, bloody weird actually, like, I've carried it around for years without knowing it.' I take the clock outta the bag, open it and show him the instructions pasted on the inside cover. 'There, under the maker's name, I thought it was just the serial number, but Evzen figured it out that it was the number of the certificate.'

'Evzen? Oh yes, the old man you mentioned?'

'Yeah, he reckons because my grandfather worked in the Ghetto print room, you know, like, during the war, he was able to print the label so it looked like the real thing.'

He studies the clock and label closely and mumbles almost to himself, 'Yes, so many things were done then to hide secrets.'

I sense there's more behind what he said as he hands the clock back.

'Yeah, well, I'm told it's the only thing left that once belonged to my grandfather, so I guess it's, like, pretty special, hey?'

'Yes, precisely…and because of you and your friend's good detective work I've managed to get you some recompense.'

He takes an envelope out of the same pocket where he put the certificate and hands it to me. I take it and look past him to give Zoja a smile at my good fortune and notice she's watching but seems unsteady on her feet. I look back to the envelope, open it and take out a cheque.

'It's a cash cheque. I presumed you don't have an account in Prague so keep it safe until you get to a bank. I trust that's acceptable.'

'Yeah, sure,' I reply glancing over it, but it's written in Czech and I've no idea of how much the six-figure amount is in Aussie dollars, and I sorta feel it's a bit rude to ask.

'I'm afraid that's the best I can do. I did have to push the limits, you understand, so much time has passed.'

'Yeah, thanks, I'm sure whatever…um…whatever…'

I'm distracted by Zoja's strange actions in the background.

'Daddy,' she calls out. 'Tell Brightlight all about…um…how…' She giggles and begins to wander around the room, running her hands over her body and down between her legs. 'How I got that…that lovely…mmm…oh so lovely little goose ring.'

Shit! What the fuck's she doing?

Doran is distracted by her request but only glances to the side without looking directly at her.

'Ring?' he says, as if he's no idea what she's taking about.

'Mm…yes…you know…' She looks down at her hands feeling her crotch. 'With…with two cute little Goosey heads side by side.' Her voice is slurred and starts to trail off. 'I…I showed…I showed my little Brightlight…didn't I?' She starts to lift up the hem of her gown.

Shit! What's she up to, telling her father that I've seen the ring while I was down on her? Jeez!

'Go on…tell how granddaddy got it.'

'Oh, that ring. Well, it was…it was a long time ago.'

He seems flustered. Maybe he knows where she's put it, shit!

'Nooo Daddy…how did he get it!' Thankfully she's raised her hands, but now she's dancing around the room. Fuck, I think she's sniffed some coke or something.

'Oh, I'm sure Briney is not interested, Zoja.'

His eyes are trying to convince me I'm not interested, but I'm very bloody interested. Shit, if it wasn't being worn as a clit ring, I'd ask him myself.

'Look," he says appearing even more edgy. "I'm sorry, but I've just remembered I have another appointment and I really must go.' He takes up his coat. 'Maybe another time, yes?'

Shit, it's so obvious he doesn't want to talk about the ring.

'You will take care of that information I've given you, won't you? You may need it on your return to Australia.'

Australia? Strange, he seems to be suggesting I go back home.

There's a crash and I look to see Zoja straightening herself up after knocking over one of the chairs at the dining table.

'Zoja, you all right?' I ask.

Doran looks around and sees his daughter waving her arms around, staggering and mumbling to herself. Again she bumps into the table. It's as if she has no idea where she is.

'Zoja!' he calls, rushing over to her.

I follow. She turns to face us but her emerald eyes are greyed over and distant as if staring into a fog. I'm sure she doesn't see us, but what I see worries me. He gown is soaked and stuck to her body. She's absolutely drenched in her own sweat.

'Zoja, what have you taken?' I ask, as flashes of the many overdoses I've seen, come to mind.

'She's having a hypoglycaemic attack,' says Doran placing a hand on her cold, sweat-covered arm.

'A what?'

'She needs sugar.'

CHAPTER 54

In the shadows of the Church of Our Lady Before Tyn, Goddard and Dasha watch the evening crowd of tourists stream through the bluestone archway of Tyn Court to the Old Town Square. Goddard waits for the group to pass then turns his attention back to the building with a curved wall and upside-down keyhole windows that houses Zoja's apartment. There's no way they'd be allowed up to her apartment because of the security intercom, so all they can do is wait in the shadows for either Briney or Doran to arrive and use one or the other to force their way in. After waiting more than an hour, Goddard spots Doran exit the Court. Moving into the doorway of the gallery next door, the pair wait for him to push the button and announce himself. The buzzer sounds, the door unlocks and they make a rush to grab him just as a group of diners leaving the adjoining restaurant block their way. By the time Goddard pushes past the diners and reaches the door, Doran has gone in and the door has locked behind him. Furious, Goddard threatens to break in, but Dasha convinces him that with so many people around it would not be wise and that they should wait till he comes back out and grab him then. Reluctantly Goddard agrees and they merge back into the shadows to wait.

But their wait is short. Surprised and amazed at his good fortune, Goddard watches Zac limp into the small plaza, stop to look around, check a card in his hand and look back to the buildings. He appears confused by the restaurant sign outside the entrance and Dasha needs to restrain Goddard from grabbing him before he has a chance to use the intercom.

Goddard can't believe the hand fate has dealt him. All his problems have come together in the one place. But where are Deratz and Stik? They were meant to be following him and there's no sign of them.

Dasha grabs Goddard's arm to draw his attention back to Zac, who's about to enter the building. Once again Goddard pushes aside some patrons leaving the gallery while Zac figures out the right button and presses it. No response. He pushes the button again, but still no buzz of the door unlocking. Goddard and Dasha look at each other, questioningly: has anyone left the building? Zac tries again. This time a voice comes through the intercom but they can't hear who it is or what's said. Zac leans forward, his mouth almost touching the intercom, and whispers into it. Goddard and Dasha can't hear what he's saying but they clearly hear the sound of the buzzer and the door unlocking. Zac's father rushes forward, placing one heavy hand over his son's mouth and with the other twisting his arm behind his back while Dasha keeps the door open. There's a muffled cry of pain as Zac's chest is stretched and he's roughly pushed inside and up the stairs to the top landing.

CHAPTER 55

I'm so bloody confused…she's having a what attack? And sugar! Why sugar? And, shit, now there's someone buzzing from downstairs. It's all bloody happening at once as Doran grabs me and points to the kitchen.

'Sugar!' he yells, unaware that Zoja has danced away towards the buzzing intercom.

From the kitchen I hear Zoja in the background singing into the intercom something about a party and everyone's welcome. I'm flustered: this urgency, in a kitchen I've never been in and frantically searching for bloody sugar. Then I hear Zoja call out 'Zac!' Nah, can't be, all this has got me so fucking confused I'm hearing things. But then, I'm sure I hear the buzz of the door down in the entrance hall.

I turn my attention back to why I'm in the kitchen and spot the coffee maker. There's gotta be sugar there somewhere, but before I can move one step, I hear someone—Doran I think—scream out *'NO!'* followed by a lot of yelling, bumping and crashing. I back up against the wall and peer around the kitchen door.

With only the main entrance area in view, I see Zoja pushed around pretty violently, but strangely enough, she seems to be enjoying it, dancing and singing with her arms flapping around. But the girl who's pushing her is familiar. Squat, short cropped hair, tats on her arms and neck, Yeah, she's one of the skinheads I saw Zac with at the pub. What the fuck is *she* doing here? Then someone else is shoved into the room. It takes a moment before I recognise Zac— what with his hair cut off and all roughed up and bloody. The guy pushing him is big and heavy and looks fucking angry. Shit! Who is he and what the Hell's goin' on? Then Zac's pushed so hard he trips and hits his head on the edge of the solid table and slumps to the floor. I half take a step to go to him, but my instinct tells me to stay in the kitchen and I slide away from the doorway hoping to stay out of sight.

Through all the yelling, I can only make out Doran saying something about no-one needs to get hurt. Hurt? Shit! There's more yelling, arguing, pushing and shoving with furniture and stuff being knocked over. Shit, I gotta see what's happening and sidle back to the door and take a quick glance into the room. The butch girl's struggling to control Zoja who just wants to dance with her and Doran is arguing, or maybe pleading, with the big guy who's now got this fucking ugly looking knife in his hand, shit! I swing back around and away from the door.

'Where's the girl?' I hear. A new voice...a rough voice...and a fucking angry voice, it's must be the big guy. *The girl?* Shit, he's talking about me! I press harder back against the wall and frantically look around the kitchen, for what, I don't know.

'Goddard, there's no need for this.' I hear Doran say. 'I've paid her off and she'll be back in Australia and out of the way.'

'And your other threat?' That's the big guy again. 'It's not just a matter of the girl now, is it?'

What the fuck is he talking about?

'That's in the hands of someone else now and if anything happens to me...' Doran's voice is cut short by a gurgling sound as if he's being choked. Zoja is still singing in the background.

'Fucking bullshit,' says the big guy. 'You go down with me if our arrangement gets out. So where is she and where's the dossier?'

Fuck, the USB stick Doran gave me. I don't believe it...he's given me this bloody dossier! I knew there was something strange about him when he handed it to me. Now I'm really shit-scared and edge away from the door. There's a clinking of glasses as I bump into a table. Suddenly there's silence from the main room. Fuck!

'In there! Get her!' I hear the big guy call out and push myself away from the door as far as I can, then this cropped and studded head peeks around the doorway and spots me.

'Got her,' she says.

'Kill her,' he says.

She steps into the kitchen with this weird look in her eyes as if she's about to do something that'll give her great pleasure. With a flick of a switch and a crisp metallic clink, the gleaming blade of the knife in her hand flicks open. I try to yell, scream, anything, but nothings coming out. I shake my head in disbelief. I'm about to be murdered. This is it... that was my life...and this is my death.

Suddenly the girl's arms are held to her, wrapped up by Zoja as she finds her missing dance partner.

'Dance, dance, dance the night away...' she's singing.

The sight of Zoja dancing with my killer, her flimsy gown soaked with sweat and clinging to every curve of her body, maybe the last image that I take to my grave. But I grab this moment of distraction to reach back and glance around as my hand touches something. It's where Zoja had been preparing some nibbles, and there, on a cutting board with the core and discarded seeds of a capsicum, is a large knife. In one smooth, continuous motion, I grab the handle and swing my arm around, feeling the blade's entry hampered for a moment by the leather vest she's wearing, then, as if in slow motion, having pierced the leather, the blade passes through the flesh of her left tit then jars through her ribs and into her heart. The look of surprise in her eyes is combined with an eerie look of pleasure on her face. Her slight smile relaxes as her mouth opens and a gush of foaming blood spews out over my hand still holding the knife that's now embedded up to the hilt. I feel her weight as she begins to collapse to the floor and let go the knife and watch her slide down out of Zoja's arms. Zoja's left standing with her head hanging and her singing voice fading. She looks up at me as if asking why I did that to her dancing partner. Her now murky grey eyes are rolling as she continues to sway on the spot to some silent music in her head. Suddenly the big guy enters the kitchen holding his knife at Doran's throat. He looks down at the girl on the floor, her legs and hands still twitching.

'You fucking bitch!' he yells and pushes Doran away into Zoja and goes for me. With the knife no longer at his throat, Doran lunges at him. The struggle is very short as the big guy whips the knife back in a flash, opening up a gaping gash in Doran's throat. I swear I heard a voice coming from this hole, but whatever it was is short-lived as blood spurts out around the kitchen. Doran is casually flung aside, leaving him clinging to his throat in a futile attempt to stop the blood.

'Daddy, you want to dance?' I hear Zoja say as she struggles to keep him on his feet.

With this big bastard coming at me, I want to beg and plead for my life, but it's as if I've accepted the inevitable and remain silent. His arm is reaching out with the knife aimed at my throat. I can already feel it slicing into me just like Doran. Then it's gone...the knife...the arm... and the big guy. Whatever space there was on the floor in this small kitchen is now covered with bodies: the skinhead chick, who's now stopped her death dance, Doran, who's slid from Zoja's arms, and now the big guy with Zac on top of him. The floor's covered in blood and the pair wrestling are smearing the red fluid in strange and weird patterns —graffiti of the worst kind. I'm hypnotised at the sight of so much bloody mayhem. I see graphic images. I see paintings. And then I see Zoja slowly sink, adding another body to the crowded floor. Her eyes are closed and her body is going into spasms. I look at her. I look at Zac. I look at the big guy. Everything is so surreal and ticking over frame by frame. I'm absorbing all before me until I jolt back to reality...the sugar!

I turn to where the coffee's made but I'm suddenly pulled back. The big guy has got to his feet and he's turned me around by the arm. I see Zac lying still on the bloodied floor with Zoja having convulsions beside him. With one arm free I reach back and grab the first thing I can and slam the glass coffee pot into his face. This time nothing is in slow motion...it's quick, as quick as his hands move from me to grab at the shard of glass sticking out of his cheek. There's no blood immediately, but I do catch a glimpse of white cheekbone under his left eye, which is now hanging out of its socket. He looks at me with his good eye, first in rage, then, as realisation sets in...fear. I'm still holding the smashed coffee pot by the handle with jagged glass still threateningly close to his face. He backs away, stumbling over the pile of bodies, turns and runs out of the kitchen and down the stairs. I hear the street door slam behind him.

All is quiet except for the pounding in my head. I'm shaking uncontrollably, befuddled and disorientated. Then Zoja has a spasm of movement that snaps me back to reality again. I place the remains of the shattered coffee pot back where it was and spot the sugar bowl.

Stepping over the skinhead chick, Doran and Zac, I kneel down beside Zoja. She's cold and damp and rigid except for the occasional spasm. Her mouth is closed and I prise open her lips to pour in some sugar but her teeth are tightly clenched together. Now I start to panic. I look back around the kitchen and hit upon a jar of honey—the English word written on the label. Is it the same in Czech, I curiously have time to wonder? Careful not to slip on the blood-covered floor while I step over bodies, get the jar, and with no other guide than instinct, part her lips and start rubbing honey over her gums. I have no idea why or what I'm doing, but continue to add more honey even though nothing is going into her mouth. The sticky nectar is oozing all over her face, over my hands and down onto the floor, the rich golden colour swirling into the dark red of the blood.

I look around at the sound of Zac coming to. He stares up at me, utterly bewildered as the bloody scene around him registers. In a rush of panic, he tries to push himself away from the lifeless, blood-covered bodies, but his feet keep slipping on the saturated floor until he's wedged against the doorframe.

'Fuckin Hell!' he calls out.

'Zac, we need an ambulance here fast.'

'Where is he? Is he fuckin' dead? Is my old man dead?' he frantically calls out while scanning the main room.

'Your fucking what?' I don't believe what I just heard. 'You…you mean that big guy's your old man?'

He says nothing but cowers away from the kitchen door.

'He's fucking gone, Zac! Now get some help, quick!'

I can tell he's lost it and I'm bloody surprised I haven't, but I can't leave Zoja.

He turns to me and snaps, 'Gone! He's fuckin' gone! Why didn't you kill the bastard?'

'Now's not the fucking time, Zac!' I shout. 'Get down to the street and yell for help…NOW!'

It seems to have some effect and he gets unsteadily to his feet.

'You sure he's gone?'

'NOW!' I yell as loud as I can.

He sways with dizziness, shakes his head and after another cautious look around the main room, gingerly heads to the stairs.

'And ya better get the cops!'

CHAPTER 56

The hour-long journey from Terezín and the short ride to the Old Town Square's nearest tram stop allowed Evzen to regain some of his strength. But now, shuffling as fast as he can through the narrow lanes and arcades of Staré Město, his erratic heart rate and wheezing lungs are once again taking their toll—not just from the physical effort, but also the stress of getting to this girl he now finds himself desperate to protect.

Night has fallen and it's a rarity for Evzen to be in Prague in the dark. The condensed layout of the Old Town and the hordes of dawdling tourists only add to the unending obstructions and he has to pause again, but the sound of a siren in a nearby accessible street, followed by another siren converging from a different direction, renews his sense of urgency. This is not good. The sirens wind to a stop not far ahead and he pushes himself to continue.

Reaching Tyn Court, panting and desperately worried, he sees, beyond the shops, crowded restaurants, the old water pump, sculptures and the gateway at the far end, flashing blue lights dancing on the walls of the Church of Our Lady Before Tyn—seemingly adding to the festivity, but clearly the deadly opposite.

Evzen pushes his way through the compacted crowd of tourists and onlookers to the other side of he gateway and is prevented from going any further by the outstretched arms of a uniformed policeman. The narrow confines behind the church is a scene of chaos as police cars and ambulances compete for access. Evzen looks up at the address he had memorised and which is now the focus of all the activity. Fearing the worst, he manages to convince the officer that his daughter could be in the building. Another officer is called over to escort him into the crowded space. They pause to allow a stretcher to be unloaded from an ambulance and rushed into the building then approach a tall thin man in an ill-fitting grey suit taking notes by the apartment entrance. The uniformed officer repeats what the old man has told him and that he could be related to someone in the building. The vulture-like plain-clothed detective looks down on the diminutive Evzen and flips over to a fresh page of his notepad. After writing down Evzen's details and who and what he may know, he finally introduces himself as a detective from the homicide section. Evzen's heart sinks and his legs go to jelly at the word *homicide* and he needs the support of the uniform policeman to stay on his feet as another stretcher is wheeled inside.

Finding strength in his desperation, Evzen insists on knowing what has happened, but the detective ignores his plea. This ignites Evzen's long-held distrust of those in authority and he erupts into an abusive tirade, insisting that his daughter does not speak Czech, and if she is inside, he must go to her. The uniformed officer is ordered to take him away until, and if, the need arises for further interrogation. As he's forcefully escorted away, Evzen looks back up to the top floor and sees moving shadows silhouetted in the window. Is Briney up there, alive and terrified? He looks away, refusing to think of the alternative.

As the first stretcher reappears from the building, Evzen shrugs off his escort and hobbles to the back of an ambulance. To his relief, the face is not covered by a sheet, and even with an oxygen mask on and eyes closed, the short spiky white hair confirms it's not Briney. But his relief is short-lived—the injured will be rushed to hospital while the dead will remain for the forensic police to do their work.

As soon as the ambulance has driven away with siren blaring, another stretcher is wheeled out of the building. It's Zac, his face bruised and bloodied wit a bandage wrapped around his head. Seeing his eyes open, Evzen tries to move closer but is held back.

'Zac!' he calls out.

Zac struggles to twist his head against the neck brace and sees the old man's frantic face peering down at him.

'Briney? Is she…?'

He's words are muffled as he disappears into the ambulance, the door closes, the siren starts and the ambulance drives off.

As the officer struggles to move Evzen back, the Detective reappears in the doorway and orders them both into the building.

Fearing he's to identify a body, Evzen struggles up each step until they reach the apartment's entrance hall and the remaining stairs. He hears movement and voices above as he takes the final steps into the main room where he pauses, his eyes lowered, afraid to look up. Then, through the murmur of activity, he hears a faint sobbing. He raises his head, his watery eyes blurring the scene. He wipes them and blinks to clear his vision. There, on the far side of the room, sitting with a woman in uniform on the leather couch, is Briney. His shoulders droop and his tired, stressed body sags with relief.

'Briney,' he calls out.

CHAPTER 57

My eyes are locked on the blue rubber gloved hand on my knee. I don't want to look up. All I want is to wake and for this horrible nightmare to be over. The hand tightens as a voice breaks through the confusion of activity and I raise my eyes from the blue glove, up a uniformed arm, to a female face. She's saying something to me but I don't understand a word. Even if she were speaking in English it wouldn't register. Now she's smiling at me…what for? What's there to smile about?

Other noises filter through, telling me I'm not asleep and the nightmare is real. I warily look around the room. People are everywhere and I try to focus on each individual, then back at the uniform beside me. The word Policie registers and I look back around the room. There's a mix of cops, plain clothes and what I reckon are medics, why? One of them is attending to someone all bloody and beaten slumped against a wall, but before I can focus on who it is, a stretcher passes, blocking my view. I'm drawn to its wheels as they roll across the floor until they're covered in red stuff and stop at two sets of legs sticking out from a doorway. I wonder at the uncomfortably way they're resting and the different footwear, one pair, shiny and business looking, the other, heavily scuffed military boots…and I start to remember.

'Zoja!' I call out. Oh fuck I hope she's alive. I hope I haven't killed her. I look back to the uniform beside me. She smiles again and taps my knee with her blue-gloved hand. I look back to see Zoja carried by two ambulance men as they gingerly step over the legs on the floor and place her on the stretcher. She's got a mask over her face and her little robe, saturated with sweat, blood and honey, is rising with each breath. I let out a sigh of relief as a blanket is placed over her and she's wheeled away.

Another stretcher arrives and stops beside the body against the wall. With a clearer view and clearing memory, I recognise Zac. I want to go to him but the firm hand on my knee stops me and I can only watch as he's attended to, placed on the stretcher, wheeled out of sight and I'm once again alone amongst all these strangers. The room starts to spin as all the gory detail of what's happened becomes gut-wrenchingly clear and that it was all because of me and that I'm to blame. I look into the face of the uniform beside me. She smiles again, but it's not her I want to see. 'No,' I say, shaking my head at her. The feeling of total isolation is unbearable. I start to sob but I want to speak, to call out for the support I never had. Then something inside me erupts like a dormant volcano and I scream out, 'RUZA…WHERE ARE YOU? WHY ARE YOU NEVER HERE WHEN I NEED YOU?' There's no reply, just the sound of sirens as they fade into the distance. The uniform tries to calm me, her smile gone, then I hear something, barely audible, but comfortably familiar.

'Briney.'

I look up but through tear-filled eyes I can only make out a hunched figure at the entrance to the apartment.

'Briney,' comes the word again. A little stronger this time, as the figure approaches. I wipe at my eyes. I need to see familiarity. I need to see family.

'Briney…you are not…' says a breathless Evzen.

No one can hold me down no matter how big or strong they are. I jump up and fling my arms around my stubbled, smelly old friend, and we cry together.

It takes some time before I let him go and we sit down on the couch in silence. Just having him beside me is enough. But now this tall skinny guy, smelling of garlic, is towering over us, wanting our attention and making us move along the couch for him to sit.

'They want ask you questions…I interpret, ya?' says Evzen.

I nod, sniffing back tears and attempting to shake off the last of the shivers. But I'm not too sure if I'm ready to talk about what's happened, or indeed if I ever will be.

'First, I need to know if Zoja will be all right.' That'll help.

There's some chat and it seems the uniform chick has the answer.

'She will be,' Evzen relates back. 'You do right thing.'

'And Zac?'

'I see him…he be fine.'

I look to where the legs are sticking out from the kitchen.

'And them?'

Evzen places his knobbly hand on my knee, a welcomed difference to the blue glove. 'You need tell what happen, ya,' he says with a nod to the guy on the other side of me. I turn to him as he flips over to a new page of his notepad.

The description I give is very short. I mean, I didn't see much until they all came into the kitchen and then everything happened so fast. But it only raised more questions from the detective. Why was I here in the first place? The skinhead girl—seems the police knew about her —what was she doing here? Who was the other man on the floor? Who killed who and who is the man seen leaving with blood all over his face? And on and on it went. For something that happened so fast there was a shitload of questions. But damned if I can remember who killed the girl. Then, as I'm telling about smashing the big guy in the face with the coffee pot, it hits me. I killed her. I had actually killed someone. I feel like throwing up…and I do.

The detective cops most of it. He jumps up off the couch like a stork in flight, screaming out something in Czech and getting everyone's attention. The police chick, luckily still wearing her blue rubber gloves, starts fussing over him and trying to clean off as much vomit as she can. Evzen has escaped my spillage and he hands me his old handkerchief. I'm sure I detect a wry smile on his face.

The grilling goes on for a while. It seems the dead chick and her neo-nazi friends are suspects in another killing. That doesn't surprise me after seeing the look in her eyes when she came at me. But then the cop starts to question Evzen. I can't understand a word they're saying, but it seems there's a lot he knows that I don't, which surprises me. Then it's back to me again. He wants to know more about the big guy who fled and what's his connection with the skinheads. Seems that's one thing Evzen didn't know…and I'm not about to tell them he's Zac's old man…he can do that himself. I tell the cop the dead body with the shiny shoes was Zoja's old man and that he seemed to know the big guy, but that's all I tell him.

And that was it. I'm not gunna be arrested. Seems they have a pretty lenient law here when it comes to self defense, especially when it involves the neo-nazis, and me being Jewish. Shit, I never thought being Jewish would keep me out of prison. I mean, all I've learnt since being here is that in the past if you were Jewish that's where they sent you. But I had to give up my passport and not leave the Republic until there's a hearing. We're told to stay in Prague, at least for tomorrow… or is that today, I've no idea how late it is. The detective notes down my mobile phone number and hands me his card. I get Evzen to ask what hospital Zoja and Zac have gone to cuz I want to go straight there to see them. I think they want to keep an eye on us cuz a couple of uniformed cops are called over and ordered to drive us to the hospital and then to a hotel.

I'm allowed to go to the bathroom to wash the blood off and change my clothes, all the time closely watched over by the uniform chick. I avoid looking in the mirror, I just want to get out of these clothes and wash all the blood off. As I didn't have any other clothes, I grab a pair of Zoja's jeans, a T and the jacket I first saw her in and give my boots a wipe cuz Zoja's don't fit. Figuring I should take her some clothes, I grab a large soft leather bag from the bottom of her wardrobe and stuff some casual clothes in, some underwear, the pair of boots I tried on and a bottle of perfume from her dresser…giving myself a squirt in the hope of smothering the smell of death. Now all I want to do is get out of this place.

They did ask me why the bed was messed up and I had to tell them the truth, much to Evzen's amazement and difficulty in translating. But I said nothing of the ring…that was just too personal and something I'll tell Evzen about later.

We're driven to the hospital and taken to see Zac. There's a cop sitting outside his room and after getting the nod from our escort we're allowed to enter but Evzen opts to stay outside. I go in. He's cleaned up, bandaged and there's a drip going into his arm and a tube coming out of his chest dripping a murky fluid into a plastic bag hanging on the side of the bed. And he's out to it.

I move to his side and feel so sorry that I've involved him in such a bloody mess. He looks so peaceful, yet I know that when he wakes, he'll wake to his demons and whatever it was between him and his old man. Shit, whatever it was, it must have been something real fucking bad. I lean over and kiss him on his shaved head. I so owe him my life.

We're given the all clear to see Zoja, and again Evzen chooses not to go into the ward but sit beside the female guard and wait. I pause at the door, expecting her to be out to it too, but I'm surprised to see her awake and looking reasonably well, even though she's crying. I figure they've told her about her father…her *Daddy*. I'm not sure what to do or say. She sees me, her crying stops and she looks at me with a frozen stare. I reckon she must blame me for his death, and until I know differently, it probably is my fault. We look at each other, speechless. Then she raises one hand, open with her palm facing up, beckoning me. I feel a lump rising in my throat as I step closer and stretch out a hand to take hers. She pulls me to her and wraps her arms around me.

We hug and we cry. That's all that's required at this time. We're so wrung out, our thoughts and what to say to each other can wait till tomorrow.

CHAPTER 58

The hotel we're taken to is not far from the hospital. It wasn't like we had any choice. One cop stays in the car while the other comes with us while we register. After making a note of our room number, he says something to Evzen and leaves.

'What was that about?' I ask.

'They stay watch outside…for our good.'

For our good! What the fuck does that mean? Am I still in danger until this guy's caught? I mean, shit, how hard could it be to get someone who's running around the streets with his face cut wide open and an eye hanging out? I squirm at the thought. He's gotta go to a bloody hospital somewhere, which makes me think of all the cops guarding Zac and Zoja.

Our room's on the second floor, small with two single beds and a bathroom, but it's of little interest to me. Even though I'm so bloody tired, there's no way I'll sleep with all these gory images swirling around in my head and the worry that Zac's old man could still be after me. I mean, shit, where did he come from and why? And why the fuck does a guy I've never met want to kill me? Jeez, Zac's got a lot of explaining to do. I look out the window and at the cop car parked opposite…thank Christ!

Evzen comes out of the bathroom after doing his thing. He looks tired. I don't think he'll have any trouble sleeping even if I won't, but I may as well brush my teeth anyway. Hunting around in my bag for the toothbrush I always carry, I spot the USB stick Doran gave me and the word *dossier* echoes in my head. The teeth can wait. I boot up the laptop instead. As soon as I see the first page of the document, I realize I need

Evzen's help to translate and call him over, but he's already in bed.

'Evzen, I know you're tired, but Zoja's dad gave me something and I need you to translate.'

He grunts and reluctantly raises himself up while I sit beside him. He looks over the first page without a word then motions for me to show the next. On the second page is a photo of Zac's old man.

'That's him,' I say pointing. 'That's the guy who tried to kill me… that's Zac's old man.'

I look at Evzen and he's gone as white as a sheet and a quivering finger is pointing at the photo. He recognizes him?

'What?' I ask. 'You know him?'

He can only shake his head from side to side, but I'm not sure if he's saying no or shaking his head in disbelief.

'You know this guy, don't ya?'

'Ne…ne…nemožné,'

'What? English, Evzen, speak to me in English.'

'It impossible,' he says, his body stiffening with rage.

'What? What's impossible? Evzen, this is the guy who tried to kill me…tell me!'

'He…he look like Kapo.'

I look at the photo again then back to Evzen.

'What Kapo?'

He answers with an expression of utter rage and hatred.

'You mean the Kapo in the Ghetto? The one who pushed your parents under the train?'

He's still shaking his head in disbelief. I start to do the same.

'How can he be? I mean, what, he'd be in his eighties by now…if he's still alive, that is.'

'Ya,' Evzen agrees.

I look at the name attached to the photo.

'This is Goddard Klein.'

He's shaking his head.

'Boch…Albrecht Boch!' he spits out.

I open more documents and come to a photo of Doran.

'You know him?' I ask

Evzen leans forward and wipes the rage from his eyes. He studies the photo for some time, his finger tracing all of Doran's features.

'I...I not sure,' he mumbles.

'That's Zoja's father. The one I met about the property and he got me some...' Shit, I haven't told Evzen about the cheque. 'He...he managed to get some money from some fund as compensation for losing the property, here I'll show you.'

He holds up his hand.

'Ne...I no want see.'

I stop reaching for the cheque and wonder why.

'There was child in Ghetto...younger than me...but hard to say.'

I open up more pages. They're all in Czech so I decide to worry about that later and look for more photos. Another one appears. It looks to have been taken through a car window and shows some old guy coming out of a restaurant. He's wearing a brimmed hat but the streetlight has softened the shadow on his face. Under the photo a caption reads: *Is this Albrecht Boch?—Melbourne Australia 1983*. I turn the screen a little more towards Evzen. He's already focussing on it with eyes that could burn a hole right through the screen. There's no doubting the inherited features. If Goddard Klein was too young to be the Kapo, then this is his father! Suddenly, everything that's happened to me since that morning in Melbourne when I fell under the train then placed my hand on the wall, has come back to the one thing that started it all off...the Goose ring.

'Evzen, I've got something to tell you' He can't take his eyes away from the photo on the screen. 'Evzen...I've seen the ring.'

His head slowly turns to me as the words sink in.

'Zoja has it.' I'm expecting some reaction, but there is none. 'Her grandfather gave it to her.' I look back at the photo. 'I remember she said something about her dad's partner asking about it.'

Evzen's mouth is tightly closed with rage and the heavy breathing through his nose forces a drop to fall. His hand starts to flutter at the screen.

'Back,' he manages to spit out. 'I want see all pages.'

I replace each page at full screen one at a time, allowing him to scan

311

the text until he waves his finger for me to replace the page with another. Some pages he only spends a few seconds on, some longer. I'm desperate to know what's written but too scared to interrupt him.

'You say…this man, Doran…give you this?' he says, his eyes not leaving the screen.

'Yeah, he said it was just something to explain the property claim stuff. He never said anything about all this.'

'You make copy…and make safe.'

'Yeah, okay…but…' I want to ask why but he gets in first.

'This man Albrecht Boch…is wanted for war crimes. Ruza felt he in Melbourne but had no proof.' He flips his finger for me to turn back the pages until reaching the one showing Goddard Kein's photo.

'He son of Kapo…born after Ghetto…he partner with this man Doran…'

'Partner!' I interrupt. 'But he killed him. Why would he kill his own partner?'

'Their company…it the one that own much of Terezín.' He pauses for a breath. 'When flood stop sale to University…they set to lose much. This…' he waves his hand across the screen. '…this tell all…and more.'

'More?'

'That man Goddard…he finance Prague neo-nazi group…I sure his father, Albrecht Boch, behind all this.'

'But…' I struggle to accept what I'm thinking. 'But that…shit, Zac's shaved head…he's one of them!'

'Ne…ne,' he says, placing his hand on my knee. 'He came to Terezín to warn you.'

'I don't understand.'

'He beaten up bad by gang…he knew they after you.'

'You saw him?' All this is new to me and I kick myself for not once wondering why Zac turned up at Zoja's, or even Evzen for that matter.

'But the chick and his old man were with him at Zoja's?'

'Ne…I sure they use him to find you. Two others follow him to Terezín.'

'You saw them?'

'Ya.'

'Were they both big guys? Skinheads? Lots of tats?' I'm thinking of the two guys with the now-dead chic I saw at the Kain.

'Ya.'

That's got me spooked, especially now that I decked the chick. They could still be after me!

'Shit…so where are they?'

'They find new religion,' he says with a hint of a smirk on his face. 'You not worry about them.'

'So…like, you reckon Zac's got nothing to do with all this?'

'I think not.'

We remain silent while I copy the contents from the stick onto the hard drive and shut down the computer.

'I gotta be sure. We'll go see Zac first thing in the morning.'

CHAPTER 59

One of the two cops that guarded us all night is waiting for a couple of coffees in the hotel reception as we check out. He finds himself in an argument with Evzen over who's paying for the room. It was all a waste of time, and the cop finds it amusing that we expected anyone other than ourselves to pay. But any excuse to argue with the authority gives Evzen some satisfaction. But I'm eager to get to the hospital so I pay to shut them up. Obviously they haven't found this guy Goddard yet.

I'm still feeling strange and on edge. I guess it's all to do with the shock of what's happened. I've heard people are offered counselling after traumatic events like, but not here…maybe it's a Czech thing. I mean, last night was nothing compared to all the shit they've lived through over the years.

We're allowed in to see Zac, but Evzen says he'll wait for me down the hall. I reckon I understand, I mean, Zac's the son of the son of the guy who threw his parents under a train. Shit, I'm pretty unsure how to face him as well. Like, what if he *is* part of this thing with his old man? Nah, he said he left home because of him…yeah, but why? Jeez, last night I was thankful he saved my life but this morning I'm suspicious of him, so who's the one with demons now?

He's lying there with his face turned away and I can't tell if he's asleep on not, but he turns when he hears me approach and looks at me with a strange glazed expression. I feel my stomach tighten as I see some of his old man's features in his face even though he's a lot skinnier. I must stop this. Think lifesaver!

'Hi Zac, how you feeling?'

He remains silent.

'They've cleaned you…'

'He tried to kill me,' he breaks into me words. 'The fucking cunt tried to kill me.'

'Hey, cool it, Zac, it's…'

'Have they got him yet? They won't tell me anything.'

'I don't know. They haven't told me either.' But I knew they hadn't.

'Zac…' I hesitate, unsure if I should come out with this now or later…what the hell. 'Zac, did you know anything about, you know, all this shit with ya old man and property and neo-nazi stuff?'

I was ready to step back quick if he spat the dummy.

'Ya gotta be fuckin' joking.' He pushes himself up against the pillow. 'I knew he was a real brutal bastard back in Oz. You know, stand-over and all that shit, but fucked if I knew anything about that… no fuckin' way.'

As he pushes himself up, the sheet over his chest slides down and I see the heavy bandage. He sees me looking.

'You know what the bastard did?' he says pointing to his chest. 'He fuckin' ripped me nipple ring out and took the whole fuckin' nipple with it.'

I cringe at the thought.

'Then those other bastards beat into me. So does that answer ya fuckin' question?'

I look back to the door to see the cop on guard checking us out.

'Look Zac, it's just that all of a sudden your old man's in Prague causing all sorts of shit and after my bloody guts. I mean I do have reason to expect some answers, don't I?'

'Yeah, well it's all your fuckin' fault isn't it?'

'Me? Why?'

'Cuz to get the money to come here on ya fuckin' crazy Goose chase, I done a deal with the guys to steal his Merc, and in return for half of what they got for it, I told them who my dealer was...'

That's got me angry.

'Hang on. I didn't ask you for you to do anything. Fuck, I didn't even want you to come with me.'

'Yeah, and you'd still be in the shitty dump back in Melbourne trying to scrape up enough money, wouldn't ya?'

'Okay, okay, but I still don't get it. I mean, why come all the way over here to kick your arse?'

He goes quiet for a second.

'The supplier was his too. So when I told the guys who it was...that made a lot of people very un-fuckin' happy so he put the word out to find me, and shit, how the fuck was I to know that the word was getting here to the bunch I was shacked up with.'

'Okay, so he had a reason to kick your arse, but why me? Like, I know now he has some involvement in this property scam with Zoja's old man, and okay, so I may have stirred up something there, but that was all sorted and settled as far as I was concerned.'

'I know fuck-all about any property shit. All I know is that as soon as he saw the fuckin' graff ya painted all over their factory, he went ballistic and ordered the guys to get ya. That's when I got away and tried to warn ya.'

'Yeah, Evzen filled me in with that bit...thanks.'

'I must admit it was fuckin' cool though, not that I understood any of what ya painted.'

'Yeah, well I'll fill you in later,' I say, convinced he knew nothing about his old man's involvement in the neo-nazi shit. 'So, what's gunna happen now?'

'Yeah, well they haven't said anything that I can fuckin' understand yet. They took a statement through an interpreter and that's all.'

315

'How long you staying in here?'

He shrugs his shoulders and winces as a pain stabs his chest.

'Fucked if I know. A while I hope. I mean it's got all the mods and cons and plenty of food and shit.' He pauses. 'What about you?'

It's the first time I've been asked, and the first time I had to think about it.

'I'll go and see how Zoja is. Then, I don't know. I can't leave Prague until there's a hearing.'

'So, what's the story with ya dyke mate?'

I ignore his crudeness.

'I don't think she's got anything to do with anything. You know, sorta innocent bystander. But I reckon she'll be cut up for some time. She and her dad were pretty close.'

Suddenly I need to see her.

'Look, I better go, Evzen's waiting for me. I think he's itching to get outta the big city, outta all this shit and to the hospital to see Ruza.'

The look on his face shows he's got no idea what's happened to me over the past week or two.

'Look, I'll come back and check on you tomorrow and fill you in with everything then, okay?'

I can see he doesn't want me to go, and I sorta feel sorry for him, being all alone and shit.

'Hey, guess what I've got now?' I say, hoping to cheer him up a bit, but the only response is the look of loneliness in his eyes.

'I've got a mobile phone.' I pull it outta my bag. 'See!'

He's uninterested and doesn't look at it at all.

I scribble down the number and hand it to him.

'Here...you know...just in case.'

I check on Evzen before going in to see Zoja and tell him I won't be long. The poor old bugger, all he wants to do is to go and to Ruza.

I'm surprised to see Zoja dressed and sitting in the chair beside her bed. There's no smile of welcome as I enter the room and I accept that.

'You chose well,' she says with sadness in her voice and glancing down at the clothes I'd brought for her.

'Oh, I didn't know, I just grabbed some things.'

I then realize I'm still wearing her clothes.

'Look, I hope you don't mind me wearing some of yours. Mine were covered in bl…' I figured I shouldn't go any further.

'Suits you, though I would have chosen a different top.'

She's trying to be brave but I know she must be hurting.

'So, you've recovered from the, you know, um, whatever attack you had?'

'They pumped a whole tube of glucose into me apparently. But they also said that if you hadn't stuffed so much honey into my mouth, I…well it could have been worse.'

I'm still wondering if she blames me for all that's happened.

'Look, I know I said this last night, but I'm real sorry about everything,' I'm testing her.

She just gives a tight little smile as tears well up in her clear emerald eyes.

'Look, I've had a visit from one of Daddy's lawyers and…' she sniffs back a tear, '…and he's told me what the policie have managed to put together.' She holds out a hand to me. 'Brightlight, I'm so sorry you got caught up in what he was up to. I really had no idea, I hope you believe me?'

Calling me Brightlight meant a lot. I take her hand…it's cold.

'Your father gave me something last night. A USB stick, you remember?'

Her look and a shake of the head says no. I guess she was beginning to have the attack then.

'Well, it's got a lot of stuff about everything. I think he knew what a bastard this Goddard guy was and wanted to end the partnership.'

That seemed to bring a slight glow to her face, but not a lot.

'You know, I just took all he gave me without a worry where it was coming from. I didn't care. I was living a life of luxury. I had everything I wanted, and I didn't care how or where the money came from. I feel so dirty.'

'Hey, like, we're both innocent victims here.' I butt in before she gets too low.

She reaches out her arms for a hug.

'Will we see each other again?' she says over my shoulder.

I hold her while searching for the right answer. Silence makes her release her embrace.

'I have something for you. I hope you'll accept it as…as a memento of your visit.'

She reaches into the pocket of her jacket and hands me the Goose ring.

CHAPTER 60

Evzen is uptight and fidgety as he waits for Briney to finish her visits. It's now two days since he last sat by Ruza's bedside and he feels angry and ashamed that he's broken his promise to visit her every day without fail.

The two police who escorted him and Briney from the hotel are also anxious as they wait for their replacements. Evzen watches and listens as they chat with their colleagues guarding Zac and Zoja and hears that Goddard Klein is yet to be found. Then, a crackling voice comes through one of their radios that their replacements are only minutes away. Impatient to end their long shift, the two head down to the hospital entrance to wait for their replacements with the understanding that the two stationed on guard will also keep an eye on the old man and the girl for the next few minutes.

At the same time, Evzen sees Briney come out of Zoja's room. He glances back to the two remaining police and, seeing they have their backs turned, he heaves himself to his feet, and before Briney can say a word, grabs her by the arm and hurries her to an emergency exit at the other end of the corridor.

'What's happening?' asks a surprised Briney as they start heading down the stairs in the enclosed stairwell.

'We go now…go see Ruza.'

Briney stops him at the first landing.

'What about the cops? Are we allowed to leave?'

He pulls away from her hold and continues down the stairs. Nothing will stop him, not even Briney.

'I go…you stay if you want.'

She's surprised at his readiness to leave her and follows after him.

'Okay, okay I'm coming.'

Reaching ground level, they make their way to the front of the building. Evzen stops and peeks around the corner. The two replacements have just arrived and he backs away to wait for them to enter the hospital, but a call on their car radio stops them.

While they wait, Briney can no longer hold back her news.

'Evzen, I've got something to tell you before we go any further.'

He only gives her half his attention, the other half on the police.

'We'll go see Ruza, I promise, but first I've got something for you.'

He turns as Briney takes his hand and places the ring into it.

It takes a moment to register. He glances up at her and back at the ring he hasn't laid eyes on for more than sixty years. After a stunned, silent moment, he takes Briney's hand and places the ring into her palm. Their hands press together, joined as one by the force of the ring. Then she feels his hand shudder. She thinks the heart again, but this is different, this time she feels her own tremor ripple through her body and looks down at their hands and the force still holding them together. She knows this feeling. It's the same surge of energy she gets from walls. She looks up to see Evzen looking at her with determination in his moist eyes.

'You keep,' he says in a soft wavering voice. 'I want you keep.'

She's unsure of what to say as the force releases its hold and he slides his hand from hers and wraps her fingers around the ring.

'This ring now yours…it back in family,' he says with a weak smile.

Briney raises her clasped hand to her lips as his words sink in.

Evzen takes another glance around the corner and sees the two officers disappear into the hospital. 'Come, we go tell Ruza.'

They take advantage of every doorway and cover until they reach a crossroad as a number 14 tram approaches. On board, Evzen buys two tickets and remains standing, constantly looking out the tram window, up and down the street and at each person who boards at each stop. Briney can only assume he's worried the police will stop him before he can get back to his Ruza.

At the Náměstí Republiky Metro, Briney is hurried into the station, down the escalator, through the long tunnel, up and down stairs until they finally reach the yellow B line platform just as the last carriage of their train to Florenc and the bus terminal disappears into the dark tunnel. Evzen is agitated that he has to wait another ten minutes, and continues to look around nervously. His behaviour worries Briney and the sound of her phone ringing inside her bag only adds to her concern.

By the time she fumbles through her bag and finds the phone, the passengers that had alighted the now-distant train have gone and the two are alone on the eastbound side of the platform. Briney answers her phone, but all she gets is a lot of Czech words. Thinking it's probably the hospital and something is wrong, she hands the phone to Evzen. He hesitates for a moment before placing the phone to his ear. After listening to the caller without a word of reply, he hands the phone back. She sees the cloud of disbelief in his eyes and puts the phone to her ear but the caller has hung up. There's no need to discuss the message, no need for translation: the message of death has its own silent language.

Meanwhile, on the westbound platform, a crowd gathers as their train is about to arrive, while, on the eastbound side new passengers join Briney and Evzen for the train to Florenc.

With both sides of the platform crowded, Briney is distracted as a group jostle past. She looks back to Evzen, but he is no longer beside her. She spins around in all directions, but he is nowhere to be seen. She runs to the westbound side of the platform, feeling the breeze pushed ahead of the arriving train, and weaves her way through the people in a desperate search, but it's as if Evzen has just suddenly vanished.

Evzen has slipped away without Briney noticing. His Ruza is now gone forever and he needs a moment alone. He did not want Briney to speak for she had kept him away from Ruza's bedside and caused him to break a promise to be with her when the time came. Now the time had come and he feels the same as he did during all those years Ruza was far away in Australia…separated by a vast distance and the course of history.

He can see Briney looking for him as he hides behind one of the large pillars separating the east and west lines as the surge of passengers gather at the edge if the platform ready to board their train. But his focus turns to a figure approaching the frantic Briney. The long dark coat, turned-up collar and wide-brimmed hat cannot fully hide the bandage over one eye or the Roma features. He had sensed Goddard Klein was watching them as soon as he touched the Goose ring in Briney's hand. Now the son of the man who killed his parents is in range.

Briney's hair is blown back as the train emerges from the tunnel. Her mouth trembles as she tries to call Evzen's name, but an energy is all around her, an energy so strong she's confused and caught up in the rush of the train's power, until suddenly the emergency brakes are activated and the train comes to a shuddering halt. Shock silences the onlookers as if a film has skipped out of the sprocket and stopped at a single frame. The train driver leaps from his cabin as the guard appears from the rear and they run towards each other, pausing now and then to look under the train. The driver is first to stop and get down on his knees. The guard joins him and is instantly on his two-way radio. Those waiting to disembark can only watch from behind locked doors and wonder what has happened

A breeze begins to wisp the hair of those standing in shock as the Florenc train approaches the eastbound platform. They now become animated and start to edge forward in the hope of catching a glimpse of the carnage, but a group of transport guards arrive to push them back.

Within a few short minutes the police arrive and start herding those on the platform to the exit tunnel where they'll be questioned. Briney stands her ground, an obstacle to those streaming past. She studies each one, hoping to see his white scruffy hair and stubbled face. One hunched old man raises her hopes, but it's not Evzen. As the platform empties, her fears grow, but a grip on her arm makes her spin around in hope. It's one of the police pulling her to join the others. Reluctantly she allows herself to be dragged away while straining to look back towards the front of the train.

Jammed into the confines of the exit tunnel with the other shocked passengers, she overhears some of the English-speaking tourists recount what they witnessed, and with the Goose ring clutched firmly in her hand, she knew it was fate written more than sixty years ago. It was reprisal. The son who watched his parents die under a train has now taken with him the son of the Kapo who pushed them to their death, and when the news reaches Australia it is hoped will result in the final gasp of an ailing murderer.

Briney looks above the heads of the gathered crowd and takes in the solid tile-covered walls that surround them. Is this the end that was meant to be? Has her mission all along been to ensure the reprisal and for Evzen and Ruza to never to be apart again? If so, it has been accomplished.

CHAPTER 61
Eight months later

I'm nervously watching people entering the art gallery from the restaurant next door. I'm into my second beer but I better slow down if I've gotta get up and say something. My mind is as blank as the pages of the open notebook in front of me. I can't think of anything to say. Not that many will understand me anyway. I've picked up a bit of Czech over the last eight months but it's so bloody hard to learn, I guess I'll use that as an excuse and just shut up after a minute.

I told the gallery owner I don't want to be there meeting people before the show opens. Fuck that for a joke, me meeting strangers, forget it, I can hardly put two words together with people I know. I said I'd be there at seven and no earlier. But she's so bloody worried I might run off that she keeps poking her head out the front door of the gallery to check on me. *Hi*, I wave as her head pokes out again and I check the time? My old clock's sitting on the table in front of me showing I've got another ten minutes.

Every time I look at the clock it takes me back. While I never really got to know Ruza, there was a moment I felt we shared something. But it's Evzen I miss. Yeah, the silly old bugger with his dribbling nose. The cops said he died a hero saving me from that bastard Goddard Klein. Yeah, I guess he was, but I know the real reason and I reckon he died a happy man. He's now with his Ruza forever and he'll no longer crave the revenge that had been eating away at him for all those years. And I reckon he died knowing that someone would be around to remember him. I look at both my hands wrapped around the beer mug. On the index finger of my left hand is the old plastic amber ring and on the index finger of the other is the shiny platinum and gold Goose ring. Yeah, silly old bugger, I'll never forget you.

'Briney, everyone is waiting for you,' comes the voice from the present. I get lost in thought every time I look at the clock and the ring.

'Yeah, I'm coming,' I say, stuffing the clock and notebook in my bag and throwing down the rest of the beer.

'I'll fix up the account,' she says edging me out.

I pause at the gallery door and look at all the people inside. All enjoying the wine and chitchat—shit, this is so not me.

'Come now,' says the gallery lady grabbing me by the arm. 'You okay, ya?'

I nod, a fucking big lie, I'm as nervous as shit.

'We need send for more wine and beer. You attract much interest.'

Shit, that doesn't help.

As soon as I'm inside, a camera flash blinds me, followed by another and another. All I see are white dots as strange hands are grabbing mine and shaking it, slapping me on the back, on the shoulder and all I hear above the wild music is a chorus of Czech. The dots dissolve and I regain some vision. The faces are as unrecognizable as the words coming from them. The gallery is more packed than it looked from outside and I'm dragged and jostled through the smells of heavy perfume and cigarette smoke until I'm planted at the side of a small cleared area, where, sitting atop a tall thin stand, a microphone is waiting for me. Shit, I can't do this. Then a soft touch on my shoulder and the erotic whiff of a familiar peppery perfume gives me a moment of courage.

'Have a drink of Slivovitz, Brightlight. It'll get the words flowing.'

I eagerly take the small glass and throw it down as she taught me and give Zoja a smile.

The next few minutes seem to have never happened. It's as if I'd stepped out of my body and hovered, watching me from above as I do the duty. It all went so fast, the introduction, or I assume that is what it was, being half Czech and half broken English. And then, me, at a distance, mumbling something about how glad I am being here, something about thanking the gallery and all who dared come, and a lot of ums and ahs. But it seemed to do the trick. They came, they saw, they heard me speak and now it was time to see what I've done. I rejoin my body and step back from the mike as the music from a local street group drowns out the applause.

'Well done, darling,' says Zoja. 'Come, I'll introduce you to some people.'

I grab her arm as she starts to walk into the crowd.

'Look Zoja, I'm still shaking. Give me a minute to settle down will you? I just want to stand in a corner and watch for a moment, okay?'

'Sure, darling, I understand. I'll fend off anyone who comes near you.'

I smile, knowing there is no one better at fending off people. I step back into a corner and try to shrink myself to an unnoticeable shadow.

The gallery owner approaches and is the first to be fended off. I don't know what Zoja told her, maybe I've suddenly come down with the plague or something, but it worked. I know it won't last, but I just need a moment to soak up the scene, after all this is the first legitimate exhibition I've ever had, and an art exhibition at that. Never ever thought this would happen. Then again, I never ever thought what happened eight months ago would happen either.

I look at Zoja, my protector. She's had a hard time coming to grips with what happened. She adored her father, and finding out what he was up to didn't destroy that love, for he also adored her. But she changed a lot. She felt dirty for enjoying the wealth derived from cheating others, though it turned out that Doran did have a very successful legitimate business as well, and it was decided that whatever assets Zoja had were hers and deemed to be unaffected by any reversal of property ownership back to those who'd been cheated. As it turned out only a few of the properties had living owners or descendants, and practically no one had any interest in reclaiming what was now considered a financial liability due to the cost of the restoration. And, well, as far as the Terezín property goes, as Ruza had died—I wish she could be here to see this—I made the decision that I couldn't see myself living there in such a cold, grey, morbid place. So I accepted whatever the authorities offered. I'm not good at wealth, I mean anything is more than I've ever had, and I did have the cheque Doran gave me. Yeah… that's a little secret between Zoja and me.

I moved in with Zoja. She wanted to sell the apartment, but I figured no matter where she went, the memories would never go away. It took a while, but I think she's starting to relax more in the place. I mean, shit, it's so fucking Gothic, it's so her, where else could she find a place that suits her so well? Though the only thing I did insist on was that she change the bloody threatening chandelier that hung above the bed.

I had space there to work on this exhibition…an exhibition that had never entered my head. But after much pressure from her and her gallery owner friend, I ran out of excuses. Plus it was handy, the gallery being next to the apartment and all.

Zac moved in with us for a bit after all the legal shit. It gave him a place to recover from his injuries, but I don't think he'll ever get over the fact that his old man tried to kill him. I tried to get him to stay in Prague and said that I'd help him out with some money, but he wouldn't. He was so lost I really felt for him. His crazy larrikin carefree nature was totally burnt out. His old lady came over and I don't think she was all that upset about losing her husband, more about losing the wealth he provided, I reckon. Anyway, she wanted Zac to go back to Oz with her and after a while he agreed. I think he'll be okay over time… but I'm not sure about his brother. Seems he went ballistic on hearing about his old man's death. Shaved his head and covered himself with tats and left home. No one knows where he went, and every time I see a skinhead, I get this creepy feeling that he might be here in Prague. Oh…and the grandfather…I gave the cops a copy of the dossier, but he died from a stroke on hearing about Goddard, so he never went to trial for war crimes. Pity!

Yeah, well, here I am at my own exhibition with my own art hanging—not painted—on walls. Art, shit, never thought that word would ever be tagged to me. You know, I still can't help it, but looking around this gallery and watching all these strangers discussing the work and imagining the absolute crap they're coming out with, I just want to burst out laughing. These tinted rubbings I did on the walls at Terezín, are not my work. They're the result of hundreds of secrets imprisoned in the decaying bricks, mortar and plaster. It was those walls that held my hand. It was those faded and soiled walls that determined the palette. It was those witnessing walls that reached out and offered their secrets to me, and like Evzen, and all the others who witnessed such inhumane actions, the walls needed someone to be the…the…I don't know…the messenger, I suppose.

And now, all these critics and art connoisseurs are spouting their know-all wisdom and it's all a load of shit. They've no idea of the secrets those walls allowed me to convey. They see nothing but what they want to see. But that's the way I like it. That's the way the walls will like it. That's the way I started out with my spray cans beside the train tracks, letting others see what they want to see, to reveal their own secrets through their own assumptions. *SECRETSINCITY* is still alive.

———————

Also by

DENNIS OGDEN

SAVING SPADE
WWI has ended
but the battle to save a horse has just begun

"The horses stay!" came the order as men of the Australian Light
Horse are being sent home.

Trooper Lewis Dunbar will never abandon his loyal war horse
Spade. So begins a perilous journey into the Sinai Desert and his
struggles to protect his horse from a mute Bedouin girl, nomadic
tribes, and the Djinn spirits of the desert.

The winds of the Sinai whip up a gripping tale that stir the dormant
spirits within.

ISBN
Paperback - 9780648086901
Ebook - 9780648086918